'This wonderful novel is difficult to put down. There's something for everyone: br⬚⬚⬚⬚⬚⬚⬚⬚⬚⬚⬚⬚⬚⬚⬚⬚⬚⬚ plot, believable characters, ⬚⬚⬚⬚⬚⬚⬚⬚⬚⬚⬚⬚⬚⬚⬚⬚⬚⬚⬚⬚⬚⬚⬚⬚racter that ties it all together ⬚⬚⬚⬚⬚⬚⬚⬚⬚⬚⬚⬚⬚⬚⬚⬚⬚⬚⬚⬚⬚⬚⬚⬚⬚⬚

rterly

'*Fire* is fresh, interestin⬚⬚⬚⬚⬚⬚⬚⬚⬚⬚⬚⬚⬚⬚⬚⬚⬚⬚⬚⬚⬚ that, above all, will make its readers impatient for any stories that may follow'

Bookgeeks.co.uk

'The setting is rich and beautifully explored and described, the characters all multidimensional, interesting and believable, and the romance is exquisitely drawn out and developed. Cashore has created a world it's a real joy to exist in, populated with characters it's a pleasure to be among'

The Book Bag

'Its themes – embracing your talents and moving out of your parents' shadow – are similar [to those of *Graceling*], as is the absorbing quality of Cashore's prose ... Many twists propel the action ... tension that keeps the pages turning'

Publishers Weekly

'The subtle intrigues of palace plots and even the sickening horrors of open warfare are vehicles to total immersion into Fire's character ... Fire tentatively, tenderly, passionately falls in love with a family, a city, a kingdom, with the very contradictions that make them human – and, at the last, with her own place among them. Fresh, hopeful, tragic and glorious'

Kirkus Reviews

'Readers can enjoy this novel without having read *Graceling* ... and enjoy it they will, with its vivid storytelling, strongly realized alternate world, well-drawn characters, convincing fantasy elements, gripping adventure scenes, and memorable love story'

Booklist

'Readers will fall in love with *Fire* ... More adult in tone than *Graceling*, this marvellous prequel will appeal to older teens, who will not only devour it, but will also love talking about it'

School Library Journal

'Cashore is that rare gifted writer who can give a fantasy novel real depth ... One of the things Cashore does beautifully in *Fire* is to examine the workings of desire – and not always as it relates to sex ... Having created an exaggeration of female experiences in Fire's monster form, Cashore can be brutally honest about the realities of girls' lives'

Los Angeles Times

'This elegantly written prequel to the acclaimed *Graceling* blazes with the questions of young adulthood: Who am I? How do I stand in relation to my parents? What choices will define my life? Seeing those concerns played out by Fire ... and a host of memorable minor characters proves as compelling as the richly detailed medieval backdrop, the tension between battling lords and the mysterious presence of [a] strange-eyed character common to both novels'

Washington Post

Also by Kristin Cashore

Graceling

Fire

KRISTIN CASHORE

The right of Kristin Cashore to be identified as the author
of this work has been asserted by her in accordance with the
Copyright, Designs and Patents Act 1988.

First published in Great Britain in 2009 by
Gollancz
An imprint of the Orion Publishing Group
Orion House, 5 Upper St Martin's Lane,
London WC2H 9EA
An Hachette UK Company

This edition published in Great Britain in 2011 by Gollancz

1 3 5 7 9 10 8 6 4 2

A CIP catalogue record for this book
is available from the British Library

ISBN 978 0 575 09815 2

Typeset by Deltatype Ltd, Birkenhead, Merseyside

Printed in Great Britain by
Clays Ltd, St Ives plc

The Orion Publishing Group's policy is to use papers that
are natural, renewable and recyclable products and made
from wood grown in sustainable forests. The logging and
manufacturing processes are expected to conform to
the environmental regulations of the country of origin.

www.kristincashore.blogspot.com
www.orionbooks.co.uk

For my little sister Catherine,
the (Corinthian) pillar
of my heart

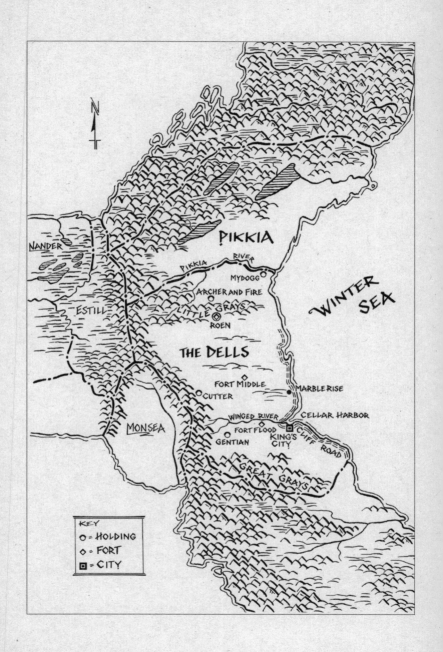

Dellian Lament

While I was looking the other way your fire went out
Left me with cinders to kick into dust
What a waste of the wonder you were

In my living fire I will keep your scorn and mine
In my living fire I will keep your heartache and mine
At the disgrace of a waste of a life

PROLOGUE

LARCH OFTEN THOUGHT that if it had not been for his new-born son, he never would have survived his wife Mikra's death. It was half that the infant boy needed a breathing, functioning father who got out of bed in the mornings and slogged through the day; and it was half the child himself. Such a good-natured baby, so calm. His gurgles and coos so musical, and his eyes deep brown like the eyes of his dead mother.

Larch was a game warden on the riverside estate of a minor lord in the south-eastern kingdom of Monsea. When Larch returned to his quarters after a day in the saddle, he took the baby from the arms of the nursemaid almost jealously. Dirty, stinking of sweat and horses, he cradled the boy against his chest, sat in his wife's old rocker, and closed his eyes. Sometimes he cried, tears painting clean stripes down a grimy face, but always quietly, so that he would not miss the sounds the child made. The baby watched him. The baby's eyes soothed him. The nursemaid said it was unusual for a baby so young to have such focused eyes. 'It's not something to be happy about,' she warned, 'a child with strange eyes.'

Larch couldn't find it within himself to worry. The nurse-maid worried enough for two. Every morning she examined the baby's eyes, as was the unspoken custom of all new parents in the seven kingdoms, and every morning she breathed more easily once she'd confirmed that nothing had changed. For the infant who fell asleep with both eyes the same colour and woke with eyes of two different colours was a Graceling; and in Monsea, as in most of the kingdoms, Graceling babies immediately became the property of the king. Their families rarely saw them again.

When the first anniversary of the birth of Larch's son had come and gone with no change to the boy's brown eyes, the nursemaid still did not leave off her muttering. She'd heard tales of Graceling eyes that took more than a year to settle, and Graceling or not, the child was not normal. A year out of his mother's womb and already Immiker could say his own name. He spoke in simple sentences at fifteen months; he left his babyish pronunciation behind at a year and a half. At the beginning of her time with Larch the nursemaid had hoped her care would gain her a husband and a strong, healthy son. Now she found the baby who conversed like a miniature adult while he drank at her breast, who made an eloquent announcement whenever his underwrappings needed to be changed, positively creepy. She resigned her post.

Larch was happy to see the sour woman go. He constructed a carrier so that the child could hang against his chest while he worked. He refused to ride on cold or rainy days; he refused to gallop his horse. He worked shorter hours and took breaks to feed Immiker, nap him, clean his messes. The baby chattered constantly, asked for the names of plants and animals, made up nonsense poems that Larch strained to hear, for the poems always made Larch laugh.

'Birdies love treetops to whirl themselves through, for inside of their heads they are birds,' the boy sang, absent-mindedly, patting his hand on his father's arm. Then, a minute later: 'Father?'

'Yes, son?'

'You love the things that I love you to do, for inside of your head are my words.'

Larch was utterly happy. He couldn't remember why his wife's death had saddened him so. He saw now that it was better this way, he and the boy alone in the world. He began to avoid the people of the estate, for their tiresome company bored him, and he didn't see why they should deserve to share in the delight of his son's company.

One morning when Immiker was three years old Larch opened his eyes to find his son lying awake beside him, staring at him. The boy's right eye was grey. His left eye was red. Larch shot up, terrified and heartbroken. 'They'll take you,' he said to his son. 'They'll take you away from me.'

Immiker blinked calmly. 'They won't, because you'll come up with a plan to stop them.'

To withhold a Graceling from the king was royal theft, punishable by imprisonment and fines Larch could never pay, but still Larch was seized by a compulsion to do what the boy said. They would have to ride east, into the rocky border mountains where hardly anyone lived, and find a patch of stone or scrub that could serve as a hiding place. As a game warden, Larch could track, hunt, build fires, and make a home for Immiker that no one would find.

IMMIKER WAS REMARKABLY calm about their flight. He knew what a Graceling was. Larch supposed the nursemaid had told him; or perhaps Larch himself had explained it and then forgotten he'd done so. Larch was growing forgetful. He sensed parts of his memory closing up on him, like dark rooms behind doors he could no longer open. Larch attributed it to his age, for neither he nor his wife had been young when she'd died birthing their son.

'I've wondered sometimes if your Grace has anything to do with speaking,' Larch said as they rode the hills east, leaving the river and their old home behind.

'It doesn't,' Immiker said.

'Of course it doesn't,' Larch said, unable to fathom why he'd ever thought it did. 'That's all right, son, you're young yet. We'll watch out for it. We'll hope it's something useful.'

Immiker didn't respond. Larch checked the straps that held the boy before him in the saddle. He bent down to kiss the top of Immiker's golden head, and urged the horse onward.

*

A GRACE WAS a particular skill far surpassing the capability of a normal human being. A Grace could take any form. Most of the kings had at least one Graceling in his kitchens, a superhumanly capable bread baker or winemaker. The luckiest kings had soldiers in their armies Graced with sword fighting. A Graceling might have impossibly good hearing, run as fast as a mountain lion, calculate large sums mentally, even sense if food was poisoned. There were useless Graces, too, like the ability to twist all the way around at the waist or eat rocks without sickening. And there were eerie Graces. Some Gracelings saw future events before they happened. Some could enter the minds of others and see things it was not their business to see. The Nanderan king was said to own a Graceling who could tell if a person had ever committed a crime, just by looking into his face.

The Gracelings were tools of the kings, and no more. They were not thought to be natural, and people who could avoid them did, in Monsea and in most of the other six kingdoms as well. No one wished the company of a Graceling.

Larch had once shared this attitude. Now he saw that it was cruel, unjust, and ignorant, for his son was a normal little boy who happened to be superior in many ways, not just in the way of his Grace, whatever it might turn out to be. It was all the more reason for Larch to remove his son from society. He would not send Immiker to the king's court, to be shunned and teased, and put to whatever use pleased the king.

THEY WERE NOT long in the mountains before Larch accepted, bitterly, that it was an impossible hiding place. It wasn't the cold that was the problem, though autumn here was as raw as midwinter had been on the lord's estate. It wasn't the terrain either, though the scrub was hard and sharp, and they slept on rock every night, and there was no place even to imagine

6

growing vegetables or grain. It was the predators. Not a week went by that Larch didn't have to defend against some attack. Mountain lions, bears, wolves. The enormous birds, the raptors, with a wingspan twice the height of a man. Some of the creatures were territorial, all of them were vicious, and as winter closed in bleakly around Larch and Immiker, all of them were starving. Their horse was lost one day to a pair of mountain lions.

At night, inside the thorny shelter Larch had built of sticks and scrub, he would pull the boy into the warmth of his coat and listen for the howls, the tumbled stones down the slope, the screeches, that meant an animal had scented them. At the first telltale sound he would strap the sleeping boy into the carrier on his chest. He would light as powerful a torch as he had the fuel for, go out of the shelter, and stand there, holding off the attack with fire and sword. Sometimes he stood there for hours. Larch didn't get a lot of sleep.

He wasn't eating much either.

'You'll make yourself sick if you keep eating so much,' Immiker said to Larch over their paltry dinner of stringy wolf meat and water.

Larch stopped chewing immediately, for sickness would make it harder to defend the boy. He handed over the majority of his portion. 'Thank you for the warning, son.'

They ate quietly for a while, Immiker devouring Larch's food. 'What if we went higher into the mountains and crossed to the other side?' Immiker asked.

Larch looked into the boy's mismatched eyes. 'Is that what you think we should do?'

Immiker shrugged his small shoulders. 'Could we survive the crossing?'

'Do you think we could?' Larch asked, and then shook himself as he heard his own question. The child was three years old and knew nothing of crossing mountains. It was a sign of

Larch's fatigue, that he groped so desperately and so often for his son's opinion.

'We would not survive,' Larch said firmly. 'I've heard of no one who has ever made it across the mountains to the east, either here or in Estill or Nander. I know nothing of the land beyond the seven kingdoms, except for tall tales the eastern people tell about rainbow-coloured monsters and underground labyrinths.'

'Then you'll have to bring me back down into the hills, Father, and hide me. You must protect me.'

Larch's mind was foggy, tired, starved, and shot through with one lightning bolt of clarity, which was his determination to do what Immiker said.

Snow was falling as Larch picked his way down a sheer slope. The boy was strapped inside his coat. Larch's sword, his bow and arrows, some blankets and bundled scraps of meat hung on his back. When the great brown raptor appeared over a distant ridge, Larch reached for his bow tiredly. But the bird lunged so fast that all in an instant it was too close to shoot. Larch stumbled away from the creature, fell, and felt himself sliding downward. He braced his arms before him to shield the child, whose screams rose above the screams of the bird: 'Protect me, Father! You must protect me, Father!'

Suddenly the slope under Larch's back gave way and they were falling through darkness. An avalanche, Larch thought numbly, every nerve in his body still focused on protecting the child under his coat. His shoulder hit against something sharp and Larch felt tearing flesh, and wetness, warmth. Strange, to be plunging downward like this. The drop was heady, dizzying, as if it were vertical, a free fall; and just before he slipped into unconsciousness Larch wondered if they were falling through the mountain to the floor of the earth.

⋆

LARCH JACKKNIFED AWAKE, frantic with one thought: Immiker. The boy's body wasn't touching his, and the straps hung from his chest, empty. Larch felt around with his hands, whimpering. It was dark. The surface on which he lay was hard and slick, like slimey ice. He shifted to extend his reach and screamed suddenly, incoherently, at the pain that ripped through his shoulder and head. Nausea surged in his throat. He fought it down and lay still again, weeping helplessly, and moaning the boy's name.

'All right, Father,' Immiker's voice said, very close beside him. 'Stop crying and get up.'

Larch's weeping turned to sobs of relief.

'Get up, Father. I've explored. There's a tunnel and we must go.'

'Are you hurt?'

'I'm cold and hungry. Get up.'

Larch tried to lift his head, and cried out, almost blacked out. 'It's no use. The pain is too great.'

'The pain is not so great that you can't get up,' Immiker said, and when Larch tried again he found that the boy was right. It was excruciating, and he vomited once or twice, but it was not so bad that he couldn't prop himself on his knees and his uninjured arm, and crawl across the icy surface behind his son.

'Where—' he gasped, and then abandoned his question. It was too much work.

'We fell through a crack in the mountain,' Immiker said. 'We slid. There's a tunnel.'

Larch didn't understand, and forward progress took so much concentration that he stopped trying to. The way was slippery and downhill. The place they went toward was slightly darker than the place they came from. His son's small form scuttled down the slope ahead of him.

'There's a drop,' Immiker said, but comprehension came so

slowly to Larch that before he understood, he fell, tumbling knees over neck off a short ledge. He landed on his injured shoulder and momentarily lost consciousness. He woke to a cold breeze and a musty smell that hurt his head. He was in a narrow space, crammed between close walls. He tried to ask whether his fall had injured the boy, but only managed a moan.

'Which way?' Immiker's voice asked.

Larch didn't know what he meant, and moaned again.

Immiker's voice was tired, and impatient. 'I've told you, it's a tunnel. I've felt along the wall in both directions. Choose which way, Father. Take me out of this place.'

The ways were identically dim, identically musty, but Larch needed to choose, if it was what the boy thought best. He shifted himself carefully. His head hurt less when he faced the breeze than when he turned his back to it. This decided him. They would walk toward the source of the breeze.

And that is why, after four days of bleeding, stumbling and starving, after four days of Immiker reminding him repeatedly that he was well enough to keep walking, Larch and Immiker stepped out of the tunnel not into the light of the Monsean foothills, but into that of a strange land on the other side of the Monsean peaks. An eastern land neither of them had heard of except for foolish tales told over Monsean dinners – tales of rainbow-coloured monsters and underground labyrinths.

LARCH WONDERED SOMETIMES if the blow to his head on the day he'd fallen through the mountain had caused some hurt to his brain. The more time he spent in this new land, the more he struggled against a fog hovering on the edge of his mind. The people here spoke differently and Larch struggled with the strange words, the strange sounds. He depended on Immiker to translate. As time passed he depended on Immiker to explain a great many things.

This land was mountainous, stormy and rough. It was

called the Dells. Variations of the animals Larch had known in Monsea lived in the Dells – normal animals, with appearances and behaviour Larch understood and recognised. But also in the Dells lived colourful, astonishing creatures that the Dellian people called monsters. It was their unusual colouration that identified them as monsters, because in every other physical particular they were like normal Dellian animals. They had the shape of Dellian horses, Dellian turtles, mountain lions, raptors, dragonflies, bears; but they were ranges of fuchsia, turquoise, bronze, iridescent green. A dappled grey horse in the Dells was a horse. A sunset orange horse was a monster.

Larch didn't understand these monsters. The mouse monsters, the fly and squirrel and fish and sparrow monsters, were harmless; but the bigger monsters, the man-eating monsters, were terribly dangerous, more so than their animal counterparts. They craved human flesh, and for the flesh of other monsters they were positively frantic. For Immiker's flesh they seemed frantic as well, and as soon as he was big enough to pull back the string of a bow, Immiker learned to shoot. Larch wasn't sure who taught him. Immiker always seemed to have someone, a man or a boy, who guarded him and helped him with this and that. Never the same person. The old ones always disappeared by the time Larch had learned their names, and new ones always took their places.

Larch wasn't even certain where the people came from. He and Immiker lived in a small house, and then a bigger house, then even bigger, in a rocky clearing on the outskirts of a town, and some of Immiker's people came from the town. But others seemed to come out of crevices in the mountains and in the ground. These strange, pallid, underground people brought medicines to Larch. They healed his shoulder.

He heard there were one or two monsters of a human shape in the Dells, with brightly coloured hair, but he never saw them. It was for the best, because Larch could never remember if the human monsters were friendly or not, and against monsters in general he had no defence. They were too beautiful. Their beauty was so extreme that whenever Larch came face to face with one of them, his mind emptied and his body froze, and Immiker and his friends had to defend him.

'It's what they do, Father,' Immiker explained to him, over and over. 'It's part of their monstrous power. They stun you with their beauty, and then they overwhelm your mind and make you stupid. You must learn to guard your mind against them, as I have.'

Larch had no doubt Immiker was right, but still he didn't understand. 'What a horrifying notion,' he said, 'a creature with the power to take over one's mind.'

Immiker burst into delighted laughter, and threw his arm around his father. And still Larch didn't understand; but Immiker's displays of affection were rare, and always overwhelmed Larch with a dumb happiness that numbed the discomfort of his confusion.

IN HIS INFREQUENT moments of mental lucidity, Larch was sure that as Immiker had grown older, Larch himself had grown stupider and more forgetful. Immiker explained to him over and over the unstable politics of this land, the military factions that divided it, the black market that flourished in the underground passages that connected it. Two different Dellian lords, Lord Mydogg in the north and Lord Gentian in the south, were trying to carve their own empires into the landscape and wrest power from the Dellian king. In the far north was a second nation of lakes and mountain peaks called Pikkia.

Larch couldn't keep it straight in his head. He knew only that there were no Gracelings here. No one would take from Larch his son whose eyes were two different colours.

Eyes of two different colours. Immiker was a Graceling. Larch thought about this sometimes, when his mind was clear enough for thought. He wondered when his son's Grace would appear.

In his clearest moments, which only came to him when Immiker left him alone for a while, Larch wondered if it already had.

IMMIKER HAD HOBBIES. He liked to play with little monsters. He liked to tie them down and peel away their claws, or their vividly coloured scales, or clumps of their hair and feathers. One day in the boy's tenth year, Larch came upon Immiker slicing stripes down the stomach of a rabbit that was coloured like the sky.

Even bleeding, even shaking and wild-eyed, the rabbit was beautiful to Larch. He stared at the creature and forgot why he'd come looking for Immiker. How sad it was, to see something so small and helpless, something so beautiful, damaged in fun. The rabbit began to make noises, horrible, panicked squeaks, and Larch heard himself whimpering.

Immiker glanced at Larch. 'It doesn't hurt her, Father.'

Instantly Larch felt better, knowing that the monster wasn't in pain. But then the rabbit let out a very small, very desperate whine, and Larch was confused. He looked at his son. The boy held a dagger dripping with blood before the eyes of the shaking creature, and smiled at his father.

Somewhere in the depths of Larch's mind a prick of suspicion made itself felt. Larch remembered why he'd come looking for Immiker.

'I have an idea,' Larch said slowly, 'about the nature of your Grace.'

Immiker's eyes flicked calmly, carefully, to Larch's. 'Do you?'

'You've said that the monsters take over my mind with their beauty.'

Immiker lowered his knife, and tilted his head at his father.

There was something odd in the boy's face. Disbelief, Larch thought, and a strange, amused smile. As if the boy were playing a game he was used to winning, and this time he'd lost.

'Sometimes I think you take over my mind,' Larch said, 'with your words.'

Immiker's smile widened, and then he began to laugh. The laughter made Larch so happy that he began to laugh as well. How much he loved this child. The love and the laughter bubbled out of him, and when Immiker walked toward him Larch held his arms open wide. Immiker thrust his dagger into Larch's stomach. Larch dropped like a stone to the floor.

Immiker leaned over his father. 'You've been delightful,' he said. 'I'll miss your devotion. If only it were as easy to control everyone as it is to control you. If only everyone were as stupid as you are, Father.'

IT WAS STRANGE, to be dying. Cold and dizzying, like his fall through the Monsean mountains. But Larch knew he wasn't falling through the Monsean mountains; in death he knew clearly, for the first time in years, where he was and what was happening. His last thought was that it hadn't been stupidity that had allowed his son to enchant him so easily with words. It had been love. Larch's love had kept him from recognising Immiker's Grace, because even before the boy's birth, when Immiker had been no more than a promise inside Mikra's body, Larch had already been enchanted.

FIFTEEN MINUTES LATER Larch's body and his house were on fire and Immiker was on his pony's back, picking his way through the caves to the north. It was a relief to be moving on. His surroundings and his neighbours had become tedious of late, and he was restless. Ready for something more.

He decided to mark this new era in his life with a change of his foolish, sentimental name. The people of this land had an odd way of pronouncing Larch's name, and Immiker had always liked the sound of it.

He changed his name to Leck.

A YEAR PASSED.

PART ONE

Monsters

CHAPTER ONE

IT DID NOT surprise Fire that the man in the forest shot her. What surprised her was that he shot her by accident.

The arrow whacked her square in the arm and threw her sideways against a boulder, which knocked the air out of her. The pain was too great to ignore, but behind it she focused her mind, made it cold and sharp, like a single star in a black winter sky. If he was a cool man, certain in what he was doing, he would be guarded against her, but Fire rarely encountered this type. More often the men who tried to hurt her were angry or arrogant or frightened enough that she could find a crack in the fortress of their thoughts, and ease her way in.

She found this man's mind instantly – so open, so welcoming, even, that she wondered if he could be a simpleton hired by someone else. She fumbled for the knife in her boot. His footfalls, and then his breath, sounded through the trees. She had no time to waste, for he would shoot her again as soon as he found her. *You don't want to kill me. You've changed your mind.*

Then he rounded a tree and his blue eyes caught hold of her, and widened in astonishment and horror.

'Not a girl!' he cried out.

Fire's thoughts scrambled. Had he not meant to strike her? Did he not know who she was? Had he meant to murder Archer? She forced her voice calm. 'Who was your target?'

'Not who,' he said. 'What. Your cloak is brown pelt. Your dress is brown. Rocks alive, girl,' he said in a burst of exasperation. He marched toward her and inspected the arrow embedded in her upper arm, the blood that soaked her cloak, her sleeve, her headscarf. 'A fellow would think you were hoping to be shot by a hunter.'

More accurately, a poacher, since Archer forebade hunting in these woods at this time of day, just so that Fire could pass through here dressed this way. Besides, she'd never seen this shortish, tawny-haired, light-eyed man before. Well. If he was not only a poacher, but a poacher who'd accidentally shot Fire while hunting illegally, then he would not want to turn himself in to Archer's famous temper; but that was what she was going to have to make him want to do. She was losing blood, and she was beginning to feel light-headed. She would need his assistance to get home.

'Now I'll have to kill you,' he said glumly. And then, before she could begin to address that rather bizarre statement: 'Wait. Who are you? Tell me you're not her.'

'Not who?' she hedged, reaching again for his mind, and finding it still strangely blank, as if his intentions were floating, lost in a fog.

'Your hair is covered,' he said. 'Your eyes, your face – oh, save me.' He backed away from her. 'Your eyes are so green. I'm a dead man.'

He was an odd one, with his talk of killing her, and himself dying, and his peculiar floating brain; and now he looked ready to bolt, which Fire must not allow. She grasped at his thoughts and slid them into place. *You don't find my eyes or my face to be all that remarkable.*

The man squinted at her, puzzled.

The more you look at me the more you see I'm just an ordinary girl. You've found an ordinary girl injured in the forest, and now you must rescue me. You must take me to Lord Archer.

Here Fire encountered a small resistance in the form of the man's fear. She pulled harder at his mind, and smiled at him, the most gorgeous smile she could muster while throbbing with pain and dying of blood loss. *Lord Archer will reward you and keep you safe, and you will be honoured as a hero.*

There was no hesitation. He eased her quiver and her fiddle case from her back and slung them over his shoulder against his own quiver. He took up both of their bows in one hand and wrapped her right arm, her uninjured arm, around his neck. 'Come along, miss,' he said. He half led her, half carried her, through the trees toward Archer's holding.

He knows the way, she thought tiredly, and then she let the thought go. It didn't matter who he was or where he came from. It only mattered that she stay awake and inside his head until he got her home and Archer's people had seized him. She kept her eyes and ears and her mind alert for monsters, for neither her headscarf nor her own mental guard against them would hide her from them if they smelled her blood.

At least she could count on this poacher to be a decent shot.

ARCHER BROUGHT DOWN a raptor monster as Fire and the poacher stumbled out of the trees. A beautiful, long shot from the upper terrace that Fire was in no state to admire, but that caused the poacher to murmur something under his breath about the appropriateness of the young lord's nickname. The monster plummeted from the sky and crashed onto the pathway to the door. Its colour was the rich orange-gold of a sunflower.

Archer stood tall and graceful on the stone terrace, eyes raised to the sky, longbow lightly in hand. He reached to the quiver on his back, notched another arrow, and swept the treetops. Then he saw them, the man dragging her bleeding from the forest. He turned on his heel and ran into the house, and even down here, even from this distance and stone walls between them, Fire could hear him yelling. She sent words and feeling into his mind, not mind control, only a message. *Don't worry. Seize him and disarm him, but don't hurt him. Please,* she added, for whatever it was worth with Archer. *He's a nice man and I've had to trick him.*

Archer burst through the great front door with his captain Palla, his healer, and five of his guard. He leapt over the raptor and ran to Fire. 'I found her in the forest,' the poacher cried. 'I found her. I saved her life.'

Once the guards had taken hold of the poacher, Fire released his mind. The relief of it weakened her knees and she slumped against Archer.

'Fire,' her friend was saying. 'Fire. Are you all right? Where else are you hurt?'

She couldn't stand. Archer grasped her, lowered her to the ground. She shook her head numbly. 'Nowhere.'

'Let her sit,' the healer said. 'Let her lie down. I must stop the flow of blood.'

Archer was wild. 'Will she be all right?'

'Most certainly,' the healer said curtly, 'if you will get out of my way and let me stop the flow of blood. My Lord.'

Archer let out a ragged breath and kissed Fire's forehead. He untangled himself from her body and crouched on his heels, clenching and unclenching his fists. Then he turned to peer at the poacher held by his guards, and Fire thought warningly, *Archer*, for she knew that with his anxieties unsoothed, Archer was transitioning now to fury.

'A nice man who must nonetheless be seized,' he hissed at the poacher, standing. 'I can see that the arrow in her arm came from your quiver. Who are you and who sent you?'

The poacher barely noticed Archer. He stared down at Fire, boggle-eyed. 'She's beautiful again,' he said. 'I'm a dead man.'

'He won't kill you,' Fire told him soothingly. 'He doesn't kill poachers, and anyway, you saved me.'

'If you shot her I'll kill you with pleasure,' Archer said.

'It makes no difference what you do,' the poacher said.

Archer glared down at the man. 'And if you were so intent

on rescuing her, why didn't you remove the arrow yourself and bind the wound before dragging her half across the world?'

'Archer,' Fire said, and then stopped, choking back a cry as the healer ripped off her bloody sleeve. 'He was under my control, and I didn't think of it. Leave him alone.'

Archer swung on her. 'And why didn't you think of it? Where is your common sense?'

'Lord Archer,' the healer said testily. 'There will be no yelling at people who are bleeding themselves to unconsciousness. Make yourself useful. Hold her down, will you, while I remove this arrow; and then you'll do best to look to the skies.'

Archer knelt beside her and took hold of her shoulders. His face was wooden but his voice shook with emotion. 'Forgive me, Fire.' To the healer: 'We're mad to be doing this outside. They smell the blood.'

And then sudden pain, blinding and brilliant. Fire wrenched her head and fought against the healer, against Archer's heavy strength. Her scarf slipped off and released the shimmering prism of her hair: sunrise, poppy, copper, fuchsia, flame. Red, brighter than the blood soaking the doorpath.

SHE ATE DINNER in her own stone house, which was just beyond Archer's and under the protection of his guard. He had sent the dead raptor monster to her kitchen. Archer was one of very few people who made her feel no shame for craving the taste of monster meat.

She ate in bed, and he sat with her. He cut her meat and encouraged her. Eating hurt, everything hurt.

The poacher was gaoled in one of the outdoor monster cages Fire's father, Lord Cansrel, had built into the hill behind the house. 'I hope there's a lightning storm,' Archer said. 'I hope for a flood. I would like the ground under your poacher to crack open and swallow him.'

She ignored him. She knew it was only hot air.

'I passed Donal in your hall,' he said, 'sneaking out with a pile of blankets and pillows. You're building your assassin a bed out there, aren't you? And probably feeding him as well as you feed yourself.'

'He's not an assassin, only a poacher with fuzzy eyesight.'

'You believe that even less than I do.'

'All right, but I do believe that when he shot me, he thought I was a deer.'

Archer sat back and crossed his arms. 'Perhaps. We'll talk to him again tomorrow. We'll have his story from him.'

'I would rather not help.'

'I would rather not ask you, darling, but I need to know who this man is and who sent him. He's the second stranger to be seen on my land these two weeks.'

Fire lay back, closed her eyes, forced her jaw to chew. Everyone was a stranger. Strangers came out of the rocks, the hills, and it was impossible to know everyone's truth. She didn't want to know – nor did she want to use her powers to find out. It was one thing to take over a man's mind to prevent her own death, and another thing entirely to steal his secrets.

When she turned to Archer again, he was watching her quietly. His white-blond hair and his deep brown eyes, his proud mouth. The familiar features she'd known since she was a toddler and he was a child, always carrying a bow around as long as his own height. It was she who'd first modified his real name, Arklin, to Archer, and he had taught her to shoot. And looking into his face now, the face of a grown man responsible for a northern estate, its money, its farms, its people, she understood his anxiety. It was not a peaceful time in the Dells. In King's City, young King Nash was clinging, with some desperation, to the throne, while rebel lords like Lord Mydogg in the north and Lord Gentian in the south built armies and thought about how to unseat him.

War was coming. And the mountains and forests swarmed

with spies and thieves and other lawless men. Strangers were always alarming.

Archer's voice was soft. 'You won't be able to go outside alone until you can shoot again. The raptors are out of control. I'm sorry, Fire.'

Fire swallowed. She'd been trying not to think about this particular bleakness. 'It makes no difference. I can't play fiddle, either, or harp or flute or any of my instruments. I have no need to leave home.'

'We'll send word to your students.' He sighed and rubbed his neck. 'And I'll see whom I can place in their houses in your stead. Until you heal, we'll be forced to trust our neighbours without the help of your insight.' For trust was not assumed these days, even among long-standing neighbours, and one of Fire's jobs as she gave music lessons was to keep her eyes and ears open. Occasionally she learned something – information, conversation, the sense of something wrong – that was a help to Archer and his father, Brocker, both loyal allies to the king.

It was also a long time for Fire to live without the comfort of her own music. She closed her eyes again and breathed slowly. These were always the worst injuries, the ones that left her unable to play her fiddle.

She hummed to herself, a song they both knew about the northern Dells, a song that Archer's father always liked her to play when she sat with him.

Archer took the hand of her uninjured arm, and kissed it. He kissed her fingers, her wrist. His lips brushed her forearm.

She stopped humming. She opened her eyes to the sight of his, mischievous and brown, smiling into hers.

You can't be serious, she thought to him.

He touched her hair, shining against the blankets. 'You look unhappy.'

Archer. It hurts to move.

'You don't have to move. And I can erase your pain.'

She smiled, despite herself, and spoke aloud. 'No doubt. But so can sleep. Go home, Archer. I'm sure you can find someone else's pain to erase.'

'So callous,' he said teasingly, 'when you know how worried I was for you today.'

She did know how worried. She merely doubted that the worry had changed his nature.

OF COURSE, AFTER he'd gone, she did not sleep. She tried, but nightmares brought her awake over and over again. Her nightmares were always worse on days when she'd spent time down among the cages, for that was where her father had died.

Cansrel, her beautiful monster father. Monsters in the Dells came from monsters. A monster could breed with a non-monster of its species – her mother had not been a monster – but the progeny was always monstrous. Cansrel had had glittery silver hair with glints of blue, and deep, dark blue eyes. His body, his face breathtaking, smooth and beautifully cut, like crystal reflecting light, glowing with that intangible something that all monsters have. He had been the most stunning man alive when he'd lived, or at least Fire had found him so. He had been better than she at controlling the minds of humans. He had had a great deal more practice.

Fire lay in her bed and fought off the dream memory. The growling leopard monster, midnight blue with gold spots, astride her father. The smell of her father's blood, his gorgeous eyes on her, disbelieving. Dying.

She wished now that she hadn't sent Archer home. Archer understood the nightmares, and Archer was alive and passionate. She wanted his company, his vitality.

In her bed she grew more and more restless, and finally she did a thing that would have turned Archer livid. She dragged herself to her closets and dressed herself, slowly, painfully, in coat and trousers, dark browns and blacks to match the night.

Her attempt to wrap her hair almost sent her back to bed, since she needed both arms to do it and lifting her left arm was an agony. Somehow she managed, capitulating at one point to the use of a mirror to be sure that no hair was showing in back. Generally she avoided mirrors. It embarrassed her to lose her own breath at the sight of herself.

She stuck a knife in her belt and hefted a spear and ignored her own conscience calling, singing, screaming to her that she couldn't even protect herself from a porcupine tonight, let alone a monster raptor or monster wolf.

Next was the hardest part of all, one-armed. She had to sneak out of her own house by way of the tree outside her window, for Archer's guards stood at all her doorways, and they would never allow her to wander the hills injured and alone. Unless she used her power to control them, and that she would not do. Archer's guards trusted her.

Archer had been the one to notice how closely this ancient tree hugged the house and how easily he could climb it in the dark, two years ago, when Cansrel had still been alive, and Archer had been eighteen and Fire had been fifteen and their friendship had evolved in a manner Cansrel's guards hadn't needed to know the particulars of. A manner that had been unexpected to her, and sweet, and boosted her small list of happinesses. What Archer hadn't known was that Fire had begun to use the route herself, almost immediately, first to skirt Cansrel's men and then, after Cansrel was dead, Archer's own. Not to do anything shocking or forbidden; just to walk at night by herself, without everyone knowing.

She pitched her spear out the window. What followed was an ordeal that involved much swearing and tearing of cloth and fingernails. On solid ground, sweating and shaking and appreciating fully now what a foolish idea this had been, she used her spear as a cane and limped away from the house. She didn't want to go far, just out of the trees so that she could see the stars. They always eased her lonesomeness. She thought of them as beautiful creatures, burning and cold; each solitary, and bleak, and silent like her.

TONIGHT THEY WERE clear and perfect in the sky.

Standing on a rocky patch that rose beyond Cansrel's monster cages, she bathed in the light of the stars and tried to soak up some of their quiet. Breathing deep, she rubbed the place in her hip that still ached sometimes from an arrow scar that was months old. Always one of the trials of a new wound: all the old wounds liked to rise up and start hurting again, too.

She'd never been injured accidentally before. It was hard to know how to categorise this attack in her mind; it almost seemed funny. She had a dagger scar on one forearm, another on her belly. An arrow gouge from years ago in her back. It was a thing that happened now and then. For every peaceful man, there was a man who wanted to hurt her, even kill her, because she was a gorgeous thing he could not have, or because he'd despised her father. And for every attack that had left a scar there were five or six other attacks she'd managed to stop.

Tooth marks on one wrist: a wolf monster. Claw marks at one shoulder: a raptor monster. Other wounds, too, the small, invisible kind. Just this morning, in the town, a man's hot eyes on her body, and the man's wife beside him, burning at Fire with jealousy and hatred. Or the monthly humiliation of needing a guard during her woman's bleedings to protect her from monsters who could smell her blood.

'The attention shouldn't embarrass you,' Cansrel would have said. 'It should gladden you. Don't you feel it, the joy of having an effect on everyone and everything simply by *being*?'

Cansrel had never found any of it humiliating. He'd kept predator monsters as pets – a silvery lavender raptor, a blood-purple mountain lion, a grass-coloured bear glinting with gold, the midnight blue leopard with gold spots. He'd underfed them on purpose and walked among their cages, his hair uncovered, scratching his own skin with a knife so that his blood beaded on the surface. It had been one of his favourite things to make his monsters scream and roar and scrape their teeth on the metal bars, wild with their desire for his monster body.

She couldn't begin to imagine feeling that way, without fear, or shame.

THE AIR WAS turning damp and cold, and peace was too far away for her to reach tonight.

Slowly she headed back to her tree. She tried to grab hold and climb, but it didn't take much scrabbling at the trunk for her to understand that she was not, under any circumstances, going to be able to enter her bedroom the way she'd exited.

Leaning into the tree, sore and weary, Fire cursed her stupidity. She had two options now, and neither was acceptable. Either she must turn herself in to the guards at her doors and tomorrow wage a battle over her freedom with Archer, or she must enter the mind of one of those guards and trick his thoughts.

She reached out tentatively to see who was around. The poacher's mind bobbed against hers, asleep in his cage. Guarding her house were a number of men whose minds she recognised. At her side entrance was an older fellow named Krell who was something of a friend to her – or would have been, did he not have the tendency to admire her too much. He was a musician, easily as talented as she and more experienced, and they played together sometimes, Fire on her fiddle and Krell on flute or whistle. Too convinced of her perfection, Krell, ever to suspect her. An easy mark.

Fire sighed. Archer was a better friend when he did not know every detail of her life and mind. She would have to do this.

She slipped up to the house and into the trees near the side door. The feeling of a monster reaching for the gates of one's mind was subtle. A strong and practiced person could learn to recognise the encroachment and slam the gates shut. Tonight Krell's mind was alert for trespassers but not for this type of invasion; he was open and bored, and she crept her way in. He noticed a change and adjusted his focus, startled, but she worked quickly to distract him. *You heard something. There it is, can you hear it again? Shouts, near the front of the house. Step away from the door and turn to look.*

Without pause he moved from the entrance and turned his back to her. She crept out of the trees toward the door.

You hear nothing behind you, only before you. The door behind you is closed.

He never swung around to check, never even doubted the thoughts she'd implanted in his mind. She opened the door behind him, slipped through, and shut herself in, then leaned against the wall of her hallway for a moment, oddly depressed at how easy that had been. It seemed to her that it shouldn't be so easy to make a man into a fool.

Rather bleak now with self-disgust, she slumped her way upstairs to her room. A particular song was stuck in her head, dully playing itself over and over, though she couldn't think why. It was the funeral lament sung in the Dells to mourn the waste of a life.

She supposed thoughts of her father had brought the song to mind. She had never sung it for him or played it on her fiddle. She'd been too numb with grief and confusion to play anything after he'd died. A fire had been lit for him, but she had not gone to see it.

It had been a gift from Cansrel, her fiddle. One of his strange kindnesses, for he'd never had patience for her music. And now Fire was alone, the only remaining human monster in the Dells, and her fiddle was one of few happy things she had to remember him by.

Happy.

Well, she supposed there was a kind of gladness in his remembrance, some of the time. But it didn't change reality. In one way or another, all that was wrong in the Dells could be traced back to Cansrel.

It was not a thought to bring peace. But delirious now with fatigue, she slept soundly, the Dellian lament a backdrop to her dreams.

CHAPTER TWO

FIRE WOKE FIRST to pain, and then to the consciousness of an unusual level of agitation in her house. Guards were bustling around downstairs, and Archer was among them.

When a servant passed her bedroom door Fire touched the girl's mind, summoning her. The girl entered the room, not looking at Fire, glaring mutinously instead at the feather duster in her own hand. Still, at least she had come. Some of them scurried away, pretending not to hear.

She said stiffly, 'Yes, Lady?'

'Sofie, why are there so many men downstairs?'

'The poacher in the cages was found dead this morning, Lady,' Sofie said. 'An arrow in his throat.'

Sofie turned on her heel, snapping the door shut behind her, leaving Fire lying heartsick in bed.

She couldn't help but feel that this was her fault somehow, for looking like a deer.

SHE DRESSED AND went downstairs to her steward, Donal, who was grizzled and strong-headed and had served her since she was a baby. Donal raised a grey eyebrow at her and cocked his head in the direction of the back terrace. 'I don't think he much cares whom he shoots,' he said.

Fire knew he meant Archer, whose exasperation she could sense on the other side of the wall. For all of his hot words, Archer did not like people in his care to die.

'Help me cover my hair, will you, Donal?'

A minute later, hair wrapped in brown, Fire went out to be with Archer in his unhappiness. The air on the terrace was wet like coming rain. Archer wore a long brown coat. Everything about him was sharp – the bow in his hand and the arrows on his back, his frustrated bursts of movement, his expression as he glared over the hills. She leaned on the railing beside him.

'I should have anticipated this,' he said, not looking at her. 'He as good as told us it would happen.'

'There's nothing you could have done. Your guard is already spread too thin.'

'I could have imprisoned him inside.'

'And how many guards would that have taken? We live in stone houses, Archer, not palaces, and we don't have dungeons.'

He swiped at the air with his hand. 'We're mad, you know that? Mad to think we can live here, so far from King's City, and protect ourselves from Pikkians and looters and the spies of rebel lords.'

'He hadn't the look or the speech of a Pikkian,' she said. 'He was Dellian, like us. And he was clean and tidy and civilised, not like any looter we've ever seen.'

The Pikkians were the boat people from the land above the Dells, and it was true that they crossed the border sometimes to steal timber and even labourers from the Dellian north. But the men of Pikkia, though not all alike, tended to be big, and lighter-skinned than their Dellian neighbours – at any rate, not small and dark like the blue-eyed poacher had been. And Pikkians spoke with a distinctive throaty accent.

'Well,' Archer said, determined not to be soothed, 'then he was a spy. Lord Mydogg and Lord Gentian have spies crawling all over the kingdom, spying on the king, spying on the prince, spying on each other – spying on you, for all we know,' he added grouchily. 'Has it never occurred to you that the enemies of King Nash and Prince Brigan might want to steal you and use you as a tool to overthrow the royal family?'

'You think everyone wants to steal me,' Fire said mildly. 'If your own father had me tied up and sold to a monster zoo for spare change, you'd claim that you'd suspected him all along.'

He spluttered at this. 'You *should* suspect your friends, or at least anyone other than me and Brocker. And you should have a guard whenever you walk out your door, and you should be quicker to manipulate the people you meet. Then I'd have less cause to worry.'

These were old arguments and he already knew her responses by heart. She ignored him. 'Our poacher was a spy of neither Lord Mydogg's nor Lord Gentian's,' she said calmly.

'Mydogg has grown quite an army for himself in the northeast. If he decided to "borrow" our more central land to use as a stronghold in a war against the king, we wouldn't be able to stop him.'

'Archer, be reasonable. The King's Army wouldn't leave us alone to defend ourselves. And regardless, the poacher was not sent here by a rebel lord; he was far too vapid. Mydogg would never employ a vapid scout, and if Gentian lacks Mydogg's intelligence, well, still, he's not fool enough to send a man with a floating, empty head to do his spying.'

'All right,' Archer said, voice rising in exasperation, 'then I return to the theory that it's something to do with you. The moment he recognised you he talked about being a dead man, and clearly he was well-informed on that point. Explain it to me, will you? Who was the man, and why the rocks is he dead?'

He was dead because he'd hurt her, Fire thought; or maybe because she'd seen him and talked to him. Little sense in it, but it would make a good joke, if Archer were in the mood for any sort of joke. The poacher's murderer was a man after Archer's own heart, for Archer also didn't like men to hurt Fire or make her acquaintance.

'And a rather good shot,' she said out loud.

He was still glowering into the distance, as if he expected the murderer to pop up from behind a boulder and wave. 'Hmm?'

'You'd get along well with this murderer, Archer. He would've had to shoot through both the bars of the outer enclosure and the bars of the poacher's cage, wouldn't he? He must be a good shot.'

Admiration for another archer seemed to cheer him slightly. 'More than that. From the depth of the wound and the angle, I think he fired long-range, from the trees beyond that rise.' He pointed to the bald patch Fire had climbed the night before. 'Through two sets of bars is impressive enough, and then into the man's throat? At least we can be sure none of our neighbours did it personally. Not one of them could have made that shot.'

'Could you?'

The question was a small gift to him to improve his mood, for there was no shot made that Archer couldn't match. He glanced at her, grinning. Looked at her again more closely. His face softened. 'I'm a beast for taking this long to ask how you feel this morning.'

The muscles of her back were tight knots of rope and her bandaged arm ached; her entire body was paying dearly for last night's abuse. 'I'm all right.'

'Are you warm enough? Take my coat.'

They sat for a while on the steps of the terrace, Fire wrapped in Archer's coat. They talked about Archer's plans for breaking ground in the fields. Soon enough it would be time for the spring planting, and northern soil, rocky and cold, always resisted the start of a new growing season.

Now and then Fire sensed a raptor monster overhead. She kept her own mind hidden from them so they wouldn't recognise her for the monster prey she was; but of course, in the absence of monster prey, they ate any living creature available. One that spotted Fire and Archer dropped down and began to circle, posing shamelessly, intangibly lovely, reaching for their minds, radiating a feeling that was hungry, primitive, and oddly soothing. Archer stood and shot it, then shot another that did the same, the first violet like sunrise, the second so pale a yellow it looked like the moon dropping from the sky.

At least fractured on the ground, Fire thought, the monsters added colour to the landscape. There was little colour in the north of the Dells in early spring – the trees were grey and the grass that tufted between cracks in the rocks was still brown from winter. Truly, even at the height of summer the north of the Dells was not what one would call colourful, but at least in summer, grey with patches of brown turned to grey with patches of green.

'Who found the poacher, anyway?' Fire asked idly.

'Tovat,' Archer said. 'One of the newer guards. You'll not have met him yet.'

'Oh, yes – the young one with the brown-orange hair that people called red. I like him. He's strong-minded and he guards himself.'

'You know Tovat? You admire his hair, do you?' Archer said in a sharp and familiar tone.

'Archer, honestly. I said nothing of admiring his hair. And I know the names and faces of all the men you station at my house. It's simple courtesy.'

'I won't be stationing Tovat at your house any longer,' he said, an unpleasant edge to his voice that drove her to silence for a moment, so that she wouldn't say anything unpleasant back about Archer's dubious – and rather hypocritical – right to jealousy. He opened a feeling to her that she didn't particularly care to feel just now. Biting back a sigh, she chose words that would protect Tovat.

'I hope you'll change your mind. He's one of the few guards who respects me both with his body and in his mind.'

'Marry me,' Archer said, 'and live in my house, and I will be your guard.'

She could not bite back this sigh. 'You know that I won't. I wish you would stop asking me.' A fat raindrop plopped onto her sleeve. 'I think I'll go and visit your father.'

She stood, creaking with pain, and let his coat slide off into his lap. She touched his shoulder once, gently. Even when she did not like Archer, she loved him.

As she went into the house, rain began to fall.

ARCHER'S FATHER LIVED in Archer's house. Fire asked a guard who was not Tovat to accompany her along the path through the rain. She carried a spear, but still, without her longbow and quiver she felt naked.

Lord Brocker was in his son's armoury, thundering instructions at a large man Fire recognised as the assistant to the blacksmith in town. At the sight of her Lord Brocker did not let off his thundering, but momentarily he lost the attention of his listener. The blacksmith turned to stare at Fire, some base thing in his eyes and in his silly, stupid smile.

He'd known Fire for long enough, this man, to have learned how to guard himself against the power of her strange monster beauty, so if he was not guarding himself, then he must not want to. His prerogative, to give up his mind in return for the pleasure of succumbing to her, but not something she cared to encourage. She kept her headscarf on. She pushed his mind away and walked past him into a side room so that she couldn't be seen. A closet really, dark, and with shelves full of oils and polish and ancient, rusted equipment no one ever used.

It was humiliating to have to retreat to a smelly old closet. The blacksmith should be the one to feel humiliated, for he was the dunce who chose to give up his self-control. What if while he gaped at her and imagined whatever his small mind cared to imagine, she convinced him to draw his knife and take out his own eye? It was the sort of thing Cansrel would have liked to do. Cansrel had never retreated.

The men's voices stopped and the blacksmith's mind

receded from the armoury. The big wheels of Lord Brocker's chair squeaked as he rolled himself toward her. He stopped in the doorway of the closet. 'Come out of there, child; he's gone. The moron. If a mouse monster stole that one's meal from under his nose, he'd scratch his head and wonder why he couldn't remember eating his food. Let's go to my rooms. You look like you should sit down.'

Archer's house had been Brocker's house before Brocker had turned the running of the estate over to his son, and Brocker had used a wheeled chair before Archer had ever been born. The house was organised such that everything but Archer's rooms and servant rooms were on the first floor, where Brocker could reach them.

Fire walked beside him down a stone hallway that was dim in the grey light seeping through tall windows. They passed the kitchen, the dining room, the stairway, and the guard room. The house was full of people, servants and guards coming in from outside, coming down from upstairs. The servant girls who passed them greeted Brocker but carefully ignored Fire, their minds guarded and cool. As always. If Archer's servants did not resent her because she was a monster and Cansrel's daughter, they resented her because they were in love with Archer.

Fire was happy to sink into a soft chair in Lord Brocker's library and drink the cup of wine an unfriendly servant clapped into her hand. Brocker positioned his chair across from hers and settled his grey eyes on her face. 'I'll leave you alone, dear,' he said, 'if you wish to nap.'

'Perhaps later.'

'When's the last time you had a good night's sleep?'

Brocker was one person she felt comfortable admitting pain to, and fatigue. 'I can't remember. It's not a thing that happens very often.'

'You know there are drugs that will put you to sleep.'

'They make me groggy, and stupid.'

'I've just finished writing a history of military strategy in the Dells. You're welcome to take it with you. It'll put you to sleep while making you clever and unbeatable.'

Fire smiled and sipped the bitter Dellian wine. She doubted that Brocker's history would put her to sleep. All she knew about armies and war came from Brocker, and he was never boring. Twenty-some years ago, in the heyday of old King Nax, Brocker had been the most brilliant military commander the Dells had ever seen. Until the day King Nax had seized him and shattered his legs – not broken them, but shattered them, eight men taking turns with a mallet – and then sent him home, half-dead, to his wife, Aliss, in the northern Dells.

Fire didn't know what terrible thing Brocker had done to justify such treatment from his king. Neither did Archer. The entire episode had taken place before they were born, and Brocker never spoke of it. And the injuries were only the beginning of it, for a year or two later, when Brocker had recovered as well as he ever would, Nax had still been angry with his commander. He'd hand-picked a brute from his prisons, a dirty, savage man, and sent him north to punish Brocker by punishing Brocker's wife. This was why Archer was brown-eyed, light-haired, handsome, and tall, while Brocker was grey-eyed and dark-haired and plain in appearance. Lord Brocker was not Archer's true father.

In some places and times Brocker's would have been a mind-boggling story, but not in King's City and not in the days when King Nax had ruled at the pleasure of his closest adviser. Cansrel.

Brocker spoke, interrupting her gruesome thoughts. 'I understand you've had the rare pleasure of being shot by a man who was not trying to kill you,' he said. 'Did it feel any different?'

Fire laughed. 'I've never been shot more pleasantly.'

He chuckled, studying her with his mild grey eyes. 'It's rewarding to make you smile. The pain in your face drops away.'

He had always been able to make her smile. It was a relief to her, his dependable light mood, especially on days when Archer's mood was heavy. And it was remarkable, since every moment he was in pain.

'Brocker,' she said. 'Do you think it could have been different?'

He tilted his head, puzzled.

'I mean Cansrel,' she said, 'and King Nax. Do you think their partnership could ever have been different? Could the Dells have survived them?'

Brocker considered her, his face gone quiet and grave at the very mention of Cansrel's name. 'Nax's father was a decent king,' he said. 'And Cansrel's father was a valuable monster adviser to him. But, darling, Nax and Cansrel were two other creatures entirely. Nax didn't inherit his father's strength, and you know as well as anyone that Cansrel didn't inherit even a touch of his father's empathy. And they grew up together as boys, so when Nax took the throne, he'd already had Cansrel living inside his head his whole life. Oh, Nax had a good heart, I'm sure of it – sometimes I saw it – but it didn't matter, because he was also just the smallest bit lazy, the smallest bit too willing to let someone else do his thinking – and that was all the opening Cansrel ever needed. Nax never had a chance,' Brocker said, shaking his head, squinting at memories. 'From the start, Cansrel used Nax to get everything he wanted, and all Cansrel ever wanted was his own pleasure. It was inevitable, sweetheart,' he said, bringing his attention back to her face. 'As long as they lived, Cansrel and Nax were always going to lead the kingdom to ruin.'

Ruin. Fire knew, for Brocker had told her, the progressive steps that had led to ruin once young Nax had taken the throne. It had started with women and parties, and that hadn't been so bad, for Nax had fallen in love with a black-haired lady from the northern Dells named Roen and married her. King Nax and Queen Roen had produced a son, a handsome, dark boy named Nash, and even with a somewhat neglectful king at its helm the kingdom had had an aura of stability.

Except that Cansrel had been bored. His gratification had always required excess, and now he began to need more women and more parties, and wine, and children from the court to alleviate the monotony of the women. And drugs. Nax had agreed to it all; Nax had been like a shell to hold Cansrel's mind and nod its head yes to whatever Cansrel said was best.

'Yet, you've told me that ultimately it was the drugs that destroyed Nax,' Fire said. 'Could Nax have held on if it hadn't been for the drugs?'

'Perhaps,' Brocker said lightly. 'Cansrel could always keep hold of himself with poison in his veins, blast him, but Nax couldn't; it made him high-strung, and paranoid, and uncontrolled, and more vindictive than he'd ever been before.'

He stopped at that, staring bleakly at his own useless legs. Fire kept her feeling tight within herself so that he would not be flooded with her curiosity. Or her pity; her pity must never touch him.

A moment later he looked up and held her eyes again. He smiled very slightly. 'Perhaps it would be fair to say that Nax mightn't have turned into a madman if it weren't for the drugs. But I believe the drugs were as inevitable as the rest. And Cansrel himself was the truest drug to Nax's mind. People saw what was happening – they saw Nax punishing law-abiding men and making alliances with criminals and wasting all the money in the king's coffers. Allies of Nax's father began to withdraw their support for Nax, as they were bound to do. And ambitious fellows like Mydogg and Gentian began to think and plot, and train squadrons of soldiers, under the guise of self-defence. And who could blame a mountain lord for that, with things so unstable? There was no law anymore, not outside the city, for Nax couldn't be troubled to attend to it. The roads were no longer safe, you had to be mad or desperate to travel the underground routes, looters and raiders and black market thugs were cropping up everywhere. Even the Pikkians. For ages, they'd been content to squabble among themselves. Now, suddenly, even they couldn't resist taking advantage of our lawlessness.'

Fire knew all of this; she knew her own history. In the end, a kingdom connected by underground tunnels and riddled with caves and hidden mountain holdings could not bear so much volatility. There were too many places for bad things to hide.

Wars had broken out in the Dells; not proper wars with well-defined political adversaries, but bungling mountain turf wars, one neighbour against another, one party of cave raiders against some poor lord's holding, one alliance of Dellian lords against the king. Brocker had been in charge of quelling all uprisings, all across the Dells. He'd been a far better military leader than Nax had deserved, and for several years, Brocker had done an impressive job of it. But he and the army had been on their own; in King's City, Cansrel and Nax had been busy, plowing their way through women and drugs.

King Nax had fathered a set of twins with a palace laundry girl. Then Brocker had committed his mysterious offense, and Nax had retaliated. And on the day that Nax had destroyed his own military commander, he'd dealt a fatal blow to any hope of rule in his kingdom. The fighting had burgeoned out of control. Roen had borne Nax another dark-haired son named Brigan. The Dells had entered a desperate time.

CANSREL HAD QUITE enjoyed being surrounded by desperation. It had entertained him to smash things apart with his power, and for entertainment he'd been insatiate.

The few women Cansrel couldn't seduce with the power

of his beauty or his mind, he raped. The few women Cansrel impregnated he killed. He didn't want monster babies growing into monster children and adults who might undermine his power.

Brocker had never been able to tell Fire why Cansrel hadn't killed Fire's mother. It was a mystery; but she knew better than to hope for a romantic explanation. Fire had been conceived in a time of depraved pandemonium. Cansrel had probably forgotten he'd taken Jessa to his bed, or never noticed the pregnancy – she was only a palace servant, after all. He'd probably not realised the pregnancy was his, until the child had been born with hair so astonishing that Jessa had named her Fire.

Why had Cansrel allowed Fire to live? Fire didn't know the answer to that, either. Curious, he'd gone to see her, probably intending to smother her. But then, looking into her face, listening to the noises she made, touching her skin – absorbing her tiny, intangible, perfect monsterness – he'd decided, for some reason, that here was a thing he didn't want to smash.

While she was still a baby, Cansrel took her away from her mother. A human monster had too many enemies, and he wanted her to grow up in a secluded place far from King's City where she would be safe. He brought her to his own estate in the northern Dells, a holding he rarely inhabited. He left her with his dumbfounded steward, Donal, and a scattering of cooks and maids. 'Raise her,' he said.

The rest Fire remembered. Her neighbour Brocker took an interest in the orphan monster and saw to her education in history and writing and mathematics. When she showed interest in music, he found her a teacher. Archer became Fire's playmate, eventually her trusted friend. Aliss died of a lingering sickness that had set in after Archer's birth. Fire learned from the reports Brocker received that Jessa had died as well. Cansrel visited often.

His visits were confusing, because they reminded her that

she had two fathers, two who never entered each other's presence if they could help it, never conversed beyond what civility demanded, and never agreed.

One was quiet and gruff and plain in a chair with big wheels. 'Child,' he'd say to her gently, 'just as we respect you by guarding our minds from you and behaving decently to you, so must you respect your friends by never using your powers deliberately against us. Does that make sense to you? Do you understand? I don't want you to do a thing unless you understand it.'

Her other father was luminous and brilliant and, in those earlier years, happy almost all of the time. He kissed her and swirled her around and carried her upstairs to bed, his body hot and electric, his hair like warm satin when she touched it. 'What has Brocker been teaching you?' he'd ask in a voice smooth as chocolate. 'Have you been practicing using the power of your mind against the servants? The neighbours? The horses and the dogs? It's right that you should do so, Fire. It's right and it's *your* right, because you're my beautiful child, and beauty has rights that plainness never will.'

Fire knew which one of the two was her true father. He was the one she called 'Father' instead of 'Brocker', and he was the one she loved the more desperately, because he was always either just arriving or just leaving, and because in their pockets of time together she stopped feeling like nature's freak. The people who despised her or loved her to excess had precisely the same feelings for Cansrel, though their behaviour towards him was different. The food her own cooks laughed at her for craving was the same food Cansrel craved, and when Cansrel was home, the cooks stopped laughing. Cansrel could sit with Fire and do something no one else could: give her lessons to improve the skill of her mind. They could communicate without saying a word, they could touch each other from opposite ends of the house. Fire's true father was like her – was, in fact, the only person in the world like her.

He always asked the same question when he first arrived: 'My darling monster girl! Was anyone mean to you while I was gone?'

Mean? Children threw stones at her in the road. She was tripped sometimes, slapped, taunted. People who liked her hugged her, but they hugged her too hard and were too free with their hands.

And still, Fire learned very young to answer no to his question – to lie, and to guard her mind from him so he wouldn't know she was lying. This was the beginning of another of her confusions, that she would want his visits so much but fall immediately to lying once he came.

When she was four she had a dog she'd chosen from a litter born in Brocker's stables. She chose him, and Brocker let her have him, because the dog had three functional legs and one that dragged, and would never be any use as a worker. He was inky grey and had bright eyes. Fire called him Twy, which was short for Twilight.

Twy was a happy, slightly brainless fellow with no idea he was missing something other dogs had. He was excitable, he jumped around a lot, and had a tendency on occasion to nip his favourite people. And nothing worked him into a greater frenzy of excitement, anxiety, joy, and terror than the presence of Cansrel.

One day in the garden Cansrel burst upon Fire and Twy unexpectedly. In confusion, Twy leapt against Fire and bit her more than nipped her, so hard that she cried out.

Cansrel ran to her, dropped to his knees, and took her into his arms, letting her fingers bleed all over his shirt. 'Fire! Are you all right?' She clung to him, because for just a moment Twy had scared her. But then, as her own mind cleared, she saw and felt Twy throwing himself against a pitch of sharp stone, over and over.

'Stop, Father! Stop it!'

Cansrel pulled a knife from his belt and advanced on the dog. Fire shrieked and grabbed at him. 'Don't hurt him, Father, please! Can't you feel that he didn't mean it?'

She scrabbled at Cansrel's mind but he was too strong for her. Hanging onto his trousers, punching him with her small fists, she burst into tears.

At that Cansrel stopped, shoved his knife back into his belt, and stood there, hands on hips, seething. Twy limped away, whimpering, his tail between his legs. And then Cansrel seemed to change, dropping down to Fire again, hugging her and kissing her and murmuring until she stopped crying. He cleaned her fingers and bandaged them. He sat her down for a lesson on the control of animal minds. When finally he let her go she ran to find Twy, who'd made his way to her room and was huddled, bewildered and ashamed, in a corner. She took him into her lap. She practised soothing his mind, so that next time she'd be able to protect him.

The following morning she woke to silence, rather than the usual sound of Twy stumping around outside her door. All day long she looked for him on her own grounds and Brocker's, but she couldn't find him. He'd disappeared. Cansrel said, with smooth sympathy, 'I suppose he's run away. Dogs do that, you know. Poor darling.'

And so Fire learned to lie to her father when he asked if anyone had hurt her.

As THE YEARS passed Cansrel's visits became less frequent but lasted longer, for the roads were unsafe. Sometimes, appearing at her door after months away, he brought women with him, or the traders who dealt his animals and drugs, or new monsters for his cages. Sometimes he spent his entire visit strung out on the poison of some plant; or, completely sober, he had strange, arbitrary, gloomy fits of temper, which he took out on everyone but Fire. Other times he was as lucid and lovely as the high notes Fire played on her flute. She dreaded his arrivals, his brassy, gorgeous, dissolute invasions of her quiet life. And after every one of his departures she was so lonesome that music was the only thing to comfort her, and she threw herself headlong into her lessons, never even minding the moments when her teacher was hateful, or resentful of her growing skill.

Brocker never spared her the truth about Cansrel.

I don't want to believe you, she'd think to him after he'd told her another tale of something Cansrel had done. *But I know it's true, because Cansrel himself tells me the stories, and he is never ashamed. He means them as lessons to guide my own behaviour. It worries him that I don't use my power as a weapon.*

'Does he not understand how different you are from him?' Brocker would ask. 'Does he not see that you're built from a different mould entirely?'

Fire couldn't describe the loneliness she felt when Brocker talked that way. How she wished at times that her quiet, plain, and good neighbour had been her true father. She wished to be like Brocker, built from his mould. But she knew what she was and what she was capable of. Even after she'd done away with mirrors, she saw it in other people's eyes, and she knew how easy it would be to make her own miserable life just a little bit more pleasant, the way Cansrel did all the time. She never told anyone, even Archer, how much the temptation of it shamed her.

When she was thirteen the drugs killed Nax, and a twenty-three-year-old Nash became king of a kingdom in shambles. Cansrel's fits of fury became even more frequent. So did his periods of melancholy.

When she was fifteen Cansrel opened the door of the cage that held back his midnight blue leopard monster, and departed from Fire for the last time.

CHAPTER THREE

FIRE DIDN'T REALISE she'd fallen asleep in Lord Brocker's library until she awoke and found herself there. It was Brocker's monster kitten that woke her, swinging from the hem of her dress like a man on the end of a rope. She blinked, adjusting her eyes to the grainy light, absorbing the baby monster's consciousness. It was still raining. No one else was in the room. She massaged the shoulder of her injured arm and stretched in her chair, stiff and achy but feeling better rested.

The kitten climbed his way up her skirts, sank his claws into her knee, and peered at her, hanging. He knew what she was, for her headscarf had slipped back a finger width. The monsters appraised each other. He was bright green with gold feet, this kitten, and his daft little mind was reaching for hers.

Of course, no animal monster could control Fire's mind, but this never stopped some of the more dim varieties from trying. He was too small and silly to think of eating her, but he would want to play, nibble her fingers, lick some blood, and Fire could do without the stings from a monster cat game. She lifted him into her lap and scratched him behind the ears and murmured nonsense about how strong and grand and intelligent he was. For good measure, she sent him a blip of mental sleepiness. He turned a circle in her lap and plopped himself down.

Housecat monsters were prized for keeping down the monster mouse population, and the regular mouse population too. This baby would grow big and fat, live a long, satisfied life, and probably father scores of monster kittens.

Human monsters, on the other hand, tended not to live long. Too many predators, too many enemies. It was for the

48

best that Fire was the only one remaining; and she had decided long ago, even before she'd taken Archer into her bed, that she would be the last. No more Cansrels.

She sensed Archer and Brocker in the hallway outside the library door, and then she heard their voices. Sharp, agitated. One of Archer's moods – or had something new happened while she was sleeping? She touched their minds to let them know she was awake.

A moment later Archer pushed the library door open and held it wide for his father. They came in together, talking, Archer jabbing the air angrily with his bow. 'Curse Trilling's guard for trying to take the man alone.'

'Perhaps he had no choice,' Brocker said.

'Trilling's men are too hasty.'

Brocker brightened with amusement. 'Interesting accusation, boy, coming from you.'

'I'm hasty with my tongue, Father, not my sword.' Archer glanced at Fire and her sleeping kitten. 'Love. How do you feel?'

'Better.'

'Our neighbour Trilling. Do you trust him?'

Trilling was one of the less foolish men Fire dealt with on a regular basis. His wife had employed Fire not only to tutor her boys in music but to teach them how to protect their minds against monster power.

'He's never given me reason to distrust him,' she said. 'What's happened?'

'He's found two dead men in his forest,' Archer said. 'One is his own guard, and I regret to say that the other is another stranger. Each with knife wounds and bruises, as if they'd been fighting each other, but what killed them both were arrows. Trilling's guard was shot from a distance in the back. The stranger was shot in the head at close range. Both arrows made of the same white wood as the bolt that killed your poacher.'

Fire's mind raced to make sense of it. 'The archer came upon them fighting, shot Trilling's guard from far away, then ran up to the stranger and executed him.'

Lord Brocker cleared his throat. 'Possibly a rather personal execution. Assuming the archer and the stranger were companions, that is, and it does seem likely that all these violent strangers in our woods have something to do with each other, doesn't it? The stranger from today had grievous knife injuries to his legs that might not have killed him, but would certainly have made it difficult for the archer to get him away once Trilling's guard was dead. I wonder if the archer shot Trilling's guard to protect his companion, then realised his companion was too injured to save, and decided to dispose of him, too?'

Fire raised her eyebrows at that, considering, and petted the monster cat absently. If the archer, the poacher, and this new dead stranger had, indeed, been working together, then the archer's responsibility seemed to be clean-up, so that no one was left behind to answer questions about why they were there in the first place. And the archer was good at his job.

Archer stared at the floor, tapping the end of his bow against the hard wood. Thinking. 'I'm going to Queen Roen's fortress,' he said.

Fire glanced at him sharply. 'Why?'

'I need to beg more soldiers of her, and I want the information of her spies. She might have thoughts about whether any of these strangers have anything to do with Mydogg or Gentian. I want to know what's going on in my forest, Fire, and I want this archer.'

'I'm going with you,' Fire said.

'No,' Archer said flatly.

'I am.'

'No. You can't defend yourself. You can't even ride.'

'It's only a day's journey. Wait a week. Let me rest, and then I'll go with you.'

Archer held up a hand and turned away from her. 'You're wasting your breath. Why would I ever allow such a thing?'

Because Roen is always unaccountably kind to me when I visit her northern fortress, Fire wanted to say. Because Roen knew my mother. Because Roen is a strong-minded woman, and there's something consoling in the regard of a woman. Roen never desires me, or if she ever does, it's not the same.

'Because,' she said out loud, 'Roen and her spies will have questions for me about what happened when the poacher shot me, and what little I managed to sense from his mind. And because,' she added, as Archer moved to object, 'you are neither my husband nor my father; I am a woman of seventeen, I have my own horses and my own money, and I decide for myself where I go and when. This is not yours to forbid.'

Archer slammed the end of his bow against the floor, but Lord Brocker was chuckling. 'Don't argue with her, boy. If it's information you're after, you're a fool not to take the monster at your disposal.'

'The roads are dangerous,' Archer said, practically spitting.

'It's dangerous here,' Brocker retorted. 'Isn't she safest with your bow to defend her?'

'She's safest inside, in a room with the door closed and locked.'

Brocker turned his chair toward the exit. 'She has precious few friends, Archer. It would be cruel for you to rush off to Roen and leave her behind.'

Fire found that she was holding the kitten close, cradling him against her breast, as if she were shielding him from something. From the way it felt to have her movements, her feelings, even, debated by two prickly men. She had the sudden mad wish that this little green-haired creature in her arms were her own baby, to hold and adore and to deliver her from people who did not understand her. Foolish, she thought to

51

herself furiously. Don't even think it. What does the world need with another mind-stealing baby?

Lord Brocker grasped Archer's hand and looked into his eyes, steadying his son, calming him. Then Brocker rolled to the exit and closed the door on their quarrel.

Archer watched Fire, his face uncertain. And Fire sighed, finally forgiving her stubborn friend and the stubborn father who'd adopted him. Their arguments, however they squashed her, were drawn from the wells of two very large hearts.

She dropped the kitten to the floor and stood, taking Archer's hand as his father had done. Archer looked down at their joined hands soberly. He brought her fingers to his mouth, kissed her knuckles, and made a show of inspecting her hand, as if he'd never seen it before.

'I'll pack my things,' Fire said. 'Just tell me when we're leaving.'

She stretched onto her toes to kiss his cheek, but he intercepted her and began to kiss her mouth, gently. She let him, for just a moment. Then she extricated herself and left the room.

CHAPTER FOUR

FIRE'S HORSE WAS named Small, and he was another of
Cansrel's gifts. She had chosen him over all the other horses
because his coat was dun and drab and because of the quiet way
he'd followed her back and forth, the pasture fence between
them, the day she'd gone to one of Cutter's shows to choose.

The other horses had either ignored her or become jumpy
and agitated around her, pushing against each other and snapping. Small had kept on the outside of the bunch of them,
where he was safe from their jostling. He'd trotted along beside Fire, stopping when she stopped, blinking at her hopefully;
and whenever she'd walked away from the fence he had stood
waiting for her until she came back.

'Small, his name is,' Cutter had said, 'because his brain's the
size of a pea. Can't teach him anything. He's no beauty, either.'

Cutter was Cansrel's horse dealer and his favourite monster smuggler. He lived in the western Great Greys and, once
a year, carted his merchandise all over the kingdom in large
caravans, showing his wares and selling them. Fire did not like
him. He was not kind to his animals. And his mouth was wide
and loose and his eyes were always settling on her in a way that
felt proprietary and disgusting, a way that made her want to
curl up into a ball to cover herself.

He was also wrong about Small. Fire knew the look of
stupid eyes and the feel of a fatuous mind, in animals and in
men, and she had sensed none of this with Small. What she had
sensed was the way the gelding trembled and balked whenever
Cutter came near, and the way the trembling stopped when
Fire touched him, and whispered her greetings. Fire was used

to being wanted for her beauty, but she was not used to being needed for her gentleness.

When Cutter and Cansrel had walked away for a moment, Small had strained his neck over the fence and rested his chin on her shoulder. She'd scratched him behind the ears, and he'd made small blissful noises and breathed spit onto her hair. She had laughed, and a door in her heart had opened. Apparently there was such a thing as love at first sight; or love at first spit, anyway.

Cutter had told her she was daft, and Cansrel had tried to talk her into a stunning black mare that suited her own flamboyant beauty. But it was Small she'd wanted, and Small that Cutter had delivered three days later. Shaking, terrified, because Cutter in his inhumanity had stuck the horse into a wagon along with a mountain lion monster Cansrel had purchased, with nothing but what amounted to a shaky arrangement of wooden slats separating them. Small had come out of the wagon rearing and screaming, and Cutter had stung him with his whip and called him a coward.

Fire had run to the horse, choked with indignation, and put all the passionate calm feeling she could into soothing his mind; and she'd told Cutter furiously, in the kind of words she never used, just what she thought of his way with his goods.

Cutter had laughed and told her she was doubly pleasing when she was angry – which had, of course, been a grave mistake on his part, for anyone with a modicum of intelligence would have known better than to treat Lady Fire with disrespect in the very presence of her father. Fire had pulled Small quickly to the side, because she'd known what was coming. First Cansrel had caused Cutter to grovel, and apologise, and weep. Then he'd caused him to believe himself to be in agonising pain from imaginary injuries. Finally he'd switched to the real thing, kicking Cutter calmly in the groin, repeatedly, until Cansrel was satisfied he understood.

Small, in the meantime, had gone quiet at Fire's first touch, and had done everything, from that first moment, that she had ever asked.

Today as she stood at Small's side, dressed warmly against the dawn, Archer came to her and offered his hand. She shook her head and grabbed the pommel one-handed. She pulled herself up, catching her breath against the pain.

She'd had only seven days of rest, and her arm, uncomfortable now, would be aching by the end of this ride. But she was determined not to be treated like an invalid. She sent a swelling of serenity to Small, a gentle plea for him to ride smoothly for her today. It was another reason Small and she were well-suited to each other. He had a warm, receptive mind.

'Give my regards to the lady queen,' Lord Brocker said from his chair in the middle of the footpath. 'Tell her, if the day ever comes when she has a moment of peace, to come visit an old friend.'

'We shall,' Archer said, pulling on his gloves. He reached behind his head to touch the fletchings of the arrows on his back, as he always did before mounting his horse – as if he had ever once in his life forgotten his quiver – and then swung himself into his own saddle. He waved the guards forward, and Fire behind them. He fell into place behind Fire, and they were off.

They rode with eight soldiers. It was more than Archer would have taken had he gone alone, but not many more. No one in the Dells travelled with fewer than six others, unless he was desperate or suicidal or had some perverse reason for wanting to be attacked by footpads. And the disadvantage of Fire's presence, as an injured rider and a popular target, was nearly negated by her ability to sense both the proximity and the attitude of the minds of approaching strangers.

Away from home, Fire did not have the luxury of avoiding the use of her mental power. Generally, minds did not draw her attention equally unless she was looking for them. A mind's palpability depended on its strength, its purpose, its familiarity, nearness, openness, awareness of her presence, and a host of other factors. On this journey she must not allow anyone to slip her notice; she would search the surroundings constantly and, if she could, take hold of every mind she encountered until she was sure of its intentions. She would hide her own mind with extra care from the recognition of monster predators. The roads were too dangerous otherwise, for everyone.

Queen Roen's fortress was a long day's ride away. The guards set a brisk pace, skirting the edges of the town, close enough to hear roosters crowing but far enough not to be seen. The best way for a traveller to get himself robbed or murdered was to make the fact of his travel public.

There were tunnels under the mountains that would have taken them faster to Roen, but these also they planned to avoid. At least in the north, the steep paths above ground were safer than the unknown that lurked in the dark.

Of course Fire's hair was tightly covered, and her riding clothes plain. Still, she hoped they would encounter no one. Predator monsters tended to overlook the charms of a face and a body if they saw no interesting hair, but this was not the way of men. If she was seen, she'd be scrutinised. Once scrutinised, she'd be recognised, and the eyes of strangers were never comfortable.

THE ABOVE-GROUND route to the fortress of Queen Roen was a high and treeless one, for mountains called the Little Grays divided the land of Fire and her neighbours from the land of the lady queen. 'Little' because they were passable by foot and because they were more easily inhabitable than the Great Grays that formed the Dells' western and southern border with the unknown land.

Hamlets balanced on top of cliffs in the Little Grays or crouched in the valleys near tunnel openings – rough-hewn, cold, colourless, and stark. Fire had watched these distant hamlets and wondered about them every time she'd travelled to Roen. Today she saw that one of them was missing.

'There used to be a village on that cliff,' she said, pointing. And then she made sense of it. She saw the broken rock foundations of the old buildings sticking out of the snow, and at the foot of the cliff on which the village had stood, a pile of rocks, wood, and rubble. And crawling all over the pile, monster wolves, and circling above it, monster raptors.

A clever new trick for the looters, to throw an entire village off a mountain, stone by stone. Archer swung down from his horse, his jaw hard. 'Fire. Are there any living human minds in that pile?'

Many living minds, but none of them human. A good many rats, monster and ordinary. Fire shook her head.

Archer did the shooting, because they hadn't any arrows to waste. First he shot the raptors. Then he wound a rag around an arrow, and set the rag on fire, and shot it into the pile of monsters and decay. He shot flaming arrow after flaming arrow into the pile until it was fully alight.

Flame was the way, in the Dells, to send the bodies of the dead where their souls had gone, into nothingness. To respect that all things ended, except the world.

The party moved on quickly, because on the wind the stench was terrible.

THEY WERE MORE than halfway to their destination when they saw a sight to bolster their spirits: the King's Army, bursting from a hole in the base of a cliff far below them, and thundering across a plain of flat rock. They stopped on their high path to watch. Archer pointed to the front of the charge.

'King Nash is with them,' he said. 'See him? The tall man, on the roan, near the standard-bearer. And that's his brother beside him, the commander, Prince Brigan, with the longbow in his hand, on the black mare. In brown, see him? Dells, isn't it a magnificent sight?'

Fire had never seen Nax's sons before, and she had certainly never beheld such a large division of the King's Army. There were thousands of them – five thousand in this branch, Archer said when she asked – some with mail flashing, others in the army's dark grey uniform, horses strong and fast, flowing across the land like a river. The one with the longbow in his hand, the prince and commander, moved to the right side and fell back; spoke to a man or two in the middle of the column; surged forward again to the front. They were so far away that they were small as mice, but she could hear the thud of the hooves of some five thousand horses, and feel the enormous presence of some ten thousand consciousnesses. And she could see the colours of the flag hoisted by the standard-bearer who stayed close to the prince's side wherever he went: a wooded valley, grey and green, with a blood red sun in an orange sky.

Prince Brigan turned in his saddle suddenly then, his eyes on some point in the clouds above him, and in that same moment Fire sensed the raptors. Brigan wheeled his black mare around and raised his hand in a signal that caused a number of the party to break off and pull arrows from their backs. Three raptors, two shades of fuchsia and violet and one apple-green, circled high over the river of soldiers, attracted by the vibrations, or by the smell of the horses.

Archer and his guards also readied arrows. Fire gripped her reins tightly with one hand, calmed Small, and tried to decide whether to put her arm through the agony of readying her own bow.

It wasn't necessary. The prince's men were efficient, and used only four arrows to bring down the fuchsia birds. The green was smarter; it circled irregularly, changing height and speed, dropping lower and lower and always closer to the column of riders. The arrow that finally caught it was Archer's, a fast shot soaring downward and over the heads of the gallop-ing army.

The bird monster fell and crashed onto the plain. The prince turned his horse and eyed the mountain paths, looking for the source of the arrow, his own arrow still notched in case he didn't like the archer he found. When he spotted Archer and the guards, he lowered his bow and raised an arm in greet-ing. Then he pointed to the carcass of the green bird on the plain and pointed back to Archer. Fire understood the gesture: Archer's kill was Archer's meat.

Archer gestured back: you take it. Brigan raised both arms in thanks, and his soldiers slung the body of the monster onto the back of a riderless horse. She saw a number of riderless horses, now that she was looking for them, carrying bags and supplies and the bodies of other game, some of it monstrous. She knew that outside King's City the King's Army housed itself and fed itself. She supposed it must take a bounty to feed so many hungry men.

She corrected herself. So many hungry men and women. Any person who could ride, fight, and hunt was welcome to join today's protectorate of the kingdom, and King Nash didn't require that person to be a man. Or, more particularly, Prince Brigan didn't. It was called the King's Army, but really it was Brigan's. People said that at twenty-seven Nash was kingly, but that when it came to bashing heads the younger brother was the one with the touch.

Far in the distance, the river of riders began to disappear into a crack at the base of another cliff. 'The tunnels would have made for safe passage today, after all,' Archer said, 'in the wake of that lot. I wish I'd known they were so near. Last I heard, the king was in his palace in King's City and the prince was in the far north, looking for Pikkian trouble.'

On the plain below, the prince turned his mare around to join the tail end of his fighting force; but first his eyes rested on Fire's form. He could not have appreciated her features from that distance, and with the light of the sun glaring into his face. He could not have ascertained much more than that she was Archer's friend, dressed like a boy for riding but female, with covered hair. Still, Fire's face burned. He knew who she was, she was sure of it. His backward glare as he swung away was evidence, and so was his ferocity as he spurred his horse forward. So was his mind, closed to her, and cold.

This was why she had avoided meeting Nash and Brigan before this. It was only natural that the sons of King Nax should despise her. She burned hot with the shame of her father's legacy.

CHAPTER FIVE

FIRE SUPPOSED IT was too much to hope that the king and the warrior would pass so close to their mother's holding without stopping. The final portion of their journey took them across rocky hills crowded with the king's resting soldiers.

The soldiers had not made camp, but they were napping, cooking meat before fires, playing cards. The sun was low. She couldn't remember in her tired mind whether armies ever travelled through darkness. She hoped this army was not staying the night on these hills.

Archer and his guards formed a wall around her as they passed the soldiers, Archer so close on her injured side that her left leg brushed against his right. Fire kept her face down, but still she felt the eyes of soldiers on her body. She was so exhausted, so impossibly sore, but she held her consciousness alert, flicking through the minds around her, looking for trouble. Looking also for the king and his brother, and wishing desperately not to find them.

There were women among the soldiers, but not many. She heard the occasional low whistle, the occasional grunt. Epithets, too, and more than one fight broke out between men as she passed, but no one threatened her.

And then as they neared the ramp to Roen's drawbridge she stirred and looked up, and was thankful, suddenly, for the presence of the soldiers. She knew that south of the Little Greys raptor monsters moved sometimes in swarms, found areas of dense population and circled there, waiting, but she had never seen anything like it before. There must have been two hundred raptors, flashing bright colours against an orange and pink sky, high up where only the luckiest of arrows could reach them. Their screeches made her cold. Her hand flew to the edges of her headscarf to check for stray hairs, for she knew that if the raptors discovered what she was, they'd cease even to notice the human army. All two hundred would turn on her.

'You're all right, love,' Archer muttered beside her. 'Quickly now. We're almost inside.'

INSIDE THE ROOFED courtyard of Queen Roen's fortress, Archer helped her as she fell more than stepped from Small's back. She balanced herself between her horse and her friend, and caught her breath. 'You're safe now,' Archer said, his arm around her, bracing her, 'and there'll be time to rest before dinner.'

Fire nodded vaguely. 'He needs a gentle hand,' she managed to say to the man who took Small's reins.

She barely noticed the girl who showed her to her room. Archer was there; he stationed his men at her doorway, and before he took his leave he warned the girl to take care with her arm.

Then Archer was gone. The girl sat Fire on the bed. She helped her out of her clothes and untied her headscarf, and Fire collapsed onto the pillows. And if the girl stared wide-eyed at Fire, touching her bright hair wonderingly, Fire didn't care. Already she was asleep.

WHEN SHE WOKE her room flickered with candles. A small woman in a brown dress was lighting them. Fire recognised Roen's mind, quick and warm. Then the woman turned to face her, and Fire recognised Roen's dark eyes, and her beautifully cut mouth, and the white streak that grew at the front and centre of her long black hair.

Roen set her candle down and sat on the edge of Fire's bed. She smiled at Fire's groggy expression. 'Well met, Lady Fire.'

'Well met, Lady Queen.'

'I spoke with Archer,' Roen said. 'How is your arm? Are you hungry? Let's have dinner now, before my sons arrive.'

Her sons. 'Haven't they already arrived?'

'They're still outside with the Fourth Branch. Brigan's passing command of the Fourth to one of his captains and sending them east tonight, and I understand it involves endless preparations. The Third comes here in a day or two. Brigan will ride with them to King's City and leave Nash in his palace, and then he'll take them south.'

King's City. It was on the green land where the Winged River met the Winter Sea. Above the waters rose the king's palace, made of brilliant black stone. People said the city was beautiful, a place of art, and medicine, and science, but Fire hadn't seen it since her infancy. She had no memory of it.

She shook herself. She was daydreaming. 'Ride with them,' she said, her mind still fuzzy with sleep. 'Them?'

'Brigan spends equal time with each division of the army,' Roen said. She patted Fire's lap. 'Come, dear. Have dinner with me. I want to hear about life on the other side of the Little Greys and our chance is now.' She stood and whisked her candle off the table. 'I'll send someone in to help you.'

Roen swept through the door, slapping it shut behind her. Fire swung her legs out from under the covers and groaned. She fantasised about a day when she would open her eyes from sleep to find that she could move her arm without this never-ending pain.

FIRE AND ARCHER ate dinner with Roen at a small table in her sitting room. Roen's fortress had been her home years ago, before she'd ever married the king of the kingdom, and was her home again now that Nax was dead. It was a modest castle with high walls surrounding it, enormous stables, lookout towers, and courtyards connecting the business quarters with the living quarters and the sleeping quarters. The castle was large enough that in the case of a siege, people from the surrounding towns for quite some distance could fit inside its walls. Roen ran the place with a steady hand, and from it dispatched assistance to those northern lords and ladies who had demonstrated a desire for peace. Guards, food, weapons, spies; whatever was needed, Roen supplied it.

'While you were resting I climbed the outer wall,' Archer told Fire, 'and waited for raptor monsters to drop low enough to shoot. I only killed two. Do you feel them? I can feel their hunger for us from this very room.'

'Vicious brutes,' Roen said. 'They'll stay up high until the army moves out. Then they'll drop down again and wait for people to emerge from the gatehouse. They're smarter in swarms, the raptors, and more beautiful, of course, and their mental draw is stronger. They're not having a beneficial effect on the moods of my people, I'll tell you that. I've two or three servants who need to be watched or they'll walk right out and offer themselves to be eaten. It's been two days now. I was so relieved when the Fourth showed up today; it's the first time in two days I've been able to send anyone outside the walls. We mustn't let the beasts spot you, my dear. Have some soup.'

Fire was grateful for the soup the servant girl spooned into her bowl, because it was food she didn't have to cut. She rested her left hand in her lap and calculated in her mind. A swarm of raptor monsters was impatient. This one would hang around for a week at most, and then it would move on; but while it lingered, she and Archer would be stuck in place. Unless they rode out in a day or two, when the next river of soldiers arrived to pick up their commander and their king.

She momentarily lost her appetite.

'On top of the hassle of being stuck inside,' Roen said, 'I hate closing the roofs. Our skies are dark enough without them. With them it's plain depressing.'

Most of the year Roen's courtyards and her passage to the stables were open to the sky; but torrential rains fell most autumns, and the raptor swarms arrived unpredictably. And so the fortress had retractable canvas roofs on hinged wooden frames that folded down across the open spaces and clicked, one frame at a time, into place, providing protection, but cutting off light from all but the outside windows.

'My father always speaks of the glass roofs of the king's palace as an extravagance,' Archer said, 'but I've spent enough time under roofs like yours to appreciate them.'

Roen smiled into her soup. 'Once about every three years, Nax did have a good idea.' She changed the subject abruptly. 'This visit will be a bit of a balancing act. Perhaps tomorrow we can sit down with my people to discuss the events on your lands. After the Third comes and goes, we'll have more time.'

She was avoiding specific mention of the thing that was on all their minds. Archer spoke plainly. 'Will the king or the prince be a danger to Fire?'

Roen didn't pretend not to understand. 'I will speak to Nash and Brigan, and I'll introduce her to them myself.'

Archer was not soothed. 'Will they be a danger to her?'

Roen regarded him for a moment in silence, and then turned her eyes to Fire. Fire saw sympathy there, possibly even apology. 'I know my sons,' she said, 'and I know Fire. Brigan will not like her, and Nash will like her overly. But neither of them will be too much for her to handle.'

Archer caught his breath and clapped his fork onto the table. He sat back, his mouth tight. Fire knew that the presence of a lady queen was the only reason he wasn't saying what she could read in his eyes: she should not have come.

A small determination flamed inside her breast. She decided to adopt Roen's attitude.

Neither the king nor the commander would be too much for her.

OF COURSE, CIRCUMSTANCES don't always align themselves with human intention, and Roen could not be everywhere at once. Fire was crossing the main courtyard with Archer after dinner, on her way to the sleeping quarters, when it happened. In the same instant that she sensed minds approaching, the gates flew open. Two men on horses clattered inside, overwhelming the space with their noise and their presence, backlit by a bonfire blazing outside the gates. Archer and everyone else in the courtyard dropped to one knee, except for Fire, who stood paralysed, shocked. The man on the first horse looked like every painting she'd ever seen of King Nax, and the man on the second horse was her father.

Her mind was on fire. Cansrel. In the light of the flames his hair flashed silver and blue, his eyes blue and beautiful. She stared into those eyes and saw them staring back at her with hatred, anger, because it was Cansrel come back from death and there was no hiding herself from him.

'Kneel,' Archer said beside her, but it was unnecessary, for she fell to both knees.

And then the gates swung shut. The white blaze of the bonfire receded, and all was yellow in the light of the courtyard torches. And still the man on the horse stared at her with hatred, but as the shadows settled it was no longer Cansrel's hatred. His hair was dark, his eyes were pale, and she saw that this was nothing but an ordinary man.

She was shaking, cold on the ground. And now of course she recognised his black mare, and his handsome brother, and his handsome brother's roan. Not Nax and Cansrel, but Nash and Brigan. They swung down from their saddles and stood arguing beside their horses. Shaking as she was, their words came to her slowly. Brigan said something about throwing someone to the raptors. Nash said that he was king, and it was his decision, and he wasn't throwing a woman who looked like that to any raptors.

Archer was crouched over Fire, repeating her name, his hand gripping her face. He said something firmly to the arguing brothers. He lifted Fire into his arms and carried her out of the courtyard.

THIS WAS SOMETHING Fire knew about herself: her mind made mistakes sometimes, but the real traitor was her body.

Archer lowered her onto her bed and sat beside her. He took her cold hands and rubbed them. Slowly, her shivering subsided.

She heard the echo of his voice in her mind. Gradually she pieced together the thing Archer had said to the king and the prince before picking her up and carrying her away: 'If you're going to throw her to the raptors you'll have to throw me as well.'

She caught his hands, and held them.

'What happened to you out there?' he asked quietly.

What had happened to her?

She looked into his eyes, which were taut with worry.

She would explain it to him, later. Right now she was stuck on something she wanted to express to him, something she wanted urgently from her living friend. She pulled on his hands.

Archer always caught on fast. He bent his face to hers and kissed her. When Fire reached to unfasten his shirt, he stopped her fingers. He told her to rest her arm, and let him do the work.

She surrendered to his generosity.

AFTERWARDS THEY HAD a whispered conversation.

'When he came into the courtyard,' she told him, lying on her side, facing him, 'I thought he was my father come back to life.'

Shock broke across his face, and then understanding. He brushed her hair with his fingers. 'Oh, Fire. No wonder. But Nash is nothing like Cansrel.'

'Not Nash. Brigan.'

'Brigan even less.'

'It was the light,' she said. 'And the hatred in his eyes.'

He touched her face and her shoulder gently, careful always of her bandaged arm. He kissed her. 'Cansrel is dead. He can't hurt you.'

She choked on the words; she couldn't say them out loud. She said them into his mind. *He was my own father.*

His arm came around her and held her tight. She closed her eyes and buried her thoughts so that all there was was the smell and the touch of Archer against her face and her breasts, her stomach, her body. Archer pushed her memories away.

'Stay here with me,' he said sometime later, still holding her, sleepily. 'You're not safe on your own.'

And how odd that his body could understand her so well; that his heart could understand her so well when it came to the truth about Cansrel, but still the simplest concepts never penetrated. There was nothing he could have said more guaranteed to make her leave.

To be fair, she probably would have gone anyway.

Out of love for her friend she waited until he was asleep.

SHE DIDN'T WANT trouble; she only wanted the stars, to tire her so that later she could sleep without dreams. She knew she would have to find her way to an outer window to see them. She decided to try the stables, because she was unlikely to run into any kings or princes there at this time of night. And at least if she found no sky-facing windows there, she would be with Small.

She covered her hair before she left, and wore dark clothing. She passed guards and servants, and of course some of them stared, but as always in this holding, no one bothered her. Roen saw to it that the people under her roofs learned how to guard their minds as best they could. Roen knew the value of it.

The roofed passageway to the stables was empty, and smelled comfortably of clean hay and horses. The stables were dark, lit by a single lantern at the near end. They were asleep, the horses, most of them, including her Small. He stood as he dozed, plain and quiet, leaning sideways, like a building about to topple. It might have worried her, except that he often slept like that, leaning one way or the other.

There was a window to the sky at the far end of the building, but when she went to it, she saw no stars. A cloudy night. She turned back down the long row of horses and stopped again before Small, smiling at his sleeping posture.

She eased the door open and sidled her way into his stall. She would sit with him for a while as he slept, and hum herself to tiredness. Even Archer couldn't object. No one would find her; curled up as she was against Small's doorway, no one who came into the stables would even see her. And if Small awoke, it would not surprise him to find his lady crooning at his feet. Small was accustomed to her night-time behaviour.

She settled herself down and breathed a song about a leaning horse.

SMALL NUDGED HER awake, and she knew instantly that she was not alone. She heard a male voice, baritone, very quiet, very near.

'I fight these looters and smugglers because they oppose the king's rule. But what right to rule do we have, really?'

'You frighten me when you talk like this.' Roen. Fire pushed herself against Small's door.

'What has the king done in thirty years to deserve allegiance?'

'Brigan—'

'I understand the motivations of some of my enemies better than I understand my own.'

'Brigan, this is your fatigue speaking. Your brother is fair-minded, you know that, and with your influence he does good.'

'He has some of Father's tendencies.'

'Well, what will you do? Let the raiders and smugglers have their way? Leave the kingdom to Lord Mydogg and his thug of a sister? Or Lord Gentian? Preserving Nash's kingship is the best hope for the Dells. And if you break with him you'll start a civil war four ways. You, Nash, Mydogg, Gentian. I fear to think who would come out on top. Not you, with the allegiance of the King's Army split between yourself and your brother.'

This was a conversation Fire should not be hearing, not under any circumstances, not in any world. She understood this now; but there was no helping it, for to reveal her presence would be disastrous. She didn't move, barely breathed. And listened hard despite herself, because doubt in the heart of the king's commander was an astonishing thing.

Mildly now, and with a tone of concession: 'Mother, you go too far. I could never break with my brother, you know that. And you know I don't want the kingship.'

'This again, and it's no comfort to me. If Nash is killed, you'll have to be king.'

'The twins are older than I.'

'You're being deliberately obtuse tonight. Garan is ill, Clara is female, and both of them are illegitimate. The Dells will not get through this time without a king who is kingly.'

'I'm not kingly.'

'Twenty-two years old, commanding the King's Army as well as Brocker did? Your soldiers would fall on their own swords for you. You are kingly.'

'All right. But rocks, Mother, I hope I'll never be called king.'

'You once hoped you'd never be a soldier.'

'Don't remind me.' His voice was tired. 'My life is an apology for the life of my father.'

A long silence. Fire sat unbreathing. A life that was an apology for the life of his father: it was a notion she could understand, beyond words and thought. She understood it the way she understood music.

Small stirred and poked his head out of his stall to examine the low-voiced visitors. 'Just tell me you'll do your duty, Brigandell,' Roen said, her use of Brigan's royal name deliberate.

A shift in his voice. He was laughing under his breath. 'I've become such an impressive warrior that you think I run around the mountains sticking swords into people because I enjoy it.'

'When you talk like this, you can't blame me for worrying.'

'I'll do my duty, Mother, as I have done every day.'

'You and Nash will make the Dells into something worth defending. You'll re-establish the order and the justice that Nax and Cansrel destroyed with their carelessness.'

Suddenly, and with no humour in his voice: 'I don't like this monster.'

Roen's voice softened. 'Nashdell is not Naxdell, and Fire is not her father.'

'No, she's worse; she's female. She's a thing I can't see Nash resisting.'

Firmly: 'Brigan. Fire has no interest in Nash. She does not seduce men and ensnare them.'

'I hope you're right, Mother, because I don't care how highly you think of her. If she's like Cansrel I'll snap her neck.'

Fire pushed herself into the corner. She was accustomed to hatred. But still it was a thing that made her cold and tired every time. She was tired thinking of the defences she would have to build against this man.

And then above her, an incongruous thing. Brigan reached a hand to the muzzle of her horse. 'Poor fellow,' he said, stroking Small's nose. 'We woke you. Go back to sleep.'

'It's her horse,' Roen said. 'The horse of the monster you threaten.'

'Ah well. You're a beauty,' Brigan said to Small, his voice light. 'And your owner is not your fault.'

Small nuzzled the hand of his new friend. And when Roen and Brigan left, Fire was gripping her skirts in both fists, swallowing an infuriating fondness that she could not reconcile.

At least if he decided to hurt her, she could trust him not to hurt her horse.

CHAPTER SIX

THIS LONG NIGHT was not over, for apparently no one in the royal family slept. Fire had just crossed the courtyard again and slipped into the corridors of the sleeping quarters when she met the prowling king, handsome and fierce in the light of the torches. His eyes glazed over when he saw her. She thought she smelled wine on his breath. When he came at her suddenly, flattened her against the wall, and tried to kiss her, she no longer had any doubt.

He had surprised her, but the wine addling his brains made her work easy. *You don't want to kiss me.*

Nash stopped trying to kiss her but continued to press himself against her, groping her breasts and her back. Hurting her arm. 'I'm in love with you,' he said, breathing sour air into her face. 'I want to marry you.'

You don't want to marry me. You don't even want to touch me. You want to release me.

Nash stepped back from her and she pushed herself away, gulping fresh air, smoothing her clothing. She turned to make her escape.

Then she swung back at him and did a thing she never did. *Apologise to me*, she thought to him fiercely. *I've had enough of this. Apologise.*

Instantly the king kneeled at her feet, gracious, gentlemanly, black eyes swimming with penitence. 'Forgive me, Lady, for my insult to your person. Go safely to your bed.'

She hurried away before anyone saw the absurd spectacle of the king on his knees before her. She was ashamed of herself.

And newly anxious for the state of the Dells, now that she'd made the acquaintance of its king.

SHE WAS ALMOST to her room when Brigan loomed out of the shadows, and this time Fire was at her wit's end.

She didn't even need to reach for his mind to know that it was closed to her control, a walled fortress with not a single crack. Against Brigan she had nothing but her small strength, and words.

He pushed her against the wall as Nash had done. He took both her wrists in one hand and yanked her arms above her head, so roughly that water sprang to her eyes from the pain of her injured arm. He crushed her with his body so she could not move. His face was a snarling mask of hatred.

'Show the slightest interest in befriending the king,' he said, 'and I will kill you.'

His superior display of strength was humiliating, and he was hurting her more even than he knew. She had no breath for speech. *How like your brother you are*, she thought hotly into his face. *Only less romantic.*

His grip on her wrists tightened. 'Lying monster-eater.'

She gasped at the pain. *You're a bit of a disappointment, aren't you? People talk about you as if you're something special, but there's nothing special about a man who pushes a defenceless woman around and calls her names. It's plain ordinary.*

He bared his teeth. 'I'm to believe that you're defenceless?'

I am against you.

'But not against this kingdom.'

I don't stand in opposition to this kingdom. At least, she added, *no more so than you, Brigandell.*

He looked as if she'd slapped him. The snarl left his face and his eyes were weary suddenly, and confused. He dropped her wrists and stepped back a hair, enough that she could push herself away from him and from the wall, turn her back to him, and cradle her left arm with her right hand. She was shaking. The shoulder of her dress was sticky; he'd made her wound bleed. And he'd hurt her, and she was angry, more than ever before.

She didn't know where her breath came from, but she let her words loose as they came. 'I can see that you studied the example of your father before deciding the man you wanted to become,' she hissed at him. 'The Dells are in fine hands, aren't they? You and your brother both – you can go to the raptors.'

'Your father was the ruin of my father *and* of the Dells,' he spat back. 'My only regret is that your father didn't die on my sword. I despise him for killing himself and denying me the pleasure. I envy the monster that ripped out his throat.'

At that she turned to face him. For the first time she looked at him, really looked at him. He breathed quickly, clenching and unclenching his fists. His eyes were clear and very light grey and flashed with something that went beyond anger, something desperate. He was little more than average in height and build. He had his mother's fine mouth, but besides that and those pale crystal eyes, he was not handsome. He stared at her, strung so tight he looked like he might snap, and suddenly to her he seemed young, and overburdened, and at the furthest edge of exhaustion.

'I didn't know you were wounded,' he added, eyeing the blood on her dress; and confusing her, because he actually sounded sorry about it. She didn't want his apologies. She wanted to hate him, because he was hateful.

'You're inhuman. You do nothing but hurt people,' she said, because it was the worst thing she could think of to say. 'You're the monster, not I.'

She turned and left him.

SHE WENT TO Archer's room first, to clean the seeping blood and rebandage her arm. Then she crept into her own room, where Archer still slept. She undressed and pulled on his shirt, which she found lying on the floor. He would like that she chose to wear it, and it would never occur to him that she only wanted to hide her wrists, blue with bruises that he must not see. She didn't have the energy for Archer's questions and his vengeful anger.

She rifled through her bags and found the herbs that prevented pregnancy. She swallowed them dry, tucked herself in beside Archer, and fell into a dreamless sleep.

IN THE MORNING, coming awake was like drowning. She heard Archer making a great clatter in the room. She fought her way to consciousness and pushed herself up, and stopped herself from groaning at the old pain in her arm and the new pain in her wrists.

'You're beautiful in the morning,' Archer said, stopping before her, kissing her nose. 'You're impossibly sweet in my shirt.'

That might be, but she felt like death. She would gladly make the trade; how blissful it would be to feel impossibly sweet, and look like death.

He was dressed, aside from his shirt, and clearly on his way out the door.

'What's the hurry?'

'A beacon fire is lit,' he said.

Towns in the mountains lit beacon fires when they were under attack, to call on the aid of their neighbours. 'Which town?'

'Grey Haven, to the north. Nash and Brigan ride out immediately, but they're sure to lose men to the raptor monsters before they get to the tunnels. I'll shoot from the wall, along with anyone else who can.'

Like a dive into cold water, she was awake. 'The Fourth has gone, then? How many soldiers do Nash and Brigan have?'

'My eight, and Roen has another forty to offer from the fortress.'

'Only forty!'

'She sent a good portion of her guard away with the Fourth,' Archer said. 'Soldiers from the Third are to replace them, but of course they're not here yet.'

'But fifty men total to two hundred raptors? Are they mad?'

'The only other option is to ignore the call for help.'

'You don't ride with them?'

'The commander believes my bow can do more damage from the wall.'

The commander. She froze. 'Was he here?'

Archer glanced at her sidelong. 'Of course not. When his men couldn't find me, Roen came herself.'

It didn't matter; already she'd forgotten it. Her mind spun with the other particular, the insanity of fifty men trying to pass through a swarm of two hundred raptor monsters. She climbed out of bed and searched for her clothes, went into her bathing room so that Archer wouldn't see her wrists as she changed. When she came out he was gone.

She covered her hair and attached her arm guard. She grabbed her bow and quiver and ran after him.

IN DESPERATE MOMENTS Archer was not above threats. In the stables, with men shouting around them and horses fidgeting, he told her that he would tie her to Small's door if he had to, to keep her off the wall.

It was bluster, and she ignored him and thought this through, step by step. She was a decent shot with a bow. Her arm was well enough to shoot as long as she could bear the pain. In the time it took the soldiers to thunder away into the tunnels she could kill two, maybe three of the monsters, and that was two or three fewer to tear into the men.

It only took one raptor to kill a man.

Some of these fifty men were going to die before they even reached whatever battle they faced at Grey Haven.

This was where panic set in and her mental reckoning fell apart. She wished they wouldn't go. She wished they wouldn't put themselves at this risk to save one mountain town. She hadn't understood before what people meant when they'd said the prince and the king were brave. Why did they have to be so brave?

She whirled around looking for the brothers. Nash was on his horse, fired up, impatient to get started, transformed from the drunken no-head of last night into a figure that at least gave the impression of kingliness. Brigan was on his feet, moving among the soldiers, encouraging them, exchanging a word with his mother. Calm, reassuring, even laughing at a joke from one of Archer's guards.

And then across the sea of clamouring armour and saddle leather he saw her, and the gladness dropped from him. His eyes went cold, his mouth hard, and he looked the way she remembered him.

The sight of her killed his joy.

Well. He was not the only person with the right to risk his life, and he was not the only person who was brave.

It all seemed to make sense in her mind as she turned to Archer, to assure him she didn't want to shoot raptors from the wall after all; and then she swung away to Small's stall to do something that had no logic whatsoever, except, perhaps, hidden very deep.

SHE KNEW THE entire enterprise would only take a few minutes. The raptors would dive as soon as they'd comprehended their own superior number. The greatest danger was to the men at the back of the line who would have to slow their pace as the horses entered the bottleneck of the nearest tunnel's entrance. The soldiers who made it into the tunnel would be safe. Raptors didn't like dark, cramped spaces, and they did not follow men into caves.

She understood from the talk she heard in the stables that Brigan had ordered the king to the front of the column and the best spearmen and swordsmen to the back, because in the moment of greatest crisis the raptors would be too close for bows. Brigan himself would bring up the rear.

The horses were filing out and gathering near the gates when she prepared Small, hooking her bow and a spear to the leather of his saddle. As she led him into the courtyard no one paid her much attention, partly because she monitored the minds around her and nudged them aside when they touched her. She led Small to the back of the courtyard, as far as she could get from the gates. She tried to express to Small how important this was, and how sorry she was, and how much she loved him. He dribbled against her neck.

Then Brigan gave the order. Servants swung the gates in and pulled the portcullis up, and the men burst into daylight. Fire pulled herself into her saddle and spurred Small forward behind them. The gates were closing again when she and Small galloped through, and rode alone, away from the soldiers, toward the empty rockiness east of Roen's holding.

The soldiers' focus was northward and up; they didn't see her. Some of the raptors did, and, curious, broke off from the surge dropping down onto the soldiers, few enough that she shot them from her saddle, clenching her teeth through the pain. The archers on the wall most certainly saw her. She knew it from the shock and panic Archer was sending at her. *I'll be most likely to survive this if you stay on that wall and keep shooting,* she thought to him fiercely, hoping it would be enough to keep him from coming out after her.

And now she was a good distance from the gates and the first soldiers had reached the tunnel, and she saw that a skirmish of monsters and men had begun at the back of the line. This was the time. She drew her brave horse up and turned him around. She yanked her scarf from her head. Her hair billowed down over her shoulders like a river of flame.

For an instant nothing happened, and she began to panic because it wasn't working. She dropped her mind's guard against their recognition. Still nothing. She reached out to grab at their attention.

Then one raptor high in the sky felt her, and then sighted her, and screamed a horrible sound, like metal screeching against metal. Fire knew what that sound meant, and so did the other raptors. Like a cloud of gnats they lifted from the soldiers. They shot into the sky, twirling desperately, searching for monster prey, finding it. The soldiers were forgotten. Every last raptor monster dove for her.

Now she had two jobs: to get herself and her horse back to the gates, if she could; and to stop the soldiers from doing something heroic and foolish when they saw what she'd done. She spurred Small forward. She slammed the thought at Brigan as hard as she could, not manipulation, which she knew would be futile – only a message. *If you don't continue onward to Grey Haven this instant, I will have done this for nothing.*

She knew he hesitated. She couldn't see him or sense his thoughts, but she could feel that his mind was still there, on his horse, not moving. She supposed she could manipulate his horse, if she had to.

Let me do this, she begged him. *My life is mine to risk, as yours is yours.*

His consciousness disappeared into the tunnel.

And now it was the speed of Fire and Small versus the swarm descending upon her from the north and from above. Under her, Small was desperate and wonderful. He had never flown so fast.

She bent herself low in her saddle. When the first raptor cut into her shoulder with its claws she threw her bow backwards at them; it was useless now, a stick of wood in her way. The quiver on her back might serve as a kind of armour. She took her spear and stuck it behind her, one more thing for the birds to have to work around. She clenched her knife in her hand and stabbed back whenever she felt a claw or a beak jabbing into her shoulder or her scalp. She didn't feel pain anymore. Only noise, that might be her own head screaming, and brightness, that was her hair and her blood, and wind that was Small's headlong speed. And arrows suddenly, flying very close past her head.

A claw caught her neck and yanked, pulled her high in her seat, and it occurred to her that she was about to die. But then an arrow struck the raptor that dragged at her, and more arrows followed it, and she looked ahead and saw the gates very near, cracked open, and Archer in the aperture, shooting faster than she'd known he could shoot.

And then he stepped aside and Small slammed through the crack, and behind her, monster bodies slammed against the closing doors. They screamed, scraped. And she left it to Small to figure out where to go and when to stop. And people were around her, and Roen was reaching for her reins, and Small was limping, she could tell; and she looked to his back and his rump and his legs and they were torn apart, sticky with blood. She cried out in distress at the sight of it. She vomited.

Someone grabbed her under the arms and pulled her out of her saddle. Archer, rigid and shaking, looking and feeling like he wanted to kill her. Then Archer went bright, and turned to black.

CHAPTER SEVEN

SHE WOKE TO stinging pain, and to the sense of a hostile mind moving down the corridor outside her room. A stranger's mind. She tried to sit up, and gasped.

'You should rest,' a woman said from a chair along the wall. Roen's healer.

Fire ignored the advice and pushed herself up gingerly. 'My horse?'

'Your horse is in about the same shape you're in,' the healer said. 'He'll live.'

'The soldiers? Did any of them die?'

'Every man made it into the tunnel alive,' she said. 'A good many monsters died.'

Fire sat still, waiting for the pounding of her head to slow, so that she could get up and investigate the suspicious mind in the hallway. 'How badly am I wounded?'

'You'll have scars on your back and your shoulders and under your hair for the rest of your life. But we have all the medicines here that they have in King's City. You'll heal cleanly, without infection.'

'Can I walk?'

'I don't recommend it; but if you must, you can.'

'I just need to check on something,' she said, breathless from the effort of sitting. 'Will you help me into my robe?' And then, noticing the skimpy sheath she wore: 'Did Lord Archer see my wrists?'

The woman came to Fire with a soft, white robe and helped her to hang it over her burning shoulders. 'Lord Archer hasn't been in.'

Fire decided to focus on the agony of putting her arms into her sleeves, rather than trying to calculate how furious Archer must be, if he hadn't even been in.

THE MIND SHE sensed was near, unguarded, and consumed with some underhanded purpose. All good reasons for it to have drawn Fire's attention, though she wasn't certain what she hoped to achieve by limping down this corridor in pursuit of it, willing to absorb whatever emotions it leaked accidentally but unwilling to take hold of it and plumb it for its true intentions.

It was a guilty mind, furtive.

She could not ignore it. I'll just follow, she thought to herself. I'll see where he goes.

She was astonished a moment later when a servant girl observing her progress stopped and offered an arm.

'My husband was at the back of that charge, Lady Fire,' the girl said. 'You saved his life.'

Fire hobbled down the hallway on the arm of the girl, happy to have saved someone's life if it meant that now she had a person to keep her from flopping onto the floor. Every step brought her closer to her strange quarry. 'Wait,' she whispered finally, leaning against the wall. 'Whose rooms are behind this wall?'

'The king's, Lady Fire.'

Fire knew with utter certainty then that a man was in the king's compartments who should not be. Haste, fear of discovery, panic: it all came to her.

A confrontation was beyond her current strength even to consider; and then down the hall, in his own room, she sensed Archer. She grasped the servant girl's arm. 'Run to Queen Roen and tell her a man is in the king's rooms who has no place there,' she said.

'Yes, Lady. Thank you, Lady,' the girl said, and scampered

away. Fire continued down the hallway alone.

When she reached Archer's room she leaned in his doorway. He stood at the window and stared into the covered courtyard, his back to her. She tapped on his mind.

His shoulders stiffened. He spun around and stalked toward her, not once looking at her. He brushed past her and stormed on down the hall. The surprise of it made her dizzy.

It was for the best. She was not in a state to face him, if he was as angry as that.

She went into his room and sat on a chair, just for a moment, to still her throbbing head.

IT TOOK HER ages to get to the stables, despite a number of helping hands; and when she saw Small she couldn't stop herself. She began to cry.

'Now, don't fret, Lady Fire,' Roen's animal healer said. 'It's all superficial wounds. He'll be right as a rainbow in a week's time.'

Right as a rainbow, with his entire back half stitched together and bandaged and his head hanging low. He was happy to see her, even though it was her doing. He pressed himself against the stall door, and when she went inside he pressed himself against her.

'I reckon he's been worrying about you,' the healer said. 'He's perked up now you're here.'

I'm sorry, Fire thought to him, her arms around his neck as best she could. *I'm sorry. I'm sorry.*

She guessed that the fifty men would remain in the Little Greys until the Third Branch arrived and drove the raptor monsters high again. The stables would be quiet until then.

And so Fire stayed with Small, leaning against him, collecting his spit in her hair and using her mind to ease his own sense of his stinging pain.

*

SHE WAS CURLED up on a fresh bed of hay in the corner of Small's stall when Roen arrived.

'Lady,' Roen said, standing outside the stall door, her eyes soft. 'Don't move,' she said as Fire tried to sit up. 'The healer told me you should rest, and I suppose resting in here is the best we can hope for. Can I bring you anything?'

'Food?'

Roen nodded. 'Anything else?'

'Archer?'

Roen cleared her throat. 'I'll send Archer to you once I'm convinced he won't say something insufferable.'

Fire swallowed. 'He's never been this angry with me before.'

Roen bent her face and considered her hands on the stall door. Then she came in and crouched before Fire. Just once she reached out and smoothed Fire's hair. She held a bit of it in her fingers, contemplating it carefully, very still on her knees in the hay, as if she were trying to work out the meaning of something. 'Beautiful girl,' she said. 'You did a good thing today, whatever Archer thinks. Next time, mention it to someone beforehand so we're better prepared.'

'Archer never would have let me do it.'

'No. But I would have.'

For a moment their eyes met. Fire understood that Roen meant what she said. She swallowed. 'Any word from Grey Haven?'

'No, but the Third has been spotted from the lookout, so we may see our fifty men back as soon as this evening.' Roen brushed off her lap and rose to her feet, all business again. 'Incidentally, we found no one in the king's rooms. And if you insist on doting on your horse in this manner I suppose the least we can do is bring you pillows and blankets. Get some sleep in here, will you? Both of you, girl and horse. And I hope you'll tell me someday, Fire, why you did it.'

With a swirl of skirts and a click of the latch, Roen was gone. Fire closed her eyes and considered the question.

She'd done it because she'd had to. An apology for the life of her father, who'd created a world of lawlessness where towns like Grey Haven fell under the attack of looters. And she'd done it to show Roen's son that she was on his side. And also to keep him alive.

FIRE WAS ASLEEP in her room that night when all fifty men clattered back from Grey Haven. The prince and the king wasted no time, departing south immediately with the Third. When Fire woke the next morning they were gone.

CHAPTER EIGHT

CANSREL HAD ALWAYS let Fire into his mind to practise changing his thoughts. He'd encouraged it, as part of her training. She went, but every time it was like a waking nightmare.

She'd heard tales of fishermen who grappled for their lives with water monsters in the Winter Sea. Cansrel's mind was like an eel monster, cold, slick, and voracious. Whenever she reached for it she felt clammy coils wrapping around her and pulling her under. She struggled madly, first simply to take hold of it; then to transform it into something soft and warm. A kitten. A baby.

The warming of Cansrel's mind took enormous burning energy. Then calm, to soothe the bottomless appetite, and then she would begin to push at its nature with all her strength, to shape thoughts there that Cansrel would never have on his own. Pity for a trapped animal. Respect for a woman. Contentment. It required all her strength. A mind slippery and cruel resists change.

Cansrel never said so, but Fire believed his favourite drug was to have her in his mind, manhandling him into contentment. He was used to thrills, but contentment was a novelty, a state Cansrel seemed never to achieve except by her help. Warmth and softness two things that rarely touched him. He never, ever refused Fire when she asked permission to enter. He trusted her, for he knew that she used her power for good and never to harm.

He only forgot to take into consideration the broken line separating good from harm.

*

TODAY THERE WAS no entering Archer's mind. He was shutting Fire out. Not that it particularly mattered, for she never entered Archer's mind to alter it, only to test the waters, and she had no interest in the nature of his waters today. She was not going to apologise and she was not going to capitulate to the fight he wanted to have. Not that she would have to stretch far to find something to accuse him of. Condescension. Imperiousness. Obstinacy.

They sat at a square table with Roen and a number of Roen's spies discussing Fire's trespassing archer, the men the archer had shot, and the fellow Fire had sensed in the king's rooms yesterday.

'There are plenty of spies out there and plenty of archers,' Roen's spymaster said, 'though perhaps few as skilled as your mysterious archer seems to be. Lord Gentian and Lord Mydogg have built up whole squadrons of archers. And some of the kingdom's finest archers are in the employ of animal smugglers.'

Yes, Fire remembered that. The smuggler Cutter had bragged of his archers. It was how he caught his merchandise, with darts tipped with sleeping poison.

'The Pikkians also have decent archers,' another of Roen's men said. 'And I know we like to think of them as clannish and simple, interested in nothing but boat-building, deep sea fishing, and the occasional sack of our border towns – but they follow our politics. They're not stupid, and they're not on the king's side. It's our taxes and our trade regulations that have kept them poor these thirty years.'

'Mydogg's sister Murgda has just married a Pikkian,' Roen said, 'a naval explorer of the eastern seas. And we have reason to believe that lately Mydogg has been recruiting Pikkians into his Dellian army. And having some success at it.'

Fire was startled; this was news, and not of the happy variety. 'How big has Mydogg's army grown?'

'It's still not as big as the King's Army,' Roen said firmly. 'Mydogg has said to my face that he has twenty-five thousand soldiers at the underside, but our spies to his holding in the northeast put the count at only twenty thousand or so. Brigan has twenty thousand patrolling in the four branches alone, and an additional five thousand in the auxiliaries.'

'And Gentian?'

'We're not certain. Our best guess is ten thousand or so, all living in caves below the Winged River near his estate.'

'Numbers aside,' the spymaster said, 'everyone has archers and spies. Your archer could be working for anyone. If you'll leave the arrow and bolt with us we may be able to eliminate some possibilities or at least determine where his gear comes from. But I'll be honest with you: I wouldn't hold out too much hope. You haven't given us much to go on.'

'The man who was killed in your cages,' Roen said. 'The one you call the poacher. He gave you no hint of his purpose? Even you, Fire?'

'His mind was blank,' Fire said. 'No evil intent, no honourable intent. He had the feel of a simpleton, someone's tool.'

'And the man in the king's rooms yesterday,' Roen said. 'Did he have that feel?'

'No. He may certainly have been working for someone else, but his mind was consumed with purpose, and with guilt. He thought for himself.'

'Nash said his belongings were disturbed,' Roen said, 'but nothing was taken. We wonder if the man was looking for a number of letters that I happened to be carrying on my own person in Nash's absence – and good thing, too. A spy – but whose? Fire, you would recognise the man if he crossed your path again?'

'I would. I don't believe he's in the castle now. Perhaps he left under cover of the Third.'

'We wasted a day,' the spymaster said. 'We could have used you yesterday to find him and question him.'

And then Fire was reminded that even when Archer wouldn't look her in the face he was her friend, for he said crisply, 'Lady Fire was in need of rest yesterday, and anyway, she is not a tool for your use.'

Roen tapped her fingernails on the table, not attending, following her own thoughts. 'Every man is an enemy,' she said grimly. 'Mydogg, Gentian, the black market, Pikkia. They've got people sneaking around trying to learn Brigan's plans for the troops, steal our allies from us, figure out a good place and time to do away with Nash or Brigan or one of the twins, or even me.' She shook her head. 'And in the meantime, we're trying to learn their numbers and their allies and their allies' numbers. Their plans for attack. We're trying to steal their spies and convert them to our side. No doubt they're doing the same with our spies. The rocks only know whom among our own people we should trust. One of these days a messenger will come through my gates to tell me my sons are dead.'

She spoke unemotionally; she wasn't trying to elicit comfort or contradiction, she was only stating fact. 'We do need you, Fire,' she added. 'And don't look all panicked like that. Not to change people's thoughts. Only to take advantage of the greater sense of people that you have.'

No doubt Roen meant her words. But with the kingdom in this unstable state the lesser expectation would grow to include the greater, sooner rather than later. Fire's head began to throb harder than she thought she could bear. She glanced at Archer, who responded by avoiding her eyes, frowning at the table, and changing the subject abruptly.

'Can you spare me any more soldiers, Lady Queen?'

'I suppose I can't deny you my soldiers when yesterday Fire saved their lives,' Roen said. 'Brigan has helped by leaving me ten dozen men from the Third. You may take eight of the soldiers from my original guard who went to Grey Haven.'

'I would prefer eight of the ten dozen from the Third,' Archer said.

'They're all in the King's Army,' Roen said, 'all trained by Brigan's people, all equally competent, and the men who went to Grey Haven already have a natural allegiance to your lady, Archer.'

Allegiance wasn't quite the word for it. The soldiers who'd gone to Grey Haven seemed to regard Fire now with something akin to worship; which was, of course, why Archer didn't want them. A number of them had sought her out today and knelt before her, kissed her hand and pledged to protect her.

'Very well,' Archer said grumpily, somewhat mollified, Fire suspected, because Roen had referred to Fire as his lady. Fire added immaturity to the things she could accuse him of in the fight they weren't going to have.

'Let's go over the encounter one more time,' the spymaster said. 'Every one of the encounters, in minute detail. Lady Fire? Please begin again in the forest.'

ARCHER SPOKE TO her finally, an entire week later, when the raptors had gone and so had much of her soreness, and their own departure was imminent. They were at the table in Roen's sitting room, waiting for Roen to join them for dinner. 'I cannot bear your silence any longer,' Archer said.

Fire had to stop herself from laughing at the joke of it. She noted the two servants standing beside the door, their faces carefully blank while their minds spun excitedly – probably with gossip to bring back to the kitchen.

'Archer,' she said. 'You're the one who's been pretending I don't exist.'

Archer shrugged. He sat back and regarded her, a challenge in his eyes. 'Can I ever trust you now? Or must I always be prepared for this brand of heroic madness?'

She had an answer to that, but she couldn't say it aloud. She leaned forward and held his eyes. *It was not the first mad thing I've ever done for this kingdom. Perhaps you who know the truth of things should not have been surprised. Brocker won't be, when we tell him what I did here.*

After a moment his eyes dropped from hers. His fingers realigned the forks on the table. 'I wish you were not so brave.'

She had no response to that. She was desperate sometimes, and a little crazy, but she was not brave.

'Are you determined to leave me in this world to live without my heart?' Archer asked. 'Because that's what you very nearly did.'

She watched her friend play with the fringe of the tablecloth, his eyes avoiding hers, his voice carefully light, trying to look as if he were speaking of something small, like an appointment she'd forgotten that had inconvenienced him.

She reached across the table and held her hand open to him. 'Make peace with me, Archer.'

At that moment Roen swept through the door and slid into a chair between them. She turned on Archer, eyes narrow and unamused. 'Archer, is there a servant girl in my fortress you haven't taken to bed? I announce you're leaving and within minutes two of them are at each other's throats, and another is crying her eyes out in the scullery. Honestly. You've been here all of nine days.' She glanced at Fire's open hand. 'I've interrupted something.'

Archer considered the table for a moment, his fingers caressing the edge of his glass, his mind clearly elsewhere. He sighed in the direction of his plate.

'Peace, Archer,' Fire said again.

Archer's eyes settled on Fire's face. 'All right,' he said reluctantly, taking her hand. 'Peace, because war is unbearable.'

Roen snorted. 'You two have the strangest relationship in the Dells.'

Archer smiled slightly. 'She won't consent to make it a marriage.'

'I can't imagine what's stopping her. I don't suppose you've considered being less munificent with your love?'

'Would you marry me, Fire, if I slept in no one's bed but yours?'

He knew the answer to that, but it didn't hurt to remind him. 'No, and I should find my bed quite cramped.'

Archer laughed and kissed her hand, then released it ceremoniously; and Fire picked up her knife and fork, smiling. Shaking her head in disbelief, Roen turned aside to take a note from an approaching servant. 'Ah,' she said, reading the note and frowning. 'It's good that you're going. Lord Mydogg and Lady Murgda are on their way.'

'On their way?' Fire said. 'You mean they're coming here?'

'Just for a visit.'

'A visit! Surely you don't visit each other?'

'Oh, it's all a farce, of course,' Roen said, waving her hand tiredly. 'Their way of showing that the royal family doesn't intimidate them, and our way of pretending that we're open to dialogue. They come and I have to let them in, because if I refuse them, it'll be taken as a hostile gesture and they'll have an excuse to come back with their army. We sit across from each other, we drink wine, they ask me nosy questions that I don't answer about Nash and Brigan and the royal twins, they tell me secrets their own spies have supposedly learned about Gentian, information that either I already know or they've fabricated. They pretend that the king's real enemy is Gentian, and that Nash should ally with Mydogg against Gentian. I pretend it's a good idea and suggest that Mydogg pass his army over to Brigan's use as a show of faith. Mydogg refuses; we agree we've reached an impasse; Mydogg and Murgda take their leave, poking their noses into as many rooms as they can on the way out.'

Archer's eyebrows were looking skeptical. 'Isn't this sort of thing a bit more risky than it's worth? For everyone?'

'They're coming at a good time – Brigan just left me all those soldiers. And when they're here, we're all so heavily guarded every minute that I don't suppose either side would ever try anything, for fear of all of us getting killed. I'm as safe as I ever am. But,' she added, studying both of them gravely, 'I want you to depart tomorrow at first light. I won't have you meeting them – there's no reason to get you and Brocker tangled up in Mydogg's nonsense, Archer. And I don't want them to see Fire.'

IT WAS ALMOST achieved. In fact, Fire, Archer, and their guards had travelled some distance from Roen's fortress and were just about to turn off onto a different path when the party from the north approached. Twenty rather fearsome soldiers – chosen because they had the aspects of pirates, with broken teeth and scars? Big and pale-ish, some of them. Pikkian? And a tough-looking man and woman who had the aura of a winter wind. Easily brother and sister, both squat and thin-lipped and icy in their expressions, until their eyes combed Fire's party and settled, with genuine and uncalculated amazement, on Fire herself.

The siblings glanced at each other. Some silent understanding passed between them.

'Come,' Archer muttered, motioning to his guards and Fire to move on. The parties clattered past each other without even a greeting.

Oddly rattled, Fire touched Small's mane, stroking his rough hair. The lord and lady had been only names before, a dot on the Dellian map and a certain unknown quantity of soldiers. Now they were real, and solid, and cold.

She had not liked the glance they'd shared at the sight of

her. Nor did she care for the feeling of their hard eyes on her back as Small carried her away.

CHAPTER NINE

IT HAPPENED AGAIN: only days after Fire and Archer returned home, another man was found trespassing in Archer's forest, a stranger. When the soldiers brought him in, Fire sensed the same mental fog she'd sensed with the poacher. And then before Fire could even begin to consider whether and how to use her power to wangle information from him, an arrow came through the open window, straight into the middle of Archer's guard room, and struck the trespasser between the shoulder blades. Archer threw himself on top of Fire, dragging her down. The trespasser toppled and fell beside her, a trickle of blood at the corner of his mouth. His empty mind fizzled into no mind at all, and from her crushed position on the floor, soldiers' feet yanking at her hair and Archer yelling orders above her, she reached for the archer who'd made the shot.

He was faint, a good distance away, but she found him. She tried to grasp hold of him but a boot trod on her finger and the explosion of pain distracted her. When she reached for him again he was gone.

He's run west into Trilling's woods, she thought to Archer, because she had no breath to speak. *And his mind is as blank as the others.*

HER FINGER WAS not broken, only beastly sore when she moved it. It was the second finger on her left hand so she put off playing harp and flute for a day or two, but she refused to spare herself when it came to her fiddle. She'd been without the instrument for too long. She simply tried not to think of the pain, because every stab of pain was accompanied now by a stab of vexation. Fire was tired of being injured.

She sat in her bedroom one day, playing a cheerful tune, a song for dancing, but something in her mood slowed the tempo and discovered sad parts in it. Eventually she found herself switching to a different song altogether, one that was manifestly sorrowful, and her fiddle cried out its feeling.

Fire stopped and lowered the instrument to her lap. She stared at it, then hugged it against her chest like a baby, wondering what was wrong with her.

She had an image in her head of Cansrel in the moment he had given her this fiddle. 'I'm told this has a nice sound, darling,' he'd said, holding it out to her almost carelessly, as if it were an inconsequential bit of rubbish that had not cost him a small fortune. She'd taken it, appreciative of its handsomeness but knowing that its real value would depend upon its tone and feeling, neither of which Cansrel could be any judge of. She'd drawn her bow across its strings as an experiment. The fiddle had responded instantly, wanting her touch, speaking to her in a gentle voice that she'd understood and recognised.

A new friend in her life.

She'd been unable to hide her pleasure from Cansrel. His own gladness had swelled.

'You're astonishing, Fire,' he'd said. 'You're a constant source of wonder to me. I'm never more happy than when I've made you happy. Isn't it peculiar?' he'd said, laughing. 'Do you really like it, darling?'

In her chair in her room, Fire forced herself to look around at the windows and walls and take stock of the present. The light was fading. Archer would be coming back soon from the fields, where he was helping with the plowing. He might have some news about the ongoing search for the archer. Or Brocker might have a letter from Roen with updates about Mydogg and Murgda, or Gentian, or Brigan, or Nash.

She found her longbow and quiver and, shaking off memories like loose hairs, left her house in search of Archer and Brocker.

THERE WAS NO news. There were no letters.

One monthly bleeding passed for Fire, with all its attendant aches and embarrassments. Everyone in her house, in Archer's house, and in the town knew what it signified whenever she stepped outside with an entourage of guards. Eventually another passed like the first. Summer was near. The farmers were willing potatoes and carrots to take hold in the rocky ground.

Her lessons progressed much as usual.

'Stop, I implore you,' she said one day at Trilling's, interrupting an earsplitting clamour of flutes and horns. 'Let's begin again at the top of the page, shall we? And, Trotter,' she begged the eldest boy, 'try not to blow so hard; I guarantee you, that shrieking noise is from blowing too hard. All right? Ready?'

The enthusiastic massacre began once more. She did love the children. Children were one of her small joys, even when they were fiends to each other; even when they imagined they were hiding things from her, like their own idleness or, in some cases, their talent. Children were smart and malleable. Time and patience made them strong and stopped them fearing her or adoring her too much. And their frustrations were familiar to her, and dear.

But, she thought, at the end of the day I must give them back. They're not my children – someone else feeds them and tells them stories. I'll never have children. I'm stuck in this town where nothing ever happens and nothing ever will happen and there's never any news. I'm so restless I could take Renner's horrible flute and break it over his head.

She touched her own head, took a breath, and made very sure that Trilling's second son knew nothing of her feeling.

I must find my even temper, she thought. What is it I'm

hoping for, anyway? Another murder in the woods? A visit from Mydogg and Murgda and their pirates? An ambush of wolf monsters?

I must stop wishing for things to happen. Because something will happen eventually, and when it does, I'll be bound to wish it hadn't.

THE NEXT DAY, she was walking the path from her house to Archer's, quiver on back and bow in hand, when one of the guards called down to her from Archer's back terrace. 'Fancy a reel, Lady Fire?'

It was Krell, the guard she'd tricked the night she'd been unable to climb up to her bedroom window. A man who knew how a flute should be played; and here he was, offering to save her from her own desperate fidgets. 'Goodness, yes,' she said. 'Just let me get my fiddle.'

A reel with Krell was always a game. They took turns, each inventing a passage that was a challenge to the other to pick up and join; always keeping in time but raising tempo gradually, so that eventually it took all of their concentration and skill to keep up with each other. They were worthy of an audience, and today Brocker and a number of guards wandered out to the back terrace for the show.

Fire was in the mood for technical gymnastics, which was fortunate, because Krell played as if he were determined to make her break a string. Her fingers flew, her fiddle was an entire orchestra, and every note beautifully brought into being struck a chord of satisfaction within her. She wondered at the unfamiliar lightness in her chest and realised she was laughing.

So great was her focus, it took her a while to register the strange expression that crept to Brocker's face as he listened, finger tapping the armrest of his chair. His eyes were fixed behind Fire and to the right, in the direction of Archer's back doorway. Fire comprehended that someone must be standing in Archer's entrance, someone Brocker watched with startled eyes.

And then everything happened at once. Fire recognised the mind in the doorway; she spun around, fiddle and bow screeching apart; she stared at Prince Brigan leaning against the door frame.

Behind her Krell's quick piping stopped. The soldiers on the terrace cleared throats and turned, falling to attention as they recognised their commander. Brigan's eyes were expressionless. He shifted and stood up straight, and she knew that he was going to speak.

Fire turned and ran down the terrace steps to the path.

ONCE OUT OF sight Fire slowed and stopped. She leaned over a boulder, gasping for air, her fiddle clunking against the stone with a sharp, dissonant cry of protest. The guard Tovat, the one with the orangish hair and the strong mind, came running up behind her. He stopped beside her.

'Forgive my intrusion, Lady,' he said. 'You left unarmed. Are you ill, Lady?'

She laid her forehead against the boulder, ashamed because he was right; in addition to fleeing like a chicken from a woman's skirts, she'd left unarmed. 'Why is he here?' she asked Tovat, still pressing fiddle and bow and forehead into the boulder. 'What does he want?'

'I left too soon to know,' Tovat said. 'Shall we go back? Do you need a hand, Lady? Do you need the healer?'

She doubted Brigan was the type to make social calls, and he rarely travelled alone. Fire closed her eyes and reached her mind over the hills. She couldn't sense his army, but she found twenty or so men in a group nearby. Outside her front door, not Archer's.

Fire sighed into the rock. She stood, checked her headscarf, and tucked fiddle and bow under her arm. She turned toward her own house. 'Come, Tovat. We'll learn soon enough, for he's come for me.'

THE SOLDIERS OUTSIDE her door were not like Roen's men or Archer's, who admired her and had reason to trust her. These were ordinary soldiers, and as she and Tovat came into their sight she sensed an assortment of the usual reactions. Desire, astonishment, mistrust. And also guardedness. These men were mentally guarded, more than she would have expected from a random assemblage. Brigan must have selected them for their guardedness; or warned them to remember it.

She corrected herself. They were not all men. Three among them had long hair tied back and the faces and the feeling of women. She sharpened her mind. Five more again were men whose appraisal of her lacked a particular focus. She wondered, hopefully, if they might be men who did not desire women.

She stopped before them. Every one of them stared.

'Well met, soldiers,' she said. 'Will you come inside and sit?'

One of the women, tall, with hazel eyes and a powerful voice, spoke. 'Our orders are to wait outside until our commander returns from Lord Archer's house, Lady.'

'Very well,' Fire said, somewhat relieved that their orders weren't to seize her and throw her into a burlap bag. She passed through the soldiers to her door, Tovat behind her. She stopped at a thought and turned again to the woman soldier. 'Are you in charge, then?'

'Yes, Lady, in the commander's absence.'

Fire touched again on the minds in the group, looking for some reaction to Brigan's election of a female officer. Resentment, jealousy, indignation. She found none.

These were not ordinary soldiers after all. She couldn't be sure of his motive, but something had gone into Brigan's choosing.

She stepped inside with Tovat and closed the door on them.

ARCHER HAD BEEN in town during the concert on the terrace, but he must have come home shortly thereafter. It was not long before Brigan returned to her door, and this time Brocker and Archer accompanied him.

Donal showed the three men into her sitting room. In an attempt to cover her embarrassment and also to reassure them that she wasn't going to make another dash for the hills, Fire spoke quickly. 'Lord Prince, if your soldiers wish to sit or take something to drink, they're welcome in my house.'

'Thank you, Lady,' he said evenly, 'but I don't expect to stay long.'

Archer was agitated about something, and Fire didn't need any mental powers to perceive it. She motioned for Brigan and Archer to sit, but both remained standing.

'Lady,' Brigan said, 'I come on the king's behalf.'

He didn't quite look her in the face as he spoke, his eyes touching on the air around her but avoiding her person. She decided to take it as an invitation to study him with her own eyes, for his mind was so strongly guarded against her that she could glean nothing that way.

He was armed with bow and sword, but unarmoured, dressed in dark riding clothes. Clean-shaven. Shorter than Archer but taller than she remembered. He held himself aloof, dark hair and unfriendly eyebrows and stern face, and aside from his refusal to look at her she could sense nothing of his feelings about this interview. She noticed a small scar cutting into his right eyebrow, thin and curved. It matched the scars on her own neck and shoulders. A raptor monster had nearly taken his eye, then. Another scar on his chin. This one straight, a knife or a sword.

She supposed the commander of the King's Army was likely to have as many scars as a human monster.

'Three weeks ago in the king's palace,' Brigan was saying, 'a stranger was found in the king's rooms and captured. The king asks you to come to King's City to meet the prisoner, Lady, and tell whether he's the same man who was in the king's rooms at the fortress of my mother.'

King's City. Her birthplace. The place where her own mother had lived and died. The gorgeous city above the sea that would be lost or saved in the war that was coming. She'd never seen King's City, except in her imagination. Certainly, no one had ever suggested before that she go there and see it for real.

She forced her mind to consider the question seriously even though her heart had already decided. She would have many enemies in King's City, and too many men who liked her too much. She would be stared at, and assaulted, and she would not ever have the option of resting her mental guard. The king of the kingdom would desire her. And he and his advisers would wish her to use her power against prisoners, enemies, every one of the million people they did not trust.

And she would have to travel with this rough man who didn't like her.

'Does the king request this,' Fire asked, 'or is it an order?'

Brigan considered the floor coolly. 'It was stated as an order, Lady, but I won't force you to go.'

And so the brother, apparently, was permitted to disobey the king's orders; or perhaps it was a measure of how little Brigan wanted to deliver her to his weak-headed brother, that he was willing to refuse the command.

'If the king expects me to use my power to interrogate his prisoners he'll be disappointed,' Fire said.

Brigan flexed and clenched his sword hand, once. A flicker of something – impatience, or anger. He looked into her eyes for the briefest of moments, and looked away. 'I don't imagine the king will compel you to do anything you don't want to do.'

By which Fire understood that the prince considered it

within her power and her intention to control the king. Her face burned, but she lifted her chin a notch and said, 'I'll go.'

Archer spluttered. Before he could speak she swung to him and looked up into his eyes. *Don't quarrel with me in front of the king's brother*, she thought to him. *And don't ruin this two months' peace.*

He glared back at her. 'I'm not the one who ruins it,' he said, his voice low.

Brocker was accustomed to this; but how must they look to Brigan, staring at each other, having one side of an argument? *I won't do this now. You may embarrass yourself, but you will not embarrass me.*

Archer drew in a breath that sounded like a hiss, turned on his heel, and stormed out of the room. He slammed the door, leaving an uncomfortable silence in his wake.

Fire touched a hand to her headscarf and turned back to Brigan. 'Please forgive our rudeness,' she said.

Not a flicker in those grey eyes. 'Of course.'

'How will you ensure her safety on the journey, Commander?' Brocker asked quietly. Brigan turned to him, then sat in a chair, resting his elbows on his knees; and his whole manner seemed to change. With Brocker he was suddenly easy and comfortable and respectful, a young military commander addressing a man who could be his mentor.

'Sir, we'll ride to King's City in the company of the entire First Branch. They're stationed just west of here.'

Brocker smiled. 'You misunderstand me, son. How will you ensure she'll be safe from the First Branch? In a force of five thousand there'll be some with the mind to hurt her.'

Brigan nodded. 'I've hand-picked a guard of twenty soldiers who can be trusted to care for her.'

Fire crossed her arms and bit down hard. 'I don't need to be cared for. I can defend myself.'

'I don't doubt it, Lady,' Brigan said mildly, looking into

his hands, 'but if you're to ride with us you'll have a guard nonetheless. I can't transport a civilian female in a party of five thousand men on a journey of nearly three weeks and not provide a guard. I trust you to see the sense in it.'

He was talking around the fact that she was a monster who provoked all the worst kinds of behaviour. And now that her temper was done flaring, she did see the sense in it. Truly, she'd never pitted herself against five thousand men before. She sat down. 'Very well.'

Brocker chuckled. 'If only Archer were here to see the powers of rational argument.'

Fire snorted. Archer wouldn't consider her allowance of the guard to be evidence of the powers of rational argument. He'd take it as proof that she was in love with whichever of her guards was most handsome.

She stood up again. 'I'll ready myself,' she said, 'and ask Donal to ready Small.'

Brigan stood with her, his face closed again, impassive. 'Very good, Lady.'

'Will you wait here with me, Commander?' Brocker said. 'I've a thing or two to tell you.'

Fire scrutinised Brocker. *Oh? What do you need to tell him?*

Brocker had too much class for a one-sided argument. He also possessed a mind so clear and strong that he could open a feeling to her with perfect precision, so that it came to her practically as a sentence. *I want to give him military advice*, Brocker thought to her.

Mildly reassured, Fire left them.

WHEN SHE GOT to her bedroom Archer was sitting in a chair against the wall. Taking a liberty with his presence, for it wasn't his room to enter without invitation. But she forgave him. Archer couldn't abandon the responsibilities of his house and farms so suddenly in order to travel with her. He would stay behind, and they would be a long time apart – almost six weeks to get there and back, and longer if she stayed any time in King's City.

When Brocker had asked her, in her fourteenth year, just how much power she had over Cansrel's mind when she was inside it, Archer had been the one to defend her. 'Where's your heart, Father? The man is her father. Don't make her relationship with him more difficult than it already is.'

'I'm only asking questions,' Brocker had responded. 'Does she have the power to shift his attitudes? Could she change his ambitions permanently?'

'Anyone can see these are not idle questions.'

'They're necessary questions,' Brocker had said, 'though I wish they were not.'

'I don't care. Leave her be,' Archer had said, so passionately that Brocker had let her be, at least for the moment.

Fire supposed she would miss Archer defending her on this trip. Not because she wanted his defence, but simply because it was what Archer did when he was near.

She unearthed her saddlebags from a pile at the bottom of her closet and began to fold underclothing and riding gear into them. There was no point in bothering with dresses. No one ever noticed what she wore, and after three weeks in her bags they would be unwearable anyway.

'You'll desert your students?' Archer said finally, leaning over his knees, watching her pack. 'Just like that?'

She turned her back to him on the pretense of searching for her fiddle, and smiled. He had never been quite so concerned for her students before.

'You didn't take long to decide,' he added.

She spoke simply; to her it was obvious. 'I've never seen King's City.'

'It's not so wonderful as all that.'

It was a thing she'd like to determine for herself. She dug through the piles on her bed and said nothing.

'It'll be more dangerous than any place you've ever been,' he said. 'Your father took you away from that place because you weren't safe there.'

She set her fiddle case beside her saddlebags. 'Shall I choose a life of bleakness, then, Archer, just to stay alive? I won't hide in a room with the doors and windows shut. That is not a life.'

He ran his finger against the ridge of a feather in the quiver beside him. He glowered at the floor, chin on fist. 'You'll fall in love with the king.'

She sat on the edge of the bed facing him, and grinned. 'I couldn't fall in love with the king. He's weak-minded and he drinks too much wine.'

He caught her eye. 'And? I'm jealous-minded and I sleep with too many women.'

Fire's smile grew. 'Luckily for you, I loved you long before you became either of those things.'

'But you don't love me as much as I love you,' he said. 'Which is what's made me this way.'

This was harsh, coming from a friend she would lose her life for. And harsh that he would say such a thing right when she was about to leave for so long. She stood and turned her back to him. *Love doesn't measure that way*, she thought to him. *And you may blame me for your feelings, but it isn't fair to blame me for how you've chosen to behave.*

'I'm sorry,' he said. 'You're right. Forgive me, Fire.'

And she forgave him again, easily, because she knew that his anger usually fizzled as quickly as it came, and behind it his heart was full to bursting. But she stopped at forgiveness. She could guess what Archer wanted, here in her bedroom before she departed, and she wasn't going to give it to him.

It had been easy once, taking Archer into her bed; not so long ago it had been simple. And then, somehow, the balance had tipped between them. The marriage proposals, the love-sickness. More and more, the simplest thing was to say no.

She would answer him gently. She turned to him and held out her hand. He stood and came to her.

'I must change into riding clothes and pull a few more things together,' she said. 'We'll say our goodbyes now. You must go down and tell the prince I'm coming.'

He stared at his shoes and then into her face, understanding her. He tugged at her headscarf until it slid away and her hair fell around her shoulders. He collected her hair in one hand, bent his face to it, kissed it. He pulled Fire to him and kissed her neck and her mouth, so that her body was left wishing that her mind were not so stingy. Then he broke away and turned to the door, his face the picture of unhappiness.

CHAPTER TEN

S HE HAD BEEN afraid the army would move too fast for her or that every one of the five thousand soldiers would have to slow down for her sake. And the army did ride fast above ground, when the land underfoot was smooth enough to allow it, but most of the time the pace was more moderate. It was partly the restrictions of tunnels and terrain and partly the objectives of an armed force, which by nature seeks out the very troubles that other travelling parties hope to avoid.

The First Branch was a wonder of organisation: a moving base divided into sections, divided again into small units that broke off periodically, sped to a gallop, disappeared into caves or up mountain paths, and reappeared some time later. Scout units rode fast ahead of them and patrol units to every side, and they sent subunits racing back sometimes to make reports, or in the case of trouble found, request support. Sometimes, the soldiers who returned were bloody and bruised, and Fire came to recognise the green tunics of the healer units that rushed to their aid.

Then there were the hunting units which moved in rotation, circling back now and then with their game. There were the supply units, which handled the pack horses and figured the inventories. The command units delivered messages from Brigan to the rest of the force. The archery units kept eyes open for animal and monster predators foolish enough to prey on the main column of riders. Fire's own guard was a unit, too. It created a barrier between her and the thousands as she rode, and assisted her with everything she needed, which at first consisted mainly of answers to her questions about why half the army seemed always to be coming or going.

'Is there a unit to keep track of all the other units?' she asked the leader of her guards, the hazel-eyed woman, whose name was Musa.

Musa laughed. Most of Fire's questions seemed to make Musa laugh. 'The commander doesn't use one, Lady. He keeps track in his head. Watch the traffic around the standard-bearer – every unit that comes or goes reports first to the commander.'

Fire had been watching the standard-bearer – and his horse – with considerable sympathy, actually, because he seemed to ride twice as far as most of the rest of the army. The standard-bearer's sole charge was to stay near the commander so that the commander could always be found; and the commander was forever doubling back, breaking off, bursting forward, depending, Fire assumed, on matters of great military import, whatever in the Dells that meant. The standard-bearer always turning circles with him, chosen for that duty, Fire supposed, because he was a fine horseman.

Then the prince and the standard-bearer came closer, and once again Fire corrected herself. A fine horsewoman.

'Musa, how many women are in the First Branch?'

'Some five hundred, Lady. Perhaps twenty-five hundred in all four branches and the auxiliaries together.'

'Where are the auxiliaries when the rest of the army is patrolling?'

'In the forts and signal stations spread throughout the kingdom, Lady. Some of the soldiers manning those posts are women.'

Twenty-five hundred women who had volunteered to live on a horse's back, and fight, and eat, dress, sleep in a mob of males. Why would a woman choose such a life? Were their natures wild and violent, as some of the men had already proven theirs to be?

When she and her entourage had first passed out of Trilling's woods onto the rocky flats where the army was stationed, there had been a single fight over Fire, short and brutal. Two men out of their minds at the sight of her and disagreeing on some point (her honour, their respective chances), enough for shoves, fists to the face, broken noses, blood. Brigan was down from his horse with three of Fire's guard before Fire had fully comprehended what was happening. And one crisp word from Brigan's mouth had ended it: 'Enough.'

Fire had kept her eyes on Small's shoulders, combing his mane with her fingers until a sense of remorse had trickled to her from the minds of both fighters. Then she'd allowed herself a surprised peek at their hanging heads, their doleful glances at Brigan, blood plopping from broken lips and noses onto the ground. They'd forgotten her. She'd sensed that clearly. In their shame before their commander, they'd forgotten all about her.

Unusual. Fire's eyes had flicked curiously to Brigan. His expression had been cool, his mind unreadable. He'd spoken to the fighters quietly, hadn't looked at her once.

Back onto their horses, and shortly thereafter word had come around from the command units that any soldier brawling over any matter relating to the Lady Fire would find himself out of the army and the army's favour, disarmed, discharged, and sent home. Fire gathered from the low whistles and high eyebrows among her guard that it was a harsh punishment for brawling.

She didn't know enough about armies to extrapolate. Did a harsh punishment make Brigan a harsh commander? Was harshness the same as cruelty? Was cruelty the source of Brigan's power over his soldiers?

And where was the hardship in discharge from a fighting force in a time of impending war? To Fire it sounded more like a reprieve.

Fire pictured Archer riding through his fields at day's end, stopping to talk with the farmers, laughing, cursing the stubborn rocky ground of the north, as he always did. Archer and Brocker sitting down to dinner without her.

When the army finally stopped for the night she insisted on currying her own horse. She leaned into Small and whispered to him, comforted herself with the feel of him, the only familiar heart in a sea of strangers.

They made camp in a gigantic underground cavern, half-way between Fire's home and Roen's fortress, the likes of which Fire had never seen. Nor could she particularly see it now, for it was dim, light glancing through cracks in the ceiling and seeping from side openings. As the sun set, the cavern turned positively dark, and the First Branch was a composition of moving shadows spread across the sloping floor of the chamber.

Sound in the cavern was thick, musical. When the commander had left the camp with a force of two hundred, two hundred had echoed like two thousand and the footfalls had chimed like bells all around her. He'd taken off just as soon as he'd seen everyone settled – his face as indecipherable as ever. A scout unit of fifty soldiers had not returned at the time and place it was meant to. He'd gone looking for it.

Fire was uneasy. The shifting shadows of her five thousand companions unsettled her. Her guard kept her apart from most of these soldiers, but she could not separate herself from the impressions she collected in her mind. It was exhausting, to keep track of so many. They were most of them aware of her on some level, even those farthest away. Too many of them wanted something from her. Some got too close.

'I like the taste of monster,' one with a twice broken nose hissed at her.

'I love you. You're beautiful,' another three or four breathed to her, seeking her out, pressing themselves against the barriers of her guard to reach her.

Brigan had given her guard strict orders before he'd ridden

away. The lady was to be housed in a tent even though the army was under a cavern's roof, and two of her female guard were to accompany her always inside the tent.

'Am I never to have privacy?' she'd put in, overhearing Brigan's order to Musa.

Brigan had taken a leather gauntlet from a young man Fire supposed was his squire, and pulled it over his hand. 'No,' he'd said. 'Never.' And before she'd even been able to take a breath to protest he'd pulled on his other gauntlet and called for his horse. The hoofbeat music had swelled, and then dissipated.

IN HER TENT the smell of roasting monster meat came to her. She crossed her arms and tried not to glare at her two female guard companions, whose names she couldn't remember. She tugged at her headscarf. Surely in the presence of these women she could have some relief from the tight wrapping around her hair. They didn't want anything from her; the strongest emotion she could sense from both of them was boredom.

Of course, once she'd uncovered her hair their boredom lessened. They watched her with curious eyes. She looked back wearily. 'I forget your names. I'm sorry.'

'Margo, Lady,' said the one with a broad, pleasant face.

'Mila, Lady,' said the other, delicate boned, light haired, and very young.

Musa, Margo, and Mila. Fire bit off a sigh. She recognised the feel of almost every one of her twenty guards at this point, but the names would take her some time.

She didn't know what else to say, so she fingered the case of her fiddle. She opened the case and inhaled the warm smell of varnish. She plucked a string and the answering acoustics, like the reverberation of a bell struck underwater, focused her disorientation. The flap of the tent was open and the tent itself was set in a niche against the side of the cavern, a low, curving roof curling above it, not unlike the shell of an instrument. She tucked the fiddle under her chin and tuned it, and then, very quietly, she began to play.

A lullaby, soothing, to calm her own nerves. The army faded away.

SLEEP DIDN'T COME easily that night, but she knew it would be pointless to seek out the stars. Rain seeped through cracks in the ceiling and trickled down the walls to the floor; the sky tonight would be black. Perhaps a midnight storm would batter away her dreams. She threw back her blanket, found her boots, slipped past the sleeping forms of Margo and Mila, and pushed open the tent flap.

Outside she took care not to trip over the other sleeping guards, who were arranged around her tent like some kind of human moat. Four of the guards were awake: Musa and three men whose names she couldn't remember. They played cards in the light of a candle. Candles flickered here and there all across the floor of the cavern. Fire supposed that most units kept some kind of watch throughout the night. She pitied the soldiers currently on guard outside this haven, in the rain. And Brigan's search party, and the scouts for whom they searched, all of whom had yet to return.

The four guards seemed a bit dazed at the sight of her. She touched her hand to her hair, remembering that it was unbound.

Musa recollected herself. 'Is anything wrong, Lady?'

'Is there an opening in this cavern to the sky?' Fire asked. 'I want to see the rain.'

'There is,' Musa said.

'Will you show me the way?'

Musa set her cards down and began to wake the guards at the furthest edges of the human moat.

'What are you doing?' Fire whispered. 'Musa, it's not necessary. Please. Let them sleep,' she said, but Musa continued to shake shoulders until four of the men were awake. She ordered two of the card players to sit and keep watch. She motioned for the others to arm themselves.

Her fatigue compounded now with guilt, Fire ducked back into the tent for a headscarf and her own bow and quiver. She emerged and joined her six armed and sleepy companions. Musa lit candles and passed them around. Quietly, in procession, the line of seven skirted the edge of the cavern.

THE NARROW, SLOPING pathway they climbed some minutes later led to a perforation in the side of the mountain. Fire could see little beyond the opening, but instinct told her not to venture too far and not to loose her hold on the edges of rock that formed a kind of doorway to either side of her. She didn't want to fall.

The night was gusty, damp, and cold. She knew it was senseless to get herself wet, but she soaked in the rain and the untamed feeling of the storm anyway, while her guard huddled just inside the opening and tried to protect the candles.

There was a shift in her consciousness: people nearing, riders. Many. Difficult to tell the difference between two hundred and two hundred and fifty at this distance, and knowing so few of them personally. She concentrated, and decided that she was sensing well more than two hundred. And they were tired, but not in any unusual state of distress. The search party must have met with success.

'The search party's returning,' she called back to her guard. 'They're close. I believe the scout unit's with them.'

At their silence she turned to glance at them, and found six pairs of eyes watching her in various states of unease. She stepped out of the rain, into the passageway. 'I thought you'd like to know,' she said more quietly. 'But I can keep my perceptions to myself, if they make you uncomfortable.'

'No,' Musa said. 'It's appropriate for you to tell us, Lady.'

'Is the commander well, Lady?' one of the men asked.

Fire had been trying to determine this for herself, finding the man irritatingly difficult to isolate. He was there, of this she was sure. She supposed the continued impenetrability of his mind must indicate some measure of strength. 'I can't quite tell, but I think so.'

And then the music of hoofbeats echoed through the corridor as somewhere, in some crevice of the mountain below them, the riders entered the tunnels that led to the sleeping cavern.

A short while later, plodding downward, Fire received an abrupt answer to her concern when she sensed the commander walking up the passageway toward them. She stopped in her tracks, causing the guard behind her to whisper something most ungentlemanly as he contorted himself to avoid lighting her headscarf with his flame.

'Is there any other route to the cavern from here?' she blurted out; then knew the answer, then shrivelled in mortification at her own display of cowardice.

'No, Lady,' Musa said, hand to her sword. 'Do you sense something ahead?'

'No,' Fire said miserably. 'Only the commander.' Come to fetch the wandering monster, who'd proven herself wild and irresponsible. He'd keep her on a chain from now on.

He came into view a few minutes later, climbing with a candle in his hand. When he reached them he stopped, nodded at the soldiers' formal greetings, spoke quietly to Musa. The scout unit had been recovered unharmed. They'd run into a nasty party of cave bandits twice their size, and after tearing up the bandits they'd got themselves turned around in the dark. Their injuries were minor. In ten minutes' time they would all be asleep.

'I hope you'll get some sleep as well, sir,' Musa said. Suddenly Brigan smiled. He stepped aside to let them by and momentarily met Fire's glance. His eyes were exhausted. He had a day-old beard and he was drenched.

And apparently he had not come to fetch her after all. Once she and her attendants had passed him he turned away, and continued up the sloping corridor.

CHAPTER ELEVEN

SHE WOKE THE next morning stiff and achy from yesterday's riding. Margo handed her bread and cheese, and a basin of water to wash her face. After this, Fire reached for her fiddle and played a single reel, slowly and then with increasing speed, to wake herself up. The effort of it crystallised her mind.

'The commander didn't mention this advantage of our guard duty,' Mila said, smiling shyly. Musa stuck her head through the flap of the tent.

'Lady,' Musa said, 'the commander bade me tell you we'll be passing near Queen Roen's fortress around midday. He has business with the horsemaster. There'll be time for you to take a short meal with the lady queen, if you like.'

'YOU'VE BEEN ON your horse since yesterday,' Roen said, taking her hands, 'so I'm guessing you don't feel as lovely as you look. There, that smile tells me I'm right.'

'I'm tight as a bowstring,' Fire admitted.

'Sit down, dear. Make yourself comfortable. Take off that scarf, I won't let any gaping no-heads in here for the next half-hour.'

Such a relief to release her hair. The weight of it was great, and after a morning of riding, the scarf was sticky, and itchy. Fire sank gratefully into a chair, rubbed her scalp, and allowed Nax's queen to shovel vegetables and casserole onto her plate.

'Haven't you ever considered cutting it short?' Roen asked.

Oh, cutting it short. Hacking it all off, throwing it once and for all on the fire. Dyeing it black, if only monster hair would take colour. When she and Archer had been very young, they'd gone so far as to shave it off once as an experiment. It had shown again on her scalp within the hour. 'It grows extremely fast,' Fire said wearily, 'and I've found it's easier to control if it's long. Short pieces break loose and escape from my scarf.'

'I suppose they would,' Roen said. 'Well. I'm glad to see you. How are Brocker and Archer?'

Fire told her that Brocker was splendid and Archer, as usual, was angry.

'Yes, I suppose it's what he would be,' Roen said robustly, 'but don't mind him. It's right for you to be doing this, going to King's City to help Nash. I believe you can handle his court. You're not a child anymore. How is your casserole?'

Fire took a bite, which was very nice, actually, and fought the disbelieving expression trying to rise to her face. Not a child anymore? Fire had not been a child for quite some time.

And then, of course, Brigan appeared in the doorway to say hello to his mother and to bring Fire back to her horse, and immediately Fire felt herself revert to a child. Some part of her brain went missing whenever this soldier came near. It froze from his coldness.

'Brigandell,' Roen said, rising from her chair to embrace him. 'You've come to steal my guest from me.'

'In exchange for forty soldiers,' Brigan said. 'Twelve injured, so I've also left you a healer.'

'We can manage without the healer, if you need him, Brigan.'

'His family's in the Little Greys,' Brigan said, 'and I promised him a stay here when I could. We'll manage with our numbers until Fort Middle.'

'Well then,' Roen said briskly. 'Are you sleeping?'

'Yes.'

'Come now. A mother can tell when her son lies. Are you eating?'

'No,' Brigan said gravely. 'I've not eaten in two months. It's a hunger strike to protest the spring flooding in the south.'

'Gracious,' Roen said, reaching for the fruit bowl. 'Have an apple, dear.'

FIRE AND BRIGAN didn't speak as they exited the fortress together to continue the journey to King's City. But Brigan ate an apple, and Fire wound up her hair, and found herself a little more comfortable beside him.

Somehow it helped to know he could make a joke.

And then, three kindnesses.

Fire's guard waited with Small near the back of the column of troops. As Fire and Brigan moved toward the spot, Fire began to know that something was wrong. She tried to focus, which was difficult with so many people milling around. She waited for Brigan to stop speaking to a captain who'd appeared alongside them with a question about the day's schedule.

'I think my guards are holding a man,' she told Brigan quietly, when the captain had gone.

His voice dropped. 'Why? What man?'

She had only the basics, and the most important assurances. 'I don't know anything except that he hates me, and he hasn't hurt my horse.'

He nodded. 'I hadn't thought of that. I'll have to do something to stop people targeting your horse.'

They had picked up their pace at Fire's warning. Now, finally, they came upon a nasty scene: Fire's guards, two of them, holding back a soldier who shouted curses and spit out blood and teeth, while a third guard cracked him across the mouth again and again to shut him up. Horrified, Fire reached for the mind of the guard to stop his fist.

And then she absorbed the details that turned the scene into a story. Her fiddle case fallen open on the ground, smeared with mud. The remains of her fiddle beside it. The instrument was smashed, splintered almost beyond recognition, the bridge rammed into the belly as if by a cruel and hateful boot.

It was worse, somehow, than being hit by an arrow. Fire stumbled to Small and buried her face in his shoulder; she had no control over the tears running down her face, and she did not want Brigan to see them.

Behind her, Brigan swore sharply. Someone – Musa – laid a handkerchief on Fire's shoulder. The captive was still cursing, screaming now that he could see Fire, horrible things about her body, what he would do to her, intelligible even through his broken, swollen mouth. Brigan strode to him.

Don't hit him again, Fire thought desperately, *Brigan, please*; for the sound of bone scraping bone was not aiding her attempts to stop crying. Brigan uttered another oath, then a sharp command, and Fire understood from the sudden formlessness of the soldier's words that the man was being gagged. And then dragged away, back toward the fortress, Brigan and a number of Fire's guard accompanying him.

The scene was suddenly quiet. Fire became conscious of her own gasping breath and forced herself calm. Horrible man, she thought into Small's mane. Horrible, horrible man. *Oh, Small. That man was horrible.*

Small made a snorting noise and deposited some very comforting drool on her shoulder.

'I'm so sorry, Lady,' Musa said behind her. 'He took us in completely. From now on we'll let no one near us who wasn't sent by the commander.'

Fire wiped her face with the handkerchief and turned sideways toward the captain of her guard. She couldn't quite look at the pile of tinder on the ground. 'I don't blame you for it.'

'The commander will,' Musa said. 'As he should.'

Fire took a steadying breath. 'I should have known playing it would be provoking.'

'Lady, I forbid you to blame yourself. Truly, I won't allow it.'

At this Fire smiled, and held the handkerchief out to Musa. 'Thank you.'

'It's not mine, Lady. It's Neel's.'

Fire recognised the name of one of her male guards. 'Neel's?'

'The commander took it from Neel and gave it to me to give to you, Lady. Keep it. Neel won't miss it, he has a thousand. Was it a very expensive fiddle, Lady?'

Yes, of course, it had been. But Fire had never valued it for that. She had valued it because of a rare and strange kindness that was gone now.

She studied Neel's handkerchief. 'It's no matter,' she said, measuring her words. 'The commander didn't hit that man. I asked him not to in his mind, and he didn't.'

Musa accepted the apparent change of subject. 'I wondered at that. He doesn't strike his own soldiers, as a rule, you know. But this time I thought we might see the exception. His face was murder.'

And he had taken the trouble to secure another man's handkerchief. And he had shared her concern for her horse. Three kindnesses.

Fire understood then that she had been afraid of Brigan, of her heart being injured by the hatred of a person she couldn't help but like; and shy, as well, of his roughness, and his impenetrability. And she was still shy. But she was no longer afraid.

THEY RODE HARD the rest of the day. As night closed in they made camp on a flat mass of rock. Tents and fires cropped up all around her, seeming to stretch on forever. It occurred to Fire that she had never been this far from home. Archer would be missing her, that she knew, and knowing it soothed her own loneliness a bit. His fury if he heard about her fiddle would be a terrible thing. Normally his furies were an aggravation to her, but she would welcome it now; if he were here, she could draw strength from his fire.

Before too long the eyes of the soldiers nearest her drove her into her tent. She could not stop thinking of the words of the man who'd destroyed the fiddle. Why did hatred so often make men think of rape? And there was the flaw in her monster power. As often as the power of her beauty made one man easy to control, it made another man uncontrollable and mad.

A monster drew out all that was vile, especially a female monster, because of the desire, and the endless perverted channels for the expression of malice. With all weak men, the sight of her was a drug to their minds. What man could use hate or love well when he was drugged?

The consciousnesses of five thousand men pressed in on her.

Mila and Margo had followed her into the tent, of course, and sat nearby, hands on swords. Silent, alert, and bored. Fire was sorry for being such a boring charge. She wished she could go out to Small without being seen. She wished she could bring Small into the tent.

Musa looked in through the flap. 'Pardon me, Lady. A soldier has come from the scout units to lend you his fiddle. The commander vouches for him, but says we're to ask your impressions before we let him near you. He's just outside, Lady.'

'Yes,' Fire said, surprised, finding the strange man among her guard. 'I believe he's harmless.'

Harmless and huge, Fire saw when she emerged from her tent. His fiddle was like a toy in his hands; this man's sword must look like a butter knife when he swung it. But the face that sat above his tree trunk of a body was quiet and thoughtful and mild. He lowered his eyes before her and held the fiddle out to her.

Fire shook her head. 'You're very generous,' she said, 'but I don't like to take it from you.'

The man's voice was so deep it sounded like it came from the earth. 'We all know the story of what you did at Queen Roen's fortress months back, Lady. You saved the life of our commander.'

'Well,' Fire said, because he seemed to expect her to say something. 'Nonetheless.'

'The men cannot stop talking about it,' he continued, bowing, then pushing the fiddle into her small hands with his enormous ones. 'And besides, you're the better fiddler.'

Fire watched the man lumber away, touched, immensely comforted by his voice, by the huge gentle feeling of him. 'Now I understand how our scout units can tear up parties of bandits twice their size,' she said aloud.

Musa laughed. 'He's a good one to have on our side.'

Fire plucked the strings of the fiddle. It was in good tune. Its tone was sharp, strident – it was no master's instrument. But it was a tool with which she could make music.

And a declaration.

Fire ducked inside her tent for her bow and came out again. Strode across the plain of soldiers toward a rise of rock that she could see some distance away. Her guard scrambled to follow her and surround her; the eyes of soldiers attached themselves to her as she passed. She reached the mound of boulders and climbed. She sat down and tucked the fiddle under her chin.

In the hearing of them all she played whatever music it pleased her to play.

CHAPTER TWELVE

IF ONLY FIRE could talk her sleeping self into the same courage. It was her father's dying eyes that never let her sleep.

The answer to Brocker's question in her fourteenth year, the question about whether she could alter Cansrel's mind lastingly, had been simple, once she'd allowed herself to consider it. No. Cansrel's mind was strong as a bear and hard as the steel of a trap, and every time she left it, it slammed back into place behind her. There were no permanent alterations to Cansrel's mind. There was no changing who he was. It had relieved her, to know there was nothing she could do, because it meant no one could ever expect it of her.

Then, in that same year, Nax had drugged himself to death. As the contours of power had shifted and resettled, Fire had seen what Brocker saw, and Archer, and Roen: a kingdom that stood on the verge of several permutations of possibility. A kingdom, suddenly, that could change.

She had been dazzlingly well-informed. On one side she'd received Cansrel's confidences; on the other she'd known all that Brocker learned from his and Roen's spies. She knew that Nash was stronger than Nax had been, strong enough sometimes to frustrate Cansrel, but a game to Cansrel still, compared with the younger brother, the prince. At eighteen the boy Brigan, the absurdly young commander, was said to be strong-minded, level, forceful, persuasive, and angry, the only person of influence in all King's City who was not influenced by Cansrel. Some among the clear-headed talked as if they expected Brigan to be the difference between a continuation of the current lawless and depraved state of things, and change.

'Prince Brigan is injured,' Brocker announced one winter day when she came to visit. 'I've just received word from Roen.'

'What happened?' Fire asked, startled. 'Is he all right?'

'There's a gala in the king's palace every January,' Brocker said. 'Hundreds of guests and dancing and a great deal of wine and nonsense, and a thousand dark corridors for people to sneak around in. Apparently Cansrel hired four men to corner Brigan and cut his throat. Brigan heard word of it and was ready for them and killed all four—'

'All four by himself?' Fire asked, distressed and confused, sitting down hard in an armchair.

'Young Brigan is good with a sword,' Brocker said grimly.

'But is he badly hurt?'

'He'll live, though the surgeons worried at first. He was stabbed in the leg in a place that bled terribly.' Brocker moved his chair to the fireplace and threw Roen's letter onto the crackling flames. 'It was very nearly the end of the boy, Fire, and I don't doubt that Cansrel will try again.'

That summer at Nash's court, an arrow from the bow of one of Brigan's most trusted captains had struck Cansrel in the back. At the start of her fifteenth year – on her fourteenth birthday, in fact – Fire had word from King's City that her father was injured and likely to die. She'd closed herself in her room and sobbed, not even knowing, for sure, what she was sobbing about, but unable to stop. She'd pressed her face against a pillow so that no one could hear.

Of course, King's City was known for its healers, for its advances in medicine and surgery. People there survived injuries people died of elsewhere. Especially people with the power to command an entire hospital's attention.

Some weeks later Fire had received the news that Cansrel was going to live. She'd run to her room again. She'd crawled onto her bed, utterly numb. As the numbness had worn off something sour had risen in her stomach and she'd begun to vomit. A vessel had burst in her eye, a blood bruise forming at the edge of her pupil.

Her body could be a powerful communicator sometimes, when her mind was trying to ignore a particular truth. Exhausted and sick, Fire had understood her body's message: it was time to reconsider the question of just how far her power over Cansrel could reach.

LURCHED INTO WAKEFULNESS again by the same tired dreams, Fire kicked her blankets away. She covered her hair, found boots and weapons, and crept past Margo and Mila. Outside, most of the army slept under canvas roofs, but her guard lay in the open, arranged again around her tent. Under the vast sky, magnificent with stars, Musa and three others played cards in the light of a candle, as they had the night before. Fire held onto the tent opening to counter the vertigo she felt when she looked up at that sky.

'Lady Fire,' Musa said. 'What can we do for you?'

'Musa,' Fire said. 'I'm afraid you have the misfortune of guarding an insomniac.'

Musa laughed. 'Is it another climb tonight, Lady?'

'Yes, with my apologies.'

'We're glad for it, Lady.'

'I expect you're saying that to ease my guilt.'

'No, truly, Lady. The commander wanders at night too, and he won't consent to a guard, even when the king orders it. If we're out with you we have an excuse to keep an eye on him.'

'I see,' Fire said, perhaps a bit sardonically. 'Fewer guards tonight,' she added, but Musa ignored this and woke as many as she'd woken the night before.

'It's orders,' Musa said, as the men sat up blearily and strapped on their weapons.

'And if the commander doesn't follow the king's orders, why should you follow the commander's?'

Her question generated more than one set of raised eyebrows. 'Lady,' Musa said, 'the soldiers in this army would follow the commander off a cliff if he asked it.'

Fire was beginning to feel irritable. 'How old are you, Musa?'

'Thirty-one.'

'Then the commander should be a child to you.'

'And you an infant, Lady,' Musa said dryly, surprising a smile onto Fire's face. 'We're ready. You lead the way.'

SHE HEADED TOWARD the same mound of rock she'd climbed earlier, because it would bring her closer to the sky and because she sensed it would also bring her guard closer to the insomniac they weren't supposed to be guarding. He was among those boulders somewhere, and the rise was broad enough that they could share it without meeting.

She found a high, flat rock to sit on. Her guard scattered themselves around her. She closed her eyes and let the night wash over her, hoping that after this she'd be weary enough for sleep.

She didn't move at the sense of Brigan's approach, but at the retreat of her guard she opened her eyes. He'd propped himself against a rock several paces from her. He was looking at the stars.

'Lady,' he said in greeting.

'Lord Prince,' she said, quietly.

He leaned there for a moment, gaze tilted upward, and Fire wondered if this was to be the extent of their conversation. 'Your horse is named Small,' he said finally, startling her with the randomness of it.

'Yes.'

'Mine is named Big.'

And now Fire was smiling. 'The black mare? Is she very big?'

'Not to my eyes,' Brigan said, 'but I did not name her.'

Fire remembered the source of Small's name. Indeed, she

could never forget the man Cansrel had abused for her sake. 'An animal smuggler gave Small his name. A brutish man called Cutter. He thought any horse that didn't respond well to flogging was small-minded.'

'Ah. Cutter,' Brigan said, as if he knew the man; which, after all, should not be surprising, as Cansrel and Nax had probably shared suppliers. 'Well, I've seen what your horse is capable of. Obviously he's not small-minded.'

It was a dirty trick, his continued kindness to her horse. Fire took a moment to swallow her gratitude, all out of proportion, she knew, because she was lonesome. She decided to change the subject. 'You can't sleep?'

He turned his face away from her, laughed shortly. 'Sometimes at night my head spins.'

'Dreams?'

'I don't get close enough to sleep for that. Worries.'

Cansrel used to lull her to sleep sometimes, on sleepless nights. If Brigan would ever let her, if he would ever in a million years, she could ease his worries for him; she could help the commander of the King's Army fall asleep. It would be an honourable use of her power, a practical one. But she knew better than to suggest it.

'And you?' Brigan said. 'You seem to do a lot of nighttime rambling.'

'I have bad dreams.'

'Dreams of pretend terrors? Or things that are true?'

'True,' she said, 'always. I've always had dreams of horrible things that are true.'

He was quiet. He rubbed the back of his head. 'It's hard to wake from a nightmare when the nightmare is real,' he said, his mind giving her nothing, still, of what he was feeling; but in his voice and his words she heard a thing that felt like sympathy.

'Good night to you, Lady,' he said a moment later. He turned and retreated to the lower ground of the camp.

Her guard trickled into place around her. She raised her face to the stars again and closed her eyes.

AFTER ABOUT A week of riding with the First Branch, Fire fell into a routine – if a continuum of unsettling experiences could be called a routine.

Watch out! She thought to her guards one morning at breakfast as they wrestled a man to the ground who'd come running at her with a sword. *Here comes another fellow with the same idea. Oh, dear*, she added. *I also sense a pack of wolf monsters at our western side.*

'Inform one of the hunting captains of the wolves, if you please, Lady,' Musa gasped, yanking at her quarry's feet and yelling at three or four guards to go punch the new attacker in the nose.

It was hard on Fire never to be allowed to be alone. Even on nights when sleep felt near, she continued her late walks with her guard, because it was the closest she could get to solitude. Most nights she crossed paths with the commander and they exchanged a few quiet lines of conversation. He was surprisingly easy to talk to.

'You let some men through your mental defences intentionally, Lady,' Brigan said to her one night. 'Don't you?'

'Some of them take me by surprise,' she said, her back resting against rock and her eyes on the sky.

'Yes, all right,' he said. 'But when a soldier marches across the entire camp with his hand on his knife and his mind wide open, you know he's coming, and in most cases you could change his intentions and turn him around if you wanted to. If that man tries to attack you, it's because you've allowed it.'

The rock on which Fire sat fit the curve of her body; she could fall asleep here. She closed her eyes and considered how to admit to him that he was right. 'I do turn a lot of men around, just as you say, and the occasional woman. My guard never even knows about them. But those are the ones who only want to look or touch or tell me things – the ones who are simply overcome, or think they love me, and are gentle in their feelings.' She hesitated. 'The ones who hate me and truly want to hurt me – yes, you're right. Sometimes I let the most malevolent men attack me. If they attack me they'll end up gaoled, and gaol is the only place other than death where they'll no longer be a danger to me. Your army's too big, Lord Prince,' she said, glancing at him. 'Too many people for me to manage all at once. I need to protect myself however I can.'

Brigan humphed. 'I don't disagree. Your guard is more than competent. As long as you can stomach the danger of it.'

'I suppose I should be more used to the feeling of danger by now,' she said. 'But it is unnerving sometimes.'

'I understand you crossed paths with Mydogg and Murgda as you left my mother's fortress in the spring,' he said. 'Did they feel dangerous to you?'

Fire remembered that unsettling double gaze. 'Obscurely. I couldn't quantify it if you asked me to, but yes, they felt dangerous.'

He paused. 'There's going to be a war,' he said quietly, 'and at the end of it I don't know who'll be king. Mydogg's a cold and greedy man and a tyrant. Gentian's worse than a tyrant, because he's also a fool. Nash is the best of the three, no contest. He can be thoughtless; he's impulsive. But he's fair and he's not motivated by self-interest, and he has a mind for peace, and flashes of wisdom sometimes—' He broke off, and when he spoke again, he sounded rather hopeless. 'There's going to be a war, Lady, and the waste of life will be terrible.'

Fire sat in silence. She hadn't expected the conversation to take such a serious turn, but it didn't surprise her. In this kingdom no one was many steps removed from grave thoughts, and this man fewer than most. This boy, she thought, as Brigan yawned and rumpled his own hair. 'We should try to get some sleep,' he said. 'Tomorrow I hope to take us as far as Grey Lake.'

'Good,' Fire said, 'because I want a bath.'

Brigan threw his head back and smiled at the sky. 'Well said, Lady. The world may be falling to pieces, but at least the lot of us can have a bath.'

BATHING IN A cold lake posed some unforeseen challenges – like the little monster fish, for example, that swarmed around her when she dunked her hair, and the monster bugs that tried to eat her alive, and the need for a special guard of archers just in case of predators. But despite the production of it all, it was good to be clean. Fire wrapped cloths around her wet hair and sat as close to the fire as she could without setting herself aflame. She called Mila to her and rebandaged the shallow cut that ran along the girl's elbow, from a man Mila had subdued three days ago, a man with a talent for knife-fighting.

Fire was coming to know her guard now, and she understood better than she had before the women who chose to ride with this army. Mila was from the southern mountains, where every child, boy or girl, learned to fight and every girl had ample opportunity to practise what she'd learned. She was all of fifteen, but as a guard she was bold and quick. She had an older sister with two babies and no husband, and her wages provided for them. The King's Army was well-paid.

The First Branch continued its journey southeast to King's City. Almost two weeks in and with about one week left to ride, they reached Fort Middle, a rough stone fortress rising out of rock with high walls and iron bars in narrow, glassless windows: the home of some five hundred auxiliary soldiers. A mean-looking, stark place, but everyone, including Fire, was happy to reach it. For one night she had a bed to sleep in and a stone roof above her head, which meant that so did her guard.

The next day the landscape changed. Very suddenly, the

ground was made of rounded rock instead of jagged: smooth rock rolling almost like hills. Sometimes the rock was bright green with moss, or with veritable stretches of grass, and even a field of tall grass once, soft to their feet. Fire had never seen so much green and she thought it the most beautiful, most astonishing landscape in the world. The grass was like brilliant hair; as if the Dells itself were a monster. It was a foolish thought, she knew, but when her kingdom turned dazzling with colour she felt suddenly that she belonged to this place.

She didn't share that thought with Brigan, of course, but she did express her shock at the world's sudden greenness. To which he smiled quietly at the night sky, a gesture she was beginning to associate with him.

'It'll keep getting greener as we approach King's City, and softer,' he said. 'You'll see there's a reason this kingdom is called the Dells.'

'I asked my father once—' she started; and then stopped tongue-tied, horrified that she had begun to speak kindly of Cansrel before him.

When he finally broke their silence, his voice was mild. 'I knew your mother, Lady. Did you realise that?'

Fire hadn't realised it, but she supposed she should have, for Jessa had worked in the royal nurseries at a time when Brigan must have been very young. 'I didn't know, Lord Prince.'

'Jessa was the person I went to whenever I'd been bad,' he said, adding wryly, 'after my mother was through with me, that is.'

Fire couldn't help smiling. 'And were you often bad?'

'At least once a day, Lady, as I remember.'

Her smile growing, Fire watched him as he watched the sky. 'Perhaps you weren't very good at following orders?'

'Worse than that. I used to set traps for Nash.'

'Traps!'

'He was five years older than I. The perfect challenge –

stealth and cunning, you see, to compensate for my lack of size. I rigged nets to land on him. Closed him inside closets.' Brigan chuckled. 'He was a good-natured brother. But whenever our mother learned of it she'd be furious, and when she was done with me I'd go to Jessa, because Jessa's anger was so much easier to take than Roen's.'

'How do you mean?' Fire asked, feeling a drop of rain, and wishing it away.

He thought for a moment. 'She'd tell me she was angry, but it didn't sit like anger. She'd never raise her voice. She'd sit there sewing, or whatever she was doing, and we'd analyse my crimes, and invariably I'd fall asleep in my chair. When I woke it'd be too late to go to dinner and she'd feed me in the nurseries. A bit of a treat for a small boy who usually had to dress for dinner and be serious and quiet around a lot of boring people.'

'A wicked boy, from the sound of it.'

His face flickered with a smile. Water splashed onto his forehead. 'When I was six Nash fell over a tripline and broke his hand. My father learned of it. That put an end to my antics for a while.'

'You gave in so easily?'

He didn't answer her teasing tone. She looked at him, his eyebrows furrowed at the sky, his face sombre, and was frightened, suddenly, of what they were talking about; for again, suddenly, it seemed they might be talking about Cansrel.

'I think I understand now why Roen lost her mind whenever I misbehaved,' he said. 'She was afraid of Nax finding out and taking it into his head to punish me. He was not ... a reasonable man, in the time I knew him. His punishments were not reasonable.'

Then they were talking about Cansrel, and Fire was ashamed. She sat, head bowed, and wondered what Nax had done, what Cansrel had told Nax to do to punish a six-year-old who probably even then had been clever enough to see Cansrel for what he was.

Drops of rain pattered onto her scarf and her shoulders.

'Your mother had red hair,' Brigan said, lightly, as if they didn't both feel the presence of two dead men among these rocks. 'Nothing like yours, of course. And she was musical, Lady, like you. I remember when you were born. And I remember that she cried when you were taken away.'

'Did she?'

'Hasn't my mother told you anything about Jessa?'

Fire swallowed a lump in her throat. 'Yes, Lord Prince, but I always like hearing it again.'

Brigan wiped rain from his face. 'Then I'm sorry I don't remember more. If we knew a person was going to die, we'd hold harder to the memories.'

Fire corrected him, in a whisper. 'The good memories.' She stood. This conversation was a mix of too many sadnesses. And she didn't mind the rain, but it seemed unfair to inflict it upon her guard.

CHAPTER THIRTEEN

THE MORNING OF her final day of riding Fire woke to an aching back, aching breasts, knotted muscles in her neck and shoulders. There was never any predicting how the time before her monthly bleeding would manifest itself. Sometimes it passed with hardly a symptom. Other times she was an unhappy captive in her own body.

And at least she'd be under Nash's roofs by the time the bleeding began; she wouldn't have to embarrass herself with an explanation for the increase in monster attacks.

On Small's back she was bleary-minded, anxious, nervous. She wished for her own bed; she wished she hadn't come. She was in no mood for beauty, and when they passed a great rocky hill with wildflowers springing from every crack she had to give herself a talking to to keep the mist out of her eyes.

The land grew greener, and finally they came upon a gorge that stretched to left and right before them, teeming with trees that reached up from the bottom, and thundering with the waters of the Winged River. A road ran east to west above the river, and a grass track, clearly much travelled, ran parallel to the road. The army turned eastward and moved fast along the grass track. The road was full of people, carts, carriages, headed in both directions. Many stopped to watch the First Branch go by, and raised arms in greeting.

Fire decided to imagine that she was out for a gallop with her guard, and none of these other thousands existed. No river or road to her right, no King's City before her. To think this way was a comfort, and her body screamed for comfort.

*

WHEN THE FIRST stopped for its midday meal, Fire had no appetite. She sat in the grass, elbows on knees, holding her throbbing head in place.

'Lady,' the commander's voice said above her.

Fire assumed a placid expression and looked up. 'Yes, Lord Prince?'

'Are you in need of a healer, Lady?'

'No, Lord Prince. I was only thinking about something.'

He didn't believe her, she could see it in the sceptical set of his mouth; but he let it go. 'I've received an urgent summons from the south,' he said. 'I'll be on my way as soon as we've reached the king's court. I wondered if there was anything you wanted, Lady, that I could provide before I go.'

Fire tugged at a patch of grass and swallowed this disappointment. She could think of nothing she wanted, not that anyone could provide, except for the answer to a question. She asked it very quietly. 'Why are you kind to me?'

He paused, watching her hands that pulled at the grass. He crouched down to her eye level. 'Because I trust you.'

The world went very still around her, and she stared hard at the grass. The green of it was radiant in the sun's light.

'Why should you trust me?'

He glanced at the soldiers around them and shook his head. 'A conversation for another time.'

'I've thought of a thing you can do for me,' she said. 'I've thought of it in this very moment.'

'Go on.'

'You can take a guard when you go wandering at night.' And then, when his eyebrows shot up and she saw him formulating his refusal: 'Please, Lord Prince. There are people who'd like to kill you, and many others who'd die to prevent it. Show some respect to those who value your life so highly.'

He turned his face away from her, frowning. His voice was not pleased. 'Very well.'

That point settled, and sorry now, most likely, that he'd ever started the conversation, Brigan went back to his horse.

IN THE SADDLE again, Fire mulled over the commander's trust, prodding and pushing it around, like a candy in her mouth, trying to decide whether she believed it. It wasn't that she thought him likely to lie. It was only that she thought him unlikely to trust – not completely, anyway, not the way Brocker or Donal did, or Archer, on the days Archer decided to trust her.

The problem with Brigan was that he was so closed. When had she ever had to judge a person by words alone? She had no formula for understanding a person like him, for he was the only one she'd ever met.

THE WINGED RIVER was so named because before its waters reached their journey's end, they took flight. At the place where the river leapt off a great green cliff and plunged into the Winter Sea, King's City had grown, starting on the north bank and spreading outward and south across the river. Joining the older city with the younger were bridges, the building of which had sent more than one unfortunate engineer over the falls to his death. A canal of steep locks on the northern side connected the city with Cellar Harbour far below.

Passing through the city's outer walls with her escort of five thousand, Fire felt herself a gawkish country girl. So many people in this city, smells and noises, buildings painted bright colours, steeply roofed, crammed together, red wooden houses with green trim, purple and yellow, blue and orange. Fire had never seen a building before that was not made of stone. It hadn't occurred to her that houses could be any colour but grey.

People hung out of windows to watch the First Branch pass. Women in the street flirted with the soldiers, and threw flowers, so many flowers Fire couldn't believe the extravagance. These people tossed more flowers over Fire's head than she had seen in a lifetime.

A flower splatted against the chest of one of Brigan's top swordfighters, riding to Fire's right. When Fire laughed at him, he beamed, and handed the flower to her. On this journey through the city streets Fire was surrounded not just by her guard but by Brigan's most proficient fighters, Brigan himself on her left. The commander wore the grey of his troops, and he'd positioned the standard-bearer some distance behind. It was all in an attempt to reduce the attention Fire drew, and Fire knew she wasn't playing her part in the charade. She should have been sitting gravely, her face bent to her hands, catching no one's eye. Instead she was laughing – laughing, and smiling, and numb to her aches and pains, and sparkling with the strangeness and the bustle of this place.

And then before too long – she couldn't have said if she sensed it or heard it first, but there was a change in their audience. A whisper seemed to work its way in among the cheers, and then a strange silence; a lull. She felt it: wonder, and admiration. And Fire understood that even with her hair covered, and even in her drab, dirty riding clothes, and even though this town hadn't seen her, possibly hadn't thought of her in seventeen years, her face and her eyes and her body had told them who she was. And her headscarf had confirmed it, for why else would she cover her hair? She became mindful of her animation that was only making her glow more brightly. She erased her smile and dropped her eyes.

Brigan signalled to his standard-bearer to come forward and ride beside them.

Fire spoke low. 'I sense no danger.'

'Nonetheless,' Brigan said grimly, 'if an archer leans out one of these windows, I want him to notice both of us. A man revenging himself on Cansrel isn't going to shoot you if he risks hitting me.'

She thought of joking about it. If her enemies were Brigan's friends and her friends were Brigan's enemies, the two of them could walk through the world arm in arm and never be hit by arrows again.

But an eerie sound rose now from the silence. 'Fire,' a woman called from an upstairs window. A cluster of barefoot children in a doorway echoed the call. 'Fire. Fire!' And other voices joined in, and the cry swelled, until suddenly the people were singing out the word, chanting it, some in veneration, some almost in accusation – some with no reason at all except that they were caught up in the captive and mindless fervour of a crowd. Fire rode toward the walls of Nash's palace, stunned, confounded, by the music of her own name.

THE FAÇADE OF the king's palace was black, this Fire had heard. But the knowledge didn't prepare her for the beauty or the luminosity of the stone. It was a black that shifted depending on the angle from which it was viewed, and that shimmered, and reflected the light of other things, so that Fire's first impression was of changing panels of black and grey and silver, and blue reflected from the eastern sky, and orange and red from the setting sun.

Fire's eyes had been starved for the colours of King's City, and she hadn't even known it. How her father must have shone in this place.

The five thousand soldiers veered off as Fire, her guard, and Brigan approached the ramp to the gates. Spears were raised and the doors swung in. The horses passed through a black stone gatehouse and emerged into a white courtyard dazzling with the reflection of the sunset on quartz walls, and the sky pink behind flashing glass roofs. Fire craned her neck and gaped at the walls and roofs. A steward approached them and gaped at Fire.

'Eyes on me, Welkley,' Brigan said, swinging down from his horse.

Welkley, short, thin, impeccably dressed and groomed, cleared his throat and turned to Brigan. 'Forgive me, Lord Prince. I've sent someone to the offices to alert Princess Clara of your arrival.'

'And Hanna?'

'In the green house, Lord Prince.'

Brigan nodded and held a hand up to Fire. 'Lady Fire, this is the king's first steward, Welkley.'

Fire knew this was her cue to dismount and give her hand to Welkley, but when she moved, a spasm of pain radiated outward from the small of her back. She caught her breath, gritted her teeth, pulled her leg over her saddle and tipped, leaving it to Brigan's instincts to keep her from landing on her backside before the king's first steward. He caught her coolly and propped her on her feet, his face impassive, as if it were routine for her to launch herself at him every time she dismounted; and scowled at the white marble floor while she presented her hand to Welkley.

A woman entered the courtyard then that Fire could not fail to sense, a force of nature. Fire turned to locate her and saw a head of bouncy brown hair, sparkling eyes, a sparkling smile, and a handsome and ample figure. She was tall, nearly as tall as Brigan. She threw her arms around him, laughing, and kissed his nose. 'This is a treat,' she said. And then, to Fire, 'I'm Clara. And now I understand Nash; you're more stunning even than Cansrel.'

Fire couldn't find words to respond to this, and Brigan's eyes, suddenly, were pained. But Clara simply laughed again and patted Brigan's face. 'So serious,' she said. 'Go on, little brother. I'll take care of the lady.'

Brigan nodded. 'Lady Fire, I'll find you before I take my leave. Musa,' he said, turning to Fire's guard, who stood quietly with the horses. 'Go with the lady, all of you, wherever Princess Clara takes her. Clara, see that a healer visits her, today. A woman.' He kissed Clara's cheek hurriedly. 'In case I don't see you again.' He spun away and practically ran through one of the arched doorways leading into the palace.

'He always has a fire under his tail, Brigan,' Clara said. 'Come, Lady, I'll show you your rooms. You'll like them, they overlook the green house. The fellow who tends the green house gardens? Trust me, Lady, you'd let him stake your tomatoes.'

Fire was speechless with astonishment. The princess grabbed the lady's arm and pulled her toward the palace.

FIRE'S SITTING ROOM did indeed overlook a curious wooden house tucked into the back grounds of the palace. The house was small, painted a deep green, and surrounded by lush gardens and trees so that it seemed to blend in, as if it had sprouted from the ground like the growing things around it.

The famous gardener was nowhere in sight, but as Fire watched from her window, the door to the house opened. A young, chestnut-haired woman in a pale yellow dress stepped outside and passed through the orchard to the palace.

'It's Roen's house, technically,' Clara said, standing at Fire's shoulder. 'She had it built because she believed the king's queen should have a place to retreat to. She lived there fully after she broke with Nax. She's given it to Brigan's use, for the moment, until Nash chooses a queen.'

And so that young woman must be associated with Brigan. Interesting, indeed, and a very pretty view, until Fire moved to her bedchamber windows and encountered a sight she appreciated even more: the stables. She stretched her mind and found Small, and was immensely comforted to know he would be near enough for her to feel.

Her rooms were too large, but comfortable, the windows

open and fitted with wire screens; a consideration someone had taken for her specially, she suspected, so she could pass her window with her hair uncovered and not have to worry about raptor monsters or an invasion of monster bugs.

It occurred to her then that perhaps these had been Cansrel's rooms, or Cansrel's screens. Just as quickly she dismissed the possibility. Cansrel would have had more rooms, and larger, closer to the king, overlooking one of the white inner court-yards, with a balcony outside each tall window, as she'd seen when she first entered the courtyard.

And then her thoughts were interrupted by the conscious-ness of the king. She looked to the door of her bedchamber, puzzled, and then startled, as Nash burst in.

'Brother King,' Clara said, much surprised. 'Couldn't wait for her to wash the road dust from her hands?'

Fire's guard of twenty dropped to their knees. Nash didn't even see them, didn't hear Clara, strode across the room to the window where Fire stood. He clamped his hand around her neck and tried to kiss her.

She'd sensed it coming, but his mind was quick and slip-pery, and she hadn't moved fast enough to take hold. And during their previous encounter he'd been drunk. He was not drunk now, and the difference was marked. To avoid his kiss she dropped to her knee in an imitation of subservience. He held on to her, struggling to make her rise.

'You're choking her,' Clara said. 'Nash. Nash, stop!'

She grabbed wildly at Nash's mind, caught hold of it, lost it again; and decided in a fit of temper that she would fall unconscious before she kissed this man. Then, quite suddenly, Nash's hand was wrenched from her throat by a new person she recognised. She took a great, relieved breath and pulled herself up by the windowpane.

Brigan's voice was dangerously calm. 'Musa, give us the room.'

The guard vanished. Brigan took a handful of Nash's shirt-front and shoved him hard against the wall. 'Look at what you're doing,' Brigan spat. 'Clear your mind!'

'Forgive me,' Nash said, sounding genuinely aghast. 'I lost my head. Forgive me, Lady.'

Nash tried to turn his face to Fire, but Brigan's fist tightened around his collar and pressed against his throat to stop him. 'If she's going to be unsafe here I'll take her away this instant. She'll come south with me, do you understand?'

'All right,' Nash said. 'All right.'

'It's not all right. This is her bedchamber. Rocks, Nash! Why are you even here?'

'All *right*,' Nash said, pushing at Brigan's fist with his hands. 'Enough. I see I was wrong. When I look at her, I lose my head.'

Brigan dropped his fist from his brother's neck. Took a step back and rubbed his face with his hands. 'Then don't look at her,' he said tiredly. 'I have business with you before I go.'

'Come to my office.'

Brigan cocked his head at the doorway. 'I'll meet you in five minutes' time.'

Nash turned and slumped out of the room, banished. A puzzle of inconsistencies, this eldest of Nax's sons, and the king in name; but which of these brothers was the king in practice?

'Are you all right, Lady?' Brigan asked, frowning after Nash.

Fire was not all right. She clutched her aching back. 'Yes, Lord Prince.'

'You can trust Clara, Lady,' Brigan said, 'and my brother Garan. And Welkley, and one or two of the king's men that Clara can point you to. In the absence of Lord Archer I'd like to escort you home myself next time I pass north through the city. It's a route I travel often. It shouldn't be more than a few weeks. Is this acceptable to you?'

It was not acceptable; it was too long by far. But Fire nodded, swallowing painfully.

'I must go,' he said. 'Clara knows how to get messages to me.'

Fire nodded again. Brigan turned and was gone.

SHE HAD A bath, and a massage and warm compress from a healer so skilled that Fire didn't care if the woman couldn't keep her hands out of her hair. Dressed in the plainest dress of the many choices a wide-eyed servant girl had brought to her, Fire felt more like herself; as much like herself as she could, in these strange rooms, and not knowing what to expect next from this strange royal family. And deprived of music, for she had returned her borrowed fiddle to its rightful owner.

The First had a week's leave in King's City, and then they'd take to the road again under whatever captain Brigan had left in command. Brigan, she discovered when she emerged from her bathing room, had decided to assign her entire guard to her permanently, with the same rules as before: six guards to accompany her wherever she went, and two women in her bedroom when she slept. She was sorry for this, that these soldiers should have to continue such a dull charge, and sorrier still at the thought of them underfoot. It was worse than a bandage that chafed at a wound, her endless lack of solitude.

At dinnertime she claimed a backache, to avoid having to appear so soon before Nash and his court. Nash sent servants to her room pushing carts bearing a feast that could have fed all the residents of her own stone house in the north, and Archer's house as well. She thought of Archer, and then cast the thought away. Archer brought the tears too near.

Welkley came with four fiddles after dinner, two hanging from the fingers of each hand. Astonishing fiddles, nothing modest about them, smelling wonderfully of wood and varnish and gleaming brown, orange, vermilion. They were the best he'd been able to find in such a short time, Welkley explained. She was to choose one of the four, as a gift from the royal family.

Fire thought she could guess which member of the royal family had spared a minute amidst his preoccupations to order a roundup of the city's finest fiddles, and again she found herself uncomfortably close to tears. She took the instruments from the steward one by one, each more beautiful than the last. Welkley waited patiently while she played them, testing their feeling against her neck, the sharpness of the strings on her fingertips, the depth of their sound. There was one she kept reaching for, with a copper-red varnish, and a clarity like the point of a star, precise and lonesome, reminding her, somehow, of home. This one, she thought to herself. This is the one. Its only flaw, she told Welkley, was that it was too good for her skill.

That night memories kept her awake, and aches, and anxiety. Shy of the court bustling with people even late into the night, and not knowing the route to any quiet view of the sky, she went with six of her guard to the stables. She leaned on the stall door before her dozing, lopsided horse.

Why have I come here? she asked herself. What have I got myself into? I don't belong in this place. *Oh, Small. Why am I here?*

From the warmth of her fondness for her horse she constructed a fragile and changeable thing that almost resembled courage. She hoped it would be enough.

CHAPTER FOURTEEN

THE SNOOP WHO'D been captured in the king's palace was not the same man Fire had sensed in the king's rooms at Roen's fortress, but his consciousness did have a similar feeling.

'What does that mean?' Nash demanded. 'Does it mean he was sent by the same man?'

'Not necessarily, Lord King.'

'Does it mean he's of the same family? Are they brothers?'

'Not necessarily, Lord King. Family members can have broadly different consciousnesses, as can two men under the same employ. At this point I can only determine that their attitudes and their aptitudes are similar.'

'And what help is that? We didn't bring you all this distance so you could tell us he's of average disposition and intelligence, Lady.'

In King Nash's office, with its stunning views of the city, its bookshelves rising from floor to mezzanine to domed ceiling, its rich green carpet and gold lamps, and most especially its handsome and high-strung monarch, Fire was in a state of mental stimulation that made it difficult for her to focus on the prisoner, or care about his claims to intelligence. The king was intelligent, and fatuous and powerful and flighty. This was what impressed Fire, that this man with the dark good looks was all things at once, open as the sky, and desperately difficult to subdue.

When she'd first come through the door of this office with six of her guard the king had greeted her glumly. 'You entered my mind before you entered this room, Lady.'

'Yes, Lord King,' she said, startled into honesty before him and his men.

'I'm glad of it,' Nash said, 'and I give you leave. Around you I cannot bear my behaviour.'

He sat at his desk, staring at the emerald ring on his finger. While they waited for the prisoner to be brought before them, the room turned to a mental battlefield. Nash was keenly aware of her physical presence; he struggled not to look at her. He was just as keenly aware of her presence inside his mind, and here was the problem, for he clung to her there, perversely, to savour the excitement of her where he could. And it did not work both ways. He could not ignore her and cling to her simultaneously.

He was too weak and too strong in all the wrong places. The harder she took hold of his consciousness the harder he pulled at her to keep taking, so that her control turned somehow into his control and his taking. And so she fought off his mental suckers, but that was no good either. It was too much like letting him go, and leaving his body to his mind's volatility.

She could not find the right way to hold him. She sensed him slipping away. And he became more and more agitated, and finally his eyes slid to her face; he stood, and began pacing. And then the prisoner arrived, and her answers to Nash's questions only added to his frustration.

'I'm sorry if I'm no help to you, Lord King,' she said now. 'There are limits to my perception, especially with a stranger.'

'We know you've caught trespassers on your own property, Lady,' one of the king's men said, 'who had a distinct feeling to their minds. Is this man like those men?'

'No, sir, he isn't. Those men had a kind of mental blankness. This man thinks for himself.'

Nash stopped before her and frowned. 'Take control of his mind,' he said. 'Compel him to tell us the name of his master.'

The prisoner was exhausted, nursing an injured arm, frightened of the lady monster, and Fire knew she could do what the king commanded easily enough. She gripped Nash's consciousness as tightly as she could. 'I'm sorry, Lord King. I only take control of people's minds for the sake of self-defence.'

Nash struck her across the face, hard. The blow threw her onto her back. She was scrambling to her feet practically before she'd hit the rug, ready to run, or fight, or do whatever she needed to do to protect herself from him, no matter who he was, but all six of her guards surrounded her now and pulled her out of the king's reach. In the corner of her vision she saw blood on her cheekbone. A tear ran into the blood, and her cheek smarted terribly. He'd cut her with the great square emerald of his ring.

I hate bullies, she thought at him furiously.

The king was crouched on the floor, his head in his hands, his men beside him, confused, whispering to each other. He raised his eyes to Fire. She sensed his mind, clear now, and understanding what he'd done. His face was broken with shame.

Her fury dropped away as quickly as it had come. She was sorry for him.

She sent him a firm message. *This is the last time I'll ever appear before you, until you've learned to guard yourself against me.*

She turned to the door without waiting for a dismissal.

FIRE WONDERED IF a bruise and a square-shaped cut on her cheek might make her ugly. In her bathing room, too curious to stop herself, she held a mirror to her face.

One glance and Fire shoved the mirror under a stack of towels, her question answered. Mirrors were useless, irritating devices. She should have known better.

Musa was perched on the edge of the bath, scowling, as she had been since her guard contingent had returned with their bleeding charge. It irked Musa, Fire knew, to be trapped between Brigan's orders and the king's sovereignty.

'Please don't tell the commander about this,' Fire said.

Musa scowled harder. 'I'm sorry, Lady, but he asked specifically to be told if the king tried to hurt you.'

Princess Clara knocked on the door frame. 'My brother tells me he's done an inexcusable thing,' she said; and then, at the sight of Fire's face, 'Oh my. That's the king's ring clear as day, the brute. Has the healer been?'

'She just left, Lady Princess.'

'And what's your plan for your first day at court, Lady? I hope you won't hide just because he's marked you.'

Fire realised that she had been going to hide, and the cut and bruising were only a part of it. How relieving, the thought of staying in these rooms with her aches and her nerves until Brigan came back and whisked her home.

'I thought you might like a tour of the palace,' Clara said, 'and my brother Garan wants to meet you. He's more like Brigan than Nash. He has control of himself.'

The king's palace, and a brother like Brigan. Curiosity got the better of Fire's apprehensions.

NATURALLY, EVERYWHERE FIRE went she was stared at.

The palace was gigantic, like an indoor city, with gigantic views: the falls, the harbour, white-sailed ships on the sea. The great spans of the city bridges. The city itself, its splendour and its dilapidation, stretching toward golden fields and hills of rocks and flowers. And of course the sky, always a view of the sky from all seven courtyards and all of the upper corridors, where the ceilings were made of glass.

'They don't see you,' Clara told Fire, when a pair of raptor monsters perched on a transparent roof made her jump. 'The glass is reflective on the outside. They only see themselves. And incidentally, Lady, every window in the palace that opens is fitted with a screen – even the ceiling windows. That was Cansrel's doing.'

It wasn't Clara's first mention of Cansrel. Every time she

said his name Fire flinched, so accustomed was she to people avoiding the word.

'I suppose it's for the best,' Clara continued. 'The palace is crawling with monster things – rugs, feathers, jewellery, insect collections. Women wear the furs. Tell me, do you always cover your hair?'

'Usually,' Fire said, 'if I'm to be seen by strangers.'

'Interesting,' Clara said. 'Cansrel never covered his hair.'

Well, and Cansrel had loved attention, Fire thought to herself dryly. More to the point, he had been a man. Cansrel had not had her problems.

PRINCE GARAN WAS too thin and didn't share his sister's obvious robustness; despite it, he was quite good-looking. His eyes were dark and burning under a thatch of nearly black hair, and there was something furious and graceful about his manner that made him intriguing to watch. Appealing. He was very like his brother the king.

Fire knew he was ill – that as a child he'd been taken by the same fever that had killed her mother, and had come out alive but with ruined health. She also knew, from Cansrel's muttered suspicions and Brocker's certainties, that Garan and his twin Clara were the nerve centre of the kingdom's system of spies. She had found it hard to believe of Clara, following the princess around the palace. But now in Garan's presence Clara's bearing changed to something shrewd and serious, and Fire understood that a woman who gabbed about satin umbrellas and her latest love affair might know quite well how to keep a secret.

Garan was sitting at a long table piled high with documents, in a heavily guarded room full of harassed-looking secretaries. The only noise, other than the rustling of paper, came, rather incongruously, from a child who seemed to be playing shoe tug-of-war with a puppy in the corner. The child stared at Fire momentarily when Fire entered, then politely avoided staring again.

Fire sensed that Garan's mind was guarded against her. She realised suddenly, with surprise, that so was Clara's, and so had Clara's been all along. Clara's personality was so open that Fire had not appreciated the degree to which her mind was closed. The child, too, was carefully shielded.

Garan, in addition to being guarded, was rather unfriendly. He seemed to make a point of not asking Fire the usual civil questions, such as how her trip had been, if she liked her rooms, and whether her face was in much pain from being punched by his brother. He appraised the damage to her cheek blandly. 'Brigan can't hear about this until he's done with what he's doing,' he said, his voice low enough that Fire's guard, hovering in the background, could not hear.

'Agreed,' Clara said. 'We can't have him rushing back to spank the king.'

'Musa will report it to him,' Fire said.

'Her reports go through me,' Clara said. 'I'll handle it.'

With ink-stained fingers Garan shuffled through some papers and slid a single page across the table to Clara. While Clara read it he reached into a pocket and glanced at a watch. He spoke over his shoulder to the child.

'Sweetheart,' he said, 'don't pretend to me that you don't know the time.'

The child gave a great gloomy sigh, wrestled the shoe from the piebald puppy, put the shoe on, and moped out the door. The puppy waited a moment, and then trotted after its – lady? Yes, Fire decided that at the king's court, long dark hair prob-ably trumped boyish clothes, and made her a lady. Five years old, possibly, or six, and presumably Garan's. Garan was not married, but that did not make him childless. Fire tried to ignore her own involuntary flash of resentment at the majority of humanity who had children as a matter of course.

'Hmm,' Clara said, frowning at the document before her. 'I don't know what to make of this.'

'We'll discuss it later,' Garan said. His eyes slid to Fire's face and she met his gaze curiously. His eyebrows snapped down, making him fierce, and oddly like Brigan.

'So, Lady Fire,' he said, addressing her directly for the first time. 'Are you going to do what the king's asked, and use your mental power to question our prisoners?'

'No, Lord Prince. I only use my mental power in self-defence.'

'Very noble of you,' Garan said, sounding exactly like he didn't mean it, so that she was perplexed, and looked back at him calmly, and said nothing.

'It *would* be self-defence,' Clara put in distractedly, frowning still at the paper before her. 'The self-defence of this kingdom. Not that I don't understand your resistance to humouring Nash when he's been such a boor, Lady, but we need you.'

'Do we? I find myself undecided on the matter,' Garan said. He dipped his pen into an inkwell. He blotted carefully, and scribbled a few sentences onto the paper before him. Without looking at Fire he opened a feeling to her, coolly and with perfect control. She felt it keenly. Suspicion. Garan did not trust her, and he wanted her to know it.

THAT EVENING, WHEN Fire sensed the king's approach, she locked the entrance to her rooms. He made no objection to this, resigned, seemingly, to holding a conversation with her through the oak of her sitting room door. It was not a very private conversation, on her side at least, for her on-duty guards could recede only so far into her rooms. Before the king spoke, she warned him that he was overheard.

His mind was open and troubled, but clear. 'If you'll bear with me, Lady, I've only two things to say.'

'Go on, Lord King,' Fire said quietly, her forehead resting against the door.

'The first is an apology, for my entire self.'

Fire closed her eyes. 'It's not your entire self that needs to apologise. Only the part that wants to be taken by my power.'

'I can't change that part, Lady.'

'You can. If you're too strong for me to control, then you're strong enough to control yourself.'

'I can't, Lady, I swear to it.'

You don't want to, she corrected him silently. *You don't want to give up the feeling of me, and that is your problem.*

'You're a very strange monster,' he said, almost whispering. 'Monsters are supposed to want to overwhelm men.'

And what could she respond to that? She made a bad monster and a worse human. 'You said it was two things, Lord King.'

He took a breath, as if to clear his head, and spoke more steadily. 'The other is to ask you, Lady, to reconsider the issue of the prisoner. This is a desperate time. No doubt you've a low opinion of my ability to reason, but I swear to you, Lady, that on my throne – when you're not in my thoughts – I see clearly what's right. The kingdom is on the verge of something important. It might be victory, it might be collapse. Your mental power could help us enormously, and not just with one prisoner.'

Fire turned her back to the door and crouched low against it. She held her head up by her hair. 'I'm not that kind of monster,' she said miserably.

'Reconsider, Lady. We could make rules, set limits. There are reasonable men among my advisers. They wouldn't ask too much of you.'

'Leave me to think about it.'

'Will you? Will you really think about it?'

'Leave me,' she said, more forcefully now. She felt his focus shift from business back to his feelings. There was a lengthy silence.

'I don't want to leave,' he said.

Fire bit down on her mounting frustration. 'Go.'

'Marry me, Lady,' he whispered, 'I beg you.'

His mind was his own as he asked it, and he knew how foolish he was. She sensed plain and clear that he simply couldn't help himself.

She pretended hardness, though hardness was not what she felt. *Go, before you ruin the peace between us.*

ONCE HE'D GONE she sat on the floor, face in hands, wishing herself alone, until Musa brought her a drink, and Mila, shyly, a hot compress for her back. She thanked them, and drank; and because she had no choice, eased into their quiet company.

CHAPTER FIFTEEN

Fire's ability to rule her father had depended upon his trust.

As an experiment, in the winter after his accident, Fire got Cansrel to stick his hand into his bedroom fire. She did it by making his mind believe that it was flowers in the grate, and not flame. He reached in to pick them and recoiled; Fire took stronger hold and made him more determined. He reached in again, obstinately resolved to pick flowers, and this time believed he was picking them, until pain brought his mind and his reality crashing back to him. He screamed and ran to the window, threw it open, thrust his hand into the snow piled against the windowpane. He turned to her, cursing, almost crying, to demand what in the Dells she thought she was doing.

It was not an easy thing to explain, and she burst into quite authentic tears that came from the confusion of conflicting emotions. Distress at the sight of his blistered skin, his blackened fingernails, and a terrible smell she hadn't anticipated. Terror of losing his love now that she'd compelled him to hurt himself. Terror of losing his trust, and with it her power to compel him ever to do it again. She threw herself sobbing onto the pillows of his bed. 'I wanted to see what it was like to hurt someone,' she spat at him, 'like you always tell me to. And now I know, and I'm horrified with both of us, and I'll never do it again, not to anyone.'

He came to her then, the anger gone from his face. It was clear that her tears grieved him, so she let the tears come. He sat beside her, his burned hand clutched to his side but his focus clearly on her and her sadness. He stroked her hair with his unhurt hand, trying to soothe her. She took the hand, pressed it to her wet face, and kissed it.

After a moment of this he shifted, extricating his hand from hers. 'You're too old for that,' he said.

She didn't understand him. He cleared his throat. His voice was rough from his own pain.

'You must remember that you're a woman now, Fire, and an unnatural beauty. Men will find your touch overwhelming. Even your father.'

She knew that he meant it plainly, that it contained no threat, no suggestion. He was only being frank, as he was with all matters relating to her monster power, and teaching her something important, for her own safety. But her instincts saw an opportunity. One way to secure Cansrel's trust was to turn this around: make Cansrel feel the need to prove his own trustworthiness to her.

She pushed herself away from him, pretending horror. She ran from the room.

That evening Cansrel stood outside Fire's closed door, pleading with her to understand. 'Darling child,' he said. 'You need never fear me; you know I'd never act on such base instincts with you. It's only that I worry about the men who would. You must understand the dangers of your power to yourself. If you were a son I would not be so worried.'

She let him make his explanations for a while, and was stunned, inside her room, with how easy it was to manipulate the master manipulator. Astonished and dismayed. Understanding that she'd learned how to do this from him.

Finally she came out and stood before him. 'I understand,' she said. 'I'm sorry, Father.' Tears slid down her face and she pretended they were on account of his bandaged hand, which, in part, they were.

'I wish you would be more cruel with your power,' he

said, touching her hair and kissing her. 'Cruelty is strong self-defence.'

And so, at the end of her experiment, Cansrel still trusted her. And he had reason to, for Fire didn't think she could go through with anything like that again.

Then, in the spring, Cansrel began to talk of his need for a new plan, an infallible plan this time, to do away with Brigan.

WHEN FIRE'S BLEEDING began she felt compelled to explain to her guard why bird monsters had begun to gather outside her screen windows, and why raptor monsters swooped down occasionally, ripped apart the smaller birds, and then perched on the sills to stare inside, screeching. She thought the guards took it rather well. Musa sent the two with the best aim to the grounds below the rooms to do some raptor hunting rather perilously close to the palace walls.

The Dells was not known for hot summers, but a palace made of black stone with glass ceilings will get warm; on clear days the ceiling windows were levered open. When Fire passed through a courtyard or corridor during her bleeding the birds chirped and the raptors screeched through those screens as well. Sometimes flying monster bugs trailed in her wake. Fire didn't imagine it did much for her reputation around the court, but then again, very little did. The square mark on her cheek was recognised and much talked of. She could sense the spinning gossip that stopped whenever she entered a room and started up again as she left.

She had told the king that she would think about the issue of the prisoner, but she didn't, not really; she didn't need to. She knew her mind. She spent a certain amount of energy monitoring his whereabouts so she could avoid him. A good bit more deflecting the attention of people of the court. She sensed curiosity from them foremost, and admiration; some hostility, especially from servants. She wondered if the court's servants had clearer recollections of the particulars of Cansrel's cruelty. She wondered if he had been crueller to them.

People followed her sometimes, at a distance, both men and women, servants and nobles, usually without any definite antagonism. Some of them tried to talk to her, called out to her. A grey-haired woman walked right up to her once, said, 'Lady Fire, you are like a delicate blossom,' and would have embraced her if Mila hadn't held out a restraining hand. Fire, her abdomen heavy and aching with cramps and her skin tender and burning, felt the furthest thing from a delicate blossom. She couldn't decide whether to slap the woman or fall into her embrace, weeping. And then a raptor monster scratched on a window screen above and the woman looked up and raised her arms to it, just as entranced with the predator as she had been with Fire.

From other ladies of the court Fire sensed envy and resentment, and jealousy for the heart of the king, who fretted over her from a distance like a stallion behind a fence and did little to hide his frustrated regard. When she met the eyes of these women, some of them with monster feathers in their hair or shoes of lizard monster skins, she lowered her eyes and moved on. She took her meals in her rooms. She was shy of the severe city fashion of the court, sure of the impossibility of herself ever blending in, and besides, it was a way to avoid the king.

CROSSING A BRIGHT white courtyard one day, Fire witnessed a spectacular fight between a pack of small children on one side and Prince Garan's daughter, passionately assisted by her puppy, on the other. Garan's daughter was the instigator of the swinging fists, this Fire saw plainly; and from the broiling emotions in the bunch Fire sensed that she herself might be the matter of dispute. *Stop*, she thought to the children from across the courtyard, *now*; at which every one of them save Garan's girl froze, turned to stare, and then ran shrieking into the palace.

Fire sent Neel for a healer and rushed with the rest of her guard to the girl, whose face was swelling and whose nose ran with blood. 'Child,' Fire said, 'are you all right?'

The girl was engaged in an argument with her puppy, who jumped and yapped and strained against her hand on his collar. 'Blotchy,' she said, crouching to his level, her voice congested with blood, 'down. Down, I say! Stop it! Monster rocks!' This last as Blotchy jumped and banged against her bloody face.

Fire took hold of the puppy's mind and soothed him to calmness.

'Oh, thank goodness,' the child said woefully, plopping down on the marble floor beside Blotchy. She ran searching fingers over her cheeks and nose. She winced and pushed her sticky hair out of her face. 'Papa will be disappointed.'

As before, this child was quite closed to Fire mentally, impressively so, but Fire had understood enough of the other children's feelings to interpret what she meant. 'Because you came to my defence, you mean.'

'No, because I forgot to guard my left side. He reminds me all the time. I think my nose is broken. He'll punish me.'

It was true Garan was not the personification of kindness, but still, Fire couldn't imagine him punishing a child for not winning a fight against approximately eight adversaries. 'Because someone else broke your nose? Surely not.'

The child gave a mournful sigh. 'No, because I threw the first punch. He said I mustn't do that. And because I'm not in my lessons. I'm supposed to be in my lessons.'

'Well, child,' Fire said, trying not to be amused. 'We've fetched you a healer.'

'It's just there are so many lessons,' the girl went on, not much interested in the healer. 'If Papa were not a prince I wouldn't have all these lessons. I love my riding lessons but I could die from my history lessons. And now he won't let me ride his horses, ever. He lets me name his horses but he never lets me ride them, and Uncle Garan will tell him I missed my lessons, and Papa'll say I can't ride them ever. Does Papa ever let you ride his horses?' the girl asked Fire tragically, as if she knew she was bound to receive the most calamitous of responses.

But Fire could not answer, for her mouth was hanging open, her mind scrambling to make sense of the thing she'd thought she understood. This child with dark eyes and hair and a mashed-up face, and an Uncle Garan and a princely father, and an unusual propensity for mental closedness. 'I've only ridden my own horse,' she managed to say.

'Have you met his horses? He has many. He's crazy for horses.'

'I think I've only met one,' Fire said, still disbelieving. Sluggishly she began to strain through some mental arithmetic.

'Was it Big? Big's a mare. Papa says most soldiers favour stallions, but Big is fearless and he wouldn't trade her for any stallion. He says you're fearless, too. He says you saved his life. That's why I defended you,' she said dismally, her current dilemma rounding back to her again. She touched the vicinity of her nose. 'Perhaps it's not broken. Perhaps it's only sprained. Do you think he'll be less angry if my nose is only sprained?'

Fire had begun to clutch her forehead. 'How old are you, child?'

'Six come winter.'

Neel came trotting across the courtyard then with a healer, a smiling man in green. 'Lady Fire,' the healer said, nodding. He crouched before the child. 'Princess Hanna, I think you'd best come with me to the infirmary.'

The two of them shuffled away, the child still chattering in her stuffed-nose voice. Blotchy waited a moment, then trailed after them.

Fire was still gaping. She turned to her guard. 'Why did no one tell me the commander had a daughter?'

Mila shrugged. 'Apparently he keeps it quiet, Lady. All we've ever heard is rumours.'

Fire thought of the woman at the green house with the chestnut hair. 'The child's mother?'

'Word is she's dead, Lady.'

'How long?'

'I don't know. Musa might know, or Princess Clara could tell you.'

'Well,' Fire said, trying to remember what she'd been doing before all of this had happened. 'We may as well go someplace where the raptors aren't screeching.'

'We were on our way to the stables, Lady.'

Ah, yes, to the stables, to visit Small. And his many horsey friends – a number of which, presumably, had short, descriptive names.

FIRE COULD HAVE gone to Clara immediately to hear the story of how a prince of twenty-two had ended up with a secret daughter nearing six. Instead she waited until her bleeding was over, and then she went to Garan.

'Your sister tells me you work too much,' she said to the spymaster.

He looked up from his long table of documents and narrowed his eyes. 'Indeed.'

'Will you come for a walk with me, Lord Prince?'

'Why should you want to walk with me?'

'Because I'm trying to decide what I think of you.'

His eyebrows shot up. 'Oh, a test, is it? Do you expect me to perform for you, then?'

'I don't care what you do, but I'm going regardless. I haven't been outside in five days.'

She turned and left the room; and was pleased, as she moved through the corridor, to feel him weaving through her guard and falling into place beside her.

'My reason is the same as yours,' he said in a patently un-friendly voice.

'Fair enough. I could perform for you if you like. We could stop for my fiddle.'

He snorted. 'Your fiddle. Yes, I've heard all about it. Brigan thinks we're made of money.'

'You hear about everything, I suppose.'

'It's my job.'

'Then perhaps you can explain why no one's ever told me about Princess Hanna.'

Garan glanced at her sideways. 'Why should you care about Princess Hanna?'

It was a reasonable question, and it pricked at a hurt Fire hadn't quite acknowledged yet. 'Only to wonder why people like Queen Roen and Lord Brocker have never made mention of her.'

'Why should they mention her?'

Fire rubbed her neck under her headscarf and sighed, understanding now why her heart had wanted to have this conversation with Garan of all people.

'The lady queen and I speak freely with each other,' she said, 'and Brocker shares all he learns with me. The question isn't why they should have mentioned her. It's why they've taken care not to.'

'Ah,' Garan said. 'This is a conversation about trust.'

Fire took a breath. 'And why should the child be kept secret? She's only a child.'

Garan was silent for a moment, thinking, now and then glancing at her. He steered her across the palace's central courtyard. She was happy to let him choose the route. Fire still got lost in the labyrinths of this place, and only this morning had found herself in the laundry when she'd been aiming for the blacksmith's shop.

'She is just a child,' Garan said finally, 'but her identity has been kept quiet since before she was born. Brigan himself didn't know about her until she'd been alive four months.'

'Why? Who was the mother, an enemy's wife? A friend's wife?'

'No one's wife. A stable girl.'

'Then why—'

'The child was born the third heir to the throne,' Garan said, very low, 'and she was born to Brigan. Not Nash, not Clara, not I. Brigan. Think of the time, Lady, six years ago. If, as you claim, you've been educated by Brocker, you'll know the danger Brigan faced as he grew into adulthood. He was the only one of the court who was Cansrel's open enemy.'

This silenced Fire. She listened, shamed, as Garan unfolded the story.

'She was the girl who cared for his horses. He was sixteen, barely, and she was, too, a pretty thing; goodness knew there was little joy in his life. Her name was Rose.'

'Rose,' Fire repeated, woodenly.

'No one knew of them but four in the family: Nash, Clara, Roen, and I. Brigan kept her quiet to keep her safe. He wanted to marry her.' Garan laughed shortly. 'He was an impossible romantic rockhead. Luckily he couldn't, and keep her secret.'

'And why was that lucky?'

'The son of a king and a girl who slept with the horses?'

It seemed to Fire it was rarely enough one knew a person one wished to marry. How unjust then to meet that person, and be kept from it because one's bed was made of hay and not feathers.

'Anyway,' Garan continued. 'Around that time Cansrel convinced Nax to throw Brigan into the army and send him off to the borders, where presumably Cansrel hoped he'd get himself killed. Brigan was angry as a hornet, but he had no choice but to go. Shortly thereafter it became clear to those of us who knew Rose that he'd left part of himself behind.'

'She was pregnant.'

'Precisely. Roen arranged for her needs, everything secret of course. And Brigan didn't get himself killed after all, but Rose died giving birth to the child; and Brigan came home, all of seventeen years old, to learn in one day that Rose was dead, he had a child, and Nax had named him Commander of the King's Army.'

Fire remembered this part. Cansrel had convinced Nax to promote Brigan far beyond his capability, in the hopes that Brigan would destroy his own reputation with a show of military incompetence. Fire recalled Brocker's pleasure and his pride when Brigan, through some impossible feat of determination, had turned himself first into a credible leader and then into an uncommon one. He'd mounted the entire King's Army, not just the cavalry but the infantry and bow-men. He'd raised the standards of their training and raised their pay. He'd increased their ranks, invited women to join, built signal stations in the mountains and all across the kingdom so that distant places could communicate with each other. He'd planned new forts with vast grain farms and enormous stables to care for the army's greatest asset, the horses that made it mobile and swift. All to the effect of creating new challenges indeed for the smugglers, looters, Pikkian invaders – and for rebel lords like Mydogg and Gentian who were forced now to take pause and reassess their own small armies and dubious ambitions.

Poor Brigan. Fire almost couldn't fathom it. Poor heart-broken boy.

'Cansrel was after everything of Brigan's,' Garan said, 'especially as Brigan's power increased. He poisoned Brigan's horses, out of spite. He tortured one of Brigan's squires and killed him. Obviously we who knew the truth of Hanna knew not to breathe a word.'

'Yes,' Fire whispered. 'Of course.'

'Then Nax died,' Garan said, 'and Brigan and Cansrel spent the next two years trying to kill each other. And then Cansrel killed himself. Finally Brigan was able to name the child his heir, and the second heir now to the throne. But he did so only among the family. It's no official secret – much of the court knows she's his – but it's continued to remain quiet. Partly out of habit, and partly to divert attention from her. Not all of Brigan's enemies died with Cansrel.'

'But how can she be an heir to the throne,' Fire asked, 'if you're not? Nax was your father, and you're no more illegitimate than she is. Plus, she's female, and a child.'

Garan pursed his lips and looked away from her. When he spoke, it wasn't to answer her question. 'Roen trusts you,' he said, 'and Brocker trusts you, so you needn't worry your monster heart. If Roen never told you about her grandchild, it's because she's in the habit of never telling anyone. And if Brocker never told you, it's probably because Roen never told him. And Clara trusts you too, because Brigan trusts you. And I'll admit Brigan's trust is a strong recommendation, but of course, no man is infallible.'

'Of course,' Fire said, dryly.

One of Fire's guards brought down a raptor monster then. It fell from the sky, golden green, and landed in a patch of trees out of their sight. Fire became aware suddenly of their surroundings. They stood in the orchard behind the palace, and beyond the orchard sat the little green house.

Fire stared in astonishment then at the tree beside the house, wondering how she'd failed to notice it from her window. She realised it was because she'd assumed from above that it was a grove of trees and never a single organism. Its mammoth trunk split off in six directions, the limbs so many and so massive that some of them bent with their weight down to the ground, burrowed into the grass, and rose up again to the sky. Supports had been built for some of the heaviest limbs to hold them up and prevent them from breaking.

Beside her, Garan watched the amazement on her face. Sighing, he walked to a bench beside the pathway to the house, where he sat with his eyes closed. Fire noticed his drawn face and his slumped posture. He looked washed out. She went and sat next to him.

'Yes, it's extraordinary,' he said, opening his eyes. 'It's grown so big it'll kill itself. Every father names his heirs. Surely you know that.'

Fire turned from the tree to glance at him, startled. Garan looked back at her coolly.

'My father never named me,' he said. 'He named Nash, and Brigan. Brigan did differently. Hanna will be his first heir even after he marries and has an army of sons. Of course I never minded. I've never once wanted to be king.'

'And of course,' Fire said smoothly, 'none of it will matter once the king and I marry and produce a jungle of monster heirs.'

He hadn't been expecting that. He sat still for a moment, measuring, and then half smiled, despite himself, understanding that it was a joke. He changed the subject again. 'And what have you been doing with yourself, Lady? You've been ten days at court with little but a fiddle to occupy you.'

'And why should you care? Is there something you want me to do?'

'I've no employment for you until you decide to help us.'

Help them – help this strange royal family. She found herself wishing that it weren't so impossible. 'You said you didn't want me to help you.'

'No, Lady, I said I was undecided. I remain undecided.'

The door of the green house swung open then and the lady with the chestnut hair walked down the path toward them. And suddenly the feeling of Garan's mind changed to something lighter. He jumped up and went to the woman and reached for her hand. He walked her back to Fire, his face alight; and Fire understood that of course he'd steered their walk in this direction intentionally. She'd been too wrapped up in their conversation to notice.

'Lady Fire,' Garan said, 'this is Sayre. Sayre has the misfortune of being Hanna's history tutor.'

Sayre smiled up at Garan, a smile that had everything in the world to do with Garan, so that Fire couldn't fail to understand what she was seeing. 'It's not so bad as all that,' Sayre said. 'She's more than capable. It's just she gets restless.'

Fire held out her hand. The two ladies greeted each other, Sayre exceedingly polite and ever so mildly jealous. Understandable. Fire would have to advise Garan not to cart lady monsters along on his trips to visit his sweetheart. Some of the smartest men had a hard time comprehending the obvious.

Then Sayre took her leave and Garan watched her go, rubbing his head absently and humming.

The son of a king and a woman who's a palace tutor? Fire thought to him, propelled by some strange joy into cheekiness. *Shocking.*

Garan lowered his eyebrows and tried to look stern. 'If you're desperate for something to do, Lady, go to the nurseries and teach guarding against monster animals. Get the children on your side so Brigan's daughter still has some teeth in her mouth next he sees her.'

Fire turned to go, a smile playing around her lips. 'Thank you for walking with me, Lord Prince. I should tell you I'm difficult to deceive. You may not trust me, but I know you like me.'

And she told herself it was Garan's regard that had buoyed her mood, and nothing to do with a woman whose significance had been reassigned.

CHAPTER SIXTEEN

F IRE WAS, IN fact, in need of something to do, because without an occupation all she could do was think. And thinking brought her back, over and over, to her lack of occupation, and the question of how much help, in fact, she would be capable of offering this kingdom – if her heart and her mind didn't positively forbid it. The matter plagued her at night when she couldn't sleep. She had bad dreams of what it meant to trick people and hurt people, nightmares of Cansrel making Cutter grovel in imagined pain.

Clara took Fire sightseeing. The city folk adorned themselves with even more monster trappings than the court folk, and with much less concern for the aesthetic integration of the whole. Feathers jammed randomly into buttonholes; jewellery, quite stunning really, necklaces and earrings made of monster shells, worn by a baker woman over her mixing bowl and covered in flour dust. A woman wearing a blue-violet wig from the fur of some silky monster beast, a rabbit or a dog, the hair short and uneven and sticking out in spikes. And the woman's face underneath quite plain, the overall effect tending to an odd caricature of Fire herself; but still, there was no denying she had something lovely atop her head.

'Everyone wants a bit of something beautiful,' Clara said. 'Among the wealthy it's the rare skins and furs sold on the black market. With everyone else it's whatever they find clogging the gutters or killed in the housetraps. It all amounts to the same thing, of course, but the rich people feel better knowing they've paid a fortune.'

Which was, of course, silly. This city, Fire saw, was part

sober and part silly. She liked the gardens and the old crumbling sculptures, the fountains in the squares, the museums and libraries and bright rows of shops that Clara led her through. She liked the bustling cobbled streets where people were so busy with their noisy living that sometimes they didn't even notice the lady monster's guarded walking tour. Sometimes. She calmed a team of horses once that panicked when some children ran too close to their heels, murmuring to them, petting their necks. Business stopped on that street, and didn't resume until she and Clara had rounded a corner.

She liked the bridges. She liked standing in the middle and looking down, feeling she could fall but knowing she wouldn't. The bridge farthest from the falls was a drawbridge; she liked the bells that rang when it rose and fell, soft, almost melodic, whispering around and through the other city noises. She liked the warehouses and docks along the river, the aqueducts and sewers, and the locks, creaking and slow, that brought supply ships up and down between river and harbour. She especially liked Cellar Harbour, where the falls created a mist of seawater and drowned out all sound and feeling.

She even, hesitatingly, liked the feel of the hospitals. She wondered which one had cured her father of the arrow in his back, and she hoped that the surgeons brought good folk back to life too. There were always people outside the hospitals, waiting and worrying. She glanced at them, touching them with surreptitious wishes that their worry should come to a happy ending.

'There used to be medical schools all over the city,' Clara told her. 'Do you know of King Arn and his monster adviser, Lady Ella?'

'I remember the names from my history lessons,' Fire said, reflecting, but not coming up with much.

'They ruled a good hundred years ago,' Clara said. 'King Arn was an herbalist and Lady Ella a surgeon, and they became a bit obsessive about it, really – there are stories about them doing bizarre medical experiments on people who probably wouldn't have consented to it if a monster hadn't been the one making the suggestions, if you know what I mean, Lady. And they'd cut up dead bodies and study them, but no one was ever sure where they were getting the dead bodies from. Ah, well,' Clara said, with a sardonic lift of the eyebrows. 'Be that as it may, they revolutionised our understanding of doctoring and surgery, Lady. It's thanks to them we know the uses for all the strange herbs that grow in the crevices and caves at the edges of the kingdom. Our medicines to stop bleeding and keep wounds from festering and kill tumours and bind bones together and do just about everything else came from their experiments. Of course, they also discovered the drugs that ruin people's minds,' she added darkly. 'And anyway, the schools are closed now; there's no money for research. Or for art, for that matter, or engineering. Everything goes to policing – to the army, the coming war. I suppose the city will begin to deteriorate.'

It already was, Fire thought but didn't say. She saw the seedy, sprawling neighbourhoods that abutted the docks on the south side of the river, and the tumbledown alleyways that popped up in parts of the city centre where it seemed they shouldn't. Many, many sections of the city that were not devoted to knowledge or beauty, or any kind of goodness.

Clara took her to lunch once with the twins' mother, who had a small and pleasant home on a street of florists. She also had a husband, a retired soldier who moonlighted as one of the twins' most reliable spies.

'These days, my focus is smuggling,' he told them in confidence over their meal. 'Almost every wealthy person in the city dips into the black market now and then, but as often as not, when you find someone who's very deeply involved, you've also found someone who's the king's enemy. Especially if they're smuggling weapons or horses or anything Pikkian.

If we're lucky, we're able to trace a buyer to the fellow he's buying for, and if that turns out to be one of the rebel lords, we bring the buyer in for questioning. Can't always trust their answers, of course.'

Unsurprisingly, this sort of talk was always fuel for Clara's pressure tactics with Fire. 'With your power, it'd be easy for us to learn who's on whose side. You could help us find out if our allies are true,' she'd say, or, 'You could figure out where Mydogg's planning to attack first.' Or, when that didn't work, 'You could uncover an assassination plot. Wouldn't you feel terrible if I were assassinated because you weren't helping?' And in a moment of desperation: 'What if they're planning to assassinate you? There have to be some who are, especially now that people think you might marry Nash.'

Fire never responded to the endless battery, never admitted the doubt – and guilt – she was beginning to feel. She only filed the arguments away to mull over later, along with the ongoing arguments of the king. For occasionally after dinner – often enough that Welkley had installed a chair in the hallway – Nash came to speak to her through the door. He conducted himself decently, talked of the weather and stately visitors to the court; and always, always tried to convince her to reconsider the matter of the prisoner.

'You're from the north, Lady,' he'd say to her, or something like it. 'You've seen the loose hold the law has outside this city. One misstep, Lady, and the entire kingdom could fall through our fingers.'

And then he'd grow quiet, and she would know the marriage proposal was coming. She would send him away with her refusal and take what comfort she could in the company of her guard; and consider very seriously the state of the city, and the kingdom, and the king. And what her own place should be.

To busy herself and ease her sense of uselessness, she took Garan's advice in the nurseries. Entering cautiously at first, sitting quietly on a chair and watching the children as they played, read, squabbled, for this was where her mother had worked, and she wanted to take in its feeling slowly. She tried to picture a young, orange-haired woman in these rooms, counselling children with her even temper. Jessa had had a place in these noisy, sunlit rooms. Somehow the very thought made Fire feel like less of a stranger here. Even if it also made her more lonely.

Teaching guarding against animal monsters was delicate work, and Fire came up against some parents who wanted nothing of her association with their children. But a mix of royal and servant children did become her pupils.

'Why are you so fascinated with insects?' she asked one of her cleverest students one morning, an eleven-year-old boy named Cob who could build a wall in his mind against raptor monsters, and resist the urge to touch Fire's hair when he saw it, but would not kill a monster bug even if it was camped out on his hand making a dinner of his blood. 'You have no trouble with the raptors.'

'Raptors,' Cob said with high-pitched scorn. 'They have no intelligence, only a big meaningless surge of feeling they think they can mesmerise me with. They're completely unsophisticated.'

'True,' Fire said. 'But compared to monster bugs, they're veritable geniuses.'

'But monster bugs are so perfect,' Cob said wistfully, going cross-eyed as a dragonfly monster hovered at the tip of his nose. 'Look at their wings. Look at their jointed legs and their beady little eyeballs and look how *smart* they are with their pinchers.'

'He loves all bugs,' Cob's younger sister said, rolling her eyes. 'Not just monster bugs.'

Perhaps his problem, Fire thought to herself, is that he's a scientist. 'Very well,' she said. 'You may allow monster bugs to sting you, in appreciation of their excellent pinchers. But,' she added sternly, 'there are one or two bugs that would do you harm if they could, and those you must learn to guard yourself against. Do you understand?'

'Must I kill them?'

'Yes, you must kill them. But once they're dead, you could always dissect them. Had you thought of that?'

Cob brightened. 'Really? Will you help me?'

And so Fire found herself borrowing scalpels and clips and trays from a healer in the castle infirmary and engaging in some rather peculiar experimentation, perhaps along the lines of what King Arn and Lady Ella had done one hundred years before. On a smaller scale, of course, and with much less brilliant results.

She crossed paths often with Princess Hanna. From her windows she saw the girl running to and from the little green house. She also saw Sayre, and other tutors, and sometimes Garan, and even Clara's legendary gardener, who was blond and bronzed and muscular, like something out of a heroic romance. And sometimes an old woman, tiny and bent, who wore an apron and had pale green eyes and was the frequent stopping block to Hanna's headlong rushes.

She was strong, this little woman, always carrying Hanna around, and it appeared she was the housekeeper of the green house. Her love for the child was obvious, and she had no love for Fire. Fire had encountered her once in the orchard and found her mind as closed as Brigan's. Her face, at the sight of the monster lady, had gone cold and unhappy.

The palace had outside walkways built into the stone portions of the roof. At night, far from sleep, Fire walked them with her guard. From the heights she could see the glimmer of the great torches on the bridges, kept lit throughout the night so that boats on the fast-running waters below always knew exactly how close they were to the falls. And from the heights she could hear those falls roaring. On clear nights she watched the city spread sleeping around her and the flash of stars on the sea. She felt like a queen. Not like a real queen, not like the wife of King Nash. More like a woman at the top of the world. At the top of a city, in particular, where the people were becoming real to her; a city of which she was growing rather fond.

Brigan RETURNED TO court three weeks from the day he'd left. Fire knew the instant he arrived. A consciousness was like a face you saw once and forever recognised. Brigan's was quiet, impenetrable, and strong, and indubitably his from the instant her mind tripped over it.

She happened to be with Hanna and Blotchy at the time, in the morning sun of a quiet courtyard corner. The little girl was examining the raptor scars on Fire's neck and trying to wheedle from her, not for the first time, the story of how she'd got those scars and saved Brigan's soldiers. When Fire declined, the girl wheedled at Musa.

'You weren't even there,' Fire objected, laughing, when Musa began the tale.

'Well,' Musa said, 'if no one who *was* there will tell it—'

'Someone's coming who knows it to tell it,' Fire said mysteriously, causing Hanna to freeze, and stand bolt upright.

'Papa?' she said, turning in circles now, spinning to look at each of the entrances. 'Do you mean Papa? Where?'

He came through an archway on the other side of the court-yard. Hanna shrieked and bolted across the marble floor. He caught her up and carried her back the way she'd come, nodding to Fire and the guard, smiling through Hanna's stream of chatter.

And what was it with Brigan every time he reappeared? Why this instinct to bolt? They were friends now, and Fire should be beyond this fear of him. She forbade herself to move and focused on Blotchy, who offered his ears to be petted.

Brigan put Hanna down and crouched before the child. He touched his fingers to her chin and moved her face one way and the other, surveying her still-bruised and bandaged nose. He interrupted her quietly. 'And tell me what happened here?'

'But Papa,' she said, changing subject in mid-sentence. 'They were saying bad things about Lady Fire.'

'Who were?'

'Selin and Midan and the others.'

'And what? Then one of them punched you in the nose?'

Hanna scuffed her shoes at the ground. 'No.'

'Tell me what happened.'

Another scuff at the ground, and then Hanna spoke dismally. 'I hit Selin. He was wrong, Papa! Someone had to show him.'

Brigan was silent for a moment. Hanna rested one hand on either of his bent knees and dropped her eyes to the floor. She sighed dramatically behind her curtain of hair.

'Look at me, Hanna.'

The girl obeyed.

'Was hitting Selin a reasonable way to show him he was wrong?'

'No, Papa. I did badly. Are you going to punish me?'

'I'm going to take away your fighting lessons for now. I didn't agree to them so that you might misuse them.'

Hanna sighed again. 'For how long?'

'Until I'm convinced you understand what they're for.'

'And will you take away my riding lessons?'

'Have you ridden over anyone you shouldn't?'

A small giggle. 'Of course not, Papa!'

'Then you'll keep your riding lessons.'

'Will you let me ride your horses?'

'You know the answer to that. You must grow bigger before you ride warhorses.'

Hanna reached her hand out and rubbed her palm on the

stubble of his face with an ease and affection Fire found hard to bear, so that she had to look away and stare fiercely at Blotchy, who was shedding silky hairs all over her skirt. 'How long do you stay, Papa?'

'I don't know, love. I'm needed in the north.'

'You have a wound, too, Papa.' Hanna took Brigan's left hand, which was wrapped in a bandage, and inspected it. 'Did you throw the first punch?'

Brigan twitched a smile at Fire. Focused on the lady more closely. And then his eyes went cold and his mouth formed a hard line; and Fire was frightened, and hurt by his disregard.

And then reason returned, and she understood what he saw. It was the lingering square mark of Nash's ring on her cheek.

It was weeks ago, Fire thought to him. *He's behaved himself since.*

Brigan stood, lifting Hanna with him. He spoke to the girl quietly. 'I did not throw the first punch. And right now I must have a chat with your uncle the king.'

'I want to come,' Hanna said, wrapping arms around him.

'You may come as far as the hall, but there I must leave you.'

'But why? I want to come.'

'It's a private chat.'

'But—'

Firmly: 'Hanna. You heard me.'

There was a sullen silence. 'I can walk for myself.'

Brigan lowered Hanna to the floor. Another sullen silence as they regarded each other, the taller side much more calmly than the shorter.

Then a small voice. 'Will you carry me, Papa?'

Another flicker of smile. 'I suppose you're not too big yet.'

Brigan carried Hanna back across the courtyard and Fire listened to the receding music of Hanna's voice. Blotchy was doing as he always did – sitting, and considering, before following his lady. Knowing it was unethical, Fire reached out to his mind and convinced him to stay. She couldn't help it; she needed him. His ears were soft.

Brigan had been unshaven, in black clothing, his boots spattered with mud. His light eyes standing out in a weary face.

She'd very much come to like his face.

And of course she understood now why her body wanted to run whenever he appeared. It was a correct instinct, for there was nothing to be got from this but sadness.

She wished she hadn't seen his gentle way with his child.

FIRE WAS SPECTACULARLY good at not thinking about a thing when she chose, if the thing was hurtful, or just plain stupid. She manhandled, pummelled, packed this thing away. His own brother in love with her, and she Cansrel's daughter?

It was not to be thought of.

What she did think of, more urgently now, was the question of her purpose at this court. For if Brigan's next responsibility took him north, then surely he meant to deposit her home. And she was not ready to go.

She had grown up between Brocker and Cansrel and she was not naïve. She'd seen the parts of the city with the abandoned buildings and the smell of filth; she understood the look and feel of city people who were hungry, or lost to drugs. She understood what it meant that even with a military force in four large pieces, Brigan couldn't stop looters from knocking a town off a cliff. And these were only the small things, these were mere policing. War was coming, and if Mydogg and Gentian overran this city and this kingdom with their armies, if one of them made himself king, how much lower would that push those already at the bottom?

Fire couldn't imagine leaving, going all the way back to her stone house where the reports came slowly and the only variance in her routine was the occasional empty-headed trespasser whom no one knew the significance of. How could she refuse to help when there was so much at stake here? How could she go away?

'You're wasting something you have,' Clara had said to her once, almost with resentment. 'Something the rest of us could only imagine possessing. Waste is criminal.'

Fire hadn't responded. But she'd heard, more deeply than Clara had realised.

TONIGHT, WHILE SHE was fighting with herself on the roof, Brigan appeared beside her and leaned on the railing. Fire took a steadying breath and watched the glimmer of torches in the city, trying not to look at him, or be pleased of his company.

'I hear you're crazy for horses,' she said lightly.

He broke into a smile. 'Something's come up and I'm leaving tomorrow night, following the river west. I'll be back two days later, but Hanna won't forgive me. I'm in disgrace.'

Fire remembered her own experience of being five. 'I expect she misses you terribly when you go.'

'Yes,' he said, 'and I'm always going. I wish it weren't the way of things. But I wanted to check with you before I left, Lady. I travel north soon, this time without the army. It'll be faster, and safer, if you'd like to return home.'

Fire closed her eyes. 'I suppose I should say yes.'

He hesitated. 'Would you prefer me to arrange for a different escort?'

'Goodness, no,' she said, 'it's not that. It's only that every one of your siblings is pressuring me to stay at court and use my mental power to help with the spy work. Even Prince Garan, who hasn't decided yet if he trusts me.'

'Ah,' he said, understanding. 'Garan doesn't trust anyone, you know. It's his nature, and his job. Does he give you a hard time?'

'No. He's kind enough. Everyone is, really. I mean, it's no harder for me here than it's been anywhere else. Just different.'

He thought about that for a moment. 'Well. You mustn't let them bully you; they see only their side of it. They're so embroiled in the matters of the kingdom that they can't imagine any other way of living.'

Fire wondered what other way of living Brigan imagined; what life he dreamed of, if he hadn't been born to this one. She spoke carefully. 'Do you think I should stay and help them as they ask?'

'Lady, I can't say what you should do. You must do whatever you think is right.'

She caught something defensive in his tone, but she wasn't certain which one of them he was defending. She pressed him again. 'And do you have an opinion as to what is right?'

He was flustered. He looked away from her. 'I don't wish to influence you. If you stay, I'll be terribly pleased. You'll be such invaluable help. But I'll also be sorry for what we would ask of you, truly sorry.'

It was a rare outburst – rare because he wasn't one for outbursts, and rare because it wasn't likely to occur to anyone else to be sorry. Rather at a loss, Fire gripped her bow tightly and said, 'Taking someone's mind and changing it is a trespass. A violence. Can I ever use such a thing without overstepping my right? How will I know if I'm going too far? I'm capable of so many horrors.'

Brigan took a minute to think, staring intently into his hands. He tugged at the edge of his bandage. 'I understand you,' he said, speaking quietly. 'I know what it's like to be capable of horrors. I'm training twenty-five thousand soldiers for a bloodbath. And there are things I've done I wish I'd never had to do. There are things I'll do in future.' He glanced at her, then looked back into his hands. 'No doubt this is presumptuous, Lady. But for whatever it's worth, if you'd like, I could promise to tell you if I ever believed you to be overstepping the rights of your power. And whether or not you choose to accept that promise, I'd very much like to ask you to do the same for me.'

Fire swallowed, hardly believing that he was entrusting her with so much. She whispered, 'You honour me. I accept your promise, and I give you my own in return.'

The lights in the city houses were dimming one by one. And part of avoiding thoughts about something was not encouraging opportunities for that something to make itself felt.

'Thank you for the fiddle,' she said. 'I play it every day.'

And she left him, and walked with her guard back to her rooms.

IT WAS IN the great hall the next morning that she came to understand what had to be done.

The walls of this cavernous room were made of mirrors. Passing through, on sudden impulse, Fire looked at herself.

She caught her breath and kept looking, until she was beyond that first staggering moment of disbelief. She crossed her arms and squared her feet, and looked, and looked. She remembered a thing that made her angry. She'd told Clara her intention never to have children; and Clara had told her of a medicine that would make her very sick, but only for two or three days. After she recovered, she'd never have to worry again about the chance of becoming pregnant, no matter how many men she took to her bed. The medicine would make her permanently unable to bear children. One of the most useful discoveries of King Arn and Lady Ella.

It made Fire so angry, the thought of such a medicine, a violence done to herself to stop her from creating anything like herself. And what was the purpose of these eyes, this impossible face, the softness and the curves of this body, the strength of this mind; what was the point, if none of the men who desired her were to give her any babies, and all it ever brought her was grief? What was the purpose of a woman monster?

It came out in a whisper. 'What am I for?'

'Excuse me, Lady?' Musa said.

Fire shook her head. 'Nothing.' She took a step closer and pulled off her headscarf. Her hair slid down, shimmering. One of her guards gasped.

She was fully as beautiful as Cansrel. Indeed, she was very like him.

Behind her Brigan entered the great hall suddenly and stopped. In the mirror their eyes met, and held. It was clear he was in the middle of a thought or a conversation – one that her appearance had interrupted completely.

It was so rarely he held her eyes. All the feeling she'd been trying to batter away threatened to trickle back.

And then Garan caught up with Brigan, speaking sharply. Nash's voice behind Garan, and then Nash himself appeared, saw her, and stopped cold beside his brothers. In a panic Fire grabbed at her hair to collect it, steeling herself against whatever stupid way the king intended to behave.

But it was all right, they were safe, for Nash was trying very hard to close himself. 'Well met, Lady,' he said with considerable effort. He threw his arms around both of his brothers' shoulders and moved with them out of the hall, out of her sight.

Fire was impressed, and relieved. She pushed her feelings back into their cell. And then, just before the brothers disappeared, her eyes caught the flash of something at Brigan's hip.

It was the hilt of his sword. The sword of the commander of the King's Army. And all at once, Fire understood.

Brigan did terrible things. He stuck swords into men in the mountains. He trained soldiers for war. He had enormous destructive power, just as his father had had – but he didn't use that power the way his father had done. Truly, he would rather not use it at all. But he chose to, so that he might stop other people from using power in even worse ways.

His power was his burden. He accepted it.

And he was nothing like his father. Neither were Garan or Clara; neither, really, was Nash. Not all sons were like their fathers. A son chose the man he would be.

Not all daughters were like their fathers. A daughter monster chose the monster she would be.

Fire looked into her face. The beautiful vision blurred suddenly behind her own tears. She blinked the tears away. 'I've been afraid of being Cansrel,' she said aloud to her reflection. 'But I'm not Cansrel.'

At her elbow, Musa said blandly, 'Any one of us could have told you that, Lady.'

Fire looked at the captain of her guard and laughed, because she wasn't Cansrel – she wasn't anyone but herself. She had no one's path to follow; her path was her own to choose. And then she stopped laughing, because she was terrified of the path she suddenly knew herself to be choosing. I can't do this, she thought. I'm too dangerous. I'll only make things worse.

No, she said back to herself. Already I'm forgetting. I'm not Cansrel; at every step on this path I create myself. And maybe I'll always find my own power horrifying, and maybe I can't ever be what I'd most like to be.

But I can stay here, and I can make myself into what I *should* be.

Waste is criminal. I'll use the power I have to undo what Cansrel did. I'll use it to fight for the Dells.

PART TWO

Spies

CHAPTER SEVENTEEN

As MUCH AS Fire had known about the play of power in the Dells, her knowledge had been drawn in broad strokes. She understood this now, because now she held a minute and specific map in her mind. The focal points were King's City; Mydogg's holding on the Pikkian border; and Gentian's land in the southern mountains below the river, not far from Fort Flood. There were places in between: Brigan's many other forts and outposts, the estates of lords and ladies with tiny armies and shifting alliances, the Great Greys in the south and west, the Little Greys in the north, the Winged River, the Pikkian River, the high, flat area north of King's City called Marble Rise. Rocky patches of poverty, flashes of violence, plundering, desolation; landscapes and landmarks that were bound to be keystones in the war between Nash, Mydogg, and Gentian.

Her work was never the same from day to day. She never knew what kind of folk Garan and Clara's people would pick up: Pikkian smugglers, common soldiers of Mydogg's or Gentian's, messengers of either, servants who had worked for them once. Men suspected of being their spies or the spies of their allies. Fire came to see that in a kingdom balanced delicately atop a pile of changing associations, the most critical commodity was information. The Dells spied on their friends and on their enemies; they spied on their own spies. And indeed, all players in the realm did the same.

The very first man they brought before her, an old servant of a neighbour of Mydogg's, opened wide at the sight of her and spilled every thought that bubbled into his head. 'Both Lord Mydogg and Lord Gentian are rightly impressed with

Prince Brigan,' the man told her, staring, quivering. 'Both have been buying horses and mounting their armies for the past few years like the prince did, and recruiting mountain folk and looters as soldiers. They respect the prince as an opponent, Lady. And did you know there are Pikkians in Lord Mydogg's army? Big, pale men hulking around his land.'

This is easy, Fire thought to herself. I only have to sit here and they blurt everything out.

But Garan was unimpressed. 'He told us nothing we didn't already know. Did you plumb him for more – names, places, secrets? How do you know you've learned every part of his knowledge?'

The next couple of fellows were less forthcoming – a pair of convicted spies, resistant to her, and strong. Both bruised around the face, both gaunt, and one of them limping and stoop-shouldered, wincing as he eased back in his chair, as if he had cuts or bruises on his back. 'How were you injured?' she asked them, suspicious. 'And where?' They sat before her mutely, eyes averted, stony-faced, and answered neither that question nor any other question she put to them.

When the interrogation was over and the two spies had gone back to the dungeons, she made her excuses to Garan, who'd sat in on the entire thing. 'They were too strong for me, Lord Prince. I could get nothing from them.'

Garan eyed her moodily over a sheaf of papers. 'Did you try?'

'Of course I tried.'

'Really? How hard did you try?' He stood, lips tight. 'I have neither energy nor time to waste, Lady Fire. When you decide that you're actually going to do this thing, let me know.'

He shoved his papers under his arm and pushed through the questioning room door, leaving her with her own indignation. He was right, of course. She hadn't tried, not really. She'd poked at their minds and, finding them closed, done nothing to force an opening. She hadn't even tried to get them to look into her face. How could she? Was she honestly expected to sit before men weakened by ill treatment and abuse them even further?

She jumped up and ran after Garan, finding him at a desk in his offices, scribbling madly in coded letters.

'I have rules,' she said to him.

He stilled his pen, raised expressionless eyes to her face, and waited.

'When you bring me an old servant who's come willingly where the king's men have bidden him, a man who's never been convicted, or even accused, of a crime,' Fire said, 'I will not take his mind. I'll sit before him and ask questions, and if my presence makes him more talkative, very well. But I will not compel him to say things he would otherwise not have said. Nor,' she added, voice rising, 'will I take the mind of a person who's been fed too little, or denied medicines, or beaten in your gaols. I won't manipulate a prisoner you've mistreated.'

Garan sat back and crossed his arms. 'That's rich, isn't it? Your own manipulation is mistreatment; you've said it yourself.'

'Yes, but mine is meant to be for good reason. Yours is not.'

'It's not *my* mistreatment. I don't give the orders down there, I've no idea what goes on.'

'If you want me to question them, you'd best find out.'

To Garan's credit, the treatment of Dellian prisoners did change after that. One particularly laconic man, after a session in which Fire learned positively nothing, thanked her for it specifically. 'Best dungeons I ever been in,' he said, chewing on a toothpick.

'Wonderful,' Garan grumbled when he'd gone. 'We'll grow a reputation for our kindness to lawbreakers.'

'A prison with a monster on its staff of interrogators is not likely to grow a reputation for kindness,' Nash responded, quietly. Some loved to be brought before her, loved her presence too much to care what she caused them to reveal; but for the most part, Nash was right. She met with tens, gradually hundreds, of different spies and smugglers and soldiers who came into the room sullenly, sometimes even fighting the guards, needing to be dragged. She asked them questions in their minds. *When did you last speak to Mydogg? What did he say? Tell me every word. Which of our spies is he trying to turn? Which of our soldiers are traitors?* She took a breath and forced herself to plumb and twist and pound – sometimes even to threaten. *No, you're lying again. One more lie and you'll start to feel pain. You believe that I can make you feel pain, don't you?*

I'm doing this for the Dells, she told herself over and over when her own capacity for bullying made her numb with shame and panic. I'm doing this to protect the Dells from those who would destroy it.

'In a three-way war,' said a prisoner who'd been caught smuggling swords and daggers to Gentian, 'it seems to me that the king has the advantage of numbers. Doesn't it seem that way to you, Lady? Does anyone know Mydogg's numbers for sure?'

He was a fellow who kept tearing away from her hold, polite and pleasant and cloud-brained one moment, the next moment clear-headed, fighting against the shackles around his wrists and ankles, whimpering at the sight of her.

She nudged at his mind now, pushing him away from his own empty speculations and centering him on his actual knowledge.

'Tell me about Mydogg and Gentian,' she said. 'Do they intend to mount an attack this summer?'

'I don't know, Lady. I've heard nothing about it but rumours.'

'Do you know Gentian's numbers?'

'No, but he buys an infinite number of swords.'

'How many is "infinite"? Be more specific.'

'I don't know specifics,' he said, still speaking truthfully, but beginning to break free again, the reality of his situation in this room coming back to him. 'I have nothing more to say to you,' he announced suddenly, staring at her big-eyed, beginning to shake. 'I know what you are. I won't let you use me.'

'I don't enjoy using you,' Fire said tiredly, allowing herself, for a moment at least, to say what she felt. She watched him as he yanked at his wrists and gasped and fell back in his chair, exhausted and sniffling. Then she reached up and tugged at her headscarf so that her hair came tumbling down. The brightness startled him; he gaped at her, astonished; in that instant, she pushed into his mind again and grabbed hold easily. 'What are these rumours you've heard about the plans of the rebel lords?'

'Well, Lady,' he said, transformed again, smiling cheerfully. 'I hear that Lord Mydogg wants to make himself the king of the Dells and Pikkia. Then he wants to use Pikkian boats to explore the sea and find new lands to conquer. A Pikkian smuggler told me that, Lady.'

I'm getting better at this, Fire thought to herself. I'm learning all the cheap, disgusting little tricks.

And the muscles of her mind were stretching; practice was making her quicker, stronger. Control was becoming an easy – even *comfortable* – position for her to assume.

But all she ever learned were vague plans for attack someplace sometime soon, random violent intentions against Nash or Brigan, sometimes against herself. Swift changes in alliance that changed back again just as swiftly. Like Garan and Clara and everyone else, she was waiting to discover something solid, something large and treacherous that could serve as a call to action.

They were all waiting for a breakthrough. But sometimes Fire just wished desperately that she were allowed the occasional moment of solitude.

SHE HAD BEEN a summer baby and in July her birthday passed – with little fanfare, for she kept the fact of it to herself. Archer and Brocker both had flowers sent. Fire smiled at this, for they would have sent something else had they known how many men of the court and the city had been sending her flowers, constantly, endlessly, flowers and more flowers, since her arrival two months ago. Her rooms were always a hothouse. She would have pitched them, the cut orchids and lilies and fine tall roses, for she had no interest in the attentions of these men; except that she loved the flowers, she loved being surrounded by the beauty of them. She found she had a knack for arranging them, colour to colour.

The king never sent flowers. His feelings had not changed, but he had stopped begging her to marry him. In fact, he'd asked her to teach him guarding against monsters. So over a series of days and weeks, each on either side of her door, she had taught him what he already knew but needed a push to remember. Intention, focus, and self-control. With practice, and with his new gloomy commitment to discipline, his mind became stronger and they moved the lessons to his office. He could be trusted now not to touch her, except when he'd had too much wine, which he did on occasion. They were irritating, his drunken tears, but at least drunk he was easy to control.

Of course, everyone in the palace noticed every time they were together, and thoughtless talk was easy. It was a solid spoke in the rumour wheel that the monster would eventually marry the king.

Brigan was away most of July. He came and went constantly, and now Fire understood where he was always going. Aside from the considerable time he spent with the army, he met with people: lords, ladies, businessmen of the black market, friends, enemies, talking this one or that one into an alliance, testing the loyalty of another. In some cases, spying was the only word for what he was doing. And sometimes fighting himself out of traps he wittingly or unwittingly walked into, coming back with bandages on his hand, black eyes, a cracked rib one time that would have stopped any sane person from riding. It was horrendous, Fire thought, some of the situations Brigan bounded off to throw himself into. Surely someone else should handle negotiations with a weapons dealer who was known to perform favours for Mydogg on occasion. Surely someone else should go to the well-guarded and isolated manor of Gentian's son, Gunner, in the southern peaks, to make clear the consequences if Gunner remained loyal to his father.

'He's too good at it,' Clara told her, when Fire questioned the wisdom of these meetings. 'He has this way of convincing people they want what he wants. And where he can't persuade with his words he often can with his sword.'

Fire remembered the two soldiers who'd brawled at the sight of her on the day she'd joined the First Branch. She remembered how their viciousness had turned to shame and regret after Brigan had spoken to them for only a few moments.

Not all people who inspired devotion were monsters.

And apparently he was renowned for his skill with a blade. Hanna, of course, talked as if he were unbeatable. 'I get my fighting skill from Papa,' she said, and clearly she had it from somewhere. It seemed to Fire that most five-year-olds in a skirmish against a mob of children would have emerged with more than a broken nose, if they'd emerged at all.

On the last day of July, Hanna came to her with a bright fistful of wildflowers, collected, Fire guessed, from the grasses of the cliff above Cellar Harbour, at the back of the green house. 'Grandmother said in a letter she thought your birthday was in July. Did I miss it? Why does no one know your birthday? Uncle Garan said ladies like flowers.' She scrunched her nose doubtfully at this last, and stuck the flowers in Fire's face, as if she thought flowers were for eating and expected Fire to lean in and munch, like Small would have done.

With Archer's and Brocker's, they were her favourite flowers in all of her rooms.

ONE TROUBLING DAY at the end of August, Fire was in the stables, brushing Small to clear her head. Her guard receded as Brigan ambled over, a collection of bridles slung on his shoulder. He leaned on the stall door and scratched Small's nose. 'Lady, well met.'

He had only just returned that morning from his latest excursion. 'Prince Brigan. And where's your lady?'

'In her history lesson. She went without complaint and I've been trying to prepare myself for what it might mean. Either she's planning to bribe me about something or she's ill.'

Fire had a question to ask Brigan, and the question was awkward. There was nothing to do but imitate dignity and fling it at him. She lifted her chin. 'Hanna's asked me several times now why the monsters go crazy for me every month, and why I can't step outside for four or five days at a time unless I bring extra guards. I'd like to explain it to her. I'd like your permission.'

It was impressive, his reaction – the command he had over his expression, emotionless as he stood on the other side of the door. He stroked Small's neck. 'She's five years old.'

Fire said nothing to this; only waited.

He scratched his head then, and squinted at her, uncertain. 'What do you think? Is five too young to understand? I don't want her to be frightened.'

'They don't frighten her, Lord Prince. She talks of guarding me from them with her bow.'

Brigan spoke quietly. 'I meant the changes that will happen to her own body. I wondered if the knowledge of it might frighten her.'

'Ah.' Fire's own voice was soft. 'But then, perhaps I'm the right person to explain it, for she's not so guarded that I can't tell if it upsets her. I can suit my explanation to her reaction.'

'Yes,' Brigan said, still hesitant and squinting. 'But you don't think five is very young?'

How odd it was, how dangerously dear, to find him so out of his element, so much a man, and wanting her advice on this thing. Fire spoke her opinion frankly. 'I don't think Hanna is too young to understand. And I think she should have an honest answer to a thing that puzzles her.'

He nodded. 'I wonder she hasn't asked me. She's not shy with questions.'

'Maybe she senses the nature of it.'

'Can she be so sensitive?'

'Children are geniuses,' Fire said firmly.

'Yes,' Brigan said. 'Well. You have my permission. Tell me afterwards how it goes.'

But suddenly Fire wasn't listening, because she was unsettled, as she had been several times that day, by the sense of a presence that was strange, familiar, and out of place. A person who should not be here. She gripped Small's mane and shook her head. Small took his nose away from Brigan's chest and peered back at her.

'Lady,' Brigan said. 'What is it?'

'It almost seems – no, now it's gone again. Never mind. It's nothing.'

Brigan looked at her, puzzled. She smiled, and explained. 'Sometimes I have to let a perception sit for a while before it makes sense to me.'

'Ah.' He considered the span of Small's long nose. 'Was it something to do with my mind?'

'What?' Fire said. 'Are you joking?'

'Should I be?'

'Do you think I sense anything at all of your mind?'

'Don't you?'

'Brigan,' she said, startled out of her manners. 'Your consciousness is a wall with no cracks in it. Never once have I had the slightest hint of anything from your mind.'

'Oh,' he said eloquently. 'Hmm.' He rearranged the straps of leather on his shoulder, looking rather pleased with himself.

'I'd assumed you were doing it on purpose,' Fire said.

'I was. Only it's hard to know how successful one is at such things.'

'Your success is complete.'

'How about now?'

Fire stared. 'What you mean? Are you asking if I sense your feelings now? Of course I don't.'

'And now?'

It came to her like the gentlest wave from the deep ocean of his consciousness. She stood quiet, and absorbed it, and took hold of her own feelings; for the fact of Brigan releasing a feeling to her, the first feeling he'd ever given her, made her inordinately happy. She said, 'I sense that you're amused by this conversation.'

'Interesting,' he said, smiling. 'Fascinating. And now that my mind is open, could you take it over?'

'Never. You've let a single feeling out, but that doesn't mean I could march in and take control.'

'Try,' he said; and even though his tone was friendly and his face open, Fire was frightened.

'I don't want to.'

'It's only as an experiment.'

The word made her breathless with panic. 'No. I don't want to. Don't ask me to.'

And now he was leaning close against the stall door, and speaking low. 'Lady, forgive me. I've distressed you. I won't ask it again, I promise.'

'You don't understand. I would never.'

'I know. I know you wouldn't. Please, Lady – I wish it unsaid.'

Fire found that she was gripping Small's mane harder than she meant to be. She released the poor horse's hair, and smoothed it, and fought against the tears pushing their way to her surface. She rested her face against Small's neck and breathed his warm horsey smell.

And now she was laughing, a breathy laugh that sounded like a sob. 'I'd thought once, actually, of taking your mind, if you asked. I'd thought I could help you fall asleep at night.'

He opened his mouth to say something. Shut it again. His face closed for a moment, his unreadable mask falling into place. He spoke softly. 'But that wouldn't be fair; for after I slept you'd be left awake, with no one to help you sleep.'

Fire wasn't certain what they were talking about anymore. And she was desperately unhappy, for it was not a conversation to distract her from how she felt about this man.

Welkley walked in then with a summons for Brigan to go to the king. Fire was relieved to see him go.

ON HER WAY to her own rooms with her guard, that strange and familiar consciousness flitted again across her mind. The archer, the empty-headed archer.

Fire let out a frustrated breath of air. The archer was in the palace or on the grounds, or nearby in the city, or at least she'd thought so at times today; and he never stayed in her mind long enough for her to catch hold, or to know what to do. It was not normal, these prowling men and these minds as blank as if they were mesmerised by monsters. The sense of him here after all these months was not welcome.

Then in her rooms, she found the guards who were stationed there in a peculiar state. 'A man came to the door, Lady,' Musa said, 'but he made no sense. He said he was from the king and he'd come to examine the view from your windows, but I didn't recognise him as a king's man and I didn't trust what he wanted. I didn't let him in.'

Fire was rather astonished. 'The view from my windows? Why on earth?'

'He didn't feel right, Lady,' Neel said. 'There was something funny about him. Nothing he said made any sense.'

'He felt well enough to me,' another guard said gruffly. 'The king will not be pleased that we disobeyed.'

'No,' Musa said to her soldiers. 'Enough of this argument. Neel is right, the man had a bad feeling to him.'

'He made me dizzy,' Mila said.

'He was an honourable man,' another said, 'and I don't believe we have the authority to turn the king's men away.'

Fire stood in her doorway, her hand on the door frame to steady herself. She was certain as she listened to the disagreement between her guards – her guards, who never argued in front of their lady, and never talked back to their captain – that something was wrong. It wasn't just that they argued, or that this visitor sounded a suspicious fellow. Neel had said the man hadn't felt right; well, a number of her guards at this moment didn't feel right. They were much more open to her than usual, and a fog hovered in their minds. The most affected were the guards who argued now with Musa.

And she knew through some instinct, monster or human, that if they spoke of this man as honourable, they were reading him wrong. She knew with a certainty that she couldn't explain that Musa had been right to turn the man away.

'What did he look like, this fellow?'

A few of the guard scratched their heads and grumbled that they couldn't remember; and Fire could almost reach out and touch the fog of their minds. But Musa's mind was clear. 'He was tall, Lady, taller than the king, and thin, wasted. He had white hair and dark eyes and he was not well. His colour was off, he was grey-like, and he had marks on his skin. A rash.'

'A rash?'

'He wore plain clothing, and he had a positive armament of bows on his back – crossbow, short bow, a truly gorgeous longbow. He had a full quiver and a knife, but no sword.'

'The arrows in his quiver. What were they made of?'

Musa pursed her lips. 'I didn't notice.'

'A white wood,' Neel said.

And so the foggy-headed archer had come to her rooms to see her views. And had left a number of her guards with puzzled expressions, and foggy heads.

Fire walked to the foggiest guard, the first who'd raised an argument, a fellow named Edler who was normally quite amiable. She put her hand to his forehead. 'Edler. Does your head hurt?'

It took Edler a moment to process his answer. 'It doesn't exactly hurt, Lady, but I don't feel quite like myself.'

Fire considered how to word this. 'May I have your permission to try to clear the discomfort?'

'Certainly, Lady, if you wish.'

Fire entered Edler's consciousness easily, as she had the poacher's. She played around with his fog, touched it and twisted it, trying to decide what exactly it was. It seemed like a balloon that was filling his mind with emptiness, pushing his own intelligence to the edges.

Fire jabbed the balloon hard and it popped, and fizzled. Edler's own thoughts rushed forward and fell into place; and he rubbed his head with both hands. 'It does feel better, Lady. I can picture that man clearly. I don't think he was the king's man.'

'He wasn't the king's man,' Fire said. 'The king wouldn't send a sickly fellow armed with a longbow to my rooms to admire my views.'

Edler sighed. 'Rocks, but I'm tired.'

Fire moved on to her next foggy guard, and thought to

herself that here was a thing more ominous than anything she'd uncovered yet in the questioning rooms.

On her bed later she found a letter from Archer. Once the summer harvest was through, he intended to visit. It was a happiness, but it did not lighten the state of things.

She had thought herself the only person in the Dells capable of altering minds.

CHAPTER EIGHTEEN

THE YEAR FIRE spent training her father to experience things that didn't exist was also, thankfully, the year her relationship with Archer found a new happiness.

Cansrel hadn't minded experiencing non-existent things, for it was a time when existing things depressed him. Nax had been his conduit to all pleasures, and Nax was gone. Brigan grew more influential and had escaped another attack uninjured. It was some relief for Cansrel to feel sun on his skin in the midst of weeks of drizzle, or taste monster meat when it was not being served. There was solace in the touch of his daughter's mind – now that she knew better than to turn flames into flowers.

On her side of things, Fire's body suffered; she lost her appetite, grew thin, had attacks of dizziness, got cramps in her neck and shoulders that made playing music painful and brought on splitting headaches. She avoided contemplation of the thing she was thinking of doing. She was certain that if she looked at it straight on she'd lose control of herself.

Archer was not, in fact, the only person that year to bring her comfort. A young woman named Liddy, sweet and hazel-eyed, was the maid of Fire's bedrooms. She came upon Fire one spring day curled on the bed, fighting off a whirling panic. Liddy liked her mild young lady, and was sorry at her distress. She sat beside Fire and stroked her hair, at Fire's forehead and behind her ears, against her neck, and down to the small of her back. The touch was kindly meant, and the deepest and tenderest comfort in the world. Fire found herself resting her head in Liddy's lap while Liddy continued stroking. It was a gift, offered unjealously, and Fire accepted it.

That day, from that moment, something quiet grew between them. An alliance. They brushed each other's hair sometimes, helped each other dress and undress. They stole time together, whispering, like little girls who've discovered a soul mate.

Some things could not happen in Cansrel's proximity without Cansrel knowing; monsters knew things. Cansrel began to complain about Liddy. He did not like her, he did not like the time they spent together. Finally he lost patience and arranged a marriage for Liddy, sending her away to an estate beyond the town.

Fire was breathless, astounded, and heartbroken. Certainly she was glad that he'd merely sent Liddy away, not killed her or taken her into his own bed to teach her a lesson. But still, it was a bitter and selfish cruelty. It did not make her merciful.

Perhaps her lonesomeness after Liddy prepared her for Archer, though Liddy and Archer were manifestly different.

During that spring and into the summer she turned fifteen, Archer knew what mad thing Fire was contemplating. He knew why she couldn't eat and why her body suffered. It tormented him, took him out of his mind with fear for her. He fought with her about it; he fought with Brocker, who was also worried but who nonetheless refused to interfere. Over and over he begged Fire to release herself from the entire endeavour. Over and over Fire refused.

One August night during a frantic whispered battle under a tree outside her house, he kissed her. She stiffened, startled, and then knew, as his hands reached for her and he kissed her again, that she wanted this, she needed Archer, her body needed this wildness that was also comfort. She burrowed herself against him; she brought him inside and upstairs. And that was that; child companions became lovers. They found a place where they could agree, a release from the anxiety and unhappiness that threatened to overwhelm them. After making love with her friend, Fire often found herself wanting to eat. Kissing her and laughing, Archer would feed her in her own bed with food he carried in through the window.

Cansrel knew, of course, but where her gentle love of Liddy had been intolerable to him, her need for Archer roused nothing stronger than an amused acceptance of the inevitable. He didn't care, as long as she took the herbs when she needed to. 'Two of us is enough, Fire,' he'd say smoothly. She heard the threat in his words toward the baby she wasn't going to have. She took the herbs.

Archer did not act jealous in those days, or domineering. That came later.

Fire knew too well that things didn't ever stay the same. Natural beginnings came to natural or unnatural ends. She was eager to see Archer, more than eager, but she knew what he would come to King's City hoping for. She wasn't looking forward to putting this end into words for him.

FIRE HAD TAKEN to describing the foggy archer to everyone she questioned, very briefly at the end of each interview. So far it was to no avail.

'Lady,' Brigan said to her today in Garan's bedroom. 'Have you learned anything yet about that archer?'

'No, Lord Prince. No one seems to recognise his description.'

'Well,' he said, 'I hope you'll keep asking.'

Garan's health had had a setback, but he refused to go into the infirmary or stop working, which meant that in recent days his bedchamber had become quite a hub of activity. Breathing was a difficulty and he had no strength to sit up. Despite this, he remained more than capable of holding his side of an argument.

'Forget the archer,' he said now. 'We have more important matters to discuss, such as the exorbitant cost of your army.'

He glared at Brigan, who'd propped himself against the wardrobe, too directly in Fire's line of vision to ignore, tossing a ball back and forth in his hands that she recognised as a toy she'd seen Blotchy and Hanna fighting over on occasion. 'It's far too expensive,' Garan continued, still glaring from his bed. 'You pay them too much, and then when they're injured or dead and no use to us you continue to pay them.'

Brigan shrugged. 'And?'

'You think we're made of money.'

'I will not cut their pay.'

'Brigan,' Garan said wearily. 'We cannot afford it.'

'We must afford it. The eve of a war is not the time to start cutting an army's pay. How do you think I've managed to recruit so many? Do you really think them so shot through with loyalty for the bloodline of Nax that they wouldn't turn to Mydogg if he offered more?'

'As I understood it,' Garan said, 'the lot of them would pay for the privilege of dying in defence of none other than you.'

Nash spoke from his seat in the window, where he was a dark shape outlined in the light of a blue sky. He'd been sitting there for some time. Fire knew he was watching her. 'And that's because he always sticks up for them, Garan, when brutes like you try to take their money away. I wish you would rest. You look like you're about to pass out.'

'Don't patronise me,' Garan said; and then dissolved into a fit of coughing that had the sound of a saw blade tearing through wood.

Fire leaned forward in her chair and touched Garan's damp face. She'd come to an understanding with him regarding this bout of illness. He insisted on working, and so she agreed to bring him her reports from the questioning rooms; but only if he allowed her into his mind, to ease his sense of his throbbing head and burning lungs.

'Thank you,' he said to her softly, taking her hand and

holding it to his chest. 'This conversation rots. Lady, give me some good news from the questioning rooms.'

'I'm afraid there isn't any, Lord Prince.'

'Still coming up with contradiction?'

'Most certainly. A messenger told me yesterday that Mydogg has definite plans to make an attack against both the king and Lord Gentian in November. Then today a new fellow told me Mydogg has definite plans to move his entire army north into Pikkia and wait for a war between Gentian and the king to play out before he so much as raises a sword. Plus, I spoke to a spy of Gentian's who says Gentian killed Lady Murgda in an ambush in August.'

Brigan was spinning the ball now on the end of his finger, absentmindedly. 'I met with Lady Murgda on the fifteenth of September,' he said. 'She wasn't particularly friendly, but she was plainly not dead.'

It was a tendency in the questioning rooms that had arisen suddenly in recent weeks, contradiction and misinformation, coming from all sides and making it very difficult to know which sources to trust. The messengers and spies Fire questioned were clear-headed and truthful with their knowledge. It was simply that their knowledge was wrong.

All at the Dellian court knew what it meant. Both Mydogg and Gentian were aware that Fire had joined the ranks of the enemy. To lessen the advantage she gave the Dellian throne, both rebel lords had begun misinforming some among their own people, and then sending them out to get caught.

'There are people close to both men,' Garan said, 'people who know the truth of their plans. We need those people – a close ally of Mydogg's, and one of Gentian's. And they have to be people we'd never suspect normally, for neither Mydogg nor Gentian must ever suspect us of questioning them.'

'We need an ally of Mydogg's or Gentian's pretending to be among the most loyal allies of the king,' Brigan said. 'Shouldn't be so hard, really. If I shot an arrow out the window I'd probably hit one.'

'It seems to me,' Fire said carefully, 'that if I take a less direct approach, if I question every person we're holding about things I haven't bothered to investigate before – every party they've ever been to, every conversation they've ever overheard but perhaps not understood the significance of, every horse they've ever seen heading south when it should've been heading north—'

'Yes,' Brigan said. 'It might yield something.'

'And where are the women?' Fire asked. 'Enough men. Give me the women Mydogg and Gentian've taken to bed, and the barmaids who've had to serve them their wine. Men are daft around women, incautious and boastful. There must be a hundred women out there carrying information we could use.'

Nash spoke soberly. 'That seems good advice.'

'I don't know,' Garan said. 'I'm offended.' He stopped, choked by a spasm of coughing. Nash moved to his brother's bed, sat beside him, and held his shoulder to steady him. Garan reached a shaky hand to Nash. Nash clasped it in his.

It always struck Fire, the physical affection between these siblings, who as often as not were at each other's throats over one thing or another. She liked the way the four of them shifted and changed shape, bumping and clanging against each other, sharpening each other's edges and then smoothing them down again, and somehow always finding the way to fit together.

'And,' Brigan said, returning quietly to his previous topic, 'don't give up on the archer, Lady.'

'I won't, for he troubles me much,' Fire said; and then sensed the approach of an altogether different archer. She looked into her lap to hide her flush of joy. 'Lord Archer has just arrived at court,' she said. 'Welkley is bringing him here now.'

'Ah,' Brigan said. 'And here's the man we should recruit to shoot arrows out the window.'

'Yes,' Garan said wickedly, 'I hear his arrow is always finding new targets.'

'I'd hit you if you weren't flat on your back,' Brigan said, suddenly angry.

'Behave yourself, Garan,' Nash hissed. Before Fire could even begin to react to the argument, which struck her as rather funny, Welkley and Archer were through the door, and everyone but Garan was standing.

'Lord King,' Archer said immediately, dropping to his knee before Nash. 'Lord Princes,' he said next, standing to take Brigan's hand and stooping to take Garan's.

He turned to Fire. With great propriety he took her hands in his. And the instant their eyes met he was laughing and glinting with mischief, his face so happy and Archer-like that she began to laugh as well.

He lifted her up to give her a proper hug. He smelled like home, like the northern autumn rains.

SHE WENT FOR a walk with Archer around the palace grounds. The trees were blazing with autumn colour. Fire was astonished now, and thrilled, with the tree beside the green house, because in recent days it had transformed into the closest natural thing she'd ever seen to her hair.

Archer told her how bleak the north was in comparison. He told her about Brocker's activities, and the year's good harvest, and his passage south with ten soldiers through the rain. 'I've brought your favourite musician,' Archer said, 'and he's brought his whistle.'

'Krell,' Fire said, smiling. 'Thank you, Archer.'

'This guard on our heels is all very well,' Archer said, 'but when can we be alone?'

'I'm never alone. I always have a guard, even in my bed-chamber.'

'Surely that can change now I'm here. Why don't you tell them to go away?'

'They're under Brigan's orders, not mine,' Fire said lightly. 'And as it turns out, he's quite stubborn. I haven't been able to change his mind about it.'

'Well,' Archer said, smirking, '*I* will change his mind. I daresay he understands our need of privacy. And his authority over you must lessen now that I'm here.'

Of course, Fire thought, and Archer's own authority must rise up to replace it. Her temper flared out; she caught at the ends of it and hauled it back in. 'There's something I must tell you, Archer, and you're not going to like it.'

His entire manner changed instantly, mouth hard, eyes flashing, and Fire was amazed at how fast their reunion had turned to this. She stopped and stared at him in exasperation, spoke over him to stop him. 'Archer, stay within your rights. Don't you dare start accusing me of taking some man to my bed.'

'A woman, then? It wouldn't be entirely without precedent, would it?'

She clenched her fists so hard her nails hurt the palms of her hands; and suddenly she was no longer concerned with holding on to the ends of her fury. 'I was so excited for you to come,' she said. 'I was so happy to see you. And now already you've started in on me, and I wish you would leave. You understand me, Archer? When you get like this I wish you would leave. The love I give you, you take, and you use it against me.'

She swung away from him, strode away, came back again and stood furious before him, aware that this was the first time she'd ever spoken to him this way. She should have spoken like this more. She'd been too generous with her patience.

We're not lovers anymore, she thought at him. *This is the thing I needed to tell you. The closer you get to me the harder you pull, and your grip is too tight. You hurt me with it. You love me so much you've forgotten how to be my friend. I miss my friend,* she thought at him fiercely. *I love my friend. We're through as lovers. Do you understand?*

Archer stood dazed, breathing heavily, eyes stony. Fire could see that he did understand.

And now Fire saw Hanna, and sensed her at the same time, coming over the hill at the archery range and bolting toward them with all her small speed.

Fire began a battle for her composure. 'There's a child coming,' she told Archer hoarsely, 'and if you take your vile mood out on her I won't speak to you again.'

'Who is she?'

'Brigan's daughter.'

Archer stared at Fire very hard.

And then Hanna reached them, Blotchy careening close behind. Fire knelt to meet the dog. Hanna stopped before them, smiling and gasping, and Fire sensed her sudden confusion as she took in their silence. 'What's wrong, Lady Fire?' Hanna asked.

'Nothing, Lady Princess. I'm happy to see you and Blotchy.'

Hanna laughed. 'He's getting your dress muddy.'

Yes, Blotchy was destroying her dress, and practically bowling her over as he bounced in and out of her lap, for in his mind he was still a puppy, even though his body had grown. 'Blotchy is much more important than my dress,' Fire said, taking the wriggling dog in her arms, wanting his muddy joy.

Hanna came close and whispered in her ear. 'Is that angry man Lord Archer?'

'Yes, and he is not angry with you.'

'Do you think he would shoot for me?'

'Shoot for you?'

'Papa says he's the best in the kingdom. I want to see.'

Fire couldn't have explained why this made her so sad, that Archer should be the best in the kingdom, and Hanna should want to see. She burrowed her face for a moment against Blotchy. 'Lord Archer, Princess Hanna would like to see you shoot, for she's heard you're the best in all the Dells.'

Archer was hiding his feelings from her mind, but Fire knew how to read his face. She knew how his eyes looked when he was blinking back tears, and the muted voice he used when he was too miserable for anger. He cleared his throat now, and spoke in that voice. 'And what kind of bow do you favour, Lady Princess?'

'A longbow, like the one you carry, only yours is much bigger. Will you come? I'll show you.'

Archer didn't look at Fire. He turned and followed Hanna up the hill, Blotchy bounding after them. Fire stood, and watched them go.

Quite unexpectedly, Musa took her arm. Fire placed her hand on Musa's, grateful to be touched, fiercely glad to think that her guard might be overpaid.

It was a very hard thing to have crushed the heart, and the hopes, of a friend.

After dark, unable to sleep, she went to the roofs. Eventually Brigan came wandering by and joined her. Now and then, since their conversation in the stables, he opened a flash of feeling to her. Tonight she could tell he was surprised to see her.

Fire knew why he was surprised. After her quarrel with Archer, Musa had told her, matter-of-factly, that at Fire's request Fire actually was permitted to be alone with Archer; that in the very beginning, in his instructions, Brigan had made an exception for Archer, as long as the grounds outside the windows were guarded and guards stood outside every door. She should have informed the lady of this before, Musa said, but she hadn't expected Lord Archer so soon. And once Fire and Archer had begun to argue, she hadn't wanted to interrupt.

Fire's face had burned at this knowledge. And here was why

Brigan had defended Archer in Garan's bedroom earlier: he'd seen Garan's jibe as an offense to Fire, believed, even, that Fire was in love with Archer.

Fire told Musa, 'The exception is not necessary.'

'Yes, I got that sense,' Musa said. Then Mila brought Fire a cup of wine in the timid, comprehending way Mila had. The wine was a comfort. Fire's head had begun to ache, and she recognised the onset of her pre-bleeding time.

Now, on the roof, Fire was silent. She said nothing, not even when Brigan greeted her. He seemed to accept her silence and was rather quiet himself, filling the space occasionally with the gentle patter of his conversation. He told her that Hanna was bedazzled by Archer, that they'd shot so many arrows together she had blisters between her fingers.

Fire was thinking about Archer's fear. She thought it was Archer's fear that made his love so hard to bear. Archer was controlling and imperious, and jealous and suspicious, and Archer always held her too near. Because he was afraid of her dying.

She broke a long silence with her first words of the night, spoken so quietly he moved closer to hear. 'How long do you think you'll live?'

His breath was a surprised laugh. 'Truly, I don't know. Many mornings I wake knowing I might die that day.' He paused. 'Why? What's on your mind tonight, Lady?'

Fire said, 'It's likely one of these days a raptor monster will get me, or some arrow will find its way past my guard. It doesn't seem to me a morbid thought; only realistic.'

He listened, leaning against the railing, his head propped on his fist.

'I only hope it won't cause my friends too much pain,' she continued. 'I hope they'll understand it was inevitable.'

She shivered. Summer was well over, and if she'd had half a mind tonight she would have brought a coat. Brigan had remembered his coat, a fine long coat that Fire liked, because Brigan was wearing it, and Brigan was quick and strong, and always seemed comfortable whatever he was wearing. And now his hands reached for the buttons and he shrugged himself out of the coat, for try as she might, Fire couldn't hide her shivers.

'No,' Fire said. 'It's my own fault for forgetting the season.'

He ignored this and helped her into the coat, which was too big; and its warmth and bigness were welcome, and so was its smell, of wool, and campfires, and horses. She whispered it into his mind. *Thank you.*

After a moment, he said, 'It seems we're both afflicted with sober thoughts tonight.'

'What have you been thinking?'

That unhappy laugh again. 'Nothing that will cheer you. I've been trying to find a way around this war.'

'Oh,' Fire said, rising for a moment from her self-absorption.

'It's a fruitless line of thought. There's no way around it, not with two enemies bent on fighting.'

'It isn't your fault, you know.'

He glanced at her. 'Reading my mind, Lady?'

She smiled. 'Lucky guess, I suppose.'

He smiled, too, and raised his face to the sky. 'I understand you rank dogs above dresses, Lady.'

Fire's own laughter was a balm to her heart. 'I explained about the monsters, by the way. She already knew a bit about it. I think your housekeeper takes good care of her.'

'Tess,' Brigan said. 'She's taken good care since the day Hanna was born.' He seemed to hesitate then, his voice carefully inscrutable. 'Have you met her?'

'No,' Fire said; for indeed, Brigan's housekeeper still looked upon Fire with cold eyes whenever she looked upon her at all. As Brigan must know, judging by his manner of asking.

'I think it's good for Hanna to have someone old in her life,' Brigan said, 'who can talk of all different times, not just the last thirty years. And Hanna loves Tess, and all of her stories.' He yawned and rubbed his hair. 'When will you start your new line of questioning?'

'Tomorrow, I suppose.'

'Tomorrow,' he said, sighing. 'Tomorrow I go away.'

CHAPTER NINETEEN

FIRE HAD COME to know more about the insignificant habits and tastes of Lord Mydogg, Lord Gentian, Murgda, Gunner, all their households and all their guests than any person could care to know. She knew Gentian was ambitious but also slightly feather-brained at times and had a delicate stomach, ate no rich foods, and drank only water. She knew his son Gunner was cleverer than his father, a reputable soldier, a bit of an ascetic when it came to wine and women. Mydogg was the opposite, denied himself no pleasure, was lavish with his favourites but stingy with everyone else. Murgda was stingy with everyone including herself, and known to be exceedingly fond of bread pudding.

This was not helpful information. Clara and the king had better things to do than sit and witness its discovery, and Garan was still confined to his bed. More and more Fire was left alone in the questioning rooms, excepting, of course, Musa, Mila, and Neel. Brigan had ordered these three to attend Fire in any of her confidential court business, and they spent the greater part of every day with her.

Archer stood sometimes with her guard while she worked. He had asked permission to do so, and Clara had granted it, and so, rather absently, had Fire. She didn't mind Archer's presence. She understood that he was curious. She only minded the sense she got that Clara was more likely to join the interrogation if Archer was there.

Archer was quiet these days, keeping to himself, his thoughts hidden behind a closed door. Confusion obvious, at times, in his manner. Fire was as gentle with him as she could be, for she appreciated what she knew must be a conscious effort on his part, to suppress his own instinct for furious outbursts. 'How long will you be able to stay at court?' she asked him, so that he would know she didn't really want him to leave.

He cleared his throat uncomfortably. 'Now that the harvest is over, Brocker is well able to handle affairs. I could stay for some time, if I were wanted.'

She made no answer to that, but touched his arm and asked him if he'd like to sit in on the afternoon's interrogations.

She learned that Mydogg favoured the smuggled wine of an obscure Pikkian vineyard where frost came early and the grapes were left to freeze on the vine. She learned that Murgda and her Pikkian husband, the naval explorer, were thought to be very much in love. Finally and at long last, she learned something useful: the name of a tall, dark-eyed archer with spot-on aim who was old enough by now to have white hair.

'Jod,' her informant grunted. 'Knew him some twenty years ago. We were together in old Nax's dungeons, 'til Jod got out. He was in for rape. Didn't know he was sick. Not surprised, the way they piled us on top of each other, the things went on in there. You know what I'm talking about, you monster freak bitch.'

'Where is he now?'

It wasn't easy with this man, or pleasant. At every question he fought against her hold, and then lost the fight and succumbed, ashamed and hateful. 'How should I know? I hope he's hunting monster-eating bitch dogs like you. I'd like to watch him—'

What followed was a description of a violation so graphic Fire couldn't help but feel the force of its malice. But the prisoners who spoke to her like this only made her patient, and oddly depressed. It seemed to Fire that they had a right to their words, the only defence they had against her ill use. And of course these were the men who would be dangerous to her if ever released, some of them so dangerous she was compelled to recommend they never be released; and this did not help to soothe her guilt. True, these were not men whose freedom would be a boon to society. Nonetheless, they would not be so inhumanly vile had she not been around to provoke them.

This man today fared worse than most others, for Archer came forward suddenly and punched him in the face. 'Archer!' Fire exclaimed. She called for the dungeon guards to take the man away, which they did, lifting him from the floor, where he lay dizzy and bleeding. Once he was gone Fire gaped at Archer, then glared, too exasperated to trust herself to speak.

'I'm sorry,' he said sullenly, yanking his collar loose, as if it choked him. 'That one got under my skin more than the others.'

'Archer, I simply can't—'

'I said I was sorry. I won't do it again.'

Fire crossed her arms and stared him down. After a few moments, Archer actually began to smile. He shook his head, sighing hopelessly. 'Perhaps it's the promise of your angry face that keeps me misbehaving,' he said. 'You're so beautiful when you're angry.'

'Oh, Archer,' she snapped, 'flirt with someone else.'

'I will, if you command it,' he quipped, with a goofy grin that caught her off guard, so that she had to stop her own face from twitching into a smile.

For a moment, it was almost as if they were friends again.

SHE HAD A serious conversation with Archer a few days later on the archery range, where she had come with her fiddle looking for Krell. She found Krell with Archer, Hanna, and the king, all four of them shooting at targets and Hanna well boosted by advice from all sides. Hanna concentrated hard, her feet planted stubbornly, miniature bow in her hands, miniature arrows on her back, and she was not talking. It was a characteristic Fire had noted: in riding, swordplay, and archery, and any other lesson that interested her, Hanna ceased her chatter, and showed a surprising capacity for focus.

'Brigan used to focus like that in his lessons too,' Clara had told Fire, 'and when he did, it was a great relief to Roen; for otherwise, guaranteed, he was plotting some kind of trouble. I believe he used to provoke Nax on purpose. He knew Nax favoured Nash.'

'Is that true?' Fire asked.

'Oh yes, Lady. Nash was better-looking. And Brigan was better at everything else, and more like his mother than his father, which I don't think worked in his favour. Ah well, at least he didn't start the brawls Hanna starts.'

Yes, Hanna started brawls, and it could not be because her father favoured anyone over her. But today she was not brawling, and once she woke from the daze of her bow and arrows enough to notice the lady and the fiddle, the girl begged a concert, and got one.

Afterward Fire walked around the archery range with Archer and Nash, her guard trailing behind.

The simultaneous company of these two men was a funny thing, for they mirrored each other. Each in love with her, gloomy and moping; each resigned to hopelessness and each subdued, but resenting the presence of the other. And neither doing much to hide any of this from her, for as usual Nash's feelings were open, and Archer's body language unmistakable.

But Nash's manners were better than Archer's, at least for the moment, and the court had a greater hold on his time. As Archer's choice of conversation became less inclusive, Nash took his leave.

Fire considered Archer, so tall and fine-looking beside her, his bow in hand. She spoke quietly. 'You drove him away, with your talk of our childhood in the north.'

'He wants you, and he doesn't deserve you.'

'As you deserve me?'

Archer's face took on a grim smile. 'I've always known I don't deserve you. Every regard you've ever shown me has been a gift undeserved.'

That is not true, she thought to him. *You were my loyal friend even before I could walk.*

'You've changed,' Archer said. 'Do you realise how much? The more time I spend with you here the less I know you. All these new people in your life, and your happiness in this princess child – and her dog, of all things. And the work you do every day – you use your power, every day. I used to have to fight with you to use it even to defend yourself.'

Fire took a careful breath. 'Archer. Sometimes in the courtyards or the hallways, I've taken to changing people's attentions so they don't notice me. So I can walk by without being hassled, and everyone else can continue their work without distraction.'

'You're not ashamed of your abilities anymore,' Archer said. 'And the sight of you – you're glowing. Truly, Fire. I don't recognise you.'

'But the ease with which I've come to use my power. Can you understand how it frightens me, Archer?'

Archer stopped for a moment, his gaze fierce, his eyes on three dark dots in the sky. The archery range stood at a high point overlooking the sea. A trio of raptor monsters circled now over some trade boat below, and arrows flew from the bows of its sailors. It was a rough autumn sea and a blustery autumn wind, and arrow after arrow failed to hit its mark.

Archer took one stunning, lazy shot. A bird fell. Then Fire's guard Edler connected with a shot of his own, and Archer clapped him on the shoulder to congratulate him.

Fire thought her question forgotten, and so she was surprised when he spoke.

'You've always been far more afraid of yourself than of any

of the terrors in the world outside yourself. Were it the other way around, we'd both have peace.'

He said it kindly, not critically; it was his forlorn wish for peace. Fire hugged her fiddle now with both arms, muting the strings with the fabric of her dress. 'Archer, you know me. You recognise me. We must get past this thing between us, you must accept how I've changed. I could not bear it if by refusing your bed I should also lose your friendship. We were friends before. We must find the way to be friends again.'

'I know,' he said. 'I know, love. I'm trying. I am.'

He walked away from her then and stared at the sea. He stood for some time, silent. When he walked back she was still standing there, holding her fiddle to her breast. After a moment something like a smile eased the sadness in his face.

'Will you tell me why you're playing a different fiddle?' he said.

It was a good story to tell, and distant enough from today's feelings that it calmed her in the telling.

THE COMPANY OF Brigan and Garan was a great relief, compared to that of Archer and Nash. They were so easy. Their silences never felt loaded with grave things they yearned to say, and if they brooded, at least it had no connection to her.

The three sat in the sunny central courtyard, deliciously warm, for with the approach of winter there were advantages to a black palace with glass roofs. It had been a day of difficult and unproductive work that for Fire had yielded little more than a reiteration of Mydogg's preference for frozen-grape wine. An old servant of Gentian's had reported it to her; the servant had read a line or two about it in a letter Gentian had instructed him to burn, a letter from Mydogg. Fire still couldn't understand this propensity of sworn enemies in the Dells to visit each other and send each other letters. And how frustrating that all the servant had seen was a bit about wine.

She slapped at a monster bug on her arm. Garan played absently with his walking stick, which he'd used to walk slowly to this spot. Brigan sat stretched out with his hands clasped behind his head, watching Hanna scuffle with Blotchy on the other side of the courtyard.

'Hanna will never have friends who are people,' Brigan said, 'until she stops getting into scraps.'

Blotchy was whirling in circles with his mouth clamped around a stick he'd just found at the base of a courtyard tree – a branch, really, quite enormous, that swept a wide and multi-pronged radius as he spun. 'This won't do,' Brigan said now. He jumped up, went to the dog, wrestled the branch away and broke it into pieces, then gave Blotchy back a stick of less hazardous dimensions. Determined, apparently, that if Hanna should have no friends, at least she should keep both eyes.

'She has many friends who are people,' Fire said gently when he got back.

'You know I meant children.'

'She's too precocious for the children her age, and she's too small for the other children to tolerate.'

'They might tolerate her if she would tolerate them. I fear she's becoming a bully.'

Fire spoke with certainty. 'She is not a bully. She doesn't pick on the others or single them out; she isn't cruel. She fights only when she's provoked, and they provoke her on purpose, because they've decided not to like her, and they know that if she does fight, you'll punish her.'

'The little brutes. They're using you,' Garan muttered to Brigan.

'Is this just a theory, Lady? Or something you've observed?'

'It's a theory I've developed on the basis of what I've observed.'

Brigan smiled soberly. 'And have you developed a theory

about how I might teach my daughter to harden herself to taunts?'

'I'll think on it.'

'Thank the Dells for your thinking.'

'Thank the Dells for my health,' Garan said, rising to his feet at the sight of Sayre, who'd entered the courtyard, looking very pretty in a blue dress. 'I shall now bound away.'

He did not bound, but his steady walking was progress, and Fire watched his every step, as if her eyes on his back could keep him safe. Sayre met him and took his arm, and the two set off together.

His recent setback had frightened her. Fire could admit this to herself, now that he was improved. She wished that old King Arn and his monster adviser, conducting their experiments a hundred years ago, had discovered just a few more medicines, found the remedies to one or two more illnesses.

Hanna was the next to leave them, running to take Archer's hand as he passed through with his bow.

'Hanna's announced her intentions to marry Archer,' Brigan said, watching them go.

Fire smiled into her lap. She crafted her response carefully – but spoke it lightly. 'I've seen plenty of women fall into an infatuation with him. But your heart can be easier than most other fathers, for she's much too young for his brand of heart-break. I suppose it's a harsh thing to say of one's oldest friend, but were she twelve years older I would not let them meet.'

True to her expectation, Brigan's face was unreadable. 'You're little more than twelve years older than Hanna yourself.'

'I'm a thousand years old,' Fire said, 'just like you.'

'Hmm,' Brigan said. He didn't ask her what she meant, which was for the best, because she wasn't exactly sure. If she was suggesting she was too wise with the weight of her experience to fall prey to infatuation – well, the disproof was sitting before her in the form of a grey-eyed prince with a thoughtful set to his mouth that she found quite distracting.

Fire sighed, trying to shift her attention. Her senses were overloaded. This courtyard was one of the palace's busiest, and, of course, the palace as a whole swarmed with minds. And just outside the palace grounds was stationed the entire First Branch, with which Brigan had arrived yesterday and would depart the day after tomorrow. She sensed minds more easily now than she had used to. She recognised a good many members of the First Branch, despite their distance.

She tried to push the feeling of them away. It was tiring, holding everything at once, and she couldn't decide where to rest her focus. She settled on a consciousness that was bothering her. She leaned forward and spoke low to Brigan.

'Behind you,' she said, 'a boy with very odd eyes is talking with some of the court children. Who is he?'

Brigan nodded. 'I know the boy you mean. He came with Cutter. You remember the animal trader, Cutter? I want nothing to do with the man, he's a monster smuggler and a brute – except that he happens to be selling a very fine stallion that almost has the markings of a river horse. I'd buy him in a breath if the money didn't go to Cutter. It's a bit tacky, you know, me buying a horse that's likely to have been stolen. I may buy him anyway; in which case Garan will have a conniption at the expense. I suppose he's right. I'm not in need of another horse. Though I wouldn't hesitate if he really were a river horse – do you know the dappled grey horses, Lady, that run wild at the source of the river? Splendid creatures. I've always wanted one, but they're no easy thing to catch.'

Horses were as distracting to the man as to his child. 'The boy,' Fire prompted dryly.

'Right. The boy's a strange one, and it isn't just that red eye. He was lurking around when I went to look at the stallion, and I tell you, Lady, he gave me a funny feeling.'

'What do you mean, a funny feeling?'

Brigan squinted at her in perplexity. 'I can't exactly say. There was something . . . disquieting . . . about his manner. The way he spoke. I did not like his voice.' He stopped, somewhat exasperated, and rubbed his hair so it stood on end. 'As I say it, I hear it makes no sense. There was nothing solid about him to fix on as troublesome. But still I told Hanna to stay away from him, and she said she already met him and didn't like him. She said he lies. What do you think of him?'

Fire applied herself to the question with concerted effort. His mind was unusual, unfamiliar, and she wasn't sure how to connect to it. She wasn't even sure how to comprehend the borders of it. She couldn't *see* it.

His mind gave her a very funny feeling indeed. And it was not a *good* funny feeling.

'I don't know,' she said. 'I don't know.' And a moment later, not quite knowing why: 'Buy the stallion, Lord Prince, if it will get them out of this court.'

Brigan left, presumably to do what Fire said; and Fire sat alone, puzzling over the boy. His right eye was grey and his left eye was red, which was strange enough in itself. His hair was blond like wheat, his skin light, and he had the appearance of being ten or eleven. Could he be some kind of Pikkian? He was sitting facing her, a rodent monster in his lap, a mouse with glimmering gold fur. He was tying a string around its neck. Fire knew somehow that the creature was not his pet.

He pulled the string, too tight. The mouse's legs began to jerk. *Stop it*, Fire thought furiously, aiming her message at the strange presence that was his mind.

He loosened the string immediately. The mouse lay in his lap, heaving with tiny breaths. Then the boy smiled at Fire, and stood up, and came to stand before her. 'It doesn't hurt him,' he said. 'It's only a choking game, for fun.'

His very words grated against her ears; grated, it seemed,

against her brain, so horribly, like raptor monsters screeching, that she had to resist the impulse to cover her ears. Yet when she recalled the timbre of his voice, the voice itself was neither unusual nor unpleasant.

She stared at him coolly, so he would not see her bewilderment. 'A choking game? All the fun of it is on your side, and it's a sick kind of fun.'

He smiled again. His lopsided, red-eyed smile was somehow distressing. 'Is it sick? To want to be in control?'

'Of a helpless, frightened creature? Let it go.'

'The others believed me when I said it didn't hurt him,' he said, 'but you know not to. Plus, you're awfully pretty. So I'll give you what you want.'

He bent to the ground and opened his hand. The monster mouse fled, a streak of gold, disappearing into an opening in the roots of a tree.

'You have interesting scars on your neck,' he said, straightening. 'What cut you?'

'It's none of your affair,' Fire said, shifting her headscarf so that it covered her scars, very much disliking his gaze.

'I'm glad I got to talk to you,' he said. 'I've wanted to for some time. You're even better than I hoped.' He turned around, and left the courtyard.

WHAT AN UNPLEASANT child.

It had never happened before, that Fire should not be able to form a conception of a consciousness. Even Brigan's mind, which she couldn't enter, offered the shape and feeling of its barricades to her perception. Even the foggy archer, the foggy guards; she couldn't explain their minds, but she could perceive them.

Reaching for this boy's mind was like walking through a collection of twisted mirrors facing other twisted mirrors, so that all was distorted and misleading, and befuddling to the senses, and nothing could be known or understood. She couldn't get a straight look at him, not even his outline.

And this was what she stewed over for some time after the boy left; and this stewing was why it took her so long to attend to the condition of the children he'd been talking to. The children in the courtyard who'd believed what he'd said. Their minds were blank, and bubbling with fog.

Fire could not fathom this fog. But she was certain she'd found its source.

By the time she realised she mustn't let him go, the sun was setting, the stallion was bought, and the boy was already gone from the court.

CHAPTER TWENTY

THAT SAME NIGHT brought information that distracted everyone from the matter of Cutter's boy.

It was late evening and Fire was in the stables when she sensed Archer returning from the city to the palace. It was not a thing she would have sensed so forcefully, not searching for it particularly; except that he was eager to talk to her, and open as an infant, and also slightly drunk.

Fire had only just begun to brush Small, who was standing with eyes closed from the bliss of it and drooling onto his stall door. And she wasn't anxious to see Archer if he was both eager and drunk. She sent him a message. *We'll talk when you're sober.*

Some hours later with her regular guard of six, Fire followed the maze from her rooms to Archer's. But then outside his door she was perplexed, for she sensed that her Mila, who was off-duty, was inside Archer's chamber.

Fire's thoughts groped for an explanation, any explanation other than the obvious. But Mila's mind was open, as even strong minds tended to be when they were experiencing what Mila was experiencing just now on the other side of this door; and Fire remembered how sweet and pretty her guard was, and how many opportunities Archer had had to notice her.

Fire stood staring at Archer's door, silent and shaking. She was quite certain he had never done anything to make her this angry before.

She turned on her heel and marched down the hallway. She found the stairs and marched up them, and up, and up, until she burst onto the roof, where she set to marching back and forth. It was cold and damp, and she had no coat, and it smelled like coming snow. Fire didn't notice, didn't care. Her baffled guard stood out of her way so she wouldn't trample them.

After some time the thing happened she'd been waiting for: Mila fell asleep. And none too soon, for it was late now, and Brigan was climbing wearily to the roofs. She mustn't meet Brigan tonight. She would not be able to stop herself from telling him everything, and Archer might deserve to have his laundry aired, but Mila did not.

She marched down by a stairway that Brigan was not taking up. She traced the maze again to Archer's rooms and stood outside his door. *Archer*, she thought to him. *Get out here, now.*

He emerged quickly, if barefoot and confused and a bit hastily thrown together; and Fire for the first time exercised her privilege of being alone with him, sending her guards to either end of the long corridor. She could not quite force herself to appear calm, and when she spoke, her voice was scathing. 'Must you prey on my guard?'

The puzzlement left his face and he spoke hotly. 'I'm not a predator, you know. Women come to me quite willingly. And why should you care what I do?'

'It hurts people. You're careless with people, Archer. Mila, why Mila? She's fifteen years old!'

'She's sleeping now, happy as a kitten in a patch of sun. You're stirring up trouble over nothing.'

Fire took a breath, and spoke low. 'And in a week's time, when you grow tired of her, Archer, because someone else has captured your fancy; when she becomes despondent or depressed, or pathetic, or furious, because you've snatched the thing away that makes her so happy – I suppose then she'll be stirring up trouble over nothing?'

'You talk as if she's in love with me.'

He was maddening; she would like to kick him. 'They always fall in love with you, Archer, always. Once they've known the warmth of you, they always fall in love with you, and you never do with them, and when you drop them it breaks their hearts.'

He bit the words off. 'A curious accusation, coming from you.'

She understood him, but she would not let him turn this into that. 'We're talking about my friends, Archer. I beg you – if you must have the entire palace in your bed, leave the women who are my friends out of it.'

'And I don't see why this should matter to you now, when it never did before.'

'I never had friends before!'

'You keep using that word,' he said bitterly. 'She's not your friend, she's your guard. Would your friend do what she's done, knowing your history with me?'

'She knows little about it, except that it is history. And you forget I'm in a position to know how she regards me.'

'But there must be plenty she hides from you – as she's been hiding her meetings with me all this time. A person may have many feelings about you that you don't know.'

She watched him, crestfallen. He was so physical in his arguments. He loomed and gestured, his face went dark or burned with light. His eyes blazed. And he was just as physical with his love and his joy, and this was why they all fell in love with him, for in a world that was dismal he was alive and passionate, and his attentions, while they lasted, were intoxicating.

And she hadn't missed the meaning in his words: this thing with Mila had been going on for some time. She turned away from him, held a hand up against him. She couldn't fight with the appeal of Lord Archer to a fifteen-year-old soldier girl from the impoverished southern mountains. And she couldn't quite forgive herself for not realising this might happen, for not paying closer attention in her mind to Archer's whereabouts and his company.

She dropped her hand, turned back, and spoke with weariness. 'Of course she has feelings about me I don't know. But whatever those feelings are, they don't negate the feeling she does show me, or the friendship in her behaviour that goes beyond the loyalty of a guard. You will not turn my anger away from you and onto her.'

Archer seemed to deflate then. He slumped against his door and stared at his bare toes in the manner of a man accepting that he has lost. 'I wish you would come home,' he said weakly; and for a panicked moment Fire thought he was going to cry.

But then he seemed to take hold of himself. He looked up at her quietly. 'So you have friends now. And a protective heart.'

She matched his quietness. 'I've always had a protective heart. Only now I have more people inside it. They've joined you there, Archer – never replaced you.'

He thought about that for a moment, staring at his feet. 'You needn't worry about Clara, anyway,' he said. 'She ended it almost the moment it began. I believe it was out of loyalty to you.'

Fire deliberately chose to think of this as good news. She would focus on it ending, whatever *it* had been, and ending by Clara's choice – rather than on the small matter of it having begun.

There was a short, sad pause. He said, 'I'll end things with Mila.'

'The sooner you do, the sooner it'll be behind her. And you've lost your questioning-room privileges with this thing, Archer. I'll not have you there plaguing her with your presence.'

He glanced up sharply then, and stood straight. 'A relieving change of topic. You remind me of the reason I wanted to talk to you. Do you know where I was today?'

Fire couldn't turn away from the subject so easily. She rubbed both temples. *I've no idea, and I'm exhausted, so whatever it is, have out with it quickly.*

'I was visiting the house of a retired captain who was an ally of my father's,' Archer said. 'By the name of Hart. A rich man, and a great friend to the crown. His young wife sent the invitation. Hart himself was not home.'

Fire rubbed her temples harder. 'You do Brocker's ally great honour,' she said dryly.

'Well, but listen to this. She's quite a drinker, Hart's wife, and do you know what we were drinking?'

'I've no energy for riddles.'

He was smiling now. 'A rare Pikkian wine made from the juice of frozen grapes,' he said. 'They've a whole case of it hidden at the back of their wine cellar. She didn't know where it came from – she only just discovered it while I was there. She seemed to find it odd, that her husband should've hidden it away, but I think it was a wise thing for a known ally of the king to do, don't you?'

NASH FELT CAPTAIN Hart's treachery very personally. For indeed, it took little more than a week of redirected questioning, and of watching Hart while seeming not to watch him, to learn that Lord Mydogg on occasion made a present of his favourite wine; and to learn that the messengers Hart sent south to deal with his speculations in the gold mines met with interesting and obscure fellows along the way, at inns, or over drinking games, who were then seen to strike out in a northerly direction that was the straightest path to Mydogg.

It was enough for Garan and Clara to decide Hart must be questioned. The matter on the table next was how.

ON A MOONLIT night in mid-November, Captain Hart set south along the cliff road that led to his second home – a pleasant, seaside cottage to which he retreated on occasion to find respite from his wife, who drank far more than was good for the health of her marriage. He rode in his very fine carriage and was attended, as usual, not only by his drivers and footmen but by a guard of ten men on horseback. It was how a wise man travelled the cliff road in the dark, so that he could defend himself from all but the largest company of bandits.

Unfortunately, the company of bandits that hid behind the rocks on that particular night was quite large indeed; and led by a man who, if shaved, and dressed at the height of fashion, and seen in daylight engaged in some highly correct activity, might bear a resemblance to the king's steward Welkley.

The bandits set upon the travelling party with great, bandit-like howls. While the majority of the ne'er-do-wells roughed up the members of Hart's entourage, went through their pockets, bound them with ropes, and collected Hart's very fine horses, Welkley and several others entered the carriage. Inside, an irate Captain Hart was waiting for them, brandishing sword and dagger. Welkley, with a highly athletic dodge to left and right that many at court would have found quite surprising, stabbed the captain in the leg with a dart tipped with sleeping poison.

One of Welkley's fellows, Toddin, was a man whose shape, size, and bearing were quite similar to Hart's. After a patch of speedy undressing and dressing inside the carriage, Toddin was wearing Hart's hat, coat, muffler, and yellow monster skin-boots, whereas Hart was wearing much less than he had been before, and lying insensible in a pile of Toddin's clothing. Toddin now grabbed Hart's sword and rolled with Welkley out of the carriage. Cursing and grunting, they set to sword fighting very near the cliff, in full view of Hart's bound servants, who watched with horror as the man who appeared to be Hart fell to the ground, clutching his side. A trio of bandits picked him up and hurled him into the sea.

The company of bandits now fled, with their plunder of miscellaneous coinage, fourteen horses, one carriage, and one captain inside the carriage sleeping like the dead. Closer to the city Hart was slipped into a sack and passed to a delivery man who would bring him into the palace with the night's grain. The rest of the booty was rushed away, to be sold on the black market. And finally the bandits returned to their homes, transformed themselves into milkmen, storekeepers, farmers, gentlemen; and threw themselves down for a short night's sleep.

In the morning Hart's men were found by the road, bound and shivering, much ashamed of the story they had to tell. When the news reached the palace, Nash sent a convoy to investigate the incident. Welkley arranged a bouquet of flowers to be sent to Hart's widow.

And everyone was relieved that afternoon, when word finally came from Toddin's wife that Toddin was in good health. He was a phenomenal ocean swimmer with a great tolerance for cold, but the night had clouded over, and the boat sent to pick him up had taken a long time to find him. Naturally, everyone had worried.

WHEN THEY FIRST dragged Captain Hart before Fire, his mind was a closed box and his eyes were screwed shut. For days Fire could get nowhere with him. 'I suppose I shouldn't be surprised that an old friend and colleague of Lord Brocker's should be so strong,' she said to Musa, Mila, and Neel in the questioning room, after yet another session during which Captain Hart hadn't looked at her once.

'Indeed, Lady,' Musa said. 'A man who accomplished all that Commander Brocker accomplished in his time would have chosen strong captains.'

Fire had been thinking more of what Brocker had endured personally than what he had accomplished militarily – King Nax's mad punishment for Brocker's mysterious crime. Fire watched her three guards absently as they brought out a quick meal of bread and cheese. Mila handed Fire a plate, avoiding her eyes.

This was Mila's way now. In the last few weeks, since Archer had ended things, she'd shrunk somehow – gone silent and contrite around her lady. Fire, in turn, had been trying to be extra kind, careful not to subject Mila to Archer's presence any more than was necessary. Not a word had passed between the two women on the subject, but both of them knew that the other knew.

Ravenous, Fire tore off a piece of bread and bit into it; and noticed Mila sitting mutely, staring at her own food but not eating it. I could flay Archer, Fire thought. Sighing, she pushed her attention back to the matter of Captain Hart.

He was a man who had achieved much wealth after retiring from the army, gradually accustoming himself to comfort. Might comfort soften him now?

Over the next couple of days, Fire arranged for Hart's cell in the dungeons to be cleaned and improved. He was given fine bedding and carpets, and books, and lighting, and good food and wine, and warm water to wash whenever he asked for it; and rat traps, which were perhaps the greatest luxury of all. One day with her hair swirling around her shoulders, and wearing a dress perhaps a bit more low-cut than was her usual style, she wandered down to his underground lair to visit.

When her guard opened the door for her, he looked up from his book to see who was there. His face slackened. 'I know what you're doing,' he said. And perhaps he did. But it wasn't enough to stop him staring, and Fire knew she'd found her way in.

She imagined a man in prison might be lonely, especially if he had a pretty wife at home who preferred wine and young men to her husband. She sat next to him on his bed during her visits. She ate whatever food he offered her, and accepted cushions for her back. Her nearness loosened him, and a battle began that was far from easy. At his weakest, Hart was still strong.

CLARA, GARAN, AND Nash soaked up what Fire learned like the sand of Cellar Harbour during a rainstorm.

'I still can't get him to say anything useful about Mydogg,' Fire said. 'But truly, we're in luck, for he happens to know a great deal about Gentian, and he's less unwilling to spill Gentian's secrets.'

'He's Mydogg's ally,' Clara said. 'Why should we trust what he thinks he knows about Gentian? Couldn't Gentian be sending out false messengers for Mydogg to catch, just as he does with us?'

'He could,' Fire said, 'but I can't quite explain it – the certainty with which Hart speaks. The confidence in his assertions. He knows the tricks Mydogg and Gentian have been playing on us. He's quite positive his knowledge of Gentian is not of that ilk. He won't tell me his sources, but I'm inclined to believe his information.'

'All right,' Clara said. 'Tell us what you've learned, and we'll use whatever means we can to confirm it.'

'He says Gentian and his son, Gunner, are coming north to attend the palace gala that happens in January,' Fire said.

'That's nervy,' Clara said. 'I'm impressed.'

Garan snorted. 'Now that we know about his indigestion, we can torture him with cake.'

'Gentian will pretend to apologise to the court for his rebel activities,' Fire said. 'He'll talk of renewed friendship with the crown. But in the meantime his army will move north-east from his estate and hide in the tunnels of the Great Greys near Fort Flood. Sometime in the days after the gala, Gentian intends to assassinate both Nash and Brigan. Then he'll ride like blazes to the location of his army, and attack Fort Flood.'

The twins' eyes were wide. 'Not nervy after all,' Garan said. 'Stupid. What kind of commander starts a war in the middle of winter?'

'The kind that's trying to catch his enemy by surprise,' Clara said.

'In addition to which,' Garan continued, 'he should send someone anonymous and expendable to do his assassinating. What'll happen to his clever plan when he gets himself killed?'

'Well,' Clara said, 'it's no news Gentian's stupid. And thank the Dells for Brigan's foresight. The Second is already at Fort Flood, and he's taking the First quite near there as we speak.'

'What of the Third and the Fourth?' Fire asked.

'They're in the north,' Clara said, 'patrolling, but in readiness to fly wherever they're needed. You must tell us where they're needed.'

'I've no idea,' Fire said. 'I cannot get him to tell me Mydogg's plans. He says Mydogg intends to do nothing – sit back while Gentian and the king reduce each other's numbers – but I know he's lying. He also says Mydogg's sending his sister, Murgda, south to the gala, which is true; but he won't tell me why.'

'Lady Murgda to the gala as well!' Clara exclaimed. 'What's got into everyone?'

'What else?' Garan said. 'You must give us more.'

'I've nothing more,' Fire said. 'I've told you everything. Apparently Gentian's plans have been in place for some time.'

Nash was clutching his forehead. 'This is very grim. Gentian has a force of some ten thousand, supposedly, and we've ten thousand at Fort Flood to meet him. But in the north we've ten thousand scattered far and wide—'

'Fifteen thousand,' Fire said. 'We can call on the auxiliaries.'

'All right then, we've fifteen thousand scattered far and wide, and Mydogg has what? Do we even know? Twenty thousand? Twenty-one thousand? To attack wherever takes his fancy – my mother's fortress, or Fort Middle, Fort Flood if he wishes, the city itself – with days, possibly weeks, before our troops can organise to meet him.'

'He can't hide twenty thousand soldiers,' Clara said, 'not if we're looking for them. Even in the Little Greys, he can't hide them, and he could never get all the way to the city without being seen.'

'I need Brigan,' Nash said. 'I want Brigan here, now.'

'He'll come when he can, Nash,' Garan said, 'and we're keeping him informed.'

Fire found herself stretching out with the feelers of her mind to soothe a king who was frightened. Nash perceived what she was doing. He reached for her hand. With thanks, and with something else he couldn't help, he kissed her fingers.

CHAPTER TWENTY-ONE

IT WAS A curious matter of Dellian politics, the yearly gala at court to which everyone of any significance was invited. The seven courtyards were converted to ballrooms, and loyalists and traitors came together to dance, to sip from goblets of wine while pretending to be friends. Almost everyone capable of travel attended, though Mydogg and Gentian generally didn't dare, a pretense of friendship on their parts being a mite too incredible; and for a week or so the palace was bursting with the servants and guards and pets, and the endless requirements of guests. The stables were too crowded, and the horses fidgety.

Brocker had explained to Fire once that the gala was always held in January, to celebrate the lengthening of days. She learned now that December was a month of preparation. On every level of the palace, Fire saw workmen engaged in repairs. Window-washers hung from the courtyard ceilings and wall-washers from the balconies, polishing glass and stone.

Garan, Clara, Nash, and Fire were also preparing. If Gentian intended to kill Nash and Brigan in the days after the gala and then ride to Fort Flood to start a war, then Gentian and Gunner must be killed the day *of* the gala – and Lady Murgda might as well be disposed of, too, as long as she was around. Then Brigan must fly to Fort Flood and start the war himself, surprising Gentian's armies in their tunnels and caves.

'Tunnel fighting,' Garan said, 'and in January. I don't envy them.'

'What'll we do about the north?' Nash kept asking.

'Maybe we can learn something about Mydogg's plan from

Lady Murgda at the gala,' Garan said, 'before we kill her.'

'And how exactly are we going to pull off these assassinations?' Nash said, pacing, wild-eyed. 'They'll be constantly guarded, they'll let no one near them, and we can't start a war in the court. I can't think of a worse time or place to have to murder three people in secret!'

'Sit down, brother,' Clara said. 'Calm down. We've time yet to sort it out. We'll think of something.'

Brigan PROMISED TO return to court by the end of December. He wrote, from wherever he was, that he had sent a force north to collect Lord Brocker and bring him south, for apparently the old commander had offered his assistance to the younger in the event of actual war. Fire was stunned. She had never known Brocker to travel further than the neighbouring town.

At night with her guard on the roof, and missing Brigan's company, she stared at the city before her, trying to comprehend what was coming.

In the north, troops of the king's soldiers searched the mountains and tunnels and all of Mydogg's usual stomping grounds for his army. Spies searched Pikkia and the south and west. All to no avail: either Mydogg was hiding his men very well or he'd vanished them with magic. Brigan sent reserves to fortify Roen's fortress, Fort Middle, and the southern gold mines. The number of soldiers stationed in the city rose noticeably.

For her part, Fire had taken to grilling Captain Hart about the animal trader Cutter and his young fog maker with mismatched eyes. But Hart claimed to know nothing of it, and finally Fire had to believe him. After all, the boy didn't seem to fit in to the war plans, and neither did the poacher or stranger in her woods up north, nor the archer who'd wanted a look at her view. As to where they did fit in, Fire was alone in her speculations.

'I'm sorry, Fire,' Clara said flatly. 'I'm sure it's as creepy as you say, but I've no time for it if it's nothing to do with the war or the gala. We'll focus on it afterwards.'

The only person who cared was Archer, who was little help, for true to his nature, he only assumed that at the base of the matter was someone's intention to steal Fire from him.

As it turned out, Clara's preoccupation did extend beyond the war and the gala, on one point. She was pregnant.

The princess brought Fire to Cellar Harbour to tell her, so that the roar of the falls would keep everyone, even Fire's guard, from overhearing the conversation. Clara was dry-eyed and straight about it. And once Fire had adjusted to the news, she found that she was not particularly surprised.

'I was careless,' Clara said. 'I've never liked those herbs; they nauseate me. And I've never fallen pregnant before. I suppose I convinced myself I couldn't. And now I'm paying for my stupidity, for everything nauseates me.'

She hadn't seemed nauseated to Fire; in recent weeks she'd seemed nothing but calm and well. She was a fine actress, Fire knew this, and probably the best woman for this accident to befall. She was not lacking in money or support, and she would do her work up to the very day the child was born, and start again right after, and she would be a strong mother, and practical.

'Archer is the father,' Clara said.

Fire nodded. She'd assumed this. 'He'll be generous once you tell him. I know he will.'

'I don't care about that. What I care about is your feeling. Whether I've hurt you, by jumping into his bed, and then being stupid enough for this to happen.'

Fire was startled by this, and touched. 'You've certainly not hurt me,' she said firmly. 'I have no hold on Archer, and no jealousy where he's concerned. You mustn't worry on my account.'

Clara's eyebrows rose. 'You're very strange.'

Fire shrugged. 'Archer has always had enough jealousy of his own to turn me off to the feeling of it.'

Clara looked into Fire's face, into her eyes, and Fire looked back, quiet and matter-of-fact, determined that Clara should see that she meant it. Finally Clara nodded. 'This is a great relief to me. Please don't tell my brothers,' she added, sounding anxious for the first time. 'They'll all rise up determined to hack him to pieces, and I'll be furious with them. We've too much else to be thinking about. This couldn't have been more ill-timed.' She paused for a moment, then spoke plainly. 'And besides, I don't want any harm to come to him. Perhaps he didn't give me everything I hoped he would. But I can't help thinking that what he did give me is rather marvellous.'

IT WAS NOT the type of gift everyone could welcome in such a way.

Fire's guard Margo slept in Fire's bedchamber, and Musa and Mila did too on alternating nights. One dawn Fire woke to the feeling of someone out of place, and perceived that Mila was vomiting in the bathing room.

Fire rushed to the girl and held her pale hair away from her face. She rubbed Mila's back and shoulders, and as she came fully awake, began to understand what she was seeing.

'Oh, Lady,' Mila said, beginning to cry. 'Oh, Lady. What you must think of me.'

Fire was, indeed, thinking a great many hurried thoughts, and her heart was bursting with compassion. She put an arm around Mila. 'I have nothing but sympathy for you. I'm going to help you however I can.'

Mila's tears turned to sobs and she wrapped both arms around Fire. She held on to Fire's hair, speaking raggedly. 'I ran out of the herbs.'

Fire was horrified at this. 'You could have asked me for them, or any of the healers.'

'I could never, Lady. I was too ashamed.'

'You could have asked Archer!'

'He is a lord. How could I trouble him?' She was crying so hard she was choking. 'Oh, Lady. I've ruined my life.'

And now Fire was furious over Archer's lack of trouble, for most certainly, all of this had happened at little inconvenience to him. She held the girl tight and rubbed her back and made hushing noises to soothe her. It seemed to comfort Mila to hold on to her hair.

'There's something I want you to know,' Fire said, 'and you must remember it now more than ever.'

'Yes, Lady?'

'You may always ask me for anything.'

IT WAS IN the coming days that Fire began to feel the lie in her words to Clara. It was true she was not jealous of Clara or Mila for anything they'd done with Archer. But she was not immune to the feeling of jealousy. Though she was brainstorming, plotting, planning with the royal siblings, her outward self focused on the details of the coming gala and the war, inside, in her moments of quiet, Fire was grievously distracted.

She imagined what it would be like if her own body were a garden of brown soil sheltering a seed. How she would warm that seed if it were hers, and feed it, and how ferociously she would protect it; how ferociously she would love that dot, even after it left her body, and grew away from her, and chose the way it would wield an enormous power.

When she became nauseated and fatigued, her breasts swollen and sore, she even began to think of herself as pregnant, even though she knew it was impossible. The pain was a joy to her. And then, of course, her bleeding came, and tore her pretending apart, and she knew it had only been the usual symptoms of her pre-bleeding time. And she found herself crying as bitterly to know she wasn't pregnant as Mila had cried to know she was.

And her grief was frightening, because it had its own will. Her grief filled her mind with comforting, terrible ideas.

In the middle of December planning, Fire made a choice. She hoped she chose right.

On the very last day of December, which happened to be Hanna's sixth birthday, Hanna appeared at Fire's door, tattered and crying. Her mouth bled, and bleeding knees peeked through holes in both trouser legs.

Fire sent for a healer. When it was determined that Hanna was not crying over any injury to her body, Fire sent the healer away, knelt before the girl, and hugged her. She deciphered Hanna's feelings and gasps as best she could. Finally she came to understand what had happened. The others had taunted Hanna about her father, because he was always away. They'd told Hanna that Brigan was forever leaving because he wanted to get away from her. Then they'd told her he wasn't coming back this time. That was when she'd started hitting them.

In her gentlest voice and with her arms around the girl, Fire told Hanna over and over that Brigan loved her; that he hated to leave her; that the first thing he always did on his return was go find her; that indeed, she was his favourite topic of conversation, and his greatest happiness. 'You wouldn't lie to me,' Hanna said to Fire, her sobs coming quiet. Which was true; and which was the reason Fire said nothing on the point of Brigan coming home this time. It seemed to her that to assure anyone Brigan was ever coming home was always to risk a lie. He'd been gone now nearly two months, and in the last week, no one had heard a word from him.

Fire gave Hanna a bath and dressed her in one of her own shirts that made a long-sleeved dress that Hanna found quite funny. She fed Hanna dinner, and then, still sniffling, the girl fell asleep in Fire's bed. Fire sent word with one of her guards so that no one would be alarmed.

When Brigan's consciousness appeared suddenly in her range, she took a moment to calm her own shaking relief. Then she sent him a message in his mind. He came to her rooms immediately, unshaven and smelling of the cold, and Fire had to stop herself from touching him. When she told him what the children had told Hanna, his face closed and he seemed very tired. He sat on the bed, touched Hanna's hair, leaned down to kiss her forehead. Hanna woke up. She said, 'You're cold, Papa,' crawled into his arms, and fell asleep again.

Brigan rearranged Hanna in his lap then, and looked over her head at Fire. And Fire was so struck by how much she liked having this grey-eyed prince on her bed with his child that she sat down, hard. Luckily there was a chair behind her.

'Welkley tells me you've not been out of your rooms much this week, Lady,' Brigan said. 'I hope you're not unwell.'

'I was quite ill,' Fire croaked, and then bit her tongue, because she hadn't meant to tell him.

His worry was instant. He opened the feeling of it to her.

'No,' she said. 'Don't fret, it was a small thing. I'm recovered.' Which was a lie, for her body was sore still and her heart raw as Hanna's knees. But it was what she hoped would be the truth, eventually.

He studied her, unconvinced. 'I suppose if that's what you say, I'll have to believe you. But do you have the care you need?'

'Yes, of course. I beg you to forget it.'

He lowered his face to Hanna's hair. 'I'd offer you birthday cake,' he said. 'But it looks like we'll have to wait until tomorrow.'

★

THAT NIGHT THE stars were cold and brittle, and the full moon seemed very far away. Fire bundled herself up so that she was twice as wide around as usual.

On the roof she found Brigan standing contentedly hatless in a draft. She blew warm air into her mittened hands. 'Are you immune to winter, then, Lord Prince?'

He led her to a place protected from the wind by a broad chimney. He encouraged her to lean back against the chimney. When she did, she was surprised, for it was lovely and warm, like leaning against Small. Her guard faded into the background. The tinkling sound of the drawbridge bells whispered over the rumble of the falls. She closed her eyes.

'Lady Fire,' Brigan's voice said. 'Musa told me about Mila. Would you care to tell me about my sister?'

Fire's eyes flashed open. There he was at the railing, his eyes on the city, his breath shooting out like steam. 'Hmm,' she said, too astonished to build a proper defence. 'And what would you like to know about her?'

'Whether or not she's pregnant, of course.'

'Why should she be pregnant?'

He turned then to look at her, and their eyes met. Fire had a feeling her unreadable face was not as successfully unreadable as his. 'Because outside of her work,' he said dryly, 'she's overly fond of a gamble. And she's thinner, and tonight she ate little, and turned green at the sight of the carrot cake, which I assure you is something I've never seen her do once in my life. Either she's pregnant or she's dying.' His eyes turned back to the city and his voice went smooth. 'And don't tell me the father of these babies, because then I'd be tempted to harm him, and that would be inconvenient, don't you think, what with Brocker expected, and all these people about who adore him?'

If he'd deciphered this much, then there was no point in pretense. She said mildly, 'Nor would it set an example for Hanna.'

'Humph.' He leaned his mouth on his fist. His breath steamed out in every direction. 'I take it they don't know about each other yet? And I take it I'm to keep all of it secret. Is Mila as unhappy as she looks?'

'Mila is devastated,' Fire said softly.

'I could kill him for that.'

'I believe she's too angry, or too despairing, to think straight. She won't take his money. So I'm taking it myself, and I'll hold it for her, and hope she changes her mind.'

'She may keep her job if she wants it; I won't force her out of it. We'll work something out.' He shot her a wry glance. 'Don't tell Garan.' And then, grimly: 'Ah, Lady. It's a mean time to be welcoming babies to the world.'

Babies, Fire thought to herself. Babies to the world. She sent it out into the air: *Welcome to you, babies*. And found, with great frustration, that she was crying. It seemed a symptom of her friends' pregnancies that Fire should not be able to stop crying.

Brigan was transformed from hard to soft, his hands scrambling through pockets for a handkerchief that wasn't there. He came to her. 'Lady, what is it? Please tell me.'

'I've missed you,' she blubbered, 'these past two months.'

He took her hands. 'Please tell me what's wrong.'

And then, because he was holding her hands, she told him all of it, quite simply: how desperately she wanted children, and why she'd decided she mustn't have them, and how out of fear of changing her mind, she'd arranged quietly, with Clara and Musa's help, to take the medicines that would make it forever impossible. And she hadn't recovered, not nearly, for her heart was small and shivering, and it seemed that she couldn't stop crying.

He listened, quietly, growing more and more amazed; and when she finished he was silent for some time. He considered her mittens with something of a helpless expression. He said, 'I was insufferable to you the night we met. I've never forgiven myself.'

It was the last thing Fire had expected him to say. She looked into his eyes, which were pale as the moon.

'I'm so sorry for your sadness,' he said. 'I don't know what to tell you. You must live where many people are having babies, and adopt them all. We must keep Archer around – he's quite a useful chap, really, isn't he?'

At that she smiled, almost laughed. 'You've made me feel better. I thank you.'

He gave her her hands back then, carefully, as if he were afraid they might drop to the roof and shatter. He smiled at her softly.

'You never used to look at me straight, but now you do,' she said, because she remembered it, and was curious.

He shrugged. 'You weren't real to me then.'

She wrinkled her forehead. 'What does that mean?'

'Well, you used to overwhelm me. But now I've got used to you.'

She blinked, surprised into silence by her own foolish pleasure at his words; and then laughed at herself for being pleased with the suggestion that she was ordinary.

CHAPTER TWENTY-TWO

THE NEXT MORNING Fire walked to Nash's office with Musa, Mila, and Neel to meet the royal siblings and Archer.

The gala was only weeks away and the extent of Fire's involvement in the assassination plan was a matter of ongoing debate. To Fire's mind it was simple. She should be the assassin in all three cases because she was far more likely than anyone else to be able to lure each victim to a solitary and unguarded place, and she might also manage to learn a great deal from them before killing them.

But when she stated her case Garan argued that Fire was no sword fighter, and if any of the three proved to be strong-minded she would end up on someone's blade. And Clara did not want the assassin to be a person with no killing experience. 'You'll hesitate,' Clara said today. 'When you see what it really means to stick a knife in someone's chest, you won't be able to do it.'

Fire knew herself to be more experienced than anyone in this room save Archer realised. 'It's true I won't *want* to do it,' she responded calmly, 'but when I have to, I will do it.'

Archer was fuming darkly in a corner. Fire ignored him, for she knew the futility of appealing to him – especially these days, when his attitude toward her ranged from high dudgeon to shame, because her sympathies and her time were tied up with Mila, and he sensed it, and resented it, and knew it was his own fault.

'We can't send a novice to kill three of our most fearsome enemies,' Clara said again.

For the first time since the topic had been broached, Brigan was present in person to convey his opinion. He leaned a shoulder against the wall, arms crossed. 'But it's obvious she must be involved,' he said. 'I don't think Gentian'll give her much resistance, and Gunner's clever, but ultimately he's led by his father. Murgda may prove difficult, but we're desperate to learn what she knows – where Mydogg's hiding his army, in particular – and Lady Fire is the person most qualified for that job. And,' he said, raising his eyebrows to stop Clara's objections, 'the lady knows what she's capable of. If she says she'll go through with it, she will.'

Archer wheeled on Brigan then, snarling, for his mood had found what it was looking for: an outlet that was not Fire. 'Shut up, Archer,' Clara said blandly, cutting him off before he even began.

'It's too dangerous,' Nash said from his desk, where he sat gazing worriedly at Fire. 'You're the swordsman, Brigan. You should do it.'

Brigan nodded. 'All right, well, what if the lady and I did it together? She to get them to a private place and question them, and I to kill them, and protect her.'

'Except that I'll find it much harder to trick them into trusting me if you're there,' Fire said.

'What if I hid?'

Archer had been approaching Brigan slowly from across the room, and now he stood before the prince, barely seeming to breathe. 'You've no compunctions whatsoever about putting her in danger,' he said. 'She's a tool to you and you're heartless as a rock.'

Fire's temper flared. 'Don't you call him heartless, Archer. He's the only person here who believes me.'

'Oh, I believe you can do it,' Archer said, his voice filling the corners of the room like a hiss. 'A woman who can stage the suicide of her own father can certainly kill a few Dellians she's never met.'

IT WAS AS if time slowed down, and everyone else in the room disappeared. There was only Fire, and Archer before her. Fire gaped at Archer, disbelieving, and then understanding, like coldness that starts in your extremities and seeps to your core, that he truly had just said aloud the words she'd thought she'd heard.

And Archer gaped back, just as stunned. He slumped, blinking back tears. 'Forgive me, Fire. I wish it unsaid.'

But she thought it through in slow time, and understood that it couldn't be unsaid. And it was less that he'd exposed the truth, and more the way he'd exposed it. He'd accused her, he who knew all that she felt. He'd taunted her with her own shame.

'I'm not the only one who's changed,' she whispered, staring at him. 'You've changed too. You've never been cruel to me before.'

She turned, still with that sense that time had slowed. She glided out of the room.

TIME CAUGHT UP with Fire in the frozen gardens of the green house, where it occurred to her after a single shivering minute that she had a compulsive inability to remember her coat. Musa, Mila, and Neel stood quietly around her.

She sat on a bench under the big tree, great round tears seeping down her cheeks and plopping into her lap. She took the handkerchief Neel offered. She looked into the faces of her guard, one after the other. She was searching their eyes to see if behind the quiet of their minds they were horrified, now that they knew.

Each of them looked calmly back. She saw that they were not horrified. They met her eyes with respect.

It struck her that she was very lucky in her life's people, that they should not mind the company of a monster so unnatural that she'd murdered her only family.

A thick, wet snow began to fall, and finally the side door of the green house opened. Bundled in a cloak, Brigan's housekeeper, Tess, marched out to her. 'I suppose you intend to freeze to death under my nose,' the woman snapped. 'What's wrong with you?'

Fire looked up without much interest. Tess had soft green eyes, deep as two pools of water, and angry. 'I murdered my father,' Fire said, 'and pretended it was a suicide.'

Clearly, Tess was startled. She crossed her arms and made indignant noises, determined, it seemed, to disapprove. And then all at once she softened, like a clump of snow in a thaw that collapses from a roof, and shook her head, bewildered. 'That does change things. I suppose the young prince'll be telling me, "I told you so". Well, look at you, child – soaked right through. Pretty as a sunset, but no brain in your head. You didn't get that from your mother. You may as well come inside.'

Fire was mildly dumbfounded. The little woman pulled her under the cloak and pushed her into the house.

THE QUEEN'S HOUSE – for Fire reminded herself that this was Roen's house, not Brigan's – seemed a good place to soothe an unhappy soul. The rooms were small and cozy, painted soft greens and blues and full of soft furniture, the fireplaces huge, the January fires in them roaring. It was obvious a child lived here, for her school papers and balls and mittens and playthings, and Blotchy's nondescript chewed-up belongings, had found their way into every corner. It was less obvious Brigan lived here, though there were clues for the discerning observer. The blanket Tess wrapped Fire in looked suspiciously like a saddle blanket.

Tess sat Fire on a sofa before the fireplace, and her guard in armchairs around their lady. She gave all of them cups of hot wine. She sat with them, folding a pile of very small shirts.

Fire shared the sofa with two monster kittens she'd never seen before. One was crimson and the other copper with crimson markings, and they were sleeping tangled together, so that it was hard to tell which head or tail belonged to which. They reminded Fire of her hair, which was bound now under a scarf that was clammy and cold. She pulled the scarf free and spread it beside her to dry. Her hair slid down, a blaze of light and colour. One of the kittens raised its head at the brightness, and yawned.

She wrapped her hands around her warm cup and blinked wearily into its steam; and found, once she'd started talking, that confession was a comfort to her small and ragged heart. 'I killed Cansrel to stop him from killing Brigan. And to stop Brigan from killing Cansrel, because that would have damaged his chance for any alliance with Cansrel's friends. And, oh, for other reasons. I doubt I need to explain to any of you why it was best for him to die.'

Tess stopped her work, her hands resting on the pile in her lap, and watched Fire closely. Her lips moved as Fire talked, as if she were testing the words in her own mouth.

'I tricked him into thinking his leopard monster was a baby,' Fire said. 'His own human monster baby. I stood outside the fence and watched him open the door of the cage, cooing to it, as if it were helpless, and harmless. The leopard was hungry. He always kept them hungry. It— it happened very fast.'

Fire went silent for a moment, struggling against the picture that haunted her dreams. She spoke with her eyes closed. 'Once I was sure he was dead, I shot the cat. Then I shot the rest of his monsters, because I hated them, I'd always hated them, and I couldn't stand them screaming for his blood. And then I called the servants, and told them he'd killed himself and I hadn't been able to stop him. I entered their minds and made full sure they believed me, which wasn't difficult. He'd been unhappy since Nax's death, and they all knew he was capable of mad things.'

The rest of the story, she kept to herself. Archer had come and found her kneeling in Cansrel's blood, staring at Cansrel, tearless. When he'd tried to pull her away she'd fought against him desperately, screamed at him to leave her alone. For several days she'd been savage to Archer, and Brocker, too, vicious, out of her mind and her body; and they'd stayed with her and taken care of her until she'd come back into herself. Then had followed weeks of listlessness and tears. They'd stayed with her through that as well.

She sat numbly on the sofa. She wanted Archer's company, suddenly, so that she could forgive him for telling the truth. It was time other people knew. It was time everyone knew what she was, and what she was capable of.

She didn't notice herself nodding off to sleep, even when Musa jumped forward to stop her drink from spilling.

SHE WOKE HOURS later to find herself stretched out on the sofa, covered in blankets, kittens sleeping in the tangle of her hair. Tess was absent, but Musa, Mila, and Neel had not moved from their seats.

Archer stood before the fireplace, his back to her.

Fire half sat up and tugged her hair out from under the kittens. 'Mila,' she said. 'You don't have to stay if you don't want to.'

Mila's voice was stubborn. 'I want to stay and guard you, Lady.'

'Very well,' Fire said, studying Archer, who'd swung around at the sound of her voice. His left cheekbone was bruised purple, which alarmed her at first, and then struck her as intensely interesting.

'Who hit you?' she asked.

'Clara.'

'Clara!'

'She whaled me one in return for upsetting you. Well,' he added, his voice dropping low. 'At least, that was the main reason. I suppose Clara has several to choose from.' He glanced at Mila, who'd suddenly taken on the look of a boxer who'd been punched in the stomach one too many times. 'This is awkward.'

By your own doing, Fire thought to him furiously, *and your careless words only make it worse. They don't know about each other yet, and it's not yours to reveal their secrets.*

'Fire,' he said, his eyes low and dismal. 'It's been some time since I did anyone any good. When my father arrives I won't be able to look him in the face. I'm dying to do something worthwhile, something I needn't be ashamed of, but I don't seem to be capable of it while you're within my view, and not needing me anymore, and in love with someone else.'

'Oh, Archer,' she said, and then stopped, choked up with how frustrating he was. And how funny it seemed, and sad, that he should accuse her of love, and for once in his life be right.

'I'm going west,' he said, 'to Cutter.'

'What?' she cried, dismayed. 'Now? By yourself?'

'No one's paying any attention to that boy and that archer, and I know it's a mistake. The boy's not to be trifled with, and maybe you've forgotten, but twenty-some years ago that archer was in gaol for rape.'

And now Fire was near crying again. 'Archer, I don't think you should. Wait until after the gala and let me come with you.'

'I believe it's you they're after.'

'Please, Archer. Don't go.'

'I must,' he said, suddenly, explosively. He turned away from her, held up a hand against her. 'Look at you,' he said, tears thick in his voice. 'I can't even bear to look at you. I must do something, don't you see? I must get away. They're going to let you do it, you know, you and Brigan together, the grand assassination team. Here,' he said, yanking a folded paper from his coat pocket and pitching it savagely onto the sofa beside her.

'What's that?' Fire asked, bewildered.

'A letter from *him*,' Archer practically yelled. 'He was at the desk just before you woke, writing it. He told me if I didn't give it to you he'd break both my arms.'

Tess appeared suddenly in the doorway and jabbed a finger at Archer. 'Young man,' she barked, 'there's a child that lives in this house, and you've got no cause to yell the roof off.' She turned and stomped away. Archer stared after her in amazement. Then he spun to the fireplace and leaned against the mantle, head in hands.

'Archer,' Fire pleaded. 'If you must do this, take as many soldiers as you can. Ask Brigan for a convoy.'

He didn't answer. She wasn't even sure he'd heard. He turned to face her and said, 'Goodbye, Fire.' He stalked out of the room, abandoning her to her panic.

Her thoughts clamoured after him desperately. *Archer! Keep a strong mind. Go safely.*

I love you.

Brigan's letter was short.

Lady:

I have a confession. I knew that you killed Cansrel. Lord Brocker told me the day I came to your house to escort you here. You must forgive him for betraying the confidence. He told me so that I might understand what you were, and treat you accordingly. In other words, he told me in order to protect you, from me.

You asked me once why I trust you. This is not the entire

reason, but it's a part. I believe you have shouldered a great deal of pain for the sake of other people. I believe you're as strong and as brave as anyone I've met or heard of. And wise and generous in the use of your power.

I must ride suddenly to Fort Flood, but will return in time for the gala. I agree you must be involved in our plan – though Archer is wrong if he thinks it pleases me. My siblings will tell you our thoughts. My soldiers are waiting and this is hastily written, but meant sincerely.

  Yours,
  Brigan.

P.S. Do not leave this house until Tess has told you the truth, and forgive me for keeping it from you. I made a promise to her, and have been chafing under it ever since.

Fire breathed shakily as she walked to the kitchen, where she sensed Tess to be. The old woman raised green eyes from the work of her hands.

'What does Prince Brigan mean,' Fire said, frightened of the question, 'when he says you must tell me the truth?'

Tess put down the dough she was kneading and wiped her palms on her apron. 'What an upside-down day this is,' she said. 'I never saw this coming. And now that we're here, you're such a sight I'm intimidated.' She shrugged, quite at a loss. 'My daughter Jessa was your mother, child,' she said. 'I'm your grandmother. Would you care to stay for dinner?'

CHAPTER TWENTY-THREE

FIRE GLIDED THROUGH the following days in a state of wonderment. To learn that she had a grandmother was staggering enough. But to sense, from their first hesitant dinner together, that her grandmother was curious to know her, and open to her company? This was almost too much for one young human monster who'd experienced so little joy to bear.

She ate dinner every night in the kitchen of the green house with Tess and Hanna. Hanna's stream of chatter filled the spaces in the conversation between grandmother and granddaughter, and soothed, somehow, their awkwardness as they tried to find the way to relate to each other.

It helped that Tess was straightforward and honest, and that Fire could sense the sincerity of every mixed-up thing she said. 'I'm mostly unflappable,' Tess said over their first dinner of dumplings and raptor monster stew. 'But you've flapped me, monster Lady. I told myself all these years you were Cansrel's daughter, and not truly Jessa's. A monster, not a girl, that we were better off without. I tried to tell Jessa, too, though she would never listen, and she was right. Plain as day I can see her in your face.'

'Where?' Hanna demanded. 'What parts of her face?'

'You have Jessa's forehead,' Tess said, brandishing a spoon at Fire helplessly. 'And the same expression in your eyes, and her lovely, warm skin. You take after her eye and hair colouring, though yours is a hundred times what hers was, of course. The young prince told me he trusted you,' she finished weakly. 'But I couldn't believe him. I thought he was ensnared.

I thought you'd marry the king, or worse, him, and it would begin all over.'

'It's all right,' Fire said softly, immune to grudges, because she was newly fallen in love with having a grandmother.

She wished she could thank Brigan, but he was still away from court and unlikely to return before the gala. She wished more than anything that she could tell Archer. Whatever else he might feel, he would share her joy in this – he would laugh in astonishment at the news. But Archer was bumbling around somewhere west with the smallest of guards – according to Clara, he'd only taken four men – getting into who knew what kind of trouble. Fire determined to make a list of all the delights and the confusions of having a grandmother, to tell him when he returned.

She was not the only person worried about Archer. 'It wasn't such a terrible thing, really, that he told your secret,' Clara said – forgetting, Fire thought dryly, that at the time Clara had found it terrible enough to punch him. 'We're all more content with you in the plan now we know. And we admire you for it. Truly, Lady, I wonder you never told us before.'

Fire didn't respond to this, for she couldn't explain that the admiration was part of the reason she hadn't told. It was not rewarding to be the hero of other people's hatred for Cansrel. She had not killed him out of hatred.

'Archer's an ass, but still I hope he'll be careful,' Clara finished, one hand resting absently on her belly while the other rifled through a pile of floor plans. 'Does he know the terrain in the west? There are great crevices in the ground. Some of them open to caves, but some of them are bottomless. Trust him to fall into one.' She stopped rifling for a moment, closed her eyes, and sighed. 'I've decided to be grateful to him for supplying my child with a sibling. Gratitude takes less energy than anger.'

When the truth had come out, Clara had indeed, accepted

it with a generous equanimity. It had not been so easy for Mila, though she hadn't taken to anger either. In her chair now beside the door, more than anything, Mila looked dazed.

'Ah, well,' Clara said, still sighing. 'Have you memorised anything above level six? You're not afraid of heights, are you?'

'No more than the next person. Why?'

Clara pulled two enormous, curling pages from the pile of floor plans. 'Here are the layouts for seven and eight. I'll have Welkley verify I've labelled the guest rooms correctly before you start learning all the names. We're trying to keep those floors empty for your use, but there are those who like the views.'

Memorising the palace's floor plans was different for Fire from what it would be for other people, because Fire couldn't get herself to conceive of the palace as a map, flat on the page. The palace was a three-dimensional space that whirled out from her head, full of moving minds walking down corridors, passing laundry chutes and climbing stairways Fire couldn't sense but was expected to fill in now from her memory of a map on a page. It wasn't enough now for Fire to know, for example, that Welkley was on the eastern end of the palace's second level. Where was he, precisely? What room was he in, and how many doors and windows did it have? How close was it to the nearest servants' closet, or the nearest stairway? The minds that she sensed near Welkley – were they in the room with him, or were they in the hallway, or the next room over? If Fire needed to give Welkley mental directions to guide him to her own rooms this instant without anyone seeing him, could she do it? Could she keep eight levels, hundreds of hallways, thousands of rooms, doorways, windows, balconies, and her perception of a court-full of consciousnesses all in her mind at once?

The simple answer was that no, she couldn't. But she was going to have to learn to do it as best she could, because the assassination plan for gala night depended on it. In her rooms, in the stables with Small, on the roofs with her guard, she practised and practised, all day long, constantly – proud of herself, sometimes, for how far she'd moved beyond her early days in this palace. She would certainly never get lost wandering these halls again.

The success of the plan hinged rather nerve-rackingly on Fire's ability to isolate Gentian, Gunner, and Murgda, separately or together, secretly, somewhere in the palace. It was imperative that she manage to do this, because the backup plans were messy, involved too many soldiers and too many scuffles, and would be next to impossible to keep quiet.

Once alone with them, Fire would learn whatever she could from each and all of them. In the meantime Brigan would find a discreet way to join her and ensure that the information exchange ended with Fire alive and the other three dead. And then news of the entire escapade would have to be contained somehow, for as long as possible. This would also be one of Fire's jobs: monitoring the palace for people who suspected what had happened, and arranging for those people to be quietly captured before they said anything. Because no one – no one – on the wrong side of the crown could be permitted to know where matters stood or what Fire had learned. Information would only be valuable as long as no one knew they knew it.

Brigan would ride through the night to Ford Flood. The instant he got there, the war would begin.

THE DAY OF the gala, Tess helped Fire into her dress that had been commissioned, fastening hooks, smoothing and straightening bits that were already smooth and straight, and all the time murmuring her pleasure. Next, a team of hairdressers yanked and braided Fire to distraction, exclaiming at the range of reds, oranges, and golds in her hair, its occasional astonishing strands of pink, its impossibly soft texture, its luminosity. It was Fire's first experience of trying to *improve* her appearance. Very quickly the process grew tiresome.

Nonetheless, when it finally ended and the hairdressers left and Tess insisted upon pulling her to the mirror, Fire saw, and understood, that everyone had done the job well. The dress, deep shimmering purple and utterly simple in design, was so beautifully-cut and so clingy and well-fitting that Fire felt slightly naked. And her hair. She couldn't follow what they'd done with her hair, braids thin as threads in some places, looped and wound through the thick sections that fell over her shoulders and down her back, but she saw that the end result was a controlled wildness that was magnificent against her face, her body, and the dress. She turned to measure the effect on her guard – all twenty of them, for all had roles to play in tonight's proceedings, and all were awaiting her orders. Twenty jaws hung slack with astonishment – even Musa's, Mila's, and Neel's. Fire touched their minds, and was pleased, and then angry, to find them open as the glass roofs in July.

'Take hold of yourselves,' she snapped. 'It's a disguise, remember? This isn't going to work if the people meant to help me can't keep their heads.'

'It will work, Lady Granddaughter.' Tess handed Fire two knives in ankle holsters. 'You'll get what you want from whomever you want. Tonight King Nash would give you the Winged River as a present, if you asked for it. Dells, child – Prince Brigan would give you his best warhorse.'

Fire strapped a knife to each ankle and did not smile at that. Brigan couldn't give gifts until he'd returned to court, and that was a thing, two hours before the gala, he had not yet done.

ONE OF SEVERAL staging areas reserved by the royal siblings for the night was a suite of rooms on the fourth floor with a balcony overlooking the large central courtyard. Fire stood in the balcony with three of her guard, deflecting the attention of hundreds of people below.

She had never seen a party before, let alone a royal ball. The courtyard sparkled gold from the light of thousands upon thousands of candles: walls of candles behind balustrades at the edges of the dance floor so the ladies wouldn't set their dresses on fire; candles in wide lamps hanging from the ceilings by silver chains; candles melted to the railings of every balcony, including her own. Light flickered over the people, turned them beautiful in their dresses and suits, their jewellery, the silver cups they drank from. The sky was fading. Musicians tuned their instruments and began to play over and through the tinkle of laughter. The dancing began, and it was the perfect picture of a winter party.

How absolutely the look of a thing could differ from its feel. If Fire had not had such an intense need to concentrate, if she hadn't been so far from humour, she might have laughed. For she knew herself to be standing above a microcosm of the kingdom itself, a web of traitors, spies, and allies in fancy costumes, representing every side, watching each other with calculation, trying to hear each other's conversations, and keenly aware of everyone who entered or exited. It began with Lord Gentian and his son, the focal centre of the room even though they stood at its edges. Gunner, medium size and nondescript, had a way of blending into the corner, but Gentian was tall with bright white hair and too famously an enemy of this court to be inconspicuous. Surrounding him were five of his 'attendants', men with the look of vicious dogs stuffed into formal clothing. Swords were not the fashion at balls such as this; the only visible weapons were on the palace guards stationed at the doorways. But Fire knew that Gentian, Gunner, and their thinly disguised bodyguards had knives. She knew they were wound tight with distrust; she could feel it. And she saw Gentian tugging his collar, repeatedly, uncomfortably.

She saw him and his son turning sharply at every noise, their social smiles false, frozen almost to the point of crazedness. She thought that Gentian was a nice-looking man, finely dressed, seemingly distinguished, unless you were in a position to feel his screaming nerves. Gentian was regretting the plan that had brought him here.

It overwhelmed Fire to keep track of everyone in this courtyard, and stretching herself beyond this courtyard was positively dizzying. But as best as she could, and using whatever minds gave her access, she was compiling a mental list of people in the palace she thought might be sympathetic to Lord Gentian or Lady Murgda, people who were not to be trusted, and also people who were. She communicated the list to a secretary in Garan's offices who took down names and descriptions and communicated them to the master of the guard, whose many jobs this night included knowing where everyone was at all times and preventing any unplanned appearances of weapons, or disappearances of significant people.

The sky was dark now. Fire sensed archers moving into the shadows of the balconies around her. Both Gentian and Murgda had been housed on the palace's third level overlooking this very courtyard, the rooms above, below, across, and to either side of them empty of guests, and temporarily occupied with a royal military presence that made Fire's guard seem quite shabby.

These had been Brigan's orders.

Fire wasn't certain which she was dreading more: what it would mean for her and his family personally if he did not arrive in time, or what it would mean for their night's work and the war. She thought these might be pieces of the same fear. If Brigan didn't come, he was probably dead, and with that, all things would fall apart anyway, whether they be big, like tonight's plans, or small, like her heart.

And then, only a few minutes later, she stumbled upon him

as he materialised at the edges of her range on the nearest city bridge. Almost involuntarily she sent him a surge of feeling that began as fury but turned immediately to worry and also relief at feeling him, so uncontrolled that she couldn't be sure some of her deeper feeling hadn't seeped through.

He sent back assurance and exhaustion and apology, and she reached back to him with apology of her own, and he apologised again, more insistently this time. *Brigan has arrived,* she thought hurriedly to the others, and pushed their own expressions of relief out of her mind. Her focus was unravelling. She scrabbled to regain control of the courtyard.

Lady Murgda was keeping a lower profile than Gentian. Like Gentian, she'd arrived with attendants, at least twenty of them, 'servants' who had the feeling of persons used to fighting. A number of these persons were in the courtyard below. Others were spread throughout the palace, presumably watching whomever Murgda had instructed them to watch; but Murgda herself had gone straight to her rooms at her arrival and had not emerged since. She was holed up there now, a level below Fire and across from where Fire stood, though Fire could not see her. She could only feel her, sharp and intelligent, as Fire had known she would be, harder than her two enemies below and more guarded, but buzzing with a similar edginess, and burning with suspicion.

Clara, Garan, Nash, Welkley, and several guards entered Fire's room. Sensing them, but not turning from the balcony view, Fire touched their minds in greeting and, through the open balcony door, heard Clara muttering.

'I've figured out who Gentian's got tailing me,' Clara said, 'but I'm not so sure of Murgda's tail. Her people are better trained.'

'They're Pikkian, some of them,' Garan said. 'Sayre tells me she saw Pikkian-looking men, and heard their accents.'

'Is it possible Lord Gentian could be daft enough to have

no one watching Lady Murgda?' Clara said. 'His entourage is pretty obvious, and none of it seems trained on her.'

'There's no ease in watching Lady Murgda, Lady Princess,' Welkley said. 'She's barely shown her face. Lord Gentian, on the other hand, has asked for your audience three times, Lord King, and three times I've brushed him off. He's quite eager to tell you in person all kinds of made-up reasons why he's here.'

'We'll give him the opportunity to explain, once he's dead,' Garan said.

Fire listened to the conversation with one fraction of her attention and monitored Brigan's progress with another – he was in the stables now – dancing all the while around Gentian, Gunner, and Murgda. So far she had only played around their minds, searching for ways in, approaching but not taking hold. She instructed a servant below – one of Welkley's people – to offer wine to Gentian and Gunner. Both men waved the serving girl away. Fire sighed, wishing the elder were not so plagued with indigestion and the younger so austere in his habits. Young Gunner was a bit troublesome, actually, stronger-minded than she'd like. Gentian, on the other hand – she wondered if it was time to enter Gentian's mind and begin pushing. He grew more and more anxious, and she got the sense that he had wanted the wine he'd refused.

Brigan pushed into the room behind her. 'Brother,' Fire heard Garan say. 'Cutting it a bit close this time even by your standards, don't you think? Everything in place at Fort Flood?'

'Poor boy,' Clara said. 'Who punched up your face?'

'No one relevant,' Brigan said shortly. 'Where's Lady Fire?'

Fire turned from the courtyard, went to the balcony door, stepped into the room, and came face to face with Nash, very handsome, very smartly dressed, who froze, stared back at her unhappily, turned, and strode into the next room. Garan and Welkley stared also, mouths agape, and Fire remembered that she was dressed up. Even Clara seemed struck dumb.

'All right,' Fire said, 'I know. Pull yourselves together and let's get on with things.'

'Is everyone in position?' Brigan asked. Mud-splattered and radiating cold, he looked like he'd been fighting for his life not ten minutes ago and had nearly lost, his cheekbone scraped raw, his jaw bruised, and a bloody bandage across his knuckles. He directed his question at Fire, searching her face with gentle eyes that did not match the rest of his appearance.

'Everyone's in position,' she said. *Do you need a healer, Lord Prince?*

He shook his head, peering down at his knuckles with mild amusement. 'And our enemies? Anyone we weren't expecting? Any of Cutter's foggy friends about, Lady?'

'No, thank the Dells.' *Are you in pain?*

'All right,' Clara said. 'We have our swordsman, so let's get moving. Brigan, could you attempt, at least, to make yourself presentable? I know this is a war, but the rest of us are trying to pretend it's a party.'

THE THIRD TIME Fire instructed Welkley's serving girl to offer Gentian wine, Gentian grabbed the cup and downed it in two gulps.

Fire was fully inside Gentian's mind now. It was not a stable place. He kept glancing at the balcony belonging to Murgda. When he did this, his entire handsome being flashed with anxiety, and with a peculiar wishfulness.

Fire began to wonder why, if Gentian was so anxious about Lady Murgda's balcony, he'd assigned none of his men to monitor Murgda. For Clara had figured right. Fire knew the feeling of every person in Gentian's entourage, and with a small effort, she could locate each of them. They were lurking around the doors and the persons of various gala guests; they were lurking near the guarded entrances to the royal residences and offices. None of them were lurking around Murgda.

Murgda, on the other hand, had spies on everyone. Two of them were milling around Gentian this moment.

Gentian took another cup of wine and glanced once more at Murgda's empty balcony. It was so odd, the emotion that accompanied these glances. Something like a frightened child looking for reassurance from an adult.

Why would Gentian look to the balcony of his enemy for reassurance?

Suddenly Fire wanted very much to feel what would happen if Murgda came onto her balcony and Gentian saw her. But Fire was not going to be able to compel Murgda onto her balcony without Murgda knowing she was being compelled. And then it would be only one more step to Murgda figuring out why.

It seemed to Fire that if she couldn't sneak up on Murgda, she might as well be direct. She sent a message.

Come out, lady rebel, and tell me why you're here.

Murgda's response was both immediate and startling: an ironic, hard pleasure at being so hailed; an utter lack of surprise or fear; a desire, unmistakable, to meet with the lady monster in person; and a blatant and unapologetic mistrust.

Well, Fire thought, her tone deliberately careless. *I'll meet with you, if you'll go to the place I specify.*

Amusement and contempt in response to this. Murgda was not fool enough to be led into a trap.

And I'm not keen enough to see you, Lady Murgda, that I would let you choose the meeting place.

Stubborn refusal to leave her self-created fortress.

You don't imagine I'd come to you in your rooms, Lady Murgda? No, I begin to think we are not meant to meet after all.

A determination – a *need* – to meet Lady Fire, to see her.

It was intriguing, this need, and Fire was content to use it for her own purposes. She breathed to calm her nerves, for her next message must be perfect in tone: amused – delighted, even – to the point of mild acquiescence, and somewhat curious, but rather indifferent as to where all of this might lead.

I suppose we could start by getting a look at each other. I'm on the balcony just across from you and up.

Suspicion. Fire was trying to lure Murgda out again.

Very well then, Lady Murgda. If you think our plan is to kill you publicly at our winter party and start a war in the court, then by all means, don't venture onto your balcony. I cannot blame you for caution, though it does seem to disallow your own interests. Goodbye, then.

A burst of irritation in response to this, which Fire ignored. Then scorn, then mild disappointment; and finally, silence. Fire waited. Minutes passed, and her sense of Murgda shrank, as if Murgda were pulling her feelings away and closing herself tight.

More minutes passed. Fire was beginning to try to cobble together a new plan when suddenly she felt Murgda moving through her rooms toward her balcony. Fire nudged Gentian to a place in the courtyard where he would not be able to see Fire but would have an unobstructed view of Murgda's balcony door. Then Fire stepped forward into the light of the candles on her own railing.

Murgda stopped behind her balcony door and peeked out at Fire through the glass pane. She was as Fire remembered her: a short, plain-faced woman, straight-shouldered and tough-looking. Fire was pleased, oddly, by the strong and purposeful sight of her.

Murgda didn't emerge to the balcony; she didn't even crack the door open. But this was what Fire had expected and the most she dared to hope for, and it was enough, for down below, Gentian's eyes caught hold of Murgda.

His reaction came to Fire plain as a pail of water thrown in her face. His confidence surged. His nerves were immensely comforted.

She understood now why Gentian wasn't spying on Murgda, and why Lord Mydogg's ally Captain Hart had known so much about Gentian. She understood a good many things, including why Murgda had come. She had come to help Gentian see his plans through. For somewhere along the line, Mydogg and Gentian had become allies against the king.

And Fire was reading something from Murgda as well, something less surprising. Whether Gentian knew it or not, his ally had come for one other reason. Fire read it in Murgda's eyes that stared across the courtyard at her, and in the feeling Murgda was releasing now without meaning to: stupefaction, wonderment, and lust, though not the lust Fire was used to. This lust was hard and scheming, and political. Murgda wanted to steal her. Mydogg and Murgda wanted her for their very own monster tool – had wanted her since the first moment they'd seen her last spring.

Knowledge – even the knowledge that your enemies had unified to outnumber you – was strengthening. Fire saw now quite assuredly what she must do. What she *could* do, if she took care and kept hold of all the stray ends. *You see?* she thought now charmingly to Murgda. *You've shown your face, and you're still alive.*

Murgda's mind sharpened and closed. She narrowed her eyes at Fire and rested her hand on her stomach in an interesting manner Fire understood, because she'd seen it before. Murgda spun around and walked out of sight, never once noticing Gentian, who was still craning his neck at her below.

Fire stepped back into the shadows. Flatly, without dramatics, she communicated to the others all she had learned. They were surprised; horrified; unsurprised; eager to proceed. She answered as best she could what she believed to be their questions.

I don't know if I'll ever get Lady Murgda out of her rooms, she thought to them. *I don't know if Murgda will die tonight. But Lord*

Gentian will do whatever I say, and I can probably manage Gunner. Let's start with them. Lord Mydogg's allies can tell us Lord Mydogg's plans.

CHAPTER TWENTY-FOUR

FIRE WANTED GENTIAN, and more particularly Gunner, to see her clearly. So she went to the king's own living quarters, which were on the second level overlooking the courtyard, and walked right out onto the balcony. She looked straight into the dazzled faces of Gentian and Gunner, whom she'd placed in fine position to see her. She smiled suggestively at Gunner and made eyes, which was ridiculous and embarrassing but had the desired effect. And then Nash himself stormed onto the balcony, looked to see whom she was flirting with, glared at Gentian and Gunner, took Fire's arm, and yanked her back inside. The whole thing lasted possibly nine seconds, a fortunate brevity, for the mental strain on Fire was enormous.

There had been too many minds in the courtyard to control at once. She'd had help. Welkley's people had been on the floor creating distractions to deflect attention from her. But persons here and there had seen, and Fire had to make a list now of people who must be watched with extra care on the chance they'd found it interesting that the lady monster seemed to be working her charms on Gentian and Gunner – interesting enough to talk about it, or even do something about it.

Still, it had worked. Gentian and Gunner had stared, paralysed by the vision of her. *I want to talk to you*, she'd thought to them as Nash had dragged her away. *I want to join your side. But don't tell anyone, or you'll put me in danger.*

Now she sank into a chair in Nash's sitting room, her head in her hands, monitoring Gentian's eagerness, Gunner's suspicion and desire, and skimming the rest of the courtyard and the entirety of the palace for anything relevant or worrisome.

Nash went to a side table and came back, crouching before her with a cup of water.

'Thank you,' she said, glancing up gratefully and taking the cup. 'You did well, Lord King. They believe you guard me jealously and I've a wish to escape. Gentian is positively brimming with indignation.'

Clara, sprawled on a sofa, snorted in disgust. 'Gullible no-heads.'

'It's not their fault, really,' Nash said soberly, still crouched before Fire. He was having a hard time getting up and leaving her. Fire could feel that he was trying. She wanted to put a hand on his arm, out of gratitude for all the ways he always tried, but she knew her touch would be no help to him. *Why don't you take water to your brother*, she thought to him gently, for Garan had begun to sweat with one of the fevers that overtook him in moments of stress, and was resting on the sofa with his feet in Clara's lap. Nash bent his chin to his chest and stood to do what she said.

Fire considered Brigan, who'd leaned back against a bookshelf, arms crossed, eyes closed, ignoring the argument beginning now between his sister and brothers about the whys and wherefores of Gentian's stupidity. He was neatly dressed and shaved, but the bruise on his face had darkened to something purple and ugly, and he looked so tired, as if he'd like to sink into the bookshelf and become a part of its solid, inanimate bookshelfness.

When did you last sleep? she thought to him.

His pale eyes came open and regarded her. He shrugged, and shook his head, and she knew it had been too long ago.

Who hurt you?

He shook his head again, and mouthed a word across the room. Bandits.

Were you riding alone?

'I had to,' he said quietly, 'or not get here in time.'

I was not criticising you, she thought. *I trust you to do what you must.*

He opened a memory to her. He'd promised her, one green and gold day at the start of summer, not to wander alone at night. Yet he'd ridden last night alone, and most of today. It was within her right to criticise.

I wish, Fire began, and then stopped, because she could not think to him that she wished they did not have this task to do, she wished she could comfort him and help him to sleep. She wished this war away that he and Nash would fight, hacking with swords and fists on a frozen field against too many men. These brothers. How would they get out of such a thing alive?

Panic bunched inside her. Her tone grew tart. *I've grown quite fond of your warhorse, Big. Will you give her to me?*

He stared at her with about as much incredulity as such a question, posed to the army's commander on the eve of battle, rightly deserved. And now Fire was laughing, and the sudden, unexpected lightness soothed her aching brain. *All right, all right. I was only testing that you were awake and in your right mind. The sight of you taking a nap against the bookshelf doesn't inspire confidence.*

He was still looking at her as if she might be half-crazy, but he flexed his hand and rested it on his sword hilt, pushing himself upright, ready to go wherever she told him to. He cocked his head at the doorway leading to Nash's other rooms, where Fire's guard, a group of messengers, and a small army of soldiers were waiting to assist however they were needed.

Fire stood. The others stopped their chatter and looked to her.

'Levels seven and eight,' she said to Brigan, 'the far northern wing. The rooms overlooking the smallest courtyard. At this moment it's the emptiest part of the palace, and it has been all day, so that's where I'll take Gentian and Gunner. You and Clara go there now. Find whatever empty room you can, on whichever level is easiest to get to without being seen, and I'll try to lead them as close to you as I can. If you need my help getting through the halls, or if Murgda's tails give you trouble, call for me.'

Brigan nodded and went to the side rooms to collect his soldiers. Fire sat back down and dropped her head again into the palms of her hands. Every stage of this process required focus. Right now she must monitor Brigan and Clara and their soldiers and their tails and everyone who noticed any one of them. While keeping stock of Gentian, Gunner, and Murgda, of course, and perhaps sending Gentian and Gunner occasional blips of helpless desire; and holding on to a sense of the palace as a whole, in case anything anywhere, at any time, should feel wrong for any reason.

She breathed through a mild headache forming above her temples. She stretched out with her mind.

FIFTEEN MINUTES LATER, Clara, Brigan, and a number of soldiers had found their way to an unoccupied suite of rooms on level eight in the far northern wing. Three of Murgda's spies and three of Gentian's were with them also, several unconscious, and the conscious ones boiling with fury, presumably at the indignity of being bound and gagged and shoved into closets.

Brigan sent assurance that all was well. 'All right,' Fire said to Nash and Garan. *All right*, she thought to all those involved throughout the palace. *I'm beginning.*

She hunched in her chair and closed her eyes. She touched Gentian's mind and then entered it. She touched on Gunner and decided that he was not oblivious enough for sneakery.

Gunner, she thought to him, warm and flirtatious, gushing herself at him – and then thrusting herself into the cracks that opened with his involuntary rush of pleasure. *Gunner. I want you to come to me. I need to see you. Can I trust you to be kind to me?*

Suspicion washed along the edges of his gladness, but Fire

murmured at it, lulled it, and took harder hold. *You must go where I direct you and tell no one*, she told both him and Gentian. *Now, leave the courtyard through the main arch and climb the central stairway to level three, as if you were returning to your rooms. I'll lead you to a place that's safe for all of us, far away from the king and his tiresome guards.*

Gentian began to move, and then, more reluctantly, Gunner. Their five henchmen moved with them and Fire expanded her reach, stepping into each of their minds. The seven proceeded toward the exit and Fire skimmed the rest of the courtyard. It didn't matter who noticed, but it did matter very much who followed.

Three consciousnesses separated themselves casually from the dancing and fell in behind Gentian's guard. Fire recognised two as Murgda's spies and the other as a minor lord she'd identified earlier as a probable Murgda sympathiser. She touched their minds, tested, and decided that they were too guarded for her to enter without them noticing. She would have to lead the others and trust these three to follow.

Ten men. She thought she could handle that while holding the floor plan and thousands of moving figures in her mind.

How her power had grown, with practice. She could not have done this a year ago. Only last spring, the First Branch had utterly overwhelmed her.

Her party of ten ascended the steps to the third level. *Now move down the hallway and turn into the corridor containing your rooms*, Fire thought to Gentian and Gunner. Her mind raced ahead to that very corridor and found it alarmingly full of people. She sped some up, slowed some down, and sent some into their rooms, forcefully in the case of the strong-minded, for there was no time to take the proper care. When Gentian, Gunner, and their five attendants turned the corner to their rooms, the hallway stretched emptily before them.

The hallway was still empty moments later when Gentian

and Gunner came abreast of their rooms. *Stop there*, she told them. She switched to the minds of the soldiers hiding in the suites around Gentian's. When Murgda's men rounded the corner, she sent the soldiers a message: *Go now.* Soldiers piled into the hallway and set about capturing Gentian's five guards and Murgda's three spies.

Run! Fire screamed at Gentian and Gunner, perhaps unnecessarily, as they seemed already to be running. *They're onto us! Run! Run! Down the hallway! Turn left at the lantern! Now, down that corridor! Look for the green door on the left! Through the green door and you're safe! Yes, you're safe. Now up, up. Climb the stairs. Quiet, slow. Slow down. Stop*, she thought. *Stop for a minute.*

Gentian and Gunner stopped, baffled, frantic, and alone, on a spiral stairway somewhere between levels five and six. Fire kept a finger on them, petted and soothed them, and stretched back to the hallway where the short, nasty scuffle had taken place. *Did you get everyone?* she asked the soldier in charge. *Did anyone see you?*

The soldier communicated that all had gone well.

Thank you, Fire said. *Well done. If you have any trouble, call for me.* She took a long, steadying breath and returned to Gentian and Gunner on the stairway.

I'm sorry, she murmured soothingly. *Are you all right? I'm sorry. I'll take care of you.*

Gunner was in no good humour, breaking loose a bit from her hold. He was angry about the loss of his guards, angry to be huddled in a narrow stairway, furious with himself for allowing a monster to commandeer his intentions and put him in danger. Fire flooded him, overwhelming him with heat and with feelings and suggestions designed to stop him thinking. Then she sent him a steely and certain message. *You knowingly put yourself in danger when you came traipsing into the palace of the king. But you have nothing to fear. I've chosen you, and I am stronger than the king. Take hold of yourself. Think how much easier it'll be to injure him with me on your side.*

Simultaneously Fire checked the corridors to which this spiral stairway led. Gala guests walked and mingled in the corridor of level eight. Level seven was empty.

Brigan was on level eight. But Fire's mind was growing sluggish with fatigue.

Brigan, she thought, too weary to concern herself with manners. *I'm taking them to level seven, to the unoccupied rooms just below you. When the time comes, you may have to climb down by the balcony.*

Brigan's response came quickly: this was perfectly fine. Fire was not to worry about him or the balcony.

Go up, Fire told Gentian and Gunner. *Climb. Yes, one more level. Now quietly through the door. Down the corridor, yes, and turn left. Slowly ... slowly ...* Fire strained to remember the guest plan and to feel where Brigan was. *There,* she said finally, *stop. Enter the room to your right.* Gunner was still spluttering. She gave him an unaffectionate shove.

Inside the room, Gunner's anger changed to puzzlement, and then, quite abruptly, to contentment. This was odd, but Fire had no energy to contemplate it. *Sit down, gentlemen,* she told them numbly. *Stay away from the windows and the balcony. I'll be there in a few minutes and we can talk.*

Fire did one more sweep of the corridors, of the courtyards, of Murgda and Murgda's people, reassuring herself that no one was suspicious and nothing was out of place. With a great sigh she turned her mind back to the room to find Mila kneeling on the floor before her, gripping her hand, and others in her guard, and Garan and Nash, watching her anxiously. It was a comfort to find herself still with them.

'All right,' she said. 'Now for my own journey.'

*

Fɪʀᴇ ꜰʟᴏᴀᴛᴇᴅ ᴅᴏᴡɴ the hallway on Nash's arm, flanked by members of both of their guards and attracting a great deal of attention. The couple climbed the central stairway to level three, as Gentian had done, but turned in the opposite direction and wound through the corridors, stopping finally before the entrance to Fire's rooms.

'Good night to you, Lady,' Nash said. 'I hope you'll recover from your headache.'

He took her hand, raised her fingers to his mouth, and kissed them; then dropped them and slumped darkly away. Fire looked after him with true fondness, not on her face but into his mind, for he was playing his part very well tonight, and she knew it was hard on him, even if the lovestruck and jealous monarch was not much of a stretch.

Then Fire smiled sweetly at Murgda's and Gentian's tails – several of whom smiled back at her idiotically – and went into her rooms. Fingers pressed to temples, she forced her mind through an examination of the grounds and the skies outside her window.

'There's no one out there,' she told her guard, 'and no raptor monsters. Let's begin.'

Musa creaked Fire's window open and took a blade to the screen. Cold air poured into the room, bits of slush spitting onto the carpet. Fire spared a thought for Brigan and his guard, who would be riding later in that sleet. Musa and Mila lowered a rope ladder out the window.

The ladder's in place, she thought to the soldiers in the room below. She heard their window squeak open, and checked the skies and the grounds again. No one was there, not even the green house guard.

'All right,' she said. 'I'm going.'

She felt then, suddenly, how loath Musa was to let Fire go, how it pained Musa to send Fire anywhere alone and unguarded. Fire held Musa's hand harder than was necessary. 'I'll call for you if I need you,' she promised. Tight-lipped, Musa helped her out the window into the cold.

Her dress and slippers were not made for winter, nor for anything approximating weather, but rather clumsily she managed the descent to the window below. Soldiers pulled her inside and tried not to stare as she straightened her dress. Then they tucked her under the cloth of a wheeled cart bearing food bound for level seven.

It was a fine, sturdy cart, and Nash's floors were strong and smooth, and a minute or two of determined shivering under the tablecloth warmed her. A servant pushed her through the halls and then wheeled her onto the lift, which rose on its ropes without a single creak or jolt. On level seven another servant rolled her out. He followed her mental directions down hallways and around corners, finally pushing her into the far northern corridor and stopping outside the room containing Gentian and Gunner.

She reached upward to find Brigan. He was not there.

Sweeping around in a panic, she realised what she'd done. *Rocks*, she seethed to Brigan. *Monster rocks. I miscalculated. I did not send them to the rooms directly below yours. They're one suite over to the west.*

Brigan sent assurance that he wasn't worried about this. He could scale the balconies to the neighbouring rooms.

They're occupied rooms.

He was certain they weren't.

Not the ones on your level, Brigan. The ones on mine. I've led Gentian and Gunner to occupied rooms. Quisling? Quisland? Someone beginning with Q. Her head stabbed with pain. *Should I try to move them again? I think Gunner would refuse. Oh, this is dreadful. I'll spread the word that the fellow beginning with Q must be kept from his rooms somehow, and his wife and servants and guards too. I can't think what we'll do with Gentian and Gunner's bodies now*, she thought bitterly, overwhelmed almost to tears with the consequences of her mistake.

Quislam? Brigan offered. Lord Quislam from the south?

Yes, Quislam.

But isn't Quislam Gentian's ally?

Fire strained to remember. *Yes, Quislam is Gentian's ally. But it makes no difference, other than to explain why Gunner stopped fighting once he entered the room.*

But, Brigan thought, if Gunner thinks himself safe in the room of an ally, then perhaps he'll be easier to handle. Perhaps her mistake had been fortunate.

Fire was turning hysterical. *It isn't. It's not fortunate. It creates countless problems.*

Fire—

Her concentration was fracturing to pieces and she grasped wildly at a thing that seemed, suddenly and senselessly, to matter. *Brigan, your mental control is as strong as anyone's I've ever encountered. Look how well you're able to communicate – you're practically sending me sentences. And you don't need to explain why you're so strong. You made yourself that way of necessity. My father—* Fire was impossibly drained. A fist in her head was punching at her brain. *My father hated you more than anyone.*

Fire—

Brigan, I'm so tired.

Fire.

Brigan was saying her name, and he was sending her a feeling. It was courage and strength, and something else too, as if he were standing with her, as if he'd taken her within himself, letting her rest her entire body for a moment on his backbone, her mind in his mind, her heart in the fire of his.

The fire of Brigan's heart was astounding. Fire understood, and almost could not believe, that the feeling he was sending her was love.

Pull yourself together, he thought to her. Get yourself into that room.

She climbed out from under the cart. She opened the door to the room.

CHAPTER TWENTY-FIVE

Both Gentian and Gunner sat in chairs facing the entry.
As she shut the door, Gunner rose to his feet and edged sideways against the wall in a direction that brought him slightly
nearer to her.

A shield with Quislam's colours was propped against a foot-
stool. Fire saw that the carpet was a patchwork of squares in
rust, brown, and red; the curtains red; the sofa and chairs brown.
At least they wouldn't have to worry about bloodstains. She
soaked in the feeling of these two men, and knew immediately
where the trouble would lie in this room. Of course it would
not be with Gentian, so charming and so blitheringly happy
to see her, so easy for even her torpid mind to invade that she
would have wondered how such a man could ever have risen
to a place of power, had the answer not stood scowling before
her in the form of Gunner.

He was a bit like Nash used to be: unpredictable, confusing,
too much for her to control, but not entirely under his own
control either. He began to prowl back and forth along the
wall, his eyes always on her. And though he was not a big man
or imposing, something tight and smooth in his movements
caused Fire to see suddenly why the others had been worried.
He was a calculating creature with a capacity for strong, fast
viciousness.

'Won't you sit down, Gunner?' Fire murmured, moving
herself sideways, away from both of them, and seating herself
calmly on the sofa – which was a mistake, because more than
one person could fit on a sofa, and the sofa was where Gunner
now seemed inclined to sit. She fought him with her mind,

which felt puffy and stiff, pushed him back toward the seats nearer his father, but he would not sit if he couldn't sit with her. He retreated to his wall and resumed prowling.

'And what can we do for you, darling child?' Gentian said, slightly drunk and bouncing in his seat with happiness.

How she wished she could go slowly. But her time in this room was borrowed from Lord Quislam.

'I want to join your side,' she said. 'I want your protection.'

'You're not to be trusted, looking like that,' Gunner growled. 'Never trust a monster.'

Gentian chided his son. 'Gunner! Did she not prove her trustworthiness when we were set upon in the hallway? Mydogg wouldn't wish us to be rude.'

'Mydogg does not care what we do, as long as it's to his advantage,' Gunner said. 'We shouldn't trust Mydogg either.'

'Enough,' Gentian said, his voice suddenly sharp and commanding. Gunner glowered, but made no retort.

'And how long have you been allied with Mydogg?' Fire asked, turning innocent eyes to Gentian.

She latched tightly to Gentian's mind and directed him to speak.

SOME TWENTY MINUTES later she had learned, and conveyed to the siblings, that Mydogg and Gentian had allied themselves largely in response to the lady monster joining the ranks of the king, and that Hart had only told part of the story when he'd said Gentian planned to attack Fort Flood with his force of ten thousand. Really Gentian would attack Fort Flood with fifteen thousand. After they had allied, Mydogg had moved five thousand of his own Pikkian recruits piecemeal to Gentian, through the tunnels.

It had not been easy to play-act delight at that particular piece of news. It meant Brigan would be outnumbered by five thousand at Fort Flood. But perhaps it also meant that the rest of Mydogg's army, wherever it was hiding, only numbered fifteen thousand or so? Perhaps the other two branches of the King's Army plus all the auxiliaries could then meet Mydogg on equal ground . . .

'Our spies tell us you've been looking all over the kingdom for Mydogg's army,' Gentian said now, interrupting her calculations. He giggled, playing around with a knife he'd pulled from his boot because his son, pacing and snarling, was making him nervous. 'I can tell you why you haven't found it. It's on the sea.'

'On the sea,' Fire said, genuinely surprised.

'Yes,' Gentian said, 'Mydogg has twenty thousand strong – ah, I see that number impresses you? He's always recruiting, that Mydogg. Yes, he's got twenty thousand strong on the sea, just out of sight of Marble Rise, in a hundred Pikkian boats. And fifty more Pikkian boats, carry nothing but horses. They're big boat people, you know, the Pikkians. Lady Murgda's own husband's a boat type. An explorer, until Mydogg got him interested in the business of war. Sit *down*, Gunner,' Gentian said sharply, reaching out to Gunner as he loomed past, slapping Gunner's arm with the flat of his knife.

Gunner swung on his father abruptly, grappled for the knife, wrested it from Gentian's grip, and flung it at the far wall. It screeched against stone and thumped onto the rug, bent crooked. Fire kept her face still so he would not know how much he'd frightened her.

'You've lost your mind,' Gentian said indignantly, staring at his son.

'You have no mind to lose,' Gunner snarled. 'Have we any secrets you haven't told yet to the king's monster pet? Go on, tell her the rest, and when you're done, I'll break her neck.'

'Nonsense,' Gentian said sternly. 'You'll do no such thing.'

'Go on, tell her.'

'I'll tell her nothing until you've sat down, and apologised, and shown you can behave yourself.'

Gunner made a noise of impatient disgust and came to stand before Fire. He stared at her face, and then quite shamelessly at her breasts.

Gunner is unstable, Fire told Brigan. *He's winged a knife at the wall and broken it.*

Can you get more out of them about the boats? Brigan thought back. How many horses?

Before Fire could ask, Gunner touched a finger to her collarbone and Fire dropped her perception of Brigan, of Gentian, of the whole rest of the palace. She put everything into Gunner, into fighting his intent, for she knew his attention and his hand were tending downward and she thought she might lose hold of him entirely if she allowed him a handful of her breast, which was what he wanted, or more accurately, what he wanted to start with.

And she did get his hand to rise, but it rose to her throat, and encircled it, and very slightly squeezed. For a long second Fire could not breathe, she could not find her brain. He was choking her.

'Mydogg thinks the crown will send reinforcements south to Fort Flood when we attack,' Gunner said, whispering, and finally letting her go. 'Maybe even a whole branch of the King's Army, if not two branches. And when the north is less crowded with the king's soldiers, Mydogg will send word for the beacons on Marble Rise to be lit. Do you understand, monster?'

Marble Rise was a high, coastal area north of the city, and Fire did understand. 'The soldiers on the Pikkian ships will see the smoke,' she said lightly.

'Clever thing,' Gunner said, circling his hand around her throat again, then changing his mind, taking a handful of her hair and pulling on it. 'And the smoke is the signal they've been waiting for to make land and march on the city.'

'The city,' Fire whispered.

'Yes,' Gunner said, '*this* city. And why not go straight for King's City? The timing will be perfect. Nash will be dead. Brigan will be dead.'

'He means that we're killing them tomorrow,' Gentian interjected, watching his son warily. 'We have it all planned. There's to be a fire.'

Gunner yanked on Fire's hair, very hard. '*I'm* telling her, Father,' he said savagely. '*I* decide what she knows. *I* am in charge of her.'

He grabbed her neck again and pulled her against his body, rough and disgusting. Fighting for breath, Fire capitulated to old-fashioned pain, reaching for his groin, grabbing whatever she could get hold of and twisting as hard as she could. In the moment of his scream she took a swipe at his mind, but her own mind was a balloon, soft and hollow, with no sharp edges, no claws for gripping. He stepped back from her, breathing hard. His fist came out of nowhere and slammed into her face.

For an instant she lost consciousness. Then she resurfaced, to the taste of blood and the familiar feeling of pain. The rug. I'm lying on the rug, she thought. Face in agony, head in agony. She moved her mouth. Jaw intact. She wiggled her fingers. Hands intact. *Brigan?*

Brigan responded.

Good, she thought blearily. Mind intact. She began to stretch her mind out to the rest of the palace.

But Brigan wasn't through communicating. He was trying to make her understand something. He was worried. He heard noises. He was on the balcony above, ready to drop down at her command.

Fire realised that she also heard noises. She rolled her head sideways and saw Gentian and Gunner yelling at each other, pushing each other around, one pompous and outraged, the other frightening because of a deranged look in his eyes that brought the memory of why she was in this room back to Fire. She propped herself up on her elbow and dragged herself onto her knees. She sent Brigan a question.

Is there anything else you need to know about Mydogg?

There was not.

She rose to her feet, staggered to the sofa, and leaned against it, eyes closed, until the pain of her head became something she thought she could bear. *Then come down. This interview has come to the end of its usefulness. They're fighting each other.* She watched Gunner shove his father against the glass of the balcony door. *They're grappling against the balcony door this moment.*

And then, because Brigan was coming and when he did he would be in danger, she brought each of her ankles up to her hands, one at a time – vaguely suspecting that if she did it the other way, reaching hands down to feet, her head would fall off and roll away. She pulled her knives from their holsters. She stumped closer to the struggling men, both too preoccupied to notice her or the knives in her hands. She blotted her bleeding face on her gorgeous purple sleeve, and teetered, and waited.

It wasn't long. She felt Brigan and saw him almost at the same time, saw him yank the balcony door open and Gentian fall out through the opening, saw Gentian surge back in again, but different now, because his mind was gone, he was just a body now, a dagger was in his back, and Brigan was pushing him violently to get him out of the way and to give Gunner a thing to trip over as Brigan descended with his sword.

It was a horrible thing to watch, actually, Brigan killing Gunner. He smashed his sword hilt into Gunner's face, so hard Gunner's face changed shape. He kicked Gunner full onto his back and, his expression smooth and focused, drove his sword into Gunner's heart. That was it, it was so quick, and so brutal, and then he was upon her, worried, helping her to the sofa, finding a cloth for her face, all too fast for her to take control of the horror she was sending out to him.

He felt it, and understood it. His own face closed. His inspection of her injuries changed to something clinical and emotionless.

She caught his sleeve. 'It startled me,' she whispered. 'That's all.'

There was shame in his eyes. She held tighter to his sleeve.

'I won't let you be ashamed before me,' she said. 'Please, Brigan. We're the same. What I do only looks less horrible.' *And*, she added, understanding it only as she said it, *even if this part of you frightens me, I have no choice but to like it, for it's a part of you that will keep you safe in the war. I want you to live. I want you to kill those who would kill you.*

He didn't say anything. But after a moment he leaned in again to touch the bones of her cheek and chin, gently, no longer avoiding her eyes, and she knew he accepted what she'd said. He cleared his throat. 'Your nose is broken,' he said. 'I can set it for you.'

'Yes, all right. Brigan, there's a laundry chute outside, just down the hall. We need to find sheets or something to wrap up the bodies, and you need to carry them to the chute and drop them in. I'll tell Welkley to clear all the servants out of the northernmost laundry room and to get ready to deal with an enormous mess. We have to hurry.'

'Yes, good plan,' Brigan said. He took tight hold of the back of her head. 'Try to keep still.' And then he grasped her face and did something that hurt far more than Gunner's blow had, and Fire cried out, and battled him with both her fists.

'All right,' he gasped, letting go of her face and catching her arms, though not before she hit him hard in the side of the head. 'I'm sorry, Fire. It's done. Sit back and let me handle the bodies. You need to rest, so you can guide us through what's left tonight.' He jumped up and disappeared into the bedroom.

'What's left,' Fire murmured, still crying slightly from the pain. She leaned on the armrest of the sofa and breathed until the ache of her face receded and stabilised, joining the blunt throbbing rhythm of the misery of her head. Slowly, softly, she pushed her mind to travel all around the palace and the grounds, touching on Murgda, touching on Murgda's and Gentian's people, touching on their allies, latching onto Quislam and his wife. She found Welkley and conveyed her instructions.

Blood was in her mouth, dripping down the back of her throat. Just as the sensation became intolerably disgusting Brigan appeared at her elbow, sheets slung over his shoulder, and plunked a bowl of water and cups and cloths on the table before her. He moved on to the bodies of Gentian and Gunner and set to bundling them up. Fire rinsed out her mouth and ran her mind again through the palace.

For a moment at the edges of her perception she thought that someone felt wrong, out of place. On the grounds? In the green house? Who was it? The feeling disappeared, and she couldn't locate it again, which was frustrating, and unsettling, and thoroughly exhausting. She watched Brigan wrap Gunner's body in a sheet, his own face dark with bruises, his hands and his sleeves covered with Gunner's blood.

'Our army is greatly outnumbered,' she said. 'Everywhere.'

'They've been trained with that expectation in mind,' he said flatly. 'And thanks to you, we have the element of surprise on both fronts. You've done more tonight than any of us could have hoped. I've already sent messages north to the Third and Fourth and most of the auxiliaries – soon they'll be consolidated on the shore north of the city and Nash will ride to join them. And I've sent an entire battalion to Marble Rise to take charge of the beacons and pick off any messengers heading for the boats. You see how it's laid out? Once the Third and Fourth are in position, we'll light the beacons ourselves. Mydogg's army will make land, suspecting nothing, and we'll attack them, with the sea to their back. And where they outnumber us with men we'll outnumber them with horses – they can't have more than four or five thousand on the boats – and their horses will be in no state to fight after weeks on the sea. It'll help. Maybe make up a bit for our own daftness in not realising that Mydogg might be building a navy with his Pikkian friends.'

It was difficult for Fire to wipe blood from her nose without touching it. 'Murgda's a problem,' she said, gasping at the pain. 'Eventually someone's going to notice Gentian and Gunner are missing, and then Murgda will suspect what we've done and what we know.'

'It almost doesn't matter, as long as none of her messengers are able to reach those boats.'

'Yes, all right, but there are a hundred people at court this minute who'll be willing to make a go at being the one messenger who gets through.'

Brigan tore a sheet in half with a massive ripping sound. 'Do you think you could get her out of her rooms?'

Fire closed her eyes and touched on Murgda. *Any change of heart, Lady Murgda?* she thought, trying not to sound as weak as she felt. *I'm resting in my bedroom. You're welcome to join me.*

Murgda responded with scorn, and with the same recalcitrance she'd displayed before. She had no intention of going anywhere near Lady Fire's rooms.

'I don't think so,' Fire said.

'Well then, for now we'll just have to keep her from suspecting for as long as we can, however we can. The longer it takes, the more time we have to set our own wheels into motion. The shape of the war is ours to choose now, Lady.'

'We've done Mydogg an enormous favour. I suppose he'll be the commander of Gentian's army now. He'll no longer have to share.'

Brigan knotted a last sheet and stood. 'I doubt he ever meant to share for long, anyway. Mydogg was always the more real threat. Is the hallway clear? Shall I get on with this?'

A very good reason to get on with it bubbled into Fire's mind. She sighed. 'The master of the guard is calling to me. One of Quislam's servants is coming, and – and Quislam's wife, and a number of guards. Yes, go,' she said, pushing herself to her feet, dumping her bowl of bloody water into a plant beside the sofa. 'Oh! Where's my mind? How are you and I to leave this room?'

Brigan heaved one of the bundles onto his back. 'The same way I came. You're not afraid of heights, are you?'

On the balcony, tears seeped down Fire's face from the effort of detracting the attention of eight levels of potential onlookers. They put the candles out and sank into shadow.

'I won't let you fall,' Brigan said quietly. 'Nor will Clara. Do you understand?'

Fire was slightly too lightheaded to understand. She'd lost blood and she did not think she was capable of this thing just now, but it didn't matter, because Quislam's people were coming and it had to be done. She stood with her back to Brigan as he told her to, his back to the railing, and he crouched, and the next thing she knew he was lifting her up by her knees. Her palms touched the underside of the balcony above. He shifted her backward and her searching fingers found the bars to that balcony. For one horrible moment she looked down and saw what he'd done to achieve this angle; he was perched on his own railing, his feet locked around his own bars, leaning back over empty space while he lifted her. Slightly sobbing, Fire grasped the bars and held. Clara's hands came down from above and locked tight around her wrists.

'Got her,' Clara said.

Brigan abandoned her knees for her ankles and she was rising again, and suddenly the beautiful, merciful railing was before her, and she grabbed onto it, and wrapped both arms over it, and Clara was pulling at her torso and her legs and assisting her clumsy and painful climb over it. She crashed onto the balcony floor. She gasped, and with a monumental effort focused her mind, and pushed herself to a standing position so that she might aid in Brigan's ascent; and found him already standing beside her, breathing quickly. 'Inside,' he said.

Within the room, Clara and Brigan talked back and forth rapidly. Fire understood that Brigan was not waiting to see what would happen with Murgda, or with Gentian's men, or with Welkley and the bodies in the laundry room, or with anyone. Brigan was going now, this instant, across the hallway and into the opposite rooms, through the window and down a very long rope ladder to the grounds and his waiting horse, his waiting soldiers, to ride to the tunnels at Fort Flood and begin the war.

'Murgda may still light this fire Gentian spoke of,' Brigan was saying. 'They may still try to kill Nash. You must all increase your vigilance. At a certain point it might be wise if Murgda's and Gentian's thugs began to disappear, do you understand me?' He turned to Fire. 'How best for you to leave this room?'

Fire forced herself to consider the question. 'The way I came. I'll call a cart and take the lift, and climb the ladder to my window.' And then she had a night of the same work ahead of her: monitoring Murgda and everyone else, and telling Welkley, the guard – everyone – who was where, who must be stopped, and who must be killed, so that Brigan could ride to Fort Flood and his messengers could ride north and no one would learn enough about anything to know to try to pursue them, and no one would light any fires.

'You're crying,' Clara said. 'It'll only make your nose worse.'

'Not real tears,' Fire said. 'Just exhaustion.'

'Poor thing,' Clara said. 'I'll come to your rooms later and help you through this night. And now you must go, Brigan. Is the hallway clear?'

'I need a minute,' Brigan said to Clara. 'A single minute alone with the lady.'

Clara's eyebrows shot up. She glided into the next room wordlessly.

Brigan went and shut the door behind her, then turned around to face Fire. 'Lady,' he said. 'I have a request for you. If I should die in this war—'

Fire's tears were real now, and there was no helping them, for there was no time. Everything was moving too fast. She crossed the room to him, put her arms around him, clung to him, turning her face to the side, learning all at once that it was awkward to show a person all of one's love when one's nose was broken.

His arms came around her tightly, his breath short and hard against her hair. He held on to the silk of her hair and she pressed herself against him until her panic calmed to something desperate, but bearable.

Yes, she thought to him, understanding now what he'd been about to ask. *If you die in the war, I'll keep Hanna in my heart. I promise I won't leave her.*

It was not easy letting go of him; but she did, and he was gone.

IN THE CART on the way back to her rooms, Fire's tears stopped. She'd reached a point of such absolute numbness that everything, save a single living thread holding her mind to the palace, stopped. It was almost like sleeping, like a senseless, stupefying nightmare.

And so, when she stepped out of the window onto the rope ladder and heard a strange bleating on the ground below – and listened, and heard a yip, and recognised Blotchy, who sounded as if he were in some kind of pain – it was not intelligence that led her to climb down toward Blotchy, rather than up to her rooms and the safety of her guards. It was dumb bleariness that sent her downward, a dull, dumb need to make sure the dog was all right.

The sleet had turned to a light snowfall, and the grounds of the green house glowed, and Blotchy was not all right. He lay on the green house path, crying, his two front legs flopping and broken.

And his feeling contained more than pain. He was afraid, and he was trying to push himself by his back legs toward the tree, the enormous tree in the side yard.

This was not right. Something was very wrong here, something eerie and bewildering. Fire searched the darkness wildly, stretched her mind into the green house. Her grandmother was sleeping inside. So were a number of guards, which was all wrong, for the green house night guards were not meant to sleep.

And then Fire cried out in distress, for under the tree she felt Hanna, awake, and too cold, and not alone, someone with her, someone angry who was hurting her, and making her angry, and frightening her.

Fire stumbled, ran toward the tree, reaching desperately for the mind of the person hurting Hanna, to stop him. *Help me*, she thought to the guards up in her room. *Help Hanna.*

A sense of the foggy-minded archer flashed across her consciousness. Something sharp stung her chest.

Her mind went black.

PART THREE

A Graceling

CHAPTER TWENTY-SIX

SHE WOKE TO the screeching of a raptor monster, and human voices raised in alarm. The floor was lurching and creaking. A carriage, cold and wet.

'It's her blood,' yelled a familiar voice. 'The raptors smell her blood. Wash her, cover her, I don't care how, just do it—'

Men and raptors still screaming, a struggle above her. Water pouring onto her face, choking her, someone wiping at her nose, the pain so blinding that her mind spun around her and whirled her into darkness. *Hanna? Hanna, are you—*

SHE WOKE AGAIN, still crying out to Hanna, as if her mind had suspended itself in mid-cry waiting for her consciousness to return. *Are you there, Hanna? Are you there?*

No response came to her, no feeling of the child anywhere she could reach.

Her arm was trapped crookedly under her torso, her neck stiff and twisted, her face throbbing, and cold, *cold* was everywhere.

There were men in this carriage. She scrabbled among their minds for one who might be kind, who might bring her a blanket. Six men, stupid, bubbling with fog, one of them the archer with a habit of killing his friends. And the boy was here, too, the red-eyed, pale boy who made the fog, with the unreachable mind and the voice that hurt her brain. Hadn't Archer gone after this boy and this archer? *Archer? Archer? Are you anywhere?*

The floor tilted, and she became colder and wetter, and understood that she lay in a puddle of water that shifted and rocked with the floor. Everywhere she could hear the slap of water. And there were large creatures under the carriage. She could feel them.

They were fish.

This carriage was a boat.

I'm being stolen away, she thought wonderingly, in a boat. But I can't be. I need to go back to the palace, I need to watch Lady Murgda. The war. Brigan. Brigan needs me! I've got to get out of this boat!

A man near her gasped something. He was rowing, he was exhausted, he was complaining of blistered hands.

'You're not tired,' the boy said tonelessly. 'Your hands don't hurt. Rowing is fun.' He sounded bored as he said it, and thoroughly unconvincing, but Fire could feel the men experience a collective surge of enthusiasm. The creaking sound, which she recognised now as oars in oarlocks, increased its pace.

He was powerful, and she was weak. She needed to steal his foggy men away from him. But could she, while numb with pain and cold, and confusion?

The fish. She must reach for the fish lumbering enormously beneath her and urge them to the surface to capsize the boat.

A fish threw its back against the boat's underside. The men yelled, pitching sideways, dropping oars. Another hard blow, men falling and cursing, and then the boy's horrible voice.

'Jod,' he said. 'Shoot her again. She's awake and this is her doing.'

Something sharp pricked her thigh. And it was well enough, she thought as she slipped into blackness. It wouldn't solve anything to drown them if she drowned too.

SHE WOKE, AND groped for the mind of the rower nearest the boy. She stabbed at the fog she found there, and took hold. She compelled the man to stand, drop his oar, and punch the boy in the face.

The boy's scream was terrible, scratching like claws across her brain.

'Shoot her, Jod,' he gasped. 'No, *her*. Shoot the monster bitch.'

Of course, she thought to herself as the dart pierced her skin. It's the archer I need control of. I'm not thinking. They've muddied my mind so I can't think.

The boy was crying, his breath shaking with fury and pain, as she slid away.

THE NEXT TIME she woke it was to the feeling she was being dragged agonisingly back into life. Her body screamed with pain, hunger, sickness. A long time, she thought. They've been poisoning me for a long time. Too long this time.

Someone was feeding her some kind of meal cake, mushed up and dripping like a porridge. She choked on it.

'She's stirring,' the boy said. 'Shoot her again.'

This time Fire grabbed at the archer, stabbed at his fog, tried to get him to aim his darts at the boy instead of her. The sound of a struggle followed, and then the boy's screaming voice.

'I'm your protector, you fool! I'm the one who takes care of you! She's the one you want to shoot!'

A prick on her arm.

Darkness.

SHE CRIED OUT. The boy was shaking her. Her eyes opened to the sight of him leaning over her, a hand raised as if to strike her. They were on land now. She was lying on rock. It was cold and the sun was too bright.

'Wake up,' he snarled, small and ferocious, his unmatching eyes blazing at her. 'Wake up and get up and walk. And if you do anything to thwart me or any of my men I swear to you I'll hit you so hard you'll never stop hurting again. Don't trust her,' he said sharply and suddenly to his companions. 'I'm the only person you can trust. You do what I say.'

His nose and cheekbones were blue with bruises. Fire pulled her knees to her chest and kicked him in the face. As he screamed she grasped at the consciousnesses around her and tried to get up, but she was weak, and dizzy, and staggering like a person unconnected to her legs. His voice, thick with sobs, shouted orders to his men. One of them grabbed her, yanked her arms behind her back, and closed a hand around her throat.

The boy came to her, his face a mess of blood and tears. He slapped her hard across the nose and she surfaced from the shattering pain to find herself sobbing.

'Stop,' he whispered. 'Stop resisting. You will eat, and you will walk, and you will do what I say, and every time one of my men turns on me, and every time a bird pecks at me, and every time a squirrel so much as crosses my path in a way I don't like, I will hurt you. Do you understand?'

It doesn't work on me, she thought to him, gasping and furious. *The things you say don't control me.*

He spit bloody mucus onto the snow and considered her, sullenly, before turning to the path. 'Then I'll find other ways to control you.'

THE TRUTH WAS, she didn't want her body to hurt any more than it already hurt. And she didn't want them to put her to sleep again, even though sleep was peaceful darkness and waking meant inhabiting a body shaped and moulded out of pain.

She needed to possess her own mind if she wanted to get out of this. So she did what he said.

Where they were walking it was rocky and steep with such an abundance of waterfalls and streams that she thought it likely the body of water with the great fish had been the Winged River. They'd rowed west on the river, presumably, and now they were climbing north, away from the river, in some part of the kingdom near to the western Great Greys.

Sitting for a meal the first day, she sniffed a corner of her ruined purple skirts, and put it in her mouth. It did not taste clean, of course, but it also didn't taste salty. This supported her theory. The water she'd lain in for so long had been water of the river, not the sea.

Minutes later, vomiting the meal cake she'd offered her poor wrecked stomach, she found herself laughing at her attempts to be scientific. Of course they'd brought her north of the river to a place in the western Great Greys. She should not have needed a test of salinity to determine it. They were most certainly taking her to Cutter, and she'd known all her life that this was where Cansrel's monster smuggler lived.

Cutter made her think of Small, and she wished he were here – and then was glad, in the same moment, that he wasn't. It was better that she was alone, that no one she loved was anywhere near this boy.

They provided her with sturdy boots and coverings for her hair, and an odd stylish coat of white rabbit pelt that was far too beautiful for her filthy state and made for an absurd hiking costume. In their camp in the evenings, one of the men, a fellow named Sammit with gentle hands, a kind voice, and wide, empty eyes, inspected her nose, and told her what she should eat, and how much. After a day or two she began to be able to keep her food down, which went far toward helping her to feel clearer in mind. She gathered, from the way the boy spoke to Sammit, that Sammit was a healer. She also gathered that they had woken her because Sammit had thought it dangerous for her to continue any longer in her drugged stupor.

They wanted her alive then, and relatively healthy. Which was only natural, if she was a monster and they were monster smugglers.

She began to experiment.

She entered the mind of one of the men – Sammit, to start – and popped his fog, and observed as his own thoughts trickled back in. She waited – it wasn't long – for the boy to remind the men that she was not to be trusted, that he was their guardian and friend. The words brought the fog blistering, and then bulging, right back into Sammit's mind – the *words*, spoken in that voice that didn't seem to hurt Sammit's head the way it hurt hers.

This was strange to Fire at first, that his power should be in his words and his voice, rather than in his mind. But the more she considered it, the more she supposed it wasn't entirely strange. She could control with parts of her body too. She could control some people with her face alone, or with her face and a suggestion made in a certain tone of voice – a voice of pretended promises. Or with her hair. Her power was in all of those things. Perhaps it was not so different from his.

And his power was contagious. If the boy spoke words to the fellow on his left and that fellow repeated the words to Sammit, the fog passed from the fellow to Sammit. It explained why the archer had been able to infect her guards.

The boy never let more than a few minutes pass between reminders to the men that Fire was their enemy and he their friend. Which suggested to Fire that he couldn't see into their minds like she could, and know for himself if he still controlled them. This was her next experiment. She took hold of Sammit again and popped his fog, and moulded his thoughts so that he knew the boy was manipulating him. She made Sammit angry at the boy. She caused him to contemplate revenge, immediate and violent.

And the boy didn't seem to notice. He didn't even glance at Sammit sidelong. Minutes passed before he repeated his litany that erased Sammit's anger and returned Sammit to forgetfulness and fog.

The boy could not read minds. His control was impressive, but it was blind.

Which left Fire with a great deal of choice over what she could do with these men without him knowing. And without her having to worry about them resisting, for the boy's fog emptied the men so nicely of their own inclinations that might otherwise have got in her way.

At night the boy wanted her drugged with something mild to keep her from turning on him while he slept. Fire consented to this. She only made sure to occupy a corner of Sammit's mind, so that whenever Sammit reached for the mixture that the archer was to dip his darts in, he pulled out an antiseptic salve instead of a sleeping potion.

In their winter camps under white, leafless trees, while the others slept or stood watch, she pretended to sleep, and planned. She understood from the talk of the men and from a few quiet, well-placed questions that Hanna had been released unharmed, and that Fire had been drugged for almost two weeks while the boat pushed west against the current of the river. That this slow passage had not been their intention – that they'd had horses when they'd reached King's City, and meant to return the way they'd come, pounding west across the flat land north of the river; but that as they were fleeing the palace grounds with Fire tossed over someone's shoulder, Fire's guard had set upon them and chased them toward the river and away from their mounts. They'd stumbled upon a boat moored under one of the city bridges, and seized it in desperation. Two men with them had been killed.

It was as frustrating to her as it was to them, the crawling pace of their journey across black rock and white snow. It was almost too much to be borne, these days away from the city and the war, and the things she was needed for. But they were almost upon Cutter now, and she supposed it was best to submit herself to being taken to him. Her escape would be faster on a horse she could steal from Cutter. And perhaps she'd be able to find Archer, and convince him to come back with her.

The archer, Jod. The man was haggard, his skin tinged with grey, but underneath his illness he was even-featured, well-boned. He had a deep voice to him and a set to his eyes that made her uneasy. He almost reminded her of Archer.

She compelled Sammit one night, while he was on guard duty, to bring her a tiny vial of the poison they'd drugged her with for so long, and a dart. She tucked the vial into the bosom of her dress and carried the dart in her sleeve.

CUTTER HAD FORGED his small kingdom straight out of the wilderness. His land was so thick with boulders that his house seemed almost as if it were balanced upon a pile of rubble. It had a strange look, the building, constructed of enormous stacked tree trunks in some places and rock in others, all covered thickly with moss, a bright green house with blinking window eyes, icicle eyelashes, a gaping door mouth, and soft fur. It was a monster, perched precariously on a studded hill of stone.

A rock wall, high and long and incongruously neat, surrounded his property. Pens and cages dotted the grounds. Spots of colour, monsters behind bars, raptors, bears, and leopards screeching at each other. In all the strangeness of the place, this was familiar to Fire, and brought memories crowding too close.

She half expected the boy to try to force her into one of those cages. One more monster for the black market, one more catch.

She didn't really care what intentions Cutter had for her here. Cutter was nothing, he was an annoyance, a gnat, and she would disabuse him quickly of the notion that his intentions were relevant. She would leave this place and go home.

THEY DID NOT lock her in a cage. They brought her into the house and drew her a hot bath in an upstairs room with a roaring fire that quite overcame the drafts from the windows. It was a small bedroom, the walls hung with tapestries that stunned her, though she hid her surprise and pleasure. They were woven with green fields, flowers, and blue sky, and they were beautiful, and very realistic. She had thought to refuse the bath, because she sensed, and resented, that its purpose was to prettify her. But standing in a place of fields and flowers made her want to be clean.

The men left. She set her vial of poison and her dart on a table and peeled her filthy dress away from her skin. She braced herself against the painful exhilaration of scalding bathwater, finally relaxing, closing her eyes, surrendering herself to the bliss of soap that lifted sweat, old blood, and river grime from her body and hair. Every few minutes she could hear the boy shouting messages up the stairs to the guards outside her room, and just as regularly to the guards on the rocks below her window. The monster was not to be trusted or helped to escape, he yelled. The boy knew what was best. The men would avoid mistakes if they followed the boy's advice, always. It must be nerve-racking, Fire thought, to be able to manipulate minds but not sense the state of them. His shouts were unnecessary, for she was not altering any of their minds. Not yet.

She played her mind through the building and the grounds, as she'd been doing since she'd come in range of the place. She recognised Cutter, downstairs with the boy and a number of men. As foggy as everyone else, and as condescending and insincere as he'd always been. Whatever the boy's words could do, it seemed they did not alter temperament.

When she stretched to her limits she could sense possibly thirty men in the house and grounds, and a spattering of women, too. All were muddle-minded. Archer was not there.

She pushed herself further. *Archer? Archer!*

There was no response.

And she wouldn't have minded not finding him here, she would have hoped it meant he'd come to his senses and abandoned his heroic pursuit – except for an unpleasant perception she wished she were cowardly enough to ignore. One or two of the foggy men on these grounds had the feeling of people she recognised. She thought they might have been guards recently in Nash's palace. And the simplest explanation for their presence here was that they'd come with Archer as part of his guard. Which begged the question of what had happened since, and who was left guarding Archer, and where Archer was.

The bath was still the purest, hottest ecstasy but she stood, and climbed out, suddenly impatient to be done with this place. She scrubbed herself dry and dressed in the flimsy long-sleeved gown they'd left for her. It had enough the look of bedroom clothing to make her uncomfortable, in addition to which, they'd taken her boots and coat away and given her nothing for her hair. She went to a wardrobe in the corner and dug through its random assortment of items until she'd found socks, a sturdy pair of boy's boots, a man's heavy robe that was far too big, and a brown woolen scarf that would do for a head wrapping. She hoped, a bit grimly, that the ensemble looked as peculiar as it felt. She didn't need beauty to control the boy's empty-headed puppets, and she wasn't in the mood to gratify Cutter by presenting the appearance of a doe-eyed monster woman ready to be ravished by one of his disgusting male customers.

She ran her mind through the hundreds of creatures held on this estate, monster predators, horses and hunting dogs, even an odd collection of rodents she couldn't imagine the purpose of. The choice of horses satisfied her. They were none of them as sympathetic as Small, but several would suit her purposes.

She soaked the tip of her dart in the vial of sleeping poison and tucked the vial back into her gown. She held the dart in her hand, where it was hidden by the length of her heavy sleeve.

Taking a deep breath for courage, she went downstairs.

CUTTER'S SITTING ROOM was small and as warm as the bedroom had been, the walls similarly dressed, in tapestries showing fields of flowers rising to cliffs overhanging the sea. The rug here was colourful too, and it occurred to Fire that at least some of this beauty had been woven from monster fur. And the books on the bookcases, and the golden clock on the mantelpiece – Fire wondered how much of this house's richness had been stolen.

Cutter sat at the head of the room, clearly believing himself to be the room's master. The room's true master leaned against the wall to the side, small, bored, blinking unmatched eyes, and surrounded by a woven field of flowers. Jod the archer stood beside Cutter. A man was positioned at each of the room's entrances.

Cutter barely glanced at Fire's attire. His eyes were glued to her face, his mouth stretched into a jubilant and proprietary simper. He looked just as he always had, except for a new vacantness of expression that must have to do with the fog.

'It's been no easy task stealing you, girl, especially since you've taken up residence in the king's palace,' he said in the self-satisfied voice she remembered. 'It's taken a great deal of time and considerable spying. Not to mention that we had to kill a number of our own spies who were careless enough to be captured in your woods by you and your people. We seem to have the stupidest spies in the kingdom. What a lot of trouble. But it was all worth it, boy, wasn't it? Look at her.'

'She is lovely,' the boy said disinterestedly. 'You shouldn't sell her. You should keep her here with us.'

Cutter's forehead creased with puzzlement. 'The rumour

among my colleagues is that Lord Mydogg is prepared to pay a fortune for her. In fact, a number of my buyers have shown particular interest. But perhaps I should keep her here with us.' His expression brightened. 'I could breed her! What a price her babies would fetch.'

'What we do with her remains to be seen,' the boy said.

'Precisely,' Cutter said. 'Remains to be seen.'

'If she would only behave herself,' the boy continued, 'then we wouldn't have to punish her, and she might understand that we want to be friends. She might find she likes it here. Speaking of which, she's a bit too quiet for my tastes at the moment. Jod, draw an arrow. If I command it, shoot her someplace painful that won't kill her. Shoot her in the knee. It might be to our advantage to hobble her.'

This was not the job for a small dart bow. Jod swung his longbow from his back, pulled a white arrow from his quiver, and drew smoothly on a string most men wouldn't even have the strength to draw. He held the notched arrow, waiting, calm and easy. And Fire was slightly sick, and it was not because she knew that an arrow of that size shot with that bow at this range would shatter her knee. She was sick because Jod moved with his bow as if it were a limb of his body, so natural and graceful, and too much like Archer.

She spoke to placate the boy, but also because there were beginning to be questions to which she wanted answers. 'An archer shot a man imprisoned in my father's cages last spring,' she said to Jod. 'It was an uncommonly difficult shot. Were you that archer?'

Jod had no idea what she was talking about, that was plain. He shook his head, wincing, as if he were trying to remember all the things he'd ever done and could go back no further than yesterday.

'He's your man,' the boy said blandly. 'Jod does all our shooting. Far too talented to be wasted. And so delightfully malleable,' he said, tapping a fingertip to his own head, 'if you know what I mean. One of my luckiest finds, Jod.'

'And what is Jod's history?' Fire asked the boy, trying to match his bland tone.

The boy seemed delighted all out of proportion with this question. He smiled a very pleased, and unpleasant, smile. 'Interesting you should ask. Only weeks ago we had a visitor wondering the very same thing. Who knew, when we hired ourselves an archer, that he would come to be the subject of so much mystery and speculation? And I wish we could satisfy your curiosity, but it seems Jod's memory is not what it used to be. We've no idea what he was up to, what would it be, twenty-one years ago?'

Fire had taken a step toward the boy as he spoke, unable to prevent herself, clutching the dart hard in her hand. 'Where is Archer?'

At this the boy smirked, more and more happy with this turn of conversation. 'He left us. He didn't care for the company. He's gone back to his estate in the north.'

He was a terrible liar, too used to people believing him. 'Where is he?' Fire said again, her voice cracking now with a panic that made the boy smile wider.

'He left a couple of his guards behind,' the boy said. 'Kind of him, really. They were able to tell us a bit about your life at court, and your weaknesses. Puppies. Helpless children.'

Several things happened in quick succession. Fire rushed toward the boy. The boy gestured to Jod, calling, 'Shoot!' Fire smashed through Jod's fog, causing him to swing his bow wildly and release his arrow into the ceiling. The boy yelled, 'Shoot her but don't kill her!' and hurtled himself away, trying to sidestep Fire, but Fire lunged at him, reached, just barely jabbed his flailing arm with her dart. He jumped away from her, swinging fists at her, still yelling; and then his face slackened. He tipped and slumped.

Fire had clamped hold of every mind in the room before the boy even hit the floor. She bent over him, yanked a knife from his belt, walked to Cutter, and pointed the shaking blade at Cutter's throat. *Where is Archer?* she thought, because speech had become impossible.

Cutter stared back at her, entranced and stupid. 'He didn't care for the company. He's gone back to his estate in the north.'

No, Fire thought, wanting to hit him in her frustration. *Think. You know this. Where—*

Cutter interrupted, squinting at her with puzzlement, as if he couldn't remember who she was, or why he was talking to her. He said, 'Archer is with the horses.'

Fire turned and left the room and the house. She glided past men who watched her progress with vacant eyes. *Cutter is wrong*, she told herself, preparing herself with denial. *Archer is not with the horses. Cutter is wrong.*

And, of course, this was true, for it was not Archer she found on the rocks behind the stable. It was only his body.

CHAPTER TWENTY-SEVEN

WHAT HAPPENED NEXT passed in a blur of numbness and anguish.

It was a thing about being a monster. She couldn't look at a body and pretend she was looking at Archer. She knew, she could feel, that the fires of Archer's heart and mind were nowhere near. This body was a horrible thing, almost unrecognisable, lying there, mocking her, mocking Archer with its emptiness.

Nonetheless, this did not stop her dropping to her knees and stroking the cold arm of this body, over and over, breathing shallowly, not entirely sure what she was doing. Taking hold of the arm, clutching it, while confused tears ran down her face.

The sight of the arrow embedded in the body's stomach began to bring her a little too close to sensibility. An arrow shot into a man's stomach was cruel, its damage painful and slow. Archer had told her that long ago. He had taught her never to aim there.

She stood and turned away from this thinking, stumbled away, but it seemed to follow her across the yard. A great outdoor bonfire was alight between the stable and the house. She found herself standing before it, staring into the flames, fighting her mind, which seemed insistent that she contemplate the notion of Archer, dying, slowly, in pain. All alone.

At least her last words to him had been words of love. But she wished she'd told him just how much she loved him. How much she had to thank him for, how many good things he had done. She hadn't told him nearly enough.

She reached into the fire and took hold of a branch.

SHE WAS NOT entirely aware of carrying flaming branches to Cutter's green house. She wasn't aware of the men she commandeered to help her, or the trips back and forth stumbling from bonfire to house, house to bonfire. People ran frantically from the burning building. She might have spotted Cutter among them; she might have spotted Jod; she wasn't sure and she didn't care; she instructed them not to interfere. When she could no longer see the house from the black smoke billowing around it, she stopped carrying fire to it. She looked around for more of Cutter's buildings to burn.

She had mind enough to release the dogs and rodents before torching the sheds they lived in. She found the bodies of two of Archer's guards on the rocks near the predator monster cages. She took one of their bows and shot the monsters with it. She burned the men's bodies.

By the time she got to the stable the horses were panicking from the smoke and from the sounds of roaring flame, and shouting voices, and buildings falling apart. But they stilled as she entered – even the most frantic among them, even those who couldn't see her – and left their stalls when she told them to. Finally empty of horses, but full as it was of wood and hay, the stable blazed up like a mighty monster made of fire.

She bumbled around the perimeter to Archer's body. She watched, lungs hacking, until the flames reached him. Even when she could no longer see him she kept watching. When the smoke became so thick that she was choking on it, her throat burning from it, she turned her back on the fire she'd made, and walked away.

SHE WALKED WITHOUT knowing where she was going and without thinking of anyone or anything. It was cold and the terrain was hard and treeless. When she crossed paths with one of the horses, dappled and grey, it came to her.

No saddle, she thought numbly to herself as it stood before her, breathing steam and stamping its hooves against the snow. No stirrups. Hard to get on.

The horse knelt awkwardly on its forelegs before her. She hitched her gown and her robe around her knees and climbed onto its back. Balancing precariously as the horse stood, she found that a horse without a saddle was slippery and warm. And better than walking. She could wind her hands in the mane and lean her body and face forward against the aliveness of its neck, and sink into a stupor of no feeling, and let the horse decide where to go.

Her robe had not been made to serve as a winter coat and she had no gloves. Under her headscarf her hair was wet. When in darkness they came upon a plateau of stone that was oddly hot and dry, its edges running with streams of melted snow water and smoke rising from cracks in the ground, Fire didn't question it. She only slid from the horse's back and found a warm flat place to lie. *Sleep*, she told the horse. *It's time to sleep*.

The horse folded itself to the ground and nestled its back against her. Warmth, Fire thought. We'll live through this night.

It was the worst night she'd ever known, skimming hour after hour between wakefulness and sleep, jerking from dream after dream of Archer alive to remember that he was dead.

Day finally broke.

She understood, with dull resentment, that her body and the horse's body needed food. She didn't know what to do about it. She sat staring at her own hands.

She was too far beyond surprise and feeling to be startled when children appeared moments later climbing from a crevice in the ground, three of them, paler than Pikkians, black-haired, blurry at the edges from the glow of the rising sun. They were carrying things: a bowl of water, a sack, a small package wrapped in cloth. One bore the sack to the horse, dropped it near the animal, and folded the top down. The horse, which had shied away with frantic noises, now approached cautiously. It sank its nose into the sack and began to chew.

The other two carried the package and bowl to Fire, setting them before her wordlessly, staring at her with amber eyes wide. They are like fish, Fire thought. Strange and colourless and staring, on the bottom of the ocean.

The package contained bread, cheese, and salted meat. At the scent of food her stomach threatened to heave. She wished the staring children would go away so that she could have her battle with breakfast alone.

They turned and went, disappearing into the crevice from which they'd come.

Fire broke a piece of bread and forced herself to eat it. When her stomach seemed to decide it was willing to accept this, she cupped her hands into the water and took a few sips. It was warm. She watched the horse, chomping on the feed in the sack, poking its nose softly into the corners. Smoke seeped from a crack in the ground behind the animal, glowing yellow in the morning sun. Smoke? Or was it steam? This place had a strange smell to it, like wood smoke but also something else. She put her hand to the warm rock floor on which she sat and understood that there were people beneath it. Her floor was someone else's ceiling.

She was feeling the beginnings of a lustreless sort of curiosity when her stomach decided it did not want her crumbs of bread after all.

After the horse had finished its breakfast and drunk the rest of the water it came to where Fire was lying in a ball on the ground. It nudged her, and knelt. Fire uncurled herself, like a turtle ripping itself from its shell, and climbed onto the horse's back.

★

THE HORSE SEEMED to move randomly west and south across the snow. It shuffled through streams that crunched with ice, and crossed wide crevices in the rock that made Fire uneasy because she could not see to the bottoms of them.

In the early morning she felt a person on horseback approaching from behind. She didn't much care at first. But then she recognised the feel of the person and was dragged against her will into caring. It was the boy.

He was also riding saddleless, awkwardly so, and he kicked his poor frustrated horse until it brought him within shouting range. He called out angrily. 'Where are you going? And what are you doing, sending your every thought and feeling over these rocks? This is not Cutter's fortress. There are monsters out here, and wild, unfriendly people. You're going to get yourself killed.'

Fire didn't hear him, for at the sight of his mismatched eyes she found herself dropping from her horse and running at him, a knife in her hand, though she hadn't realised until that moment that she was in possession of one.

His horse chose that instant to throw the boy from its back, toward her. He fell in a bundle on the ground, clambered to his feet, and ran to escape her. There was a blundering chase across the crevices, and then an ugly scuffle that she couldn't sustain because she grew exhausted too quickly. The knife slipped from her fingers and slid into a wide crack in the earth. He pushed himself away, scrambled to his feet, choking over his words.

'You've lost your mind,' he said, touching his hand to a cut on his neck, staring incredulously at the blood that came off on his fingers. 'Take hold of yourself! I didn't come after you all this way to fight you. I'm trying to rescue you!'

'Your lies don't work on me,' she cried, her throat coarse and painful from smoke and dehydration. 'You killed Archer.'

'Jod killed Archer.'

'Jod is your tool!'

'Oh, be reasonable,' he said, his voice rising with impatience. 'You of all people should understand it. Archer was too strong-minded. It's quite a kingdom for the strong-minded you've got here, isn't it, the very toddlers taught to guard their minds against monsters?'

'You're not a monster.'

'It amounts to the same thing. You know perfectly well how many people I've had to kill.'

'I don't,' she said. 'I don't. I'm not like you.'

'Perhaps you're not, but you do understand it. Your father was like me.'

Fire stared at this boy, his sooty face, his thatch of filthy hair, his torn and bloodstained coat, oversized, as if he'd taken it from one of his own victims, from a body he'd found unburned on Cutter's grounds. The feeling of his mind bumped against hers, simmering with strangeness, taunting her with its unreachability.

Whatever he was, he was not a monster. But it amounted to the same thing. Was this what she had killed Cansrel for, so that a creature like this could rise to power in his place?

'What are you?' she whispered.

He smiled. Even in his dirty face it was a disarming smile, the delighted smile of a little boy who is proud of himself.

'I'm what is known as a Graceling,' he said. 'My name used to be Immiker. Now it is Leck. I come from a kingdom you've not heard of. There are no monsters there, but there are people with eyes of two colours who have powers, all different kinds of powers, everything you could think of, weaving, dancing, swordplay, and mental powers too. And none of the Gracelings are as powerful as I.'

'Your lies don't work on me,' Fire said automatically, feeling around for her horse, who appeared at her side for her to lean against.

'I'm not making it up,' he said. 'This kingdom does exist. Seven kingdoms, actually, and not a single monster to trouble the people. Which, of course, means that few of them have learned to strengthen their minds as people must here in the Dells. Dellians are far more strong-minded as a people, and far more vexing.'

'If Dellians vex you,' she whispered, 'go back where you came from.'

He shrugged, smiling. 'I don't know how to go back. There are tunnels, but I've never found them. And even if I did, I don't want to. There's so much potential here – so many advances in medicine, and engineering, and art. And so much gorgeousness – the monsters, the plants – do you appreciate how unusual the plants are here, how marvellous the medicines? My place is here in the Dells. And,' he said with a touch of contempt, 'don't imagine it contents me to control Cutter's vulgar smuggling operation here at the kingdom's edges. It's King's City I want, with its glass ceilings and its hospitals and its beautiful bridges all lit up at night. It's the king I want, whoever that may be at the other side of the war.'

'Are you working with Mydogg? Whose side are you on?'

He waved a dismissive hand. 'I don't care which one wins. Why should I get involved when they're doing me a favour by destroying each other? But you, don't you see the place I've made for you in my plans? You must know it was my idea to capture you – I controlled all the spies and masterminded the kidnapping, and I was never going to allow Cutter to sell you, or breed you. I want to be your partner, not your master.'

How weary Fire was of everyone, every person in this world who wanted to use her.

'Not *use* you, *work* with you to control the king,' the boy said, causing her to prickle with confusion, for she had not thought he could read minds. 'And I'm not in your mind,' he said impatiently. 'I told you before, you're sending your every

317

thought and feeling out to be felt. You're revealing things I doubt you mean to reveal, and you're also hurting my head. Pull yourself together. Come back with me, you've destroyed all my rugs and my hangings, but I'll forgive you for that. There's a corner of the house still left standing. I'll tell you my plans, and you can tell me all about yourself. Like who cut your neck, for starters. Was it your father?'

'You're not normal,' Fire whispered.

'I'll send my men away,' he continued, 'I promise. Cutter and Jod are dead, anyway – I killed them. It'll just be the two of us. No more fighting. We'll be friends.'

It was heartbreaking, the realisation that Archer had wasted himself protecting her from such a stupid, mad thing. Heartbreaking beyond endurance. Fire closed her eyes and leaned her face against the steady leg of her horse. 'These seven kingdoms,' she whispered. 'Where are they?'

'I don't know. I fell through the mountains and found myself here.'

'And is it the way, in these kingdoms you fell from, for a woman to join forces with an unnatural child who's murdered her friend? Or is that expectation unique to you, and your infinitesimal heart?'

He didn't respond. She opened her eyes to find that he'd shifted his smile, carefully, to something unpleasant that was shaped like a smile but did not have the feel of one. 'There is nothing unnatural in this world,' he said. 'An unnatural thing is a thing that could never happen in nature. I happened. I am natural, and the things I want are natural. The power of your mind, and your beauty, even when you've been drugged in the bottom of a boat for two weeks, covered in grime and your face purple and green – your unnatural beauty is natural. Nature is horrifying.

'And,' he continued, his strange smile gleaming, 'as I see it, our hearts are not so different in size. I murdered my father.

You murdered yours. Is that something you did with a large heart?'

Fire was becoming confused, because it was a cruel question, and at least one of the answers to it was yes, which she knew made no sense. She was too wild and too weak for logic. I must defend myself with illogic, she thought to herself, illogically. Archer has always been one for illogic, though he never sees it in himself.

Archer.

She had taught Archer to make his mind strong. And the strong mind she had given him had got him killed.

But he had taught her, too. He had taught her to shoot an arrow fast and with greater precision than she could ever have learned on her own.

She stood, reaching for the quiver and bow she suddenly realised she had on her back, forgetting that she was broadcasting her every intention. Leck grabbed for his own bow, and he was faster than she was – he had an arrow aimed at her knees before her own arrow was notched. She braced herself for an explosion of pain.

And then, beside her, Fire's horse erupted. The animal sprang at the boy, rearing, screaming, kicking him in the face. The boy cried out and fell, dropping his bow, clasping one eye with both hands. He scrambled away, sobbing, the horse fast after him. He seemed unable to see, there was blood in his eyes, and he tripped and sprawled headlong. Fire watched, stunned and fascinated, as he slid across a patch of ice and over the rim of a crevice, slipped through its lips, and disappeared.

Fire stumbled to the crack. She knelt, peering in. She could not see to its bottom, and she could not see the boy.

The mountain had swallowed him.

SHE WAS TOO cold. If only the boy had died in the fire and never come after her – for he'd woken her, and now she perceived things like coldness. And weakness and hunger, and what it meant to be lost in a corner of the western Great Greys.

She ate the rest of the food the children had given her, without much hope of her stomach submitting to it. She drank water from a half-frozen stream. And she tried not to think about the night that would come at the end of this day, because she had no flint, and she had never started a fire without one. She'd never even started a fire that hadn't been in a fireplace. She'd lived a pampered life.

Shaking with cold, she unwrapped her headscarf and wrapped it again so that it covered not just her hair, still slightly damp, but her face and neck as well. She killed a raptor monster before it killed her, a scarlet creature that came screeching suddenly out of the sky, but knew it was no use trying to carry the meat, for the smell of its blood would only attract more monsters.

This reminded her. The gala had taken place in the second half of January. She couldn't be certain how much time had passed, but surely it was well into February. Her bleeding was due.

Fire understood, with her new waking logic that was blunt and unsympathetic, that she was going to die soon, from one thing or another. She thought about this on her horse. It was comforting. It gave her permission to give up. I'm sorry, Brigan, she thought to herself. I'm sorry, Small. I tried.

But then a memory, and a realisation, jarred her out of this. People. She might live if she had the help of people, and there were people behind her, in the place where smoke rose from the rocks. There was warmth there, too.

Her horse was still plodding purposefully southwest. Propelled by nothing more than a drab sense of duty not to die if she didn't have to, Fire turned the animal around.

As they started back the way they'd come, snow began to fall.

HER BODY ACHED from her rattling teeth, her rattling joints and muscles. She ran through music in her mind, all the most difficult music she'd studied, forcing herself to remember the intricacies of complicated passages. She didn't know why she was doing this. Some part of her mind felt it was necessary and would not let her stop, though her body and the rest of her mind begged to be left alone.

When a golden raptor monster dove at her, screaming through falling snow, she fumbled with her bow and couldn't notch the arrow properly. The horse killed the bird, though Fire didn't know how it managed the job. She'd slid off its rearing back and was lying in a heap on the snow when it happened.

Some time later she slid off the horse's back again. She wasn't sure why. She assumed it must be another raptor monster, and waited patiently, but almost immediately her horse began pushing at her with its nose, which confused Fire, and struck her as deeply unjust. The horse blew angrily in her face and shoved her repeatedly, until, defeated, she dragged herself shaking onto its proffered back. And then she understood why she'd fallen. Her hands had stopped working. She had no grip on the animal's mane.

I'm dying, she thought, disinterestedly. Ah well. I may as well die on the back of this lovely dappled horse.

The next time she fell she was too senseless to realise that she'd fallen onto warm rock.

SHE WAS NOT unconscious. She heard the voices, sharp, urgent, and alarmed, but she could not get up when they asked her to. She heard her name and grasped that they knew who she was. She understood when a man lifted her and carried her underground, and she understood when women undressed her and undressed themselves, and wrapped themselves with her in many blankets.

She had never in her life been so cold. She shook so hard she felt she would shatter. She tried to drink the warm, sweet liquid a woman held to her face but had the impression she sprayed most of it onto her blanket companions.

After an eternity of gasping and shaking she noticed that she was no longer shaking so hard. Embraced by two pairs of arms, enfolded between the bodies of two naked women, a merciful thing happened: she fell asleep.

CHAPTER TWENTY-EIGHT

She woke to the sight of Musa's face and the feeling that her hands were being crushed by mallets.

'Lady,' Musa said grimly. 'I've never been more relieved in all my life. How do you feel?'

Her voice was a croak. 'My hands hurt.'

'Yes. They're frostbitten, Lady. You're not to worry. The people here have thawed them and bandaged them and taken very good care of you.'

Memory came back to Fire, seeping into the spaces around her. She turned her face away from Musa.

'We've been searching for you from the minute you were taken, Lady,' Musa continued. 'We wasted some time following false leads, for Princess Hanna never saw who took her, and the men we killed had no identifying marks, and your grandmother and the green house guards were drugged before they even knew it was happening. We had no idea where to look, Lady, and the king and the prince and princess were sure it was some plot of Lady Murgda's, but the commander's communications were doubtful, and it wasn't until one of the palace guards got hold of a blurry memory in his head of a red-eyed boy lurking on the grounds that we began to suspect what had happened. We reached Cutter's yesterday. I can't tell you how it frightened us, Lady, to find the place burned to the ground, and charred bodies we couldn't recognise.'

Fire spoke hollowly. 'I lit a fire for Archer. He's dead.'

Musa was startled by this. Fire felt it, and understood at once that Musa's allegiance was with Mila, not with the careless lord who'd fathered Mila's baby. This was just a death to

Musa, of someone she'd known only by bad behaviour.

Fire pushed Musa's feelings away.

'We'll send word to the commander at Fort Flood about Lord Archer, Lady,' Musa finally said. 'Everyone will be so relieved to hear you're all right. Shall I tell you of the progress the commander has made in the war?'

'No,' Fire said.

A woman appeared at Fire's side then with a bowl of soup and said gently, 'The lady must eat.' Musa rose from her chair so that the woman could sit down. She was old, her face whitish and lined, her eyes a deep yellow-brown. Her expression shifted softly in the light from a fire stoked in the middle of the stone floor, its smoke rising to the ceiling and escaping through a crack above. Fire recognised the feeling of the woman. This grandmother was one of the two who'd saved her life with the gift of her own body's heat.

The woman spoon-fed the soup to Fire, murmuring quietly, catching the bits that ran down Fire's chin. Fire consented to this kindness, and to the soup, because they came from a person who didn't want to talk about the war, and had never known Archer, and could receive her grief easily, with uncomplicated acceptance.

HER BLEEDING CAME, delaying their journey. She slept, and tried not to think, and spoke very little. She watched the lives of the people who lived in the darkness of these underground caves, poor and scrabbling through winter, but warm from their fires and from what they called the furnace of the earth, which sat very close to the surface here and heated their floors and walls. They explained the science of it to Fire's guard. They gave Fire medicinal concoctions to drink.

'As soon as you're able,' Musa said, 'we'll move you to the army healers at Fort Flood, Lady. The southern war is not going badly. The commander was hopeful, and terribly determined, when we saw him last. Princess Clara and Prince Garan are with him there. And the war is raging on the northern front as well. King Nash rode north in the days after the gala, and the Third and Fourth and most of the auxiliaries and Queen Roen and Lord Brocker met him there. Lady Murgda escaped the palace the day after the gala, Lady. There was a fire, and a terrible battle in the corridors, and in the confusion she got away. It's thought she tried to ride to the beacons at Marble Rise, but the King's Army had already taken control of the roads.'

Fire closed her eyes, trying to bear the pressure of all of this meaningless, horrible news. She did not want to go to Fort Flood. But she understood that she couldn't stay here indefinitely, imposing on these people's hospitality. And she supposed the army healers might as well look at her hands, which she herself had not yet seen, but which were obviously swollen, and useless, and ached beneath their bandages as if pain hung at the ends of her arms instead of hands.

She tried not to dwell on what it would mean if the healers told her she was going to lose them.

There was another thing she tried, and usually failed, not to dwell on – a memory of an occurrence that had taken place oh, months ago – before the gala planning, before Archer had ever found Mydogg's wine in Captain Hart's cellar. Fire had been questioning prisoners, all day, every day, and Archer had watched sometimes. And they'd talked to that foul-mouthed fellow who'd spoken of a tall archer with spot-on aim, a rapist who'd been held in Nax's dungeons some twenty years ago. Jod. And Fire had been happy, because finally she'd known the name and the nature of her foggy-minded archer.

On that day, she hadn't remembered that some twenty years ago Nax had hand-picked a brute from his dungeons and sent him north to rape Brocker's wife, the only happy consequence of which had been the birth of Archer.

The interrogation had ended with Archer punching the

informant in the face. On that day, Fire had thought it was because of the man's language.

And perhaps it had been. Fire would never know now at what point Archer had begun to suspect Jod's identity. Archer had kept his thoughts and fears to himself. For Fire had just broken his heart.

WHEN THE DAY came, her guards – nineteen of them now, for Mila was not here – wrapped her in many blankets for the journey, and strapped her arms carefully to her body so that her hands would be near her body's heat. They lifted her into Neel's saddle, and when Neel climbed up behind her they strapped her loosely to him. The party rode slowly, and Neel was strong and attentive, but still it was frightening to trust oneself entirely to someone else's balance.

And then, in time, the motion became soothing. She leaned back against him, relinquished responsibility, and slept.

The dappled grey horse, when separated from Fire and faced with the rock people, Fire's guard, and nineteen military mounts, had proven to be completely wild. It had clopped around on the rocks above ground during her illness, bolting every time a person emerged, refusing to be bridled, or stabled underground, or even approached. But nor did it seem willing to be left behind when it saw Fire being borne away. As the party picked its way east, the horse followed, tentatively, always at a safe distance.

THE BATTLES OF the southern front were waged on the land and in the caves bounded by Gentian's holding, Fort Flood, and the Winged River. Whatever ground the commander had managed to win or lose, the fort itself was still under royal control. Rising high on an outcrop of rock, surrounded by walls almost as tall as its roofs, it functioned as the army's headquarters and hospital.

Clara came running to them as they entered the gates. She stood beside Neel's horse as the guards unstrapped Fire, lowered her to the ground, and unwrapped her from her blankets. Clara was crying, and when she embraced Fire and kissed her face, taking care not to jar Fire's hands, which were still tied to her body, Fire sank numbly against her. She wished she could wrap her arms around this woman who cried for Archer and whose belly was round with Archer's baby. She wished she could melt into her.

'Oh, Fire,' Clara finally said, 'we've been out of our minds with worry. Brigan leaves tonight for the northern front. It'll relieve him greatly to see you alive before he goes.'

'No,' Fire said, pulling suddenly away from Clara, and startled by her own feeling. 'Clara, I don't want to see him. Tell him I wish him well, but I don't want to see him.'

'Oh,' Clara said, taken aback. 'Well. Are you certain? Because I can't think how we're going to stop him, once he returns from the tunnels and learns you're here.'

The tunnels. Fire sensed her own rising panic. 'My hands,' she said, focusing on a more isolated pain. 'Is there a healer with the time to attend to them?'

THE FINGERS OF her right hand were pinkish and puffy and blistered, like hunks of raw poultry. Fire stared at them, tired and sick, until she sensed that the healer was cheered by their appearance. 'It's too soon to know for sure,' the woman said, 'but we have grounds for hope.'

She smoothed a salve into the hand very, very gently, wrapped it in loose bandages, and unwrapped the other hand, humming.

The outer two fingers on Fire's left hand were black and dead-looking from the tips all the way down to the second knuckles.

The healer, no longer humming, asked if it was true what

she'd heard, that Fire was an accomplished fiddler. 'Well,' the woman said. 'All we can do now is watch them, and wait.'

She gave Fire a pill and a liquid to swallow, applied the salve, and wrapped bandages around the hand. 'Stay here,' she said. She bustled out of the small, dark room, which had a smoky fire in the grate and shutters over the windows to hold in the heat.

Fire had a vague memory of a time when she had been better at ignoring things it was no use to consider. She had been in control once, and had not sat dismal and wretched on examination tables while the entirety of her guard stood watching her with a sympathetic sort of bleakness.

And then she felt Brigan coming, an enormous moving force of emotion: concern, relief, reassurance, too intense for Fire to bear. She began to gasp; she was drowning. As he came into the room she slid off the table and ran into a corner.

No, she thought to him. *I don't want you here. No.*

'Fire,' he said. 'What is it? Please tell me.'

Please, you must go away. Please, Brigan, I beg you.

'Leave us,' Brigan said quietly to the guard.

No! I need them!

'Stay,' Brigan said in the same tone of voice, and her guard, which by now had developed a high threshold for bewilderment, turned around and filed back into the room.

Fire, Brigan thought to her. Have I done something to make you angry?

No. Yes, yes, you have, she thought wildly. *You never liked Archer. You don't care that he's dead.*

That is untrue, he thought to her with utter certainty. I had my own regard for Archer, and besides, it hardly matters, because you love him, and I love you, and your grief brings me grief. There is nothing in Archer's death but sadness.

That's why you must go, she thought to him. *There's nothing in this but sadness.*

There was a noise in the doorway and a man's harsh voice. 'Commander, we're ready.'

'I'm coming,' Brigan said over his shoulder. 'Wait for me outside.'

The man left.

Go, Fire thought to Brigan. *Don't keep them waiting.*

I will not leave you like this, he thought.

I won't look at you, she thought, pressing at the wall clumsily with her bandaged hands. *I don't want to see your new battle scars.*

He came to her in her corner, the stubborn, steady feeling of him unchanged. He touched his hand to her right shoulder and bent his face to her left ear, his stubble rough and his face cold against hers and the feel of him achingly familiar, and suddenly she was leaning back against him, her arms awkwardly embracing his left arm, stiff with leathered armour, and pulling it around her.

'You're the one with new scars,' he said very quietly, so that only she could hear.

'Don't go,' she said. 'Please don't go.'

'I desperately want not to go. But you know that I must.'

'I don't want to love you if you're only going to die,' she cried, burying her face in his arm. 'I don't love you.'

'Fire,' he said. 'Will you do something for me? Will you send me word on the northern front, so I know how you're faring?'

'I don't love you.'

'Does that mean you won't send word?'

'No,' she said confusedly. 'Yes. I'll send word. But—'

'Fire,' he said gently, beginning to untangle himself from her. 'You must feel what you feel. I—'

Another voice, sharp with impatience, interrupted from the doorway. 'Commander! The horses are standing.'

Brigan spun around to face the man, swearing with as much

exasperation and fury as Fire had ever heard anyone swear. The man scuttled away in alarm.

'I love you,' Brigan said very calmly to Fire's back. 'I hope in the coming days it may comfort you to know that. And all I ask of you is that you try to eat, Fire, and sleep, no matter how you feel. Eat and sleep. And send me word, so I know how you are. Tell me if there's anyone, or anything, I can send to you.'

Go safely. Go safely, she thought to him as he left the building and his convoy pounded through the gates.

What a silly, empty thing it was to say to anyone, anywhere.

CHAPTER TWENTY-NINE

FIRE GUESSED THAT there was little for a person with no hands to do at Fort Flood. Clara was busy with Brigan's captains and a constant stream of messengers, and Garan rarely even showed his face, scowling in his customary manner when he did. Fire avoided them, as she avoided the room where endless rows of soldiers lay suffering.

She was not permitted to step outside the walls of the fortress. She divided her time between two places: the bedroom she shared with Clara, Musa, and Margo, feigning sleep whenever Clara entered, for Clara asked too many questions about Archer. And the heavily guarded roof of the fort, where she stood in a warm hooded cloak, hands enclosed safely in her armpits, and communed with the grey dappled horse.

The mare – for Fire was clear-minded enough now to know she was a mare – was living on the rocks north of the building. She had broken away from Fire's group as they'd approached the fort and, despite the attempts of the horsemaster, would not consent to being stabled along with the other horses. Fire refused to allow anyone to subdue her with drugs, nor would Fire herself compel the horse into confinement. The horsemaster had thrown his arms in the air in disgust. This horse was obviously an uncommonly fine animal, but he was up to his elbows in injured horses and cast shoes and broken field harnesses, and had no time to waste on a recalcitrant.

And so the mare lived free on the rocks, eating food if it was left for her, finding food if it wasn't, and coming to visit Fire whenever Fire called to her. Her feeling was strange and wild, her mind a marvellous unbroken thing that Fire could touch and influence, but never truly comprehend. She belonged alone on the rocks, unconstrained, and vicious when she needed to be.

And yet there was love in the feeling of her too – constraining, in its way. This horse had no intention of leaving Fire.

They spent time within view of each other, their feelings connected by the tether of Fire's power. She was beautiful to look at, her coat soft patches and circles of grey, her mane and her tail thick and long, and tangled, and deep grey like slate. Her eyes were blue.

Fire wished she were allowed out of the fort. She would like to join the horse on the rocks, and climb onto her back, and be carried away wherever the horse wanted to go.

Garan came stalking into her bedroom one morning while she was curled under her covers, trying to numb herself to the burning of her hands and pretending to sleep. He stood over her and said without preliminary, 'Get up, Fire. We need you.'

It was not said with anger, but it didn't have the feeling of a request, either. Fire blinked up at him. 'My hands are useless,' she said.

'What we need you for does not require hands.'

Fire closed her eyes. 'You want me to question someone. I'm sorry, Garan. I don't feel well enough.'

'You'd feel better if you got up and stopped moping,' he said bluntly, 'and anyway, it's not an interrogation we need you for.'

Fire was furious. 'You never took Archer into your heart. You care nothing for what happened.'

Garan spoke hotly. 'You can't see into my heart, or you wouldn't say such a stupid thing. I'm not leaving this room until you get up. There's a war going on not a stone's throw from here, and I've enough that's heavy on my mind without you wasting yourself away like a self-absorbed brat. Do you want me to have to send a message to Brigan and Nash and Brocker one day, telling them you died, of nothing in particular? You're making me ill, Fire, and I beg you, if you won't get up for yourself, do it for me. I'm not keen on dying.'

Fire had pushed herself to a seated position somewhere in the middle of this remarkable speech, and now her eyes were open and seeing. Garan's skin was sweaty and he was breathing rapidly. He was, if possible, thinner than he had been before, and pain flickered in his face. Fire reached up to him, distressed now, and gestured for him to sit. When he did, she smoothed his hair with her own bandaged knob of a hand. She helped him to calm his breath.

'You've lost weight,' he said to her finally, his unhappy eyes on her face. 'And you have this horrible empty look in your eyes that makes me want to shake you.'

Fire smoothed his hair again, and chose her words carefully, finding ones that would not make her cry. 'I don't think I'm moping, exactly,' she said. 'I don't feel entirely connected to myself, Garan.'

'Your power is strong,' he said. 'I can feel it. You soothed me right away.'

She wondered if a person could be powerful, but inside be broken into pieces, and shaking, all the time.

She studied him again. He really didn't look well. He was carrying too much.

'What is the work you need me to do?' she asked.

He said, 'Would you be willing to ease the pain of the soldiers in this fort who are dying?'

THE HEALING WORK of the fort took place in the enormous downstairs ward that was the residence of five hundred soldiers during peacetime. There was no glass in the windows and the shutters were drawn now to conserve heat, which came from fireplaces along the walls and from a fire in the middle of the floor, its smoke billowing haphazardly toward an open flue in the ceiling that led all the way to the roof and the sky.

The room was dim, and soldiers were moaning and crying out, and the place had a smell of blood and smoke and something else cloying that stopped Fire at the entrance. It was too much like stepping into one of her nightmares. She couldn't do it.

But then she saw a man lying on his back in a bed, his nose and ears black like her fingers, and only one hand resting on his chest, for the other was gone completely, a stump wrapped with gauze. He was gritting his teeth, hot and shaking, and Fire went to him, because she could not stop her compassion.

At the very sight of her, some panic inside him seemed to still. She sat at the edge of the bed and looked into his eyes. She understood that he was exhausted, but too distracted with pain and fear to rest. She took away his sense of his pain and soothed his fear. She helped him to fall asleep.

THIS WAS HOW Fire became a fixture in the healing room; for she was even better than the surgeons' drugs at taking pain away, and every kind of pain was present in that room. Sometimes it was enough to sit with a soldier to calm him, and sometimes, as when he was having an arrow pulled, or a waking surgery, it took more. There were days when her mind was in several parts of the room at once, soothing pain where it was worst, while her body walked up and down the rows of patients, her hair loose and her eyes seeking the eyes of the men and women in the beds who felt less frightened for having seen her.

It surprised her how easy it was to talk to soldiers who were dying, or soldiers who would never be well again, or who had lost their friends, and were afraid for their families. She had thought she'd already reached her capacity for pain and had no room inside her for more. But she remembered having told

Archer once that you could not measure love on a scale of degrees, and now she understood that it was the same with pain. Pain might escalate upward and, just when you thought you'd reached your limit, begin to spread sideways, and spill out, and touch other people, and mix with their pain. And grow larger, but somehow less oppressive. She had thought herself trapped in a place outside the ordinary feeling lives of people; she had not noticed how many other people were trapped in that place with her.

She finally began to let Clara into that place. She told Clara what Clara's own grief had been yearning for: the facts of what had happened.

'He died alone,' she said to Clara quietly.

'And,' Clara said, just as quietly back, 'he died believing he'd failed you. For by then he must have known their plans to kidnap you, don't you think?'

'He certainly at least suspected it,' Fire said, realising as the story opened in words between them, just how many parts of it she didn't know. It both hurt and soothed her, like the salve the healers spread on her raw hands, to try to fill in the missing parts. She would never know how it had felt for him to be shot by his own father. Whether things would have gone differently if she'd paid more attention, if she'd fought harder to keep him from going. If years ago she'd found a way to stop him loving her so much; if Archer, no matter the strength of his mind or the depth of his affection, had ever been entirely immune to her monster beauty.

'I suppose we'll also never know what Jod was truly like,' Clara said, when Fire, quietly, had conveyed all of these thoughts. 'We know he was a criminal, of course,' she continued robustly, 'and a vicious lowlife, fit to die, even if he is my child's grandfather.' She snorted, saying as an aside, 'What a pair of grandfathers this child has. But what I mean is, we'll never know if Jod would've killed his own son if he'd been in control of his own mind instead of under the power of that horrible boy you dropped into the mountain, and good riddance. I hope that one died in terrible agony impaled upon a jagged bit of rock.'

Clara was an oddly comforting person for Fire to be with in these days. Pregnant, she was even more stunning than she had been before. Almost five months in, her hair was thicker and glossier, her skin glowing; an extra vitality fueled her usual determination. She was completely alive, which was painful sometimes for Fire to stand beside. But Clara was also angry at all the right things and fiercely honest. And she was carrying Archer's child in her body.

'Lord Brocker is also your child's grandfather,' Fire said mildly. 'And there are two grandmothers you needn't be ashamed of.'

'And anyway,' Clara said, 'if we're to be judged by our parents and grandparents, then we all may as well impale ourselves upon jagged bits of rock.'

Yes, Fire thought to herself grimly. That wasn't far from true.

When she was alone she couldn't avoid thoughts of home, memories. On the roof, visiting the mare, she fought off thinking of Small, who was far away in King's City, most certainly wondering why she had gone away and if she was ever coming back.

At night, when she struggled with sleep, Cansrel and Archer kept changing places in her nightmares. Cansrel, his throat torn apart, was suddenly Archer, staring at her just as balefully as Cansrel always had. Or sometimes she was luring Archer, rather than Cansrel, to his death, or luring them together, or sometimes Cansrel was killing Archer, or raping Archer's mother, and maybe Archer found him and killed him. Whatever happened, whichever dead man died again in her dreams, she woke to the same pitiless grief.

NEWS CAME FROM the northern front that Brigan was sending Nash down to Fort Flood and Brocker and Roen would follow him.

Garan was indignant.

'I can understand sending Nash here to take his place,' he said. 'But why is he having done with his entire strategising team? He'll be sending us the Third and Fourth next, and taking Mydogg's army on all by himself.'

'It must be becoming too dangerous there for anyone who isn't a soldier,' Clara said.

'If it's dangerous, he should tell us.'

'He *has* told us, Garan. What do you think he means when he says even in camp a night's rest is rare? Do you imagine Mydogg's soldiers are keeping ours out late with drinking games and dancing? And did you read the latest report? A soldier of the Third attacked his own company the other day, killed three of his fellow soldiers before he himself was killed. Mydogg had promised to pay a fortune to his family if he turned traitor.'

Working in the healing room, Fire could not fail to learn the things that happened in battle and in war. And she understood that despite the torn-up bodies the medics brought in from the tunnels every day, despite the difficulty of supplying food to the southern camps and carrying the injured away and repairing weapons and armour, and despite the bonfires lit every night to burn the dead, the southern war was thought to be going well. Here at Fort Flood it was a matter of skirmishes on horseback and on foot, one group of soldiers trapping another in a cave, quick strikes and retreats. Gentian's soldiers, who were led by one of Mydogg's Pikkian captains, were disorganised. Brigan's, on the other hand, were finely trained to know their responsibilities in any given situation, even in the chaos of the tunnels. Brigan had left predicting it would be only a matter of weeks before they made some kind of significant breakthrough.

But on the northern front, the fighting took place on the open, flat terrain north of the city, where there was little advantage to cleverness of strategy. The ground and the visibility warranted full-out battle, all day until dark fell. Almost every battle ended with the royal side in retreat. They were fierce, Mydogg's men, and both Mydogg and Murgda were there with them; and the snow and ice were proving to be no friends to the horses. Too often the soldiers fought on their feet, and then it began to show that the King's Army was vastly outnumbered. Very slowly, Mydogg was advancing on the city.

And of course, the north was where Brigan had gone, because Brigan always went wherever things were going most badly. Fire supposed he needed to be there in order to give rousing speeches and lead the charge into the fray, or whatever it was commanders did in wartime. She resented his competence at something so tragic and senseless. She wished he, or somebody, would throw down his sword and say, 'Enough! This is a silly way to decide who's in charge!' And it seemed to her, as the beds in the healing room filled and emptied and filled, that these battles didn't leave much to be in charge of. The kingdom was already broken, and this war was tearing the broken pieces smaller.

Cansrel would have liked it. Meaningless destruction was to his taste. The boy probably would've liked it too.

Archer would have reserved his judgment – reserved it from her, at least, knowing her scathing opinion. And whatever his opinion, he would have gone out and fought bravely for the Dells.

As Brigan and Nash were doing.

WHEN NASH'S FRONT guard clattered through the gate, Fire was ashamed to find herself running up to the roof, stumbling, uncontrolled.

Beautiful horse, she cried out to her companion. *Beautiful horse, I can't bear this. I can bear Archer and Cansrel if I must, but I cannot bear this too. Make him go away. Why must my friends be soldiers?*

Some time later, when Nash came to the roof to find her, she didn't kneel, like her own guard and the roof guard did. She kept her back turned to Nash and her eyes on the horse, her shoulders hunched as if to protect herself from his presence.

'Lady Fire,' he said.

Lord King. I mean no disrespect, but I beg you to go away.

'Certainly, Lady, if you wish it,' he said mildly. 'But first I've promised to deliver about a hundred messages from the northern front and the city – from my mother, your grandmother, Hanna, Brocker, and Mila, for starters.'

Fire imagined a message from Brocker: I blame you for the death of my son. A message from Tess: You've ruined your beautiful hands with your carelessness, haven't you, Lady Granddaughter? A message from Hanna: You left me here alone.

Very well, she thought to Nash. *Tell me your messages, if you must.*

'Well,' Nash said, somewhat bemused, 'they send their love, of course. And their heartbreak over Archer, and their relief that you're alive. And Hanna specifically asked me to tell you that Blotchy is recovering. Lady—' He stopped. 'Fire,' he said. 'Why will you talk to my sister and my brothers but not to me?'

She snapped at him. *If Brigan said we talked he was being disingenuous.*

Nash paused. 'He didn't. I suppose I assumed. But surely you've been talking to Clara and Garan.'

Clara and Garan aren't soldiers. They aren't going to die, she thought to him, realising as she conveyed it that this reasoning was flawed, for Garan could die of his illness, and Clara of childbirth. And Tess of old age, and Brocker and Roen of an attack on their travelling party, and Hanna could be thrown from a horse.

'Fire—'

Please, Nash, please. Don't make me talk about reasons, please, just let me be alone. Please!

He was stung by this. He turned to go. Then he stopped and turned back. 'Just one more thing. Your horse is in the stables.'

Fire looked across the rocks at the grey horse stamping her hooves at the snow, and didn't understand. She sent her confusion to Nash.

'Didn't you tell Brigan you wanted your horse?' he asked.

Fire spun around, looking straight at him for the first time. He struck a handsome figure and fierce, a tiny new scar running into his lip, his cloak hanging over armour of mail and leather. She said, 'You don't mean Small?'

'Of course,' he said, 'Small. Anyway, Brigan thought you wanted him. He's downstairs.'

Fire ran.

SHE HAD CRIED so often and so much since she'd found Archer's body, cried at the slightest thing, always silent tears rolling down her face. The way she began to cry when she saw Small, plain and quiet with his hair in his eyes, pressing against his stall door to reach her, was different. She thought she might choke from the violence of these sobs, or rip something inside her.

Musa was alarmed, and came into the stall with her, rubbing her back as she clung to Small's neck and gasped. Neel produced handkerchiefs. It was no use. She couldn't stop crying.

It's my fault, she said to Small over and over. *Oh Small, it's my fault. I was supposed to be the one to die, not Archer. Archer was never supposed to die.*

After a long time, she cried herself to a place where she understood that it was not her fault. And then she cried more, from the simple grief of knowing that he was gone.

SHE WOKE, NOT from a nightmare, but *to* something – something comforting. The sensation of being wrapped in warm blankets and sleeping against a warm breathing back that belonged to Small.

Musa and several other guards were having a murmured conversation with someone outside the stall. Fire's bleary mind groped its way toward them. The someone was the king.

Her panic was gone, replaced with an odd, peaceful emptiness. She pushed herself up and ran her bandaged hand lightly along Small's wonderful barrel body, swerving to touch the places where his fur grew crooked around raptor monster scars. His mind snoozed gently, and the hay near his face moved with his breath. He was a dark lump in the torchlight. He was perfect.

She touched Nash's mind. He came to the stall door and leaned over it, looking at her. Hesitation, and love, obvious on his face and in his feeling.

'You're smiling,' he said.

Naturally, tears were the response to these words. Angry with herself, she tried to stop them, but they squeezed out nonetheless.

'I'm sorry,' she said.

He came into the stall and crouched down in the space between Small's head and chest. He stroked Small's neck, considering her.

'I understand you've been crying a great deal,' he said.

'Yes,' she said, defeated.

'You must be tired and sore from it.'

'Yes.'

'And your hands. Are they still very painful?'

There was something comforting about this calm interrogation. 'They're a bit better than they were.'

He nodded gravely and continued to stroke Small's neck. He was dressed as before, except now he carried his helmet under one arm. He seemed older in the darkness and the orange light. He was older, ten years older, than herself. Almost all of her friends were older; even Brigan, the youngest sibling, was almost five years her senior. But she didn't think it was the difference in years that made her feel like such a child, surrounded by adults.

'Why are you still here?' she asked. 'Shouldn't you be in a cave somewhere inspiring people?'

'I should,' he said, shouldering her sarcasm lightly, 'and I came here for my horse so that I might ride out to the camps. But now I'm talking to you instead.'

Fire traced a long, thin scar on Small's back. She thought about her tendency lately to communicate more easily with horses and dying strangers than with the people she had thought she loved.

'It's not reasonable to love people who are only going to die,' she said.

Nash thought about that for a moment, stroking Small's neck with great deliberation, as if the fate of the Dells depended on that smooth, careful movement.

'I have two responses to that,' he said finally. 'First, everyone's going to die. Second, love is stupid. It has nothing to do with reason. You love whomever you love. Against all reason I loved my father.' He looked at her keenly. 'Did you love yours?'

'Yes,' she whispered.

He stroked Small's nose. 'I love you,' he said, 'even knowing you'll never have me. And I love my brother, more than I ever realised before you came along. You can't help whom you love, Lady. Nor can you know what it's liable to cause you to do.'

She made a connection then. Surprised, she sat back from him and studied his face, soft with shadows and light. She saw a part of him she hadn't seen before.

'You came to me for lessons to guard your mind,' she said, 'and you stopped asking me to marry you, both at the same time. You did those things out of love for your brother.'

'Well,' he said, looking a bit sheepishly at the floor. 'I also took a few swings at him, but that's neither here nor there.'

'You're good at love,' she said simply, because it seemed to her that it was true. 'I'm not so good at love. I'm like a barbed creature. I push everyone I love away.'

He shrugged. 'I don't mind you pushing me away if it means you love me, little sister.'

CHAPTER THIRTY

SHE BEGAN TO write a letter in her mind to Brigan. It wasn't a very good letter. Dear Brigan, I don't think you should be doing what you're doing. Dear Brigan, people are swirling away from me and I am swirling apart.

The swelling of her hands had gone down, and no places had blackened that hadn't been black before. There would likely be a surgery, the healers said, when more time had passed, to remove the two dead fingers on her left hand.

'With all your medicines,' Musa asked one of the healers, 'you really have nothing to help her?'

'There are no medicines to bring a dead thing back to life,' the healer said crisply. 'The best thing right now will be for Lady Fire to start using her hands again regularly. She'll find a person can manage quite well without ten fingers.'

It was not like it had been before. But what a relief to have permission to cut her food, button her own buttons, tie back her own hair, and she would do it, even if her movements were clumsy and infantile at first and her living fingers burned, even if she sensed pity in the feeling of her watching friends. The pity only made her more stubborn. She asked permission to help with practical tasks in the healing room – dressing wounds, feeding the soldiers who couldn't feed themselves. They never minded if she dribbled broth onto their clothing.

As her dexterity improved, she even began to assist with some of the simpler aspects of surgery: holding lamps, handing the surgeons their supplies. She found that she had a strong stomach for blood, and infections, and men's insides – even though men's insides were rather more messy than the insides of monster bugs. Some of these soldiers were familiar to her because of the three weeks she'd spent travelling with the First. She supposed that some of them had been her enemies once, but that feeling seemed gone from them, now that they were at war and in pain and in such need of comfort.

A soldier she remembered quite well was brought in one day, an arrow embedded in his thigh. It was the man who had once lent her his fiddle – the enormous, craggy, gentle tree of a man. She smiled to see him. They had quiet conversations now and then, she easing his pain as his wound healed. He saying little about her dead fingers, but an expression on his face, whenever he looked at them, that conveyed the depth of his empathy.

When Brocker arrived he took her hands and held them to his face, and cried into them.

WITH BROCKER CAME not only Roen but Mila, for Brocker had asked the girl to serve as his military assistant, and Mila had accepted. Brocker and Roen – old friends who had not seen each other since the time of King Nax – now were practically inseparable, and Mila was often with them.

Fire saw Nash only now and then, coming to the fort for information or to strategise with Garan and Clara, Brocker and Roen. Dirty and haggard, his smiles thin.

'I believe King Nash will come back,' Mila would say to Fire calmly every time he left again for the caves. Even though Fire knew there was no logic backing Mila's assertion, the words comforted her.

Mila had changed. She worked hard beside Brocker, quiet and intent. 'I learned that there's a drug to end a pregnancy when it first announces itself,' she told Fire lightly one day. 'It's too late for me, of course. Did you know about it, Lady?'

Fire was stunned. 'Of course not, or I would have told you, and found it for you.'

'Clara told me about it,' Mila said. 'The king's healers are impressive, but it does seem as if you need to have grown up in certain sections of King's City even to have a hope of knowing all they're capable of. I was angry when I heard,' she added. 'I was furious. But it's no use, really, to think about it now. I'm no different from anyone else, am I, Lady? We're all walking paths we would never have chosen for ourselves. I suppose I grow tired sometimes of my own complaining.'

'That boy of mine,' Brocker said, later the same day. He was sitting beside Fire in a chair on the roof, where he'd consented to be carried because he'd wanted to see the grey dappled horse. He shook his head and grunted. 'My boy. I expect I have grandchildren I'll never know about. Trust him to die, so instead of my being furious about Mila and Princess Clara, I'm comforted.'

They watched the dance taking place on the ground before them: two horses circling each other, one plain and brown who stretched his nose out occasionally in an attempt to plant a wet kiss on the other's elusive grey rump. Fire was trying to make friends of the two horses, for the mare, if she truly intended to follow Fire wherever she went, was going to need a few more souls in the world that she could trust. Today the mare had stopped trying to intimidate Small by rearing at him and kicking. This was progress.

'She's a river mare,' Brocker said.

'A what?'

'A river mare. I've seen one or two dappled greys like that before; they come from the mouth of the Winged River. I don't think there's much of a common market for river horses, despite them being so fine – they're absurdly expensive, on account of being hard to catch and even harder to break. They're not as sociable as other horses.'

Fire remembered then that Brigan had spoken once, covetously, of river horses. She also remembered that the mare had carried her stubbornly south and west from Cutter's estate, until Fire had turned her around. She had been trying to go home – to take Fire to her home where the river began. Now she was here, where she had not wanted to be, but where she'd chosen to be nonetheless.

Dear Brigan, she thought to herself. People want incongruous, impossible things. Horses do, too.

'Has the commander had a look at her yet?' Brocker asked, sounding amused by his own question. Apparently Brocker was acquainted with Brigan's stance on horses.

'I care nothing of her value,' Fire said softly, 'and I will not help him break her.'

'You're not being fair,' Brocker said mildly. 'The boy is known for his kindness to horses. He doesn't break animals that show no inclination toward him.'

'But what horse wouldn't be inclined?' Fire said, and then stopped, because she was being silly and sentimental, and saying too much.

A moment later Brocker said, in an odd, bewildered voice she didn't entirely know what to think of, 'I've made some grievous mistakes, and my mind spins when I try to comprehend all that has come of them. I have not been the man I should have been, not to anyone. Perhaps,' he said, staring into his lap, 'I have been justly punished. Oh, child, your fingers break my heart. Could you teach yourself to finger the strings with your right hand?'

Fire reached for his hand and gripped it as tightly as she could, but didn't answer. She had thought of playing her fiddle opposite-handed, but it seemed very much like starting from a base of nothing. Eighteen-year-old fingers did not learn how to fly across strings anywhere as easily as five-year-old fingers did, and besides, a bow would be a great deal for a hand with only two fingers and a thumb to manage.

Her fiddler patient had offered another suggestion. What if

she kept her fiddle in her left hand and her bow in her right, as usual, but refingered her music so that it was playable with only two fingers? How fast could she reach the strings, and how accurately? At night once, when it was dark and her guard couldn't see, she'd pretended to hold her fiddle and push her two fingers against imaginary strings. It had seemed a bumbling, useless, depressing exercise at the time. Brocker's question made her wonder if she mightn't try again.

A WEEK LATER she came to understand the rest of Brocker's words.

She had stayed late in the healing room, saving a man's life. It was a thing she was able to do very occasionally: a matter of willpower in the soldiers closest to death, some in agonies of pain and some not even conscious. In their moment of giving up she could give them mettle, if they wanted it. She could help them hold on to their disappearing selves. It didn't always work. A man who couldn't stop bleeding would never live, no matter how adamantly he fought death back. But sometimes, what she gave them was just enough.

Of course, it left her exhausted.

On this day she was hungry, and knew there would be food in the offices where Garan and Clara, Brocker and Roen spent their days waiting anxiously for messages and arguing. Except that today they weren't arguing, and as she entered with her guard she sensed an unusual lightness. Nash was there, sitting beside Mila, chatting, a truer smile on his face than Fire had seen there in some time. Garan and Clara ate peacefully from bowls, and Brocker and Roen sat together at a table, drawing lines across a topographical map of what appeared to be the bottom half of the kingdom. Roen muttered something that caused Brocker to chuckle.

'What is it?' Fire said. 'What's happened?'

Roen looked up from her map and gestured at a tureen of

stew on the table. 'Ah, Fire. Sit down. Eat something, and we'll tell you why the war isn't hopeless. What about you, Musa? Neel? Are you hungry? Nash,' she said, twisting around to regard her son critically. 'Come and get more stew for Mila.'

Nash pushed himself up from his chair. 'I see that everyone is to have stew but me.'

'I've watched you eat three bowls of stew,' Roen said severely, and Fire sat down rather hard, for the teasing in this room made her weak with a relief she wasn't sure yet it was safe to be feeling.

And then Roen explained that a pair of their scouts on the southern front had made two rather cheerful discoveries back to back. First they'd identified the labyrinthine path of the enemy's food supply route through the tunnels, and second, they'd located a series of caves east of the fighting where the enemy was stabling the majority of its horses. Commandeering both supply route and caves had been merely a matter of a couple of well-placed attacks by the king's forces. And now it would only be a matter of days before Gentian's men ran out of food; and without horses to escape on, they would be left with no option but to surrender, allowing the majority of the First and Second to race north to reinforce Brigan's troops.

Or at least, this was what the smiling faces in this office supposed would happen. And Fire had to own that it did seem likely, as long as Gentian's army didn't block the King's Army's own supply route in turn, and as long as anyone was left in the Third and Fourth to be reinforced by the First and Second by the time the First and Second reached the north.

'This is his doing,' Fire heard Roen murmur to Brocker. 'Brigan mapped these tunnels, and before he left here, he and his scouts worked out all the most likely locations for the supply routes and the horses specifically. He got it right.'

'Of course he did,' Brocker said. 'He surpassed me a long time ago.'

Something in his tone caused Fire to stop her spoon halfway to her mouth and scrutinise him, listening to his words again in her mind. It was the pride in his voice that rang strange. And of course, Brocker had always spoken proudly of the boy commander who'd followed his own path so magnificently. But today he sounded as if he were crossing over into indulgence.

He looked up at her to see why she was staring. His eyes, pale and clear, caught hers, and held.

She understood for the first time what Brocker had done twenty-some years ago to set Nax into a rage.

As she pushed away from the table Brocker's voice carried after her, tired, and oddly defeated. 'Fire, wait. Fire, love, let me talk to you.'

She ignored him. She shouldered her way through the door.

IT WAS ROEN who came to her on the roof.

'Fire,' she said. 'We'd like to talk to you, and it would be much easier for Lord Brocker if you would come down.'

Fire was amenable to this, because she had questions, and rather explosive things she found herself wanting to say. She folded her arms at Musa and looked into Musa's hazel eyes. 'Musa, you may complain to the commander all you like, but I insist on speaking to the queen and Lord Brocker alone. Do you understand me?'

Musa cleared her throat uncomfortably. 'We'll station ourselves outside the door, Lady.'

Downstairs in Brocker's living quarters with the door closed and locked, Fire stood against a wall and stared not at Brocker but at the great wheels of his chair. Every once in a while she glanced into his face, and then into Roen's, because she couldn't help herself. It seemed to her that this was happening too often lately, that she should look into a face and see someone else there, and understand pieces of the past that she had not understood before.

Roen's black hair with its white streak was pulled back tightly, and her face was also tight, with concern. She came and stood beside Brocker, gently putting a hand on his shoulder. Brocker reached up and touched Roen's hand. Even knowing what she now knew, the unfamiliarity of the gesture startled Fire.

'I have never seen the two of you together before this war,' she said.

'Yes,' Brocker said. 'You've never known me to travel, child. The queen and I haven't once been in each other's company since—'

Roen finished for him quietly. 'Since the day Nax set those brutes on you in my green house, I do believe.'

Fire glanced at her sharply. 'You saw it happen?'

Roen gave a grim nod. 'I was made to watch. I believe he hoped I would miscarry my bastard baby.'

And so Nax had been inhuman, and Fire felt the force of it; but still, she could not get around the fact of her anger.

'*Archer* is your son,' she said to Brocker, choking on her own indignation.

'Of course Archer is my son,' Brocker said heavily. 'He has always been my son.'

'Did he even know he had any kind of brother? He could've benefited from a steady brother like Brigan. And Brigan, does he know? I won't keep it from him.'

'Brigan knows, child,' Brocker said, 'though Archer never did, to my regret. When Archer died, I understood that Brigan must know. We told him, just weeks ago, when he came to the northern front.'

'And what of him? Brigan could have stood to call *you* father, Brocker, rather than a mad king who hated him because he was cleverer and stronger than his own true son. He could have grown up in the north away from Nax and Cansrel and never had to become—' She stopped and turned her face away, trying to calm her frantic voice. 'Brigan should have been a northern lord, with a farm and a holding and a stable full of horses. Not a prince.'

'But Brigandell *is* a prince,' Roen said quietly. 'He is my son. And Nax was the only one with the power to disinherit him and send him away, and Nax would never have done that. He would never have admitted publicly that he was a cuckold.'

'And so for Nax's pride,' Fire said desperately, 'Brigan has taken on the role of saviour of the kingdom. It's not fair. It's not fair,' she cried, knowing it was a child's argument but not caring, because being childish did not make it untrue.

'Oh, Fire,' Roen said. 'You can see as well as any of us that the kingdom needs Brigan exactly where he is now, just as it needs you, and every other one of us, whether or not our lots are fair.'

Roen's voice contained terrible grief. Fire looked into her face, trying to imagine the woman she had been twenty-some years ago. Intelligent, and fiercely capable, and finding herself married to a king who was puppet to a maniacal puppeteer. Roen had watched her marriage – and her kingdom – fall to ruin.

Fire's gaze moved to Brocker then, who held her eyes unhappily.

It was Brocker she could not forgive.

'Brocker, my father,' she said. 'You did such an unkind thing to your wife.'

'Would you wish it had never happened,' Roen cut in, 'and Archer and Brigan never born?'

'That is a cheater's argument!'

'But you're not the one who's been cheated, Fire,' Roen said. 'Why should it hurt you so much?'

'Would we be at war now, if you two hadn't provoked Nax into ruining his own military commander? Haven't we all been cheated?'

'Do you imagine,' Roen said with rising frustration, 'that the kingdom was headed down a path to peace?'

Fire understood, in painful fits and starts, why this hurt so much. It was not the war, or Archer or Brigan. It was not the punishments the perpetrators hadn't foreseen. It was still Brocker's wife, Aliss; it was the very small matter of what Brocker had done to Aliss. Fire had thought she had two fathers who sat on opposite poles. Yet even understanding that her bad father had been capable of kindness, she had never allowed for the possibility that her good father might be capable of cruelty or dishonour.

She understood suddenly what a useless, day-and-night way of thinking that was. There wasn't a simple person anywhere in this world.

'I'm tired of learning the truth of things,' she said.

'Fire,' Brocker said, his voice rough with a shame she had never heard there before. 'I don't question your right to be angry.'

She looked into Brocker's eyes, which were so like Brigan's. 'I find I'm not angry anymore,' she said quietly, tying her hair back, out of her face. 'Did Brigan send you away because he was angry?'

'He was angry. But no, that's not why he sent us away.'

'It was too dangerous there,' Roen said, 'for a middle-aged woman and a man in a chair, and a pregnant assistant.'

It was dangerous. And he was there all alone, fighting a war, absorbing the truth of his parentage and the truth of history, with no one to talk to. And she'd pushed him away with words of unlove she hadn't meant. In return he'd sent her Small, knowing somehow that she needed him.

She was thoroughly ashamed of herself.

And she supposed that if she were going to be in love with a man who was always where she was not, then her poor recovering fingers had better grow accustomed to holding a

pen. Which was the first thing she wrote in the letter she sent
to him that night.

CHAPTER THIRTY-ONE

THE SPRING MELT came early. On the day the First and Second left Fort Flood for the northern front the snow was shrinking in uneven crusty clumps, and the sound of trickling water was everywhere. The river roared.

Gentian's army at Fort Flood, still led by one of Mydogg's now bedraggled Pikkians, had not surrendered. Hungry and horseless, they'd done something far more desperate and foolish: they'd tried to escape on foot. It was not pleasant for Nash giving the command, but he did it, because he had to, for if they were allowed to go, they would find their way to Mydogg and his army at Marble Rise. It was a massacre. By the time the enemy laid its weapons down, they numbered only hundreds, in a force that had begun, months ago, as fifteen thousand.

Nash stopped to arrange the conveyance of prisoners and wounded back to Fort Flood. Fire helped Gentian's medics. Their need for her was overwhelming. She knelt in a sheen of water that slid across the rocks to the hungry river, and held a man's hand while he died.

FIRE, HER GUARD, several other healers, the armourers and other staff persons – and, at a distance, the dappled grey horse – rode north on the tails of the First and Second.

They passed very near the city, near enough that they could see the river swollen almost as high as the bridges. Fire stretched as hard as she could for Hanna and Tess, but though she could just make out the black turrets of the palace rising above indistinguishable buildings, she could not reach them. They were out of her range.

Soon after, they approached the vast northern camps, startlingly close to the city. The sight was not cheering – the rise was desolate, crowded with musty and soaked tents, some sitting smack in the middle of newly formed streams. Mute, exhausted-looking soldiers from the Third and Fourth wandered among the tents. At the appearance of the First and Second, their faces lit up slowly, hesitantly, as if they didn't dare to believe in the mirage of mounted reinforcements kicking up such a spray that they seemed to be emerging from a lake. Then there followed a sort of quiet and tired jubilation. Friends and strangers hugged each other. Some in the Third and Fourth wept involuntary, depleted tears.

Fire asked a soldier of the Third to take her to the army hospital. She got to work.

THE HEALING ROOMS of the northern front were situated at the south and back of the camp in hastily constructed wooden barracks with the stone plain of Marble Rise for a floor. Which meant that at the moment, the floor was slippery with seeping water, and in some places slick with blood.

She saw quickly that the work here would be no different and no more desperate than what she was used to. She uncovered her hair and moved down the rows of patients, stopping at those who were in need of more than her presence. Hope and lightness came to the rooms like a clean breeze, as it had in the camp with the arrival of reinforcements, except that here the change was her doing, and hers alone. How strange it was to understand that. How strange to have the power to cause others to feel something she herself did not feel; and then catch the hint of it in their collective minds, and begin to feel it herself.

Through an arrow loop in the wall she saw a familiar horse and rider tearing across the camp toward the healing rooms. Brigan pulled up at Nash's feet and dropped from the saddle.

The two brothers threw their arms around each other and embraced hard.

Shortly thereafter he stepped into the healing rooms and leaned in the doorway, looking across at her quietly. Brocker's son with gentle grey eyes.

She abandoned all pretense of decorum and ran at him.

AFTER SOME TIME, a cheeky fellow in a cot nearby said aloud that he was inclined to disbelieve the rumour that the lady monster was marrying the king.

'What tipped you off?' asked another fellow, one cot over.

Fire and Brigan didn't let go of each other, but Fire laughed. 'You're thin,' she said to him between kisses, 'and your colour is off. You're sick.'

'It's just a bit of dirt,' he said, kissing tears away on both of her cheeks.

'Don't joke. I can feel that you're sick.'

'It's only exhaustion,' he said. 'Oh, Fire, I'm glad you're here, but I'm not sure you should be. This isn't a fortress. They attack arbitrarily.'

'Well, if there are to be attacks, then I need to be here. I can do too much good not to be.'

His arms around her tightened. 'Tonight when you're done with your work, will you come find me?'

I will.

A voice outside the healing rooms called for the commander. Brigan sighed. 'Come straight into my office,' he said dryly, 'even if there's a queue outside the door. We'll never see each other if you wait until no one else is looking for me.'

As he left to answer the call, she heard him exclaiming in wonderment on the rise. 'Rocks, Nash. Is that a river mare out there? Do you see her? Have you ever laid eyes on a more gorgeous creature?'

*

THE KING'S ARMY'S numbers at the northern front were now practically doubled. Their plan was to launch a massive attack against Mydogg in the morning. Everyone knew that it would be the battle to determine the war. That evening, an anxious pall settled over the camp.

Fire took a break from the healing rooms and walked among the tents, through clammy patches of fog that rose from the melting water, her guard making a loose circle around her. The soldiers were untalkative, their eyes latching on to her, wide and tired, wherever she went. 'No,' she said, when her guard made a move to stop a man who reached for her arm. 'He doesn't want to hurt me.' She looked around and said with conviction, 'No one here wants to hurt me.' They only wanted a bit of reassurance on the night before a battle. Perhaps it was a thing she could give.

It was fully dark by the time she came upon Nash sitting alone in a chair outside the command tents. The stars were pricking into place in the sky, one at a time, but his head was bent into his hands, where he could not see them. Fire came to stand with him. She put her good hand on the back of his chair to steady her balance as she turned her face to the universe.

He heard her, or felt her, beside him. He reached rather absently for her other hand, stared into it, tracing the living skin at the base of her dead fingers. 'You have a reputation among the soldiers,' he said. 'Not just the injured soldiers – you've developed a reputation that's spread through the entire army. Did you know? They're saying the beauty of you is so powerful, and the mind of you so warm and insistent and strong, that you can call people back from death.'

Fire spoke quietly. 'There are many people who've died. I've tried to hold on, but still they let go.'

Nash sighed and gave her back her hand. He tilted his face up to the stars. 'We're going to win this war, you know,' he said, 'now that our army's together. But the world doesn't care who wins. It'll go on spinning, no matter how many people are slaughtered tomorrow. No matter if you and I are slaughtered.' After a moment, he added, 'I almost wish it wouldn't, if we aren't allowed to go on spinning with it.'

MOST SOLDIERS IN the camp were sleeping by the time Fire and her guard left the healing rooms and crossed again to the command tents. She stepped through the flap of Brigan's office to find him standing at a table covered with diagrams, rubbing his head while five men and three women argued a point about archers and arrows and wind patterns on Marble Rise.

If Brigan's captains did not notice her unobtrusive entry at first, they came to notice, for the tent, though large, was not so mammoth that seven newcomers could hang back in the corners. The argument dissipated and turned to stares.

'Captains,' Brigan said with obvious fatigue. 'Let this be the only time I ever have to remind you of your manners.'

Eight sets of eyes spun back to the table.

'Lady Fire,' Brigan said. He sent her a question. *How are you?*

Exhausted.

Enough for sleep?

I think so.

I'll be at this for a while yet. Perhaps you should sleep while you can.

No, I'll wait for you.

You could sleep here.

Would you wake me when you're through?

Yes.

Promise?

Yes.

Fire paused. *I don't suppose there's any way for me to walk into your sleeping quarters without everyone watching?*

A quick smile came and went across Brigan's face. 'Captains,' he said, cutting his attention back to his officers, who had been trying their hardest to bore their eyes into the diagrams on the table despite their suspicions that the commander and the monster were engaged in some outlandish manner of silent conversation. 'Kindly step outside for three minutes.'

First Brigan dismissed the majority of Fire's guard. Then he escorted Musa, Margo, and Fire through the flap that led to his sleeping tent, and lit the braziers so they wouldn't be cold.

SHE WOKE TO the light of a candle and the feel of Brigan near. Musa and Margo were gone. She turned under her blankets and saw him sitting on a chest, watching her, his features plain and dear, and soft in the candlelight. She couldn't help the tears that sprang to her eyes from the feeling of him alive.

'Did you say my name?' she whispered, remembering what had woken her.

'Yes.'

'Will you come to bed?'

'Fire,' he said. 'Will you forgive me if your beauty is a comfort?'

She propped herself on an elbow, looking back at him, astonished. 'Will you forgive me if I take my strength from yours?'

'You may always have whatever strength I have. But you're the strong one, Fire. Right now I don't feel strong.'

'I think,' she said, 'that sometimes we don't feel the things that we are. But others can feel them. I feel your strength.' And then she saw that his cheeks were wet.

She had been sleeping in a shirt of his she had found, and her own thick socks. She crawled from his bed and padded across the damp floor to him. Barelegged and wet-footed, she climbed into his lap. He took her up, cold and shaking, clinging to her. His breath was ragged. 'I'm sorry, Fire. I'm sorry about Archer.'

She could feel that it was more. She could feel how much in the world he was sorry for, and how much anguish, grief, and exhaustion he was carrying. 'Brigan,' she whispered. 'None of this is your fault. Do you understand me? It's not your fault.'

She held him tightly, pulled him into the softness of her body so that he could feel the comfort of her while he cried. She repeated it in whispers, kisses, and feeling. *Not your fault. This is not your fault. I love you. I love you, Brigan.*

After some time, he seemed to cry himself out. Holding her numbly, he came aware of her kisses, and began to return them. The pain in his feeling turned into a need that she also felt. He consented to be led to bed.

SHE WOKE, BLINKING her eyes against a torch's violent light, held over her by a man she recognised as one of Brigan's squires. Behind her Brigan stirred. 'Eyes on me, Ander,' he snarled in a voice very awake and very unambiguous about its expectations of being obeyed.

'I'm sorry, sir,' the man said. 'I have a letter, sir.'

'From whom?'

'Lord Mydogg, sir. The messenger said it's urgent.'

'What time is it?'

'Half past four.'

'Wake the king and my four first captains, take them into my office, and wait for me there. Light the lamps.'

'What is it?' Fire whispered as the soldier named Ander lit a candle for them and left. 'Does Mydogg always send letters in the middle of the night?'

'This is the first,' Brigan said, searching for his clothes. 'I expect I know the occasion.'

Fire reached for her own clothing and pulled it under the blankets so she could dress without exposing her skin to freezing air. 'What's the occasion?'

He stood and fastened his trousers. 'Love, you don't have

to get up for this. I can come back and tell you what it's about.'

'Do you think Mydogg's asking for some kind of meeting?'

In the glow of the candle he glanced at her keenly, mouth tight. 'I do.'

'Then I should be involved.'

He sighed shortly. He slapped his sword belt around his waist and reached for his shirt. 'Yes, you should.'

A MEETING WAS, indeed, what Mydogg wanted; a meeting to discuss terms of compromise with Brigan and Nash, so that all might avoid a battle that promised to be the most devastating the war had yet seen. Or at least, this was what it said in his letter.

Their breath turned to fog in the cold air of Brigan's office. 'It's a trick,' Brigan said, 'or a trap. I don't believe Mydogg would ever agree to a compromise. Nor do I believe he cares how many people die.'

'He knows that we match him in numbers now,' Nash said. 'And far exceed him in horses, which finally matters, now that it's water on the rocks instead of ice and snow.'

One of the captains, small and terse and trying not to shiver, crossed his arms. 'And he knows the mental advantage our soldiers will have with their commander and their king leading them into battle together.'

Brigan rubbed his hair frustratedly. 'For the first time, he sees that he's going to lose. So he's setting some sort of trap, and calling it compromise.'

'Yes,' Nash said. 'The meeting is a trap. But what are we to do, Brigan? You know what the cost of this battle will be, and our enemy claims to put forth an alternative. Are we to refuse to consider it?'

THE MEETING TOOK place on the plain of rock that stretched between both camps. The sun rose on Lord Mydogg, Lady

Murgda's Pikkian husband, Brigan, and Nash, making long shadows that shifted in a gloss of water. Some distance behind Mydogg and his brother-in-law a small guard of bowmen stood at attention, arrows drawn and notched. Behind Brigan and Nash a guard of bowmen did the same, the symmetry disturbed by Fire's presence, with six of her own guard, in a group behind Brigan's. Mydogg, the brother-in-law, Brigan, and Nash stood close together. This was intentional. Each was protected from his enemy's bowmen by his enemy.

Fire reached an arm to Musa on one side and Neel on the other, for she was concentrating so fiercely that she didn't trust the balance of her feet. She didn't know what Mydogg was planning; she couldn't find it in Mydogg or any of his men. But she could feel, as certain as fingers wound tight around her throat, that things on this plain of rock were not as they should be.

She was too far back to hear Brigan's quiet voice, but Brigan sent her every word. 'All right,' he said. 'You've got us out here. What do you want?'

Behind Fire, too far for Mydogg to see but not too far for Fire to feel, the King's Army stood mounted in position, ready to strike at the slightest message from Fire. The horses of the commander and the king were with them.

'I'd like to make a deal,' Mydogg said, his voice high and clear. His mind tough and impenetrable. He shifted slightly, intentionally, catching sight of Fire through the barrier of guards. His eyes narrowed on her shrewdly. Impressed and unimpressed together, and in those hard eyes, Fire could read nothing of why they were here.

Behind Lord Mydogg, too distant for Brigan to see, but definitely not too distant for Fire to feel and communicate to Brigan, Mydogg's army also stood ready. Lady Murgda at the head of it, which was to Fire's quiet astonishment. Fire didn't know how pregnant Murgda had been on the day of the January gala, but assuredly she was three more months pregnant now.

'Well then,' Brigan said, 'what deal? Out with it.'

Mydogg's steel eyes cut again to Fire. 'Give us the monster,' he said, 'and we'll surrender our position.'

It's a lie, Fire thought to Brigan. *He's made it up this moment. He wants me – certainly he'd take me if you offered – but it's not why we're here.*

Then why are we here? Can you sense anything unusual in the position of his army? What about the guard standing behind him?

Fire gripped Musa harder with her half-dead hand and leaned more heavily on Neel. *I don't know. His army seems prepared for a straightforward attack. But I can't get into Murgda's head, so I can't know for sure. His guard has no intention to strike unless you or Nash make a move. I can't find what's wrong here, Brigan, but, oh, something is wrong. I feel it. Put an end to this before we learn what it is.*

'No deal,' Brigan said. 'The lady is not a bargaining piece. Tell your archers to stand down. This meeting is over.'

Mydogg raised his eyebrows sleekly and nodded. 'Stand down,' he called to his guard of archers, and as Mydogg's archers disengaged, Fire's body clamoured with panic to find all of them so accommodating. Something was so terribly wrong here. Brigan put his hand out sideways, the signal for his own archers to disengage; and suddenly, Fire screamed with an anguish that tore through her but that she didn't know the reason for. Her cry rang out, eerie and solitary, and one of Brigan's archers shot an arrow into Nash's back.

Pandemonium. The traitorous archer was struck down by his companions, and his second arrow, surely meant for Brigan, flew wide, striking one of Mydogg's guards. Brigan spun fiercely between Mydogg and the brother-in-law, the blade of his sword on fire with morning light. Arrows soared in all directions. Mydogg and his brother-in-law lay dead on the ground. And then the King's Army came roaring onto the scene, for without meaning to, Fire had called them.

In the bedlam everything finally became clear, focused on a single pinprick of purpose. Fire dropped and crawled across rock to the place where Nash lay on his side, dying, it seemed, for the arrow was lodged deep and true. She lay next to him. She touched his face with her broken hand. *Nash. You will not die. I won't allow it. Do you hear me? Do you see me?*

His black eyes stared, conscious, but barely, and only barely did he see her. Brigan tumbled down beside them, clutching Nash's hair, kissing Nash's forehead, gasping with tears. Healers in green appeared and knelt at Nash's back.

Fire grasped Brigan's shoulder and looked into his face, his eyes blank with shock and grief. She shook him, until he saw her. *Go now and fight this battle. Brigan. Go now. We need to win the war.*

He surged up wildly. She heard him yelling for Big. Horses thundered on all sides of the sad little tableau, parting around Fire, Nash, and the healers like a river around a rise of rock. The sound was deafening and Fire was soaked, drowning in hoofbeats and water and blood, gripping Nash's face and clinging harder to his mind than she had ever clung to anything before. *Look at me, Nash. Look at me. Nash, I love you. I love you so much.*

He blinked, staring into her face, a string of blood growing at the corner of his mouth. His shoulders and neck convulsed in pain.

Living is too hard right now, he whispered into her mind. Dying is easy. Let me die.

She felt the very moment when the two armies met, an explosion taking place within her own being. So much fear and pain, and so many minds fading away.

No, Nash. I won't let you. My brother, don't die. Hold on. My brother, hold onto me.

PART FOUR

The Dells

CHAPTER THIRTY-TWO

THE RIVER HAD risen so high with the spring melt that finally one of the bridges, with great shrieks and moans, had broken loose and plunged down into the sea. Hanna said she saw it happen from the palace roof. Tess had watched it with her. Tess had said that the river was liable to wash the palace and the city and the whole kingdom off the rocks, and then there would finally be peace in the world.

'Peace in the world,' Brigan repeated musingly when Fire told him. 'I suppose she's right. That would bring peace to the world. But it's not likely to happen, so I suppose we'll have to keep blundering on and making a mess of it.'

'Oh,' Fire said, 'well put. We'll have to pass that on to the governor so he can use it in his speech when they dedicate the new bridge.'

He smiled quietly at her teasing. They stood side by side on the palace roof, a full moon and a sky of stars illuminating the city's expanse of wood, stone, and water. 'I suppose I'm a bit frightened by this new beginning we're supposed to be having,' he said. 'Everyone in the palace is so fresh and bright and confident, but it's only weeks since we were hacking each other to death. Thousands of my soldiers will never see this new world.'

Fire thought of the raptor monster that had taken her by surprise this very morning, diving upon her and her guard as she exercised Small on the road, coming so close and fast that Small had panicked and kicked at the creature, almost losing his rider. Musa had been furious with herself, furious even with Fire, or at least with Fire's headscarf, which had loosened and released part of its property and been the reason for the attack in the first place. 'It's true we've a great deal more to do than erect a new bridge,' Fire said now, 'and rebuild the parts of the palace that went up in the fire. But, Brigan, I do believe the worst is behind us.'

'Nash was sitting up when I went to the infirmary to see him today,' Brigan said, 'and shaving himself. Mila was there, laughing at his mistakes.'

Fire reached a hand to the roughness of Brigan's jaw, because he had reminded her of one of her favourite places to touch. They came together then, and forgot about the suffering kingdom for a number of minutes, while Fire's guard tried to blend even more discreetly into the background.

'My guard is another matter we need to discuss,' Fire murmured. 'I must have solitude, Brigan, and it must be when I choose it, not when you do.'

Distracted, Brigan took a moment to respond. 'You've borne your guard patiently.'

'Yes, well, I agree I do need them much of the time, especially if I'm to stand so close to the crown. And I trust them, Brigan – I'd go so far as to say I have love for some of them. But—'

'You need to be alone sometimes.'

'Yes.'

'And I've also promised you not to wander alone.'

'We must both promise each other,' Fire said, 'that we'll be thoughtful on the question, and answer it for ourselves on a case by case basis, and try not to take undue risks.'

'Yes, all right,' Brigan said. 'I'll concede this point.'

It was a piece in the structure of the ongoing conversation they had been having since the end of the war, about what it meant for them to be together.

'Could the kingdom ever bear me as its queen, Brigan?'

'Love, I'm not king. Nash is well out of danger.'

'But it could happen someday.'

He sighed. 'Yes. Well, then. We must consider it seriously.'

In the starlight she could just make out the towers of the bridge that men were building over the rush of the Winged River. In the daylight she watched them now and then, hanging from their ropes, balancing on scaffolding that barely seemed strong enough to withstand the current. She lost her breath every time one of them leapt over empty space.

THE ARRANGEMENTS AT the green house had become slightly peculiar, for Roen had decided to take the house back from Brigan and give it to Fire.

'I can understand you taking it from Brigan, if that's your pleasure,' Fire said, standing in the small green kitchen, having this argument with Roen for the third or fourth time. 'You're the queen, and it's the queen's house, and whatever Brigan may accomplish, he's highly unlikely ever to be queen. But Nash will have a queen someday, Roen, and the house by rights should be hers.'

'We'll build her something else,' Roen said with a careless sweep of her arm.

'*This* is the queen's house,' Fire repeated.

'It's *my* house,' Roen said. 'I built it, and I can give it to whomever I want, and I don't know anyone who needs a peaceful retreat from the court more than you do, Fire—'

'I have a retreat. I have a house of my own in the north.'

'Three weeks away,' Roen snorted, 'and miserable half the year. Fire. If you're to stay at court then I want you to have this house, for your own daily retreat. Take Brigandell and Hannadell in if you like, or send them out on their ears.'

'Whatever woman Nash marries is already going to resent me enough—'

Roen spoke over her. 'You are queenly, Fire, whether you see it or not. And you'd be spending most of your time here anyway if I left the house to Brigan; and I'm through with arguing. Besides, it matches your eyes.'

This last was preposterous enough to render Fire speechless, and it didn't help that Tess, kneading dough at the table, nodded her head smartly and added, 'And the flowers are all in reds and golds and pinks, Lady Granddaughter, in case you hadn't noticed, and you've seen the big tree go all red in autumn.'

'Naxdell tried to steal that tree, twice,' Roen said, careening happily off topic. 'He wanted it in his own courtyard. He set the gardeners to digging it up, but where the limbs touch the ground they take root, and it was an impossible job. And mad. How did he think he was ever going to get it into the palace – through the roofs? Nax and Cansrel could never lay eyes on a beautiful thing without needing to possess it.'

Fire gave up. The arrangement was not orderly, but the truth was that she loved the little green house, its garden, and its tree, and she wanted to live there, and she didn't want anyone who already lived there to leave. It didn't matter who owned it and who had taken in whom. It was a bit like the dappled grey horse, who, being led through the palace and shown the grounds of the green house, and being made to understand that this was Fire's home, chose it for her home, too. She grazed behind the house on the cliff above Cellar Harbour and slept under the tree, and went for rides with Fire sometimes, and Small. She belonged to herself, though it was Fire who brought her in and out, and though Hanna had named her Horse, and though Brigan sat sometimes on a bench in the garden, radiating deliberate mildness, pretending not to notice the way she edged toward him, extending her nostrils almost to his very shoulder, cautiously sniffing.

At night Fire rubbed Tess's feet and brushed out the silver-white hair that reached almost to her knees. Her grandmother insisted on being her servant, and Fire understood that. When she could, she insisted on the same thing back.

ONE PERSON FIRE spent time with had nothing to give. Lady Murgda, traitor and attempted murderer, had been kept in the dungeons since the final battle of the war. Her husband was dead. So was her brother. She was well into her pregnancy, which was the only reason she had been left alive. She lashed at Fire with bitter and hateful words when Fire visited, but still Fire continued to visit, not always certain why she did. Sympathy for a strong person who'd been brought low? Respect for a pregnant woman? At any rate, she was not afraid of Murgda's vitriol.

One day as she stepped out of Murgda's cell she met Nash being helped in by Welkley and one of the healers. Grasping his hand, looking at the message in his eyes, she understood that she was not the only person with sympathy for Murgda's miserable situation.

They didn't have a lot of words for each other these days, Fire and Nash. Something unbreakable had formed between them. A bond of memory and experience, and a desperate fondness that seemed not to require words.

How wonderful to see him on his feet.

'I'LL ALWAYS BE leaving,' Brigan said.

'Yes,' Fire said. 'I know.'

Early morning, and they were tangled together in her bed in the green house. Fire was memorising every scar on his face and his body. She was memorising the pale clear grey of his eyes, because he was leaving today with the First to the north, escorting his mother and father to their respective homes. 'Brigan,' she said, so that he would talk, and she could hear his voice and memorise it.

'Yes?'

'Tell me again where you're going.'

*

'Hanna has accepted you completely,' he said a few minutes later. 'She's not jealous, or confused.'

'She has accepted me,' Fire said. 'But she is a little jealous.'

'Is she?' he said, startled. 'Should I talk to her?'

'It's a small thing,' Fire said. 'She does allow for you loving me.'

'She loves you, too.'

'She does love me. Really, I don't think any child could see her father beginning to love someone else and not feel jealousy. At least, that's what I imagine. It never happened to me.' She lost her voice. She continued in thoughts. *I was, wholly and truly, the only person I ever knew my father to love.*

'Fire,' he whispered, kissing her face. 'You did the thing you had to do.'

He never tried to own me, Brigan. Roen said that Cansrel could never see a beautiful thing without wanting to possess it. But he did not try to possess me. He let me be my own.

On the day the surgeons removed Fire's fingers, Brigan was in the north. In the infirmary Hanna held Fire's good hand tightly, chattering her almost to dizziness, and Nash held Hanna's hand, and reached his other hand, a bit cheekily, out to Mila, who gave him a look like acid. Mila, big-eyed, big-bellied, and glowing like a person with a wonderful secret, seemed to have a curious talent for attracting the fondness of men who far outranked her. But she had learned something from the last one. She had learned propriety, which was the same as saying she had learned to trust only herself. So much so that she was not afraid to be rude to the king, when he asked for it.

Garan came in at the last minute, sat down, and, through the whole bloody thing, talked to Mila and Nash and Hanna about the plans for his wedding. Fire knew that it was an attempt to distract her. She thanked them for this kindness by trying very hard to be distracted.

It was not a pleasant surgery. The drugs were good, but they took away the pain alone, not the sensation of her fingers being stolen from her hand; and later, when the drugs wore off, the pain was terrible.

And then, over days and weeks, the pain began to fade. When no one but her guard was around to hear, she fought with her fiddle, and was astonished with how quickly the fighting turned into something more hopeful. Her changed hand couldn't do all that it had formerly done. But it could still make music.

HER DAYS WERE full. An end to the war had not put an end to treachery and lawlessness, particularly in the kingdom's far reaches, where so much went unseen. Clara and Garan often had spy-room work for her. She talked to the people they set her to, but the work she preferred was in the palace infirmary, or even better, in the city hospitals, where all kinds of folk came with all kinds of needs. It was true that some of them wanted nothing to do with her, and in the usual way, even more of them wanted her far too much, and they all made too big a fuss over the role she had played in saving the king's life. They talked about it as if it had been all her doing, and none of Nash's, and none of the kingdom's best surgeons', and when she tried to deflect their praise, they began on the subject of how she had tricked Lord Mydogg's war plans out of Lord Gentian and assured the victory of the Dells. How such rumours had been started, she didn't know, but it seemed there was no stopping them. So she moved among their moods calmly, building barriers against their admiration, helping where she could, and learning practicalities of surgery that astonished her.

'Today,' she announced triumphantly to Garan and Clara, 'a woman came in who'd dropped a cleaver on her foot and cut off her own toe. The surgeons reattached it. Can you believe it? With their tools and their drugs I almost believe they could reattach a leg. We must give more money to the hospitals, you know. We must train more surgeons and build hospitals all over the kingdom. We must build schools!'

'I wish I could take my legs off,' Clara groaned, 'until this baby is born, and then have them reattached afterwards. And my back, too. And my shoulders.'

Fire went to Clara to rub her shoulders, and to ease into Clara's mind and take away what she could of Clara's haggard feeling. Garan, who was not attending to either of them, scowled at the papers on his desk. 'All the mines in the south that were closed before the war have been reopened,' he said. 'And now Brigan believes the miners are not paid enough. Nash agrees, the vexing rockhead.'

Fire slid her knuckles against the knots of muscle in Clara's neck. The metalsmith of the palace had made two fingers for her that attached to her hand with straps and helped her with picking things up and carrying. They didn't help with massage, so she pulled them off, and pulled her headscarf off too, releasing the tension of her own scalp. 'Mining is hard work,' she said, 'and dangerous.'

Garan slapped his pen onto the table beside her metal fingers. 'We are not made of money.'

'Isn't it the kingdom's gold they're mining?'

He frowned at this. 'Clara, where do you stand?'

'I don't care,' Clara moaned. 'No, don't leave that spot. It's exactly right.'

Garan watched Fire massaging his extremely pregnant sister. When Clara moaned again, his grimace began to turn up at the corners. 'Have you heard what people are calling you, Fire?' he asked.

'What is it now?'

'"The monster life-giver". And I've also heard the term "monster protector of the Dells" bandied about.'

'Rocks,' Fire said under her breath.

'And there are ships in the harbour that have put up new sails in red, orange, pink, and green. Have you seen them?'

'Those are all colours of the Dellian standard,' Fire said – other than pink, she added quietly to herself, ignoring a streak of pink in her peripheral vision.

'Of course,' Garan said. 'And I suppose that's your explanation for what they're doing to the new bridge.'

Fire took a small breath, braced herself, and rested eyes on Garan. 'What are they doing to the bridge?'

'The builders have decided to paint the towers green,' he said, 'and line the cross-ribs with mirrors.'

Fire blinked. 'What's that got to do with me?'

'Imagine,' Garan said, 'how it will look at sunrise and sunset.'

A strange thing happened inside Fire: quite suddenly, she lost her fight. She stood back from the feeling this city bore for her and saw it plainly. It was undeserved. It was based not on her, but on stories, on an idea of her, an exaggeration. This is what I am to people, she thought to herself. I don't know what it means, but it's what I am to people.

I'm going to have to accept it.

SHE HAD SMALL things that Archer had given her that she had used every day without thinking. Her quiver and her arm guard, soft and comfortable with the wear of years – these had been gifts, ages ago, from Archer. A part of her wanted to put them aside now, because every time she saw them her heart shrank around a private pain. But she couldn't do it. Replacing them with some other quiver and arm guard was impossible.

She was touching the soft leather of her arm guard one day in a sunny corner of the main courtyard, and thinking, when she fell asleep in her chair. She woke abruptly to Hanna slapping her and yelling, which confused her entirely and alarmed her, until she understood that Hanna had found a trio of monster bugs flitting across Fire's neck and arms, eating her to pieces, and was trying to rescue her.

'Your blood must taste awfully good,' the child said doubtfully, running her fingertips over the angry welts that rose on Fire's skin, and counting.

'Only to monsters,' Fire said dismally. 'Here, give them to me. Are they utterly smashed? I have a student who'd probably like to dissect them.'

'They've bitten you one hundred and sixty-two times,' Hanna announced. 'Does it itch?'

It did itch, agonisingly, and when she came upon Brigan in his bedroom – only recently returned from his long trip north – she was more combative than usual.

'I'll always be attracting bugs,' she said to him belligerently.

He looked up, pleased to see her, if a bit surprised at her tone. 'So you will,' he said, coming to touch the bites on her throat. 'Poor thing. Is it uncomfortable?'

'Brigan,' she said, annoyed that he had not understood. 'I'll always be beautiful. Look at me. I have one hundred and sixty-two bug bites, and has it made me any less beautiful? I'm missing two fingers and I have scars all over, but does anyone care? No! It just makes me more interesting! I'll always be like this, stuck in this beautiful form, and you'll have to deal with it.'

He seemed to sense that she expected a grave response, but for the moment, he was incapable. 'I suppose it's a burden I must bear,' he said, grinning.

'Brigan.'

'Fire, what is it? What's wrong?'

'I'm not how I look,' she said, bursting suddenly into tears. 'I look beautiful and placid and delightful, but it's not how I feel.'

'I know that,' he said quietly.

'I will be sad,' she said defiantly. 'I will be sad, and confused, and irritable, very often.'

He held up a finger and went into the hallway, where he tripped over Blotchy, and then over the two monster cats madly pursuing Blotchy. Swearing, he leaned over the landing and called to the guard that unless the kingdom fell to war or his daughter was dying, he had better not be interrupted until further notice. He came back in, shut the door, and said, 'Fire. I know that.'

'I don't know why terrible things happen,' she said, crying harder now. 'I don't know why people are cruel. I miss Archer, and my father too, no matter what he was. I hate that Murgda will be killed once she's had her baby. I won't allow it, Brigan, I'll sneak her out, I don't care if I end up in prison in her place. And I'm so unbearably itchy!'

Brigan was hugging her now. He was no longer smiling, and his voice was sober. 'Fire. Do you imagine I want you to be thoughtless and chipper, and without all those feelings?'

'Well, I can't imagine that *this* is what you want!'

He said, 'The moment I began to love you was the moment when you saw your fiddle smashed on the ground, and you turned away from me and cried against your horse. Your sadness is one of the things that makes you beautiful to me. Don't you see that? I understand it. It makes my own sadness less frightening.'

'Oh,' she said, not following every word, but comprehending the feeling, and knowing all at once the difference between Brigan and the people who built her a bridge. She rested her face against his shirt. 'I understand your sadness, too.'

'I know you do,' he said. 'I thank you for it.'

'Sometimes,' she whispered, 'there's too much sadness. It crushes me.'

'Is it crushing you now?'

She paused, unable to speak, feeling the press of Archer against her heart. *Yes.*

'Then come here,' he said, a bit redundantly, as he had

already pulled her with him into an armchair and curled her up in his arms. 'Tell me what I can do to help you feel better.'

Fire looked into his quiet eyes, touched his dear, familiar face, and considered the question. *Well. I always like it when you kiss me.*

'Do you?'

You're good at it.

'Well,' he said. 'That's lucky, because I'll always be kissing you.'

EPILOGUE

FLAME WAS THE way in the Dells to send the bodies of the dead where their souls had gone, and to remember that all things came to nothingness, except the world.

They travelled north to Brocker's estate for the ceremony, because it was appropriate that it take place there and because to hold it anywhere else would be an inconvenience to Brocker, who must, of course, be present. They scheduled it for the end of summer, before the fall rains, so that Mila could attend with her newborn daughter, Liv, and Clara with her son, Aran.

Not everyone could make the journey, though practically everyone did, even Hanna, and Garan and Sayre, and quite a colossal royal guard. Nash stayed behind in the city, for someone needed to run things. Brigan promised to make every reasonable effort to attend and came tearing onto Fire's land the night before with a contingent of the army. It was all of fifteen minutes before he and Garan were quarreling over the plausibility of devoting some of the kingdom's resources to westward exploration. If through the mountains existed a land with people called Gracelings who were like that boy, Brigan said, then it would only be sensible to take a peaceful, unobtrusive interest in them – namely, to spy – before the Gracelings decided to take an unpeaceful interest in the Dells. Garan didn't want to spend the money.

Brocker, who took Brigan's side of the argument, was utterly pleased with the growing family that had descended upon him, and he talked, and so did Roen, of moving back to King's City, and leaving his estate – of which Brigan was now heir – to be handled by Donal, who had always handled Fire's capably.

The siblings had been told, quietly, of Brigan's true parentage. Hanna spent time shyly with the grandfather she had only just heard of. She liked the big wheels of his chair.

Clara teased Brigan that on the one hand, he was no technical relation to her at all, but on the other, he was doubly the uncle of her son, for, in the loosest sense, Clara was Brigan's sister and the baby's father had been Brigan's brother. 'That's how I prefer to think of it, anyway,' Clara said.

Fire smiled at all of this, and held the babies whenever anyone would let her, which turned out to be fairly often. She had a monster knack with babies. When they cried, she usually knew what was ailing them.

FIRE WAS SITTING in the bedroom of her stone house, thinking of all the things that had happened in that room.

From the doorway, Mila broke into her reverie. 'Lady? May I come in?'

'Of course, Mila, please.'

In her arms Mila carried Liv, who was asleep, smelling like lavender, and making soft breathing noises. 'Lady,' Mila said. 'You once told me I may ask you for anything.'

'Yes,' Fire said, looking at the girl, surprised.

'I'd like to ask your advice.'

'Well, you shall have it, for whatever it's worth.'

Mila dropped her face to Liv's pale, fuzzy hair for a moment. She almost seemed afraid to speak. 'Lady,' she said. 'Do you think that in his treatment of women, the king is a man like Lord Archer?'

'Goodness,' Fire said, 'no. I can't see the king being careless with a woman's feelings. It seems fairer to compare him to his brothers.'

'Do you think,' Mila began, and then sat suddenly on the bed, trembling. 'Do you think a soldier girl from the southern

Great Greys, sixteen years old with a baby, would be mad to consider—'

Mila stopped, her face buried against her child. And Fire felt the rise of her own clamouring happiness, like warm music ringing in the spaces inside her. 'The two of you seem very fond of each other's company,' she said carefully, trying not to give her feelings away.

'Yes,' Mila said. 'We were together during the war, Lady, on the northern front, when I was assisting Lord Brocker. And I found myself going to him a very great deal, when he was recovering from his injury and I was preparing for my own laying in. And when Liv was born, he visited me just as faithfully, despite all his duties. He helped me to name her.'

'And has he said anything to you?'

Mila focused on the fringe of the blanket in her arms, from which suddenly protruded a fat little foot that flexed itself. 'He's said that he'd like to spend more time in my company, Lady. As much time as I'm willing to allow him.'

Still holding back on her smile, Fire spoke gently. 'I do think it's a very large question, Mila, and one you needn't rush to answer. You might do as he asks, and simply spend more time with him, and see how that feels. Ask him a million questions, if you have them. But no, I don't think it's mad. The royal family is ... very flexible.'

Mila nodded, her face drawn in thought, seeming to consider Fire's words quite seriously. After a moment, she passed Liv into Fire's arms. 'Would you like to visit with her for a bit, Lady?'

Scrunched against the pillows of her old bed, Archer's baby sighing and yawning against her, for a short span of time Fire was shatteringly happy.

THE LANDSCAPE BEHIND what had been Archer's house was a vastness of grey rock. They waited until sunset streaked the sky with red.

They had no body to burn. But Archer had had longbows tall as he, and crossbows, short bows, bows from his childhood that he had grown out of, but kept. Brocker was not wasteful, nor did he want to destroy all of Archer's things. But he came out of the house with a bow that Archer had strongly favoured and another t hat had been a childhood gift of Aliss's, and asked Fire to lay them on top of the kindling.

Fire did as she was asked, and then lay something of her own beside the bows. It was a thing she had kept in the bottom of her bags for well over a year now: the bridge of her ruined fiddle. For she had lit a blazing fire for Archer once before, but she had never even lit a candle for Cansrel.

She understood now that while it had been wrong to kill Cansrel, it had also been right. The boy with the strange eyes had helped her to see the rightness of it. The boy who'd killed Archer. Some people had too much power and too much cruelty to live. Some people were too terrible, no matter if you loved them; no matter that you had to make yourself terrible too, in order to stop them. Some things just had to be done.

I forgive myself, thought Fire. Today, I forgive myself.

Brigan and Roen set the pyre alight and all in the party came to stand before it. There was a song played in the Dells to mourn the loss of a life. Fire took her fiddle and bow from Musa's waiting hands.

It was a haunting tune, unresigned, a cry of heartache for all in the world that fell apart. As ash rose black against the brilliant sky, Fire's fiddle cried out for the dead, and for the living who stay behind and say goodbye.

SOMETIMES ONLY A GRACE CAN SAVE YOU...

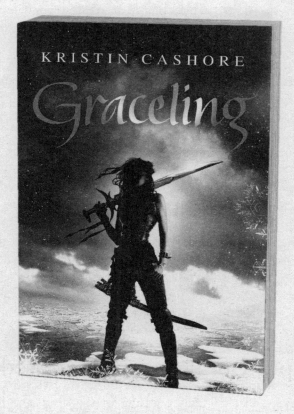

In Katsa's world some people are born with an exceptional skill, known as a Grace. Katsa's Grace is one she despises: the Grace of killing. She lives under the command of her Uncle Randa, King of the Middluns, and is expected to carry out his dirty work.

But something dark and deadly is rising in the north and creeping across the continent, and behind it all lurks the shadowy figure of a one-eyed king . . .

www.orionbooks.co.uk

VAMPIRES, MURDER, INTRIGUE . . .

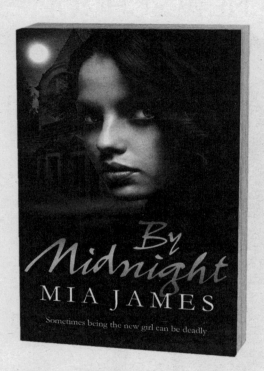

April Dunne is not impressed.

She's had to move from Edinburgh to Highgate, London, and leave behind all of her friends. Then there's Ravenwood, her prestigious new school that seems to have something sinister going on behind its glamorous façade. When the mysterious Gabriel Swift saves April from . . . something . . . . in Highgate Cemetery, she has to wonder if she will survive her new school's deadly secrets.

WELCOME TO RAVENWOOD, THE SCHOOL WITH BITE.

For a closer look at April's world visit Ravenwood at:
www.orionbooks.co.uk/ravenwood

NEW GIRL.
NEW SCHOOL.
SAME OLD MONSTERS.

As the new girl at the elite St. Sophia's boarding school,
Lily Parker thinks her classmates are the most monstrous things
she'll have to face. When a prank leaves Lily trapped in the catacombs
beneath the school, she finds herself running from a real monster.
This is a world of magic, vampires, demons and secrets.
Get ready to join the Dark Elite.

*For more information, proof giveaways, exclusive competitions and
updates please visit:* **www.orionbooks.co.uk/gollanczya**

WHAT IF EVERYTHING YOU TOUCHED WAS CURSED?

Cassel is cursed. Cursed by the memory of the fourteen year old girl he murdered. No-one at home is ever going to forget that he is a killer or that he isn't a magic worker. But Cassel is about to discover a dangerous family secret that will change everything.

www.orionbooks.co.uk

IN A WORLD SURROUNDED BY THE LIVING DEAD, WHAT DO YOU LIVE FOR?

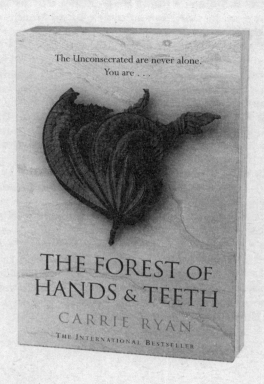

The Unconsecrated are never alone.
You are . . .

THE FOREST OF HANDS & TEETH

CARRIE RYAN

THE INTERNATIONAL BESTSELLER

In Mary's world there are simple truths. The Sisterhood always knows best. The Guardians will protect and serve. The Unconsecrated will never relent.

But Mary's truths are failing her. When the fence that surrounds and protects her town from the Unconsecrated is breached her world is thrown into chaos and she must choose between her village and her future - between the boy she loves and the one who loves her.